CRISIS OF FAITH

BENJAMIN MEDRANO

Crisis of Faith by Benjamin Medrano

© 2019 Benjamin Medrano. All rights reserved.

Contact the author at BenjaminPMedrano@gmail.com

Visit the author's website at benjaminmedrano.com

Sign up for the author's mailing list at http://eepurl.com/cGPT-b

Cover Art by June Jenssen

Editing by Picky Cat Proofreading & Copyediting

This is a work of fiction. Names, characters, places, and incidents either are the products of the author's imagination or are used fictitiously. Any resemblance to actual persons, living or dead, businesses, companies, events, or locales is entirely coincidental.

This wouldn't have been possible without the support of my family and fans.
Thank you all.

PROLOGUE

The mountain peak shattered as she slammed through it, and Medaea gasped, descending into the valley like a falling star. Trees exploded outward as she hit the ground, all their remaining leaves torn away by the shockwave. Baldwin followed her, his normally gleaming armor spattered with scorch marks, dents, and soot from their battle, his immense hammer raised in both hands as he moved to pummel Medaea into the earth.

She hadn't been idle, though. An orb of sunfire gleamed between her hands as she looked back along the path she'd traveled, still embedded in the earth. Medaea could see Baldwin's eyes widening as he saw the orb, and he tried to dodge just as she unleashed her magic. A brilliant beam of gold-white fire blasted across the sky, melting another chunk of the mountainside, which then collapsed on itself, and the forest below it ignited under the sheer heat unleashed by Medaea's magic.

Medaea didn't pause, though, and she darted out of her crater and to the side just as Baldwin erupted from her flames, his hammer still raised as he brought it down on the spot where she'd been standing a moment before. Her wings spread and she took flight, healing magic surging through her body.

Baldwin's hammer hit the ground with incredible force, and his magic erupted into the ground with the impact. A blow fit to cave in Medaea's chest hit the vulnerable ground, causing earth and stone to shatter and fly in every direction, creating a crater a hundred feet across and triggering an earthquake across the region.

Extending her hand, Medaea called for her sword, and the glowing blade unearthed itself from the mountainside as it streaked across the sky to her grasp. She studied Baldwin grimly, looking for any hint of vulnerability from her fellow deity, but not expecting to find one. His face showed a few injuries, but the man's dark eyes betrayed no fear, and his armor was barely damaged by their clash. They were mostly evenly matched, which made the battle largely fruitless for both of them. Yet at the same time, she couldn't back down, just as she knew that Baldwin couldn't.

Wordlessly, each of the deities raised their weapons, and Medaea could feel the world rippling as somewhere, far away, other deities clashed. The tragedy of their actions was obvious, yet she knew that there was little choice. So long as the other side didn't back down, neither could she and her allies.

Medaea lunged forward at Baldwin, and he yelled loudly as he struck her blade in turn, driving her back as they clashed, the force of their blows destroying anything too close to them. For several long moments they fought, Medaea's power of healing competing with Baldwin's sheer durability, then they pulled away from one another for a moment.

Just as they prepared to clash once more, though, the very aether let out a scream like nothing Medaea had ever felt before, as mana bucked and roiled around them and the ley lines themselves twisted and erupted with power. Baldwin staggered at the same time as Medaea, and both of them looked south in horror. Flames were on the horizon, and Medaea flinched as she saw the very earth itself writhing and buckling.

Baldwin paused, then spoke at last, his voice deep. "Truce?"

"Very well." Medaea replied, and both of them flew south.

There the memory ended, and Tyria frowned, slowly opening her eyes as she murmured, "What did we see there? It was when the world tree perished… I know that much, but beyond that… I cannot remember."

Tyria was standing at the very peak of Beacon, atop the tower which contained the crimson ruby namesake of the city. Below her she could see the immense city that Sistina had built from a mountain, and even now Tyria found herself with mixed feelings about her position and involvement here.

Part of Tyria knew that, as a goddess, she didn't belong here. She should return to her domain and take care of problems that had cropped up during her long millennia of sleep. It was the proper thing to do, and yet… she couldn't. Not with two different churches dedicated to two aspects of who she was. And not with how deeply she was linked to Sistina. Worse, she didn't *want* to leave.

So Tyria studied the city once more, breathing in air steeped in the mana of the dungeon, so palpable to her senses. The way Sistina's mana was controlled was breathtaking, her domain rippling with the genius loci's presence and will, yet flowing like a smooth, calm river. None of the mortals in the city could sense it as well as Tyria could, though a handful could come close, Tyria knew. Her gaze fell to the temple of Medaea located just a few hundred feet below her, and Tyria saw that a couple of priestesses were watching her. Their warm regard and whispered prayers brought a smile to the goddess's lips.

"I slept for far too long. I was such a fool… I believed that the war would leave me bereft of worshipers. I left them alone, despite their trust in me," Tyria murmured, chiding herself for what she'd done as Medaea.

The memories of Demasa, Ikora, and all the other deities who had been lost were still open wounds for her, now that she remembered them properly. Such memories didn't fade like they would have for mortals, and Tyria… she had slept instead, and hadn't built new memories to at least ease that pain. It was another mistake, and one which weighed on her. Had she not slept, Sifaren and Yisara would not have suffered as much as they had.

That self-reproach wasn't as painful as it had been when Tyria had first managed to recover her memories, but she still didn't take any pleasure in her knowledge. Many of her worshipers were even more unhappy with the situation than Tyria was as well. She needed to fix it, and the only question was how she'd go about doing so, particularly in a way she could tolerate.

A tugging sensation pulled Tyria's gaze away from the city below her, though, and she smiled again as she saw the caravan on the horizon. She could sense the calm power of Archpriestess Nadis of Yisara in the caravan, along with multiple other priestesses as well. Along with them she could feel two others, the ones who'd drawn her attention. Diane and Jaine Yisara had been changed using Tyria's blood as a catalyst, so she wasn't surprised she could sense them easily. It was more of a surprise that Diane had accompanied the caravan in returning to Beacon, considering how recently she'd left. The former queen had attended Sistina's wedding to Phynis and the Jewels, after all.

"Perhaps it does not matter," Tyria murmured, and smiled as she spread her wings to take flight, glancing toward the center of the mountains. The Godsrage Mountains were immense, and a tiny part of her wanted to investigate what was at their heart. For good or for ill, that would have to wait.

First, she needed to inform Queen Phynis of the approaching guests and prepare for the coming discussions between the priesthood of Medaea and Tyria.

The conference would be… interesting, the goddess suspected.

CHAPTER 1

Diamond opened her eyes at the knock, her eyebrows rising slightly as the door opened a moment later. She turned her head, then smiled as she saw Phynis poke her head into the room. The queen's metallic pink hair was bound back in a braid, and she was wearing an elegant but functional blue dress which suited her darker skin well, but which also told Diamond that Phynis didn't plan on having any guests today, though the lack of a presence crown was also rather telling.

"Bright the morning, Phynis," Diamond said, slowly climbing to her feet. She really shouldn't kneel on the stone floor of the chapel, but centuries of habit proved hard to break.

"I'm afraid it really isn't *morning* anymore, but the sentiment is appreciated," Phynis replied, grinning as she took a few steps forward and gave Diamond a gentle kiss. "How are you?"

The priestess enjoyed the kiss for a moment, hugging Phynis as well. It took a few moments before she broke it off, smiling happily as she did so.

"Well, on the whole," Diamond replied, feeling even better after the kiss, then glanced at the stained-glass windows that illuminated the small chapel. "I see it's rather later than I thought… I didn't think I'd been in here quite *that* long."

"I do understand. Sometimes I get involved in something, then I wonder where half the day went," Phynis agreed, her eyes dancing with amusement, her hands resting on Diamond's hips. "Alas, it appears that we're both going to have an interesting group of visitors today."

"Oh?" Diamond asked, tilting her head curiously, anticipation rising within her. "What do you mean?"

"I just had a… divine visitation by Tyria," Phynis began, then paused as Diamond laughed softly, and the queen smiled in amusement. They both knew that using such formal terms regarding Tyria was just Phynis joking, since Tyria all but lived in the palace with them. That still unsettled Diamond at times, but she'd lived under the same roof as Tyria for quite some time before, though the goddess hadn't gone by that name at the time. She also hadn't been awake, which did make things rather different.

"Sorry, you were saying?" Diamond asked, feeling a little guilty about interrupting.

"I was saying that Tyria visited and politely informed me that we have visitors on the way, and they should be able to reach the palace by an hour before dark," Phynis said, and her smile faded slightly. "She said that Archpriestess Nadis is among them, so they're going to arrive a touch sooner than expected."

"Ah, I see. That's… later than I'd prefer, if I'm being honest, since we got our first snow a few days ago," Diamond said, much of her sense of humor about the situation fading. She was concerned about how the Archpriestess would react to Tyria and everything else in Beacon, since the letters that had been exchanged had often been quite terse so far. She paused for a moment, then hugged Phynis again before asking, "Do we have any idea when High Priestess Elissa is going to arrive?"

"According to Westgate's dispatch, she should be here tomorrow or the next day," Phynis said, then smiled as she added, "There *is* one thing I'm looking forward to with Archpriestess Nadis arriving, though."

"What might that be?" Diamond asked, tilting her head curiously.

"It seems that at least Lady Diane and Lady Jaine have accompanied them. I suspect Marquis Torkal has escorted them as well, if Lady Diane is with them," Phynis said, and the explanation abruptly improved Diamond's mood, even if she had mixed feelings where Lady Diane was concerned.

Diane, the former queen of Yisara, was a tragic figure in Diamond's mind. She'd given up her freedom and surrendered to Kelvanis to rescue the abducted heirs of nearly a third of Yisara's nobles, renouncing her claim on the throne in the process as well as abdicating. As if that wasn't enough of a sacrifice, then she'd sold herself, body and soul, to a succubus named Wenris in order to save her daughter, Jaine. Wenris was now a demon lord, and though she'd granted Diane a large amount of freedom, the situation always made Diamond wish she could do something for Diane. Unfortunately, their quiet investigations when Diane had visited for the wedding had shown that the former queen's soul was irrevocably linked to that of Wenris, and even Sistina wasn't sure how to undo it.

Lady Jaine, on the other hand, had come through her captivity in astoundingly good shape, and the former princess had taken her change of roles surprisingly well. Some of that was because she'd converted to Tyria's faith, Diamond knew, but she was mostly happy that the young princess had come out of her captivity mostly intact. Considering the conference coming up, Diamond wasn't surprised that Jaine had chosen to return as well, and Diamond had enjoyed her conversations with Jaine before. Though given how things were planned to go, Jaine certainly wouldn't be attending the conference.

"I'm glad to hear that," Diamond murmured, smiling warmly. "I was happy to see them at the wedding, but with all the guests it isn't like we had much of a chance to talk. Do you know why they're coming?"

Phynis laughed and shook her head, pulling away as she replied. "Of course not! You know as much as I do, since I got word from Tyria, and you know how she is. As it is, I've only told Ruby and Isana about the caravan. Ruby went to let Lirisel and the other Jewels know, while Isana is arranging for appropriate lodging for the guests."

"Excellent. That being the case… do you know what Sistina is doing? I'd like to talk to her," Diamond asked, following Phynis out into the wide, comfortable halls of the palace.

"Oh? Going to try to convince her to mediate again?" Phynis asked, raising an eyebrow skeptically. "She's been rather resistant, and isn't the type to budge."

"I know, but if anyone can keep the conference from coming to blows, I think it'd be her," Diamond said, letting out a soft sigh as she considered how Sistina was likely to reply. She wasn't looking forward to the conversation with her.

"I know. Tyria probably will be there, but I'm not sure if she'll be able to keep the peace, either," Phynis mused, then shrugged, continuing. "As for Sistina, she's in her workshop. With Albert."

Diamond winced. She considered for a moment, then asked hesitantly, "Do you have any idea what they're up to this time? I don't want to interrupt in the middle of something liable to explode. *Again*."

"They apologized and promised to lock the door next time they were working on something like that," Phynis said, grinning broadly. "I don't know what they're up to, this time. I'd come with you, but I need to get some paperwork done and get changed. If we're going to have the archpriestess arriving today, I should dress appropriately."

"True enough. Thank you for coming to tell me," Diamond said, smiling and giving Phynis another quick kiss.

"You're welcome. Good luck with Sistina," Phynis replied, a grin playing across her lips.

"I'll certainly need it," Diamond muttered, shaking her head as she took a different hallway from Phynis. Considering how stubborn Sistina could be, Diamond didn't have high hopes of success, but she felt she had to try.

Sistina's workshop was at the very back of the palace, in a section of the building with numerous wards built into the walls to reinforce them and guarantee that explosions didn't reach into the palace, should something go wrong. That rarely made Diamond feel better about things, since in her mind it meant that Sistina expected something to go disastrously wrong at some point.

The door to the workshop was made of heavy stone, and the numerous runes carved into it were elegant, and they glittered with magic even in full daylight, prompting Diamond to study them again, feeling ever so slightly sour about them. She'd been trying to learn more about enchanting of late, but it was slow-going, and the runes that Sistina used were different than all the ones in the books Diamond was learning from. They weren't completely different, but sometimes it was hard to tell what purpose Sistina's runes had. It wasn't Sistina's fault, though, so Diamond carefully turned the doorknob, and relaxed as it moved easily.

"...alright, so we have that much dealt with. What material are you thinking to use for the rails? I'm not an engineer, mind you, but I've got a pretty good grasp of the essentials, and you're talking about a *lot* of weight." Albert's voice was calm, yet slightly eager at the same time. The human's dark hair was slightly messy, and his eyes were intense as he looked at the chalkboard in consideration. The chalkboard was covered in a diagram that Diamond couldn't quite figure out, though it had some wheels and what looked like angular boxes as well. There was also a lot of math which she couldn't understand, especially not at a glance.

"Steel," Sistina said simply, her arms crossed in front of her as she examined the chalkboard as well. While Diamond knew it wasn't Sistina's true body, she examined her wife in admiration anyway.

Sistina looked like a dryad, her skin white with the faintest hint of a wood grain to it and possessing a voluptuous figure and the ears of an elf, while she had curly golden hair that reached her knees, gold lips, and penetrating emerald eyes. The dryad was wearing a simple white dress, though one of the straps had fallen off her shoulder again.

"Steel?" Albert exclaimed, looking over in surprise, and catching a glimpse of Diamond as he did so, but he continued without pausing, his voice incredulous. "You're talking about a *lot* of metal, Sistina. Where are you going to get that much steel?"

"Am a dungeon. Have foundry, too," Sistina replied shortly, then smiled as she looked over at Diamond. "Morning, Diamond."

"You're dropping words again, Sistina," Diamond pointed

out, smiling widely in turn as she approached and gave Sistina a gentle hug, which the dryad returned eagerly.

"I can speak with perfect diction when I want to," Sistina said, her voice smooth and flawless as she leaned forward and kissed Diamond's cheek, then she pulled away and spoke more simply. "Takes concentration."

"I can understand her well enough, anyway. Good… afternoon, Diamond. Is it that late already?" Albert asked, looking out the window with a frown. "We'd probably best find lunch at some point."

"Yes, it *is* that late. I just have to give Sistina some grief for skipping words. We're trying to get her to be better about that," Diamond said, then nodded at the chalkboard. "What's all this about, anyway?"

Sistina stuck out her tongue at Diamond, then pulled away and tilted her head at Albert, asking the Guildmaster of the Adventurer's Guild, "Explain?"

"Certainly!" Albert said, his eyes brightening, and he half-sat on the table as he looked at Diamond and began speaking quickly. "So, since so many people have been frustrated about how hard it is to climb the mountain over the last few months, she's been looking at different options for a solution."

"I understand that. Most horses are somewhat exhausted by the time they reach the top, let alone people," Diamond murmured, remembering the stairs that led from Sistina's cavern in the mountain heart to the palace. *That* was a punishing climb, and one she had to take a bit more often than Diamond would prefer. Even if the exercise was good for her.

"Exactly. She considered using steam carriages, like the ones the guild uses, but those could wander off, whether by accident or design, and heavens forbid if one lost control and slammed into a house or went off a cliff. We also discussed some of the in-city carriages on rails, along the lines of mine carts, but that would take up a large part of the roads *and* would require large changes to the city in the process. I've seen those before, honestly, and favored the idea, at least at first," Albert explained, then paused, grinning as he continued. "Then she had an idea after Captain Iceheart yelled at a group of children scaling one of the walls."

Diamond winced at the memory of that incident. Beacon's walls were tall, and there was nothing below them but stone, so if any of the children had fallen they'd almost certainly have died. They might have been able to be revived if they'd been taken to the temples quickly enough, but she hadn't been happy about the thought to begin with. She nodded slightly, murmuring, "I remember hearing about that... Desa wasn't happy."

"I don't blame her. Anyway, they were climbing ropes, and coupled with the other ideas, Sistina came up with something slightly different. She's thinking to create a... *carriage* that can be hauled up and down a tunnel on rails by a steam engine. A mostly *vertical* tunnel," Albert explained eagerly, his eyes bright with excitement. "We're calling it a lift, since it lifts people. If we can build them inside the mountain, it won't take additional room, and we can make it stop at several points throughout the city."

"I... see. I think I understand, though the idea unsettles me, a little. What if it falls?" Diamond asked, frowning and reaching over to move Sistina's shoulder strap back into place.

"Brakes," Sistina chimed in, smiling at Diamond, and Albert nodded.

"Yes, we're taking precautions to make sure if it would fall, there are several sets of brakes that will bring the carriage to a stop. The entire reason I'm involved is that she wants me to check her math and point out problems she might not have noticed," Albert said, grinning more. "Besides, it'll let me learn how she does it and give us ways to build similar devices elsewhere."

"Fair, I suppose," Diamond said, a little skeptically. She wasn't too worried about the idea, not if the two were keeping people's safety in mind. She'd love to be able to travel through the city more easily, too. She set the thought aside for the moment, though, and focused on Sistina. "I'm afraid that I didn't come here to ask about your project, though. Sistina, Archpriestess Nadis will be here later today, and High Priestess

Elissa will arrive tomorrow or the next. I was curious if you'd changed your mind about mediating?"

"No," Sistina said firmly, crossing her arms and shaking her head.

Diamond suppressed her surge of disappointment and sighed, then spoke again. "May I at least ask *why*? You've been rather firm on this subject."

"Yes," Sistina replied, and frowned, tapping her lip at a slow, measured pace.

"I can leave if you need me to," Albert offered, pushing himself off the table, only to have Sistina wave him back down.

"No need," Sistina told him, shaking her head. Then she nodded. "Need proper explanation. Give time."

Diamond nodded, smiling at Sistina's attitude as she murmured softly, "Of course."

It took a minute, then Sistina finally nodded. When she spoke, it wasn't in her usual sharp, almost halting manner. It was instead in the focused, carefully enunciated words that Sistina used when she was focusing on speaking properly. It also told Diamond that she was taking this seriously.

"This meeting is a matter for mortals. I am not mortal, and quite frankly, I am too *powerful* to sit in on the meeting," Sistina said, frowning as she spoke. "If I was there, it would be seen as me trying to influence the results. With my link to Tyria, this would complicate matters further, and I do not wish that. In the end, matters of faith are something to be decided by mortals, because they are *for* mortals. I cannot allow myself to influence that, not in good conscience."

"Interesting," Albert said, looking intrigued as he sat back, watching Diamond and Sistina, tapping the table slowly.

"I… suppose it makes sense," Diamond replied and let out a soft sigh of disappointment. "Tyria is going to *be* there, though."

"Tyria is object of faith," Sistina replied, shrugging as she added, "I am not. Thank all gods for that."

"I assume you have a backup plan, since Sistina hasn't been interested in being a mediator before this," Albert said, smiling wryly. "I really don't like the idea, but if all else fails, I could try to help out."

"I'm not going to impose on you like that, though the offer is greatly appreciated Master Windgale," Diamond said, her mood brightening at the offer. She'd found herself growing to like Albert over the last few months of occasional interaction, even if they barely talked most of the time. She probably wouldn't know him more than distantly if it weren't for his utter fascination with Sistina, and that would have been unfortunate. She continued her explanation calmly after a moment. "We spoke with the priesthood of Vanir, and they've agreed to chair the conference. I expect it's going to be an unpleasant meeting to start."

"I entirely understand why that might be. The situation with Medaea being turned into Tyria... that just sounds messy," Albert said, running his fingers through his hair as he shook his head. "I'm just as glad not to be involved, to be honest."

"I'm hoping it doesn't come to blows," Diamond said, sighing heavily, then straightened. "In any case, I'll let the two of you get back to your math. If it makes it easier to move through the city, you'll have my profuse thanks."

"Oh, believe me, I'm entirely thinking about myself on this one," Albert replied, grimacing as he added, "You do remember that the guild house is at the *bottom* of the mountain, yes?"

"Of course. That would certainly give you motivation to get it right, wouldn't it?" Diamond said, smiling warmly. Then she looked at Sistina and added, "I hope you have fun, Sistina."

"Will try," Sistina said warmly, hugging Diamond again as she whispered, "Love you."

The simple phrase warmed Diamond's heart and she smiled even more as she turned her head to kiss Sistina in turn, murmuring, "I love you too."

Then she headed out to try to get things ready to meet Archpriestess Nadis. They hadn't met in close to a decade now, and Diamond couldn't help wondering how it would go. The meeting would certainly be interesting.

At least High Priestess Elissa wasn't going to be arriving at the same time.

CHAPTER 2

Diane took a breath and shivered, pulling her coat closer. She was incredibly thankful for the gift from Beryl, even if the coat *had* originally been hers before she'd surrendered to Kelvanis. The enchanted coat made it so she wasn't too uncomfortable even with the thin layer of snow on the ground, and particularly with the cold air blowing out of the mountains.

Beside her, Torkal paused as well, the two of them looking up at Beacon. After a few moments he spoke, his voice hushed. "You know, even after spending a few weeks there, looking at Beacon leaves me in awe. It also makes me feel nervous."

"What, something about a mountain being turned into a city makes you concerned?" Diane teased gently, smiling warmly at him as she examined Beacon. Truthfully, she didn't blame him in the slightest.

Five miles across and a half-mile tall at its center, the city was an incredible fortress, with five walls evenly spaced across its immense height, yet that beauty was softened by canals and waterfalls, as well as the countless buildings, many of which were beautiful. The golems standing silent guard on the walls were somewhat eerie as well, but seeing more people moving along the walls was a welcome change from Diane's last visit.

"Yes, it does," Torkal replied, smiling and giving her a gentle hug. "You're sure that Queen Phynis will welcome us for the winter?"

"Of course; she offered to let me visit for as long as I liked last time, and it isn't like she lacks space," Diane said, feeling far more at peace than she had since Kelvanis had been defeated, along with the demon queen Irethiel. "Besides, we need to give Beryl space to get Yisara in order."

"She didn't blame you for being there, and it wasn't your fault how people looked at you," Torkal replied, frowning slightly as their carriage moved toward the city.

"I know she didn't, but that doesn't change the fact it was causing problems," Diane said, her voice level. "I refuse to undermine her authority."

"Fair, fair," Torkal said, and he smiled more as he asked, "So, what do you think of her and Sir Lucien?"

The question made Diane smile as well, and much more warmly than she had before. Sir Reva Lucien had commanded one of the largest armies of Sifaren during the recent war, and he'd interacted with her daughter, Queen Beryl, during their campaign to aid Slaid Damrung in reclaiming Kelvanis and ending the majority of chaos in the human nation. How well the two got along had startled Diane, especially after how many suitors Beryl had rejected. Perhaps she should have realized sooner that her headstrong daughter would be more interested in a skilled warrior, but that was water under the bridge at this point.

"I think that she could do far, *far* worse than Sir Lucien. The biggest problem is what would happen with his father's earldom if things work out between them," Diane said, then smiled as she added, "Happily, neither you nor I have to worry about that anymore. It's Beryl's problem."

"True enough," Torkal agreed, smiling still more. Then his smile faded and he nodded ahead of them, at the wall of their carriage and the one that was leading the way, asking, "How do you think the Archpriestess is reacting?"

"Probably better than we might expect, after her conversations with Jaine," Diane said, though it was hard to keep smiling. The revelations about Tyria had caused quite a bit of chaos in Yisara, which worried her. Hopefully Jaine was helping to keep Nadis from overreacting.

~

"THAT… is an excessively large city. I heard all the descriptions, but none of them can do it justice," Archpriestess Nadis said, and Jaine nodded, looking at the city in admiration.

"I agree. I couldn't believe my eyes the first time I saw Beacon," Jaine said, smiling and leaning over to get a better look through the window. "It also looks busier than it was before. More people must have arrived over the summer."

"You're likely right. Considering what I've heard of the mage academy and many other things, I would be surprised if there weren't more people in Beacon," Nadis agreed, sitting back and steepling her hands thoughtfully. "The only question is whether that is for good or for ill."

"I can agree with that. I don't think that Queen Phynis or Sistina have anything bad planned for anyone else, but this is going to change things," Jaine said, a hint of worry making its way through her.

Ever since Jaine had returned to Yisara with her mother, aside from when they'd come to Phynis's wedding with the Jewels and Sistina, she'd spent a great deal of time with the priesthood of Medaea as they grappled with what had happened to their goddess. During that time, Jaine had ended up spending quite a bit of time with the archpriestess and had grown to know her reasonably well.

The archpriestess was beautiful, as most priestesses of Medaea were. She had a slightly darker bronze skin than most dawn elves, though not as dark as Jaine's honey-gold skin, her hair was a strawberry blonde color that reached the middle of her back, and she had bright blue eyes that were quite piercing. The priestess was wearing a warm set of robes, along with her holy symbol of Medaea and the ring of the archpriestess of the faith.

The problem was that the archpriestess was quite reserved and figuring out exactly what she was thinking was difficult at the best of times, and these weren't those. Nadis had asked Jaine questions, dozens of them if not hundreds, and she was obviously interested in what had occurred with Tyria, but beyond that… Jaine didn't know what she was thinking. If it weren't for the aspect that Tyria had been able to directly answer several of Nadis's prayers, Jaine suspected that the archpriestess would have refused to believe that Tyria had once been Medaea. It made the upcoming meeting fraught with peril, from Jaine's perspective, and she was worried about what was going to happen.

"Perhaps they don't, but even the best of intentions can lead to unexpected consequences," Nadis murmured, tilting her head. "I *am* curious about what effect the city will have on the world. For the moment, we can but wait."

"Agreed," Jaine said, then smiled as she added, "I look forward to introducing you to Lily, though. She's just a gardener, but I think she did more than anyone else in Beacon to help me relax."

"Indeed? Well, I look forward to meeting her as well," Nadis said, smiling slightly.

"I'm glad to hear that," Jaine said, glancing out at the city again, just before the carriage turned a corner that made it so she couldn't see much of it through the windows.

Soon they'd reach the city, and Jaine was looking forward to seeing the people there again. She'd made a lot of friends in Beacon after fleeing Westgate that summer, and the thought of seeing them excited Jaine. That, and where else could she see her goddess in person?

"WELCOME TO BEACON, ARCHPRIESTESS," Captain Desa Iceheart said, bowing her head courteously as Archpriestess Nadis stepped out of the carriage. Jaine Yisara had preceded her, but Desa had only spared a moment to smile warmly at the young woman before focusing on the more important guest, at least for the moment.

Desa wasn't happy with the conference that Beacon was

preparing to host. The situation with Medaea becoming Tyria could cause a religious war and having two opposing churches meeting in Beacon as a sort of neutral ground… well, it was one of those things that made her sleep a little less soundly.

"Thank you," the Archpriestess replied calmly, looking around the square with obvious interest.

Three steel-skinned golems were helping secure a perimeter around the ten carriages that had carried the priestesses and other guests, and beyond them were dozens of people, many of them dawn or dusk elves who were pausing to get a better look as they went about their business.

"May I ask who you are?" Nadis asked after a moment, then added, "Also, might I know why we're stopped at the base of the city? I was told that the temple of Medaea is much farther up the mountainside."

"Ah, my apologies, my name is Desa Iceheart, and I'm the captain of Queen Phynis's Royal Guard," Desa said, bowing more deeply, then smiled as she straightened again. "As for the temple, you're correct. However, you've had a long journey, and the horses drawing your carriages are doubtlessly fatigued. As such, we find that having fresh mounts to draw lighter carriages through the city is a faster way of reaching the city's heights. I'm told that lodging next to the temple of Medaea has been prepared for you and your companions as well, Archpriestess."

"Ah, very well," Nadis said, smiling slightly as she nodded and murmured, "I'm pleased to make your acquaintance, Captain. May I ask if my… *counterpart* has arrived yet?"

Desa felt just a hint more trepidation at the woman's slightly chillier tone, but shook her head as she replied. "She has not. I'm told that she should arrive tomorrow or the next day, weather permitting."

"I see. Now, where might these other carriages be?" Nadis asked, looking around curiously, almost imperceptibly relaxing.

"They should be coming out of the stables over there any moment," Desa explained, gesturing toward the large stables that were near the entrance of the city. More priestesses had stepped out of other carriages, as had Diane and Torkal Yisara, showing that the message Phynis had sent Desa was accurate.

The archpriestess didn't reply, simply folding her arms and waiting patiently as several acolytes rushed to pull out luggage. Carriages started emerging from the stable, these ones lighter and designed for the roads of Beacon, and Desa was relieved to see them.

In the meantime she studied Diane, Jaine, and Torkal again, always intrigued by how the two women had changed. Diane and Jaine looked more like sisters than mother and daughter, though Diane's bronzed skin was lighter than most dawn elves, while Jaine's was dark, almost honey-colored. Both had golden hair, though Jaine's had crimson highlights, and their eyes were purple, with one of Diane's eyes lighter than the other. Each had a starburst of purple in the middle of their foreheads, and they were warmly dressed for travel. Conversely, Torkal was tall and rangy, leaner than most dawn elf men Desa had known, and about as tall as most dusk elves. His hair was a sandy blond, and he had piercing blue eyes as he looked around the square, a sword at his side, just visible through his open trench coat.

"It's good to see you, Captain Iceheart," Diane said, approaching at a slow pace and smiling. "How is Lady Dayrest?"

"It's good to see you here, if somewhat surprising, Lady Diane," Desa replied warmly, conscious of how Nadis was watching her as she smiled at the two guests and Jaine. "I had expected Jaine to come for the conference, but you and the Marquis are something of a surprise. As for Isana, she's busy but doing well. I believe she's preparing lodging for the three of you, should you wish to stay separately from the priesthood of Medaea."

"That's *very* appreciated," Torkal said, smiling at Desa in obvious appreciation. "I'm sorry for dropping in on you without notice, but we decided to join the caravan at the last moment."

"Which doesn't excuse us for not having sent word ahead, perhaps. My apologies, Captain," Diane added, a touch contritely.

"I think they just wanted to avoid any accidental formality, considering Mother's current position," Jaine interjected, grinning as Desa smiled.

"Ah, much is explained. It isn't an issue, though," Desa said, smiling a little more warmly at them, her sympathy growing. "Her Majesty said that you were welcome to stay in Beacon if you chose, or to visit when you wished to, and that offer hasn't been revoked. I think she'd be scolded by Sistina if she did revoke it… or at least be the subject of a disappointed look."

"Indeed? Is… Sistina going to be involved in the conference, then?" Nadis asked, drawing Desa's attention to her again, and Desa found it harder to maintain her smile at the slight edge to the woman's voice.

"Not to my knowledge," Desa replied, letting her smile fade more gradually. "That isn't to say she'll be completely out of the way… she *is* married to the Jewels as well as Phynis, after all. However, from everything I've seen, she's been carefully avoiding having to deal directly with any part of Medaea or Tyria's churches that involves faith. She enjoys the company of any of the priesthood who I've seen visit, but that's as far as things go."

Nadis nodded slightly, and Desa studied her posture curiously. It was obvious that Archpriestess Nadis had a lot of experience in public and keeping her emotions hidden, since Desa couldn't see much of her feelings. Desa had a lot of experience in formal situations, though, so she did see a few hints, and it looked to her like Nadis was relieved.

"Indeed? I hadn't realized she wasn't involved. I'd almost thought that she'd be more heavily involved in the conference, since it *is* in Beacon," Diane said, blinking in surprise.

"I'm fairly certain that Tyria will be able to help keep the peace, at least to some degree," Desa said, relaxing slightly. "Not that she's the only one. I've heard the Jewels talking over the last few weeks, and it sounds like they've asked one of the other faiths in the city to mediate for the conference."

"Ahh," Jaine murmured, her eyes lighting up. She looked like she was about to ask another question, but one of the carriages pulled up next to them at that moment.

"Here we are," Desa said, smiling warmly as she gestured to the carriage. "I'd suggest the four of you go ahead of the others while we get your luggage organized and up to your lodging."

"Thank you, Captain," Archpriestess Nadis said, then got into the carriage carefully, the others quickly following.

"Indeed, thank you very much," Diane said, smiling warmly at Desa, which improved the captain's mood a little. Diane looked much happier than she had earlier that year when she'd taken refuge in Beacon.

"You're all quite welcome. I hope your stay in Beacon is pleasant," Desa replied, nodding to them. She stepped away so the driver could get moving and watched the carriage go for a moment, six of her best men and women escorting the carriage. It wouldn't do to have someone as important as the archpriestess attacked.

Then Desa turned to the rest of the chaos and sighed, stepping forward to get things organized properly. She was incredibly thankful that the two priesthoods weren't arriving on the same day. *That* would be awkward.

CHAPTER 3

"Medaea's archpriestess arrived," Erin said, just a few moments after closing the door behind her. Her voice was quiet, but it carried through the small room quite well.

Alexander looked up from the board game and blinked, looking at the plain brunette for a moment, then smiled. "Indeed? How was her security?"

"Surprisingly heavy. Medaea never had many knights, but I saw eight of them with her, and her robes bore subtle but strong defensive enchantments," Erin replied, frowning as she leaned against the door. "Beacon's security detail for them was disconcertingly heavy as well, as the captain of the royal guard came to meet her along with several golems and other guards, and the carriage assigned to the archpriestess and several royals had heavy defensive spells as well. I'm not certain where they're going to be lodged yet, but I'd be surprised if they weren't well defended there, too."

"I wish I could say that I was surprised," Alexander murmured, shaking his head and considering, then he carefully moved one of his pieces across the board. Bane scowled at the move, frowning as Alexander limited his options.

"What about the other faith? I heard that the church dedicated to Tyria was coming as well," Bane rumbled, running a hand over his bare head, then he moved a piece, wiping the smile from Alexander's face as he realized his own move had left a narrow but dangerous opening. One that Bane was exploiting.

"I caught enough of the conversation to know they're just a day or two away from Beacon," Erin explained, her smile widening.

"Indeed? That's good news!" Alexander said, smiling broadly as he looked away from the board. "Is Umira in position?"

"She should be," Erin said, shrugging. "I haven't gotten any messages indicating that she's been forced to move."

"Excellent. Let her know that she's allowed to strike at her discretion," Alexander said, smiling more broadly. He didn't have any personal grudge against either church, but Alexander was resigned to following orders, and he *did* like it when things went according to plan.

Erin smiled at that and nodded, pushing away from the door. "I'll let her know right away. This mission has been boring so far, anyway."

"Just don't get yourself caught," Bane said, sitting back in his chair. "We're playing a dangerous game, with everyone present in Beacon."

"I know that. I'm the one who has to go into more dangerous areas, after all," Erin retorted, then opened the door and was gone.

Alexander sighed and shook his head, scowling as he looked at Bane, and the other man's brown eyes were steady as they met his own. After a moment Alexander spoke. "You know, I really wish that we had more options for trying to get close to the rulers here. Having to rely on Erin and second-hand information is… grating. I'm used to being able to get close in person."

"Most places have more than twenty percent of the palace staff and nobility as men," Bane said, looking surprisingly calm. "The dungeon also complicates things, since we can't safely enter the palace at all, let alone spy on them. I just hope that this conference they have planned isn't inside the palace."

"You and me both," Alexander said, grimacing at the thought. "Assuming it goes off at all."

"True, true," Bane agreed, then smiled. "Now, are you going to move or not? I'd like to see you get out of *this* trap."

Alexander looked down at the board and scowled, looking at the positioning of the different pieces unhappily. After a few moments he spoke tartly. "You're way too clever for your own good, you know. Was that move I took advantage of just part of your trap?"

"Pretty much. I was more worried that you wouldn't spot it, with Erin distracting you," Bane agreed, smiling broadly.

"Damn it. Well, let's see if I can get out of this," Alexander muttered, looking at the board intently. "One of these days I'm going to beat you legitimately."

"I'll look forward to it," Bane replied with a chortle.

He never should have trusted the big man, Alexander reflected, but he couldn't help a smile. At least Bane was a good friend, as Alexander had few enough of those. Maybe Bane would even survive longer than the others had.

CHAPTER 4

"Welcome to Beacon, Your Holiness," Lirisel said, bowing her head and holding the position. To say that she wasn't nervous would be an outright lie considering the situation, and Lirisel wasn't inclined to lie to herself. Even if she *did* wish that someone else was in charge right this moment.

Lirisel had been chosen as the current high priestess in Beacon in a brief message from Nadis after they'd restored communications with Yisara the previous spring, and Lirisel wasn't entirely sure why she hadn't been replaced yet. She'd almost expected the archpriestess to replace her as soon as the dust had settled, considering how Lirisel and all the other priesthood of Medaea had failed to protect their goddess from Kelvanis.

"Rise, Lirisel," Nadis said, her voice even and clear. They were in the chapel of Medaea, and Lirisel straightened, relaxing slightly as she saw how the archpriestess was looking around the room in approval. After a moment she continued. "I must say, the temple is impressive. It's in the perfect position to greet the dawn, and I've rarely seen one so well kept, or with such lovely stained glass."

"Thank you, Your Holiness. While I cannot take credit for the position, all the priestesses drew up the plans for the temple together, and we've taken pains to ensure that it doesn't fall into disrepair," Lirisel replied, smiling warmly at the praise. "I made certain to have everyone look it over again prior to your arrival, but nothing more than minor issues were found."

"That's good to hear," the archpriestess said, nodding and slowly walking down the center of the chapel toward the altar. Lirisel accompanied her, and after a moment Nadis asked, "Did Sistina build the temple, then? That was what the reports I received said, but I wanted to ask in person."

"That's right. She originally offered last fall, if I'm remembering right… it took a few weeks for us to figure out what we wanted, and she built the temple underground, and adjusted things until it was what we wanted," Lirisel confirmed, gesturing around toward the upper reaches of the temple, particularly at the airy expanse of it and how many of the support pillars were made of stone. "That said, not everything is of her construction anymore. We needed more pews after the city was built, and she didn't have the time or mana to create them for us. We had those commissioned from some of the local craftsmen, and they've done an admirable job of assisting us."

"Interesting. Did the local craftsmen make your clothing? I don't believe I've seen that particular type of fabric before," Nadis asked, looking down at Lirisel's robes.

"Ah, these? They did, though the materials are from the farms below the city," Lirisel said, hesitating before she continued. "Miss Iris called it a satin weave, and it's quite comfortable."

"Interesting," Nadis murmured, and stopped before the altar. She examined it for several moments, then slowly knelt before the altar to pray.

Lirisel quickly followed suit, though she was careful not to lower herself too quickly. The last time she had, her knees had been extremely uncomfortable for hours, though that was mostly because Lirisel had refrained from healing them as a reminder to be more careful. Closing her eyes, Lirisel took a long moment to pray, the soft sound of bells from the city below them echoing through the chapel as well.

When she heard the archpriestess stand, Lirisel quickly opened her eyes and climbed to her feet as well. She glanced over and blinked, seeing a troubled expression on Nadis's face for the first time.

"You have interacted with Tyria more than any of the priesthood outside of Beacon, is that correct?" Nadis asked, looking at Lirisel closely.

"Yes, though my encounters with her haven't been common," Lirisel agreed, caution shadowing her thoughts, though she tried to keep her tone more upbeat. "The Jewels have spoken with her a great deal more than I have, but I understand if you don't wish to ask them. Diamond told me early on that their situation was such that she expected not to be considered part of the priesthood anymore."

"Diamond. Such a… no, it was not her choice. I should not judge Visna," Nadis said, shaking her head firmly, to Lirisel's surprise, and the archpriestess continued after a moment. "The number of our priesthood who were hurt or violated by Kelvanis's old regime are more numerous than I care to think about. Even now we're seeking those who were taken and trying to retrieve them from captivity."

"Of course. I've heard that some were sold to slave traders across the sea," Lirisel said, her eyes darkening as she thought about what might have happened to other priestesses in Medaea's service. "I can hardly imagine what happened to them."

"Fortunately or not, the *Archon* seems to have wished to keep most of the slaves in or near Kelvanis," Nadis said, her tone scathing as she referred to the former ruler of Kelvanis, Archon Ulvian Sorvos. "That helps with the search, and I'm gratified that King Damrung is doing what he can to assist us in our search. However, that wasn't what I was going to speak to you about."

"Of course, Your Holiness. My apologies," Lirisel said, feeling chastened as she looked down.

"Don't apologize, I was the one who changed the subject," Nadis scolded gently, surprising Lirisel into looking up, and the priestess blinked at the slight smile on Nadis's face as the woman continued. "You've been through much, and you don't deserve to be chided due to my own misgivings. Now, as to

Tyria. Despite every prayer and conversation with a few of your fellow priestesses who returned to Yisara, or with Lady Jaine, I find myself… I wish to hear from you. How has she interacted with you? Are you certain she was once Medaea?"

"I… I believe I understand, Your Holiness," Lirisel replied, a sense of relief rushing through her, and she straightened, looking her superior in the eyes. "As for speaking with me, Tyria asked me about who I was, and why I came to worship Medaea. She didn't talk much, but when I've spoken to her, she's been… reserved, I suppose. She listens closely, occasionally asking questions, but I've noticed how concerned she is. Some of the priestesses say that she often flies up to the top of the palace spire and stands there for hours in the wind, while other times she retreats to within the mountain, where Irethiel was defeated.

"If anything, I believe that at first she was even more concerned than you are that she might not be Medaea. I had a conversation with the demon named Wenris, the one who claimed to have sabotaged the Archon's attempt to corrupt her fully, and she claimed that what she did caused Medaea's memories to be suppressed." Lirisel paused, then looked down as she continued. "All that said, am I certain? Of course not. I never *saw* Her, before the attack on the temple. However, Diamond claims that while they changed her hair and lips, she recognized Medaea's face in Tyria's. I suppose Diamond could have had her memories of Medaea's face altered, but she never interacted with the Archon. I don't see how that could have happened. So while I'm uncertain, I've chosen to believe her."

"Interesting, though not what I wanted to hear," Nadis murmured, looking up at the stained glass, a troubled look on her face. "I'd like certainty to work off of, yet that isn't something we're allowed, is it? No matter what we choose, many of the faith are going to be shaken or worse."

"You're likely correct, Archpriestess," Lirisel agreed, looking down at the floor unhappily.

The door behind them creaked, and Lirisel looked back, only to smile as she saw the brilliant green tresses of Emerald, as the woman stepped inside, then froze in place. The other priestess was wearing a light green outfit that matched her hair, but her green eyes widened as her gaze fixed on Nadis. A moment later she quickly bowed her head and curtsied.

"Archpriestess Nadis! My apologies, I didn't expect you to be here already," Emerald said, a bit of anxiety in her voice. "I'd expected you to be at the manor, still."

"Greetings, Emerald… or Olivia, I believe your name was?" Nadis replied, a smile playing across her lips, though Lirisel thought it was somewhat mirthless.

For her part Emerald blinked as she rose, tilting her head as she replied hesitantly. "Yes… I do believe that was it. I've just grown so used to Emerald at this point that even with the changes to my mind fixed, that's what I like going by. I really wish that my memories hadn't been altered, but there's nothing I can do about it."

"May I ask what brought you here, Emerald?" Lirisel asked quickly, trying to change the subject to something more pleasant, rather than Kelvanis's enslavement of the Jewel.

"Of course! Phynis sent me to invite you to dinner tonight, and Ruby was going to your manor, Archpriestess. I suspect she'll be along shortly, assuming she learns that you've come here," Emerald said, looking much more poised, now. She smiled shyly as she added, "It's an invitation for you and whomever you'd like to bring with you, Archpriestess."

"Indeed? And whom might I expect to be present?" Nadis asked, looking at Emerald speculatively.

"Well, High Priestess Lirisel if she agrees, of course, along with Queen Phynis, Sistina, Diamond, Amethyst, Ruby, Opal, Topaz, Sapphire, and me," Emerald said, pausing as she considered, then added, "I suppose it's *possible* that Desa will join us, but that's really rare. I think Phynis is planning to invite Diane and Jaine a different night."

"Who might Desa be?" Nadis asked, pausing for a moment and frowning. "I would have sworn that I heard the name, but I can't place it."

"That would be Captain Iceheart, Archpriestess," Lirisel interjected softly. "She's a close friend of the Queen."

"I see. Now that I think of it, she *did* introduce herself, but I managed to forget her given name. Well, I believe I would like to bring two attendants with me, but would be otherwise quite interested to attend the dinner," Nadis said after a moment, then looked at Lirisel curiously. "Will you be attending as well?"

"I believe so," Lirisel agreed at the obvious implication that she should do so. Looking at Emerald, she smiled and added, "Thank you for the invitation, and please extend my thanks to Her Majesty."

"Of course, and—ah, Ruby!" Emerald's voice cut off as Ruby entered, the other woman in plain white robes rather than Emerald's more elaborate outfit, but which made her glittering red hair even more eye-catching. Emerald continued a moment later. "As you can see, I caught the Archpriestess here, and she's accepted the invitation."

"Indeed? That's good to hear, Archpriestess Nadis. It's also lovely to see that you are doing well," Ruby said, giving a half-bow, then straightening as she smiled. "I do believe it's been quite some time since we last met."

"That it has... about thirteen years, I believe," Nadis replied, smiling slowly. "You needed to discuss the budget for the temple, as I recall."

"That's right. I remember it was... an interesting conversation, and you weren't thrilled to hear that some of the funds had been siphoned off by one of the other temples," Ruby agreed, and Lirisel's eyebrows rose abruptly.

"That doesn't sound good," Emerald commented softly, and Nadis laughed.

"Oh, most definitely *not*. Priestess Malan was stripped of her position and sent to a rather spartan monastery in southern Yisara for that trespass. She has another seven years before I'll consider her requests to transfer to another temple," Nadis explained, relaxing still more, then her smile faded. "That was just before Kelvanis's first invasion... would that we'd always been able to focus on such petty matters."

"I entirely agree," Ruby said, smiling and looking to Emerald. "That said, we'd best return to the palace and inform Isana how many guests to expect. She'll appreciate additional time to prepare."

"She always does," Emerald agreed, and sighed before curtsying to Nadis again. "We'll see you this eve, Archpriestess!"

"That we will," Nadis said, looking amused as the two women walked toward the doors. Once they were gone, she remained silent, and Lirisel waited patiently. Eventually Nadis spoke, her tone amused. "At least she hasn't changed. Ruby always was the most responsible priestess in the temple, at least that I know of. Though their hair and eyes… it has to be seen to be believed."

"True enough. Ruby always did keep things running smoothly back at the temple. I never realized just how much she did until she was taken away," Lirisel admitted, shrugging uncomfortably as she realized that Nadis had been subtly checking to see if Ruby truly was who she claimed to be. "With the six highest-ranking priestesses gone, I had to shoulder a lot of duties that I had little experience with. We managed, though."

"That you did. Now, I believe that I should return to the manor to prepare for the dinner, and you should do the same," Nadis said, smiling at Lirisel as she added, "I'm glad I have the opportunity to settle in without having to worry about the priesthood of Tyria just yet. No matter how much I've spoken with Lady Jaine, I can't help feeling uneasy about them."

"I don't blame you. There *are* a few priests and priestesses of Tyria in the city, with a small chapel they tend to, but they've kept a low profile, despite her being in the city," Lirisel said, then bowed her head. "I won't keep you, Archpriestess. I look forward to joining you for dinner tonight."

"I'll see you then. May you walk in light, Lirisel," Nadis said, laying a hand on Lirisel's head for a moment, and Lirisel felt the blessing wash through her like a refreshing breeze.

"Thank you, Archpriestess," Lirisel replied, and watched the woman go, a smile flitting across her lips. Despite everything, the chance to see the archpriestess in person was a blessing all on its own.

However, after a few moments Lirisel shook off her distraction and headed for her quarters. If she was going to dine with the queen *and* the archpriestess, she wanted to be as close to immaculate as she could manage.

CHAPTER 5

The cold tried to bite at Elissa's fingertips as she touched the window, but it couldn't find purchase, and instead the traces of frost slowly melted where she was touching.

Tyria's fire blazed within Elissa, banishing the cold from her body, and she slowly breathed in and out, half-meditating to stabilize her emotions. Despite everything Elissa had done to mitigate it, the last several months had been chaos, and the amount of destruction within Kelvanis's borders was incalculable. At Tyria's command she'd done her best to reduce the violence, and Elissa knew that she *had* helped and would have even without the order, but nothing could truly stop it. Not when abused slaves had abruptly been freed, some of whom had been violent criminals in poorly guarded work camps, or when thousands of orcs abruptly lost their paymasters.

Slaid Damrung had done a lot to gain the support of the common folk of Kelvanis in that time, though, and had started in the area where his family had once ruled. The last months had allowed him to take control of the nation, though there were still two former Adjudicators at large and several pockets of resistance. Elissa wasn't happy with leaving all of that behind to attend a conference, but it was necessary.

"My goddess needs us to come to terms now, not when it's convenient for us," Elissa murmured softly.

"High Priestess?" Ollie asked, his voice pleasant. Elissa smiled at the recently ordained priest and shook her head at the sandy-haired man.

"It's nothing, Ollie. Just… thinking about everything we have yet to do," Elissa said, pulling her fingers away from the window.

"As you say," he agreed, nodding and smiling wryly as he continued. "There *is* an immense amount to do back in Kelvanath, isn't there?"

"That's putting it mildly," Elissa replied, almost grinning at his comment.

Instead of speaking further, Elissa continued to meditate on the fire within her. The blessing of Tyria was dangerous, but it also was a soothing reminder of what she'd promised the goddess. No matter what came, Elissa would remain faithful to Tyria. Even if Tyria became something other than she was now.

~

UMIRA WATCHED through the spyglass as the caravan moved slowly along the road between Westgate and Beacon, mildly annoyed by what she was seeing. The caravan wasn't quite as large or ornate as the one which had carried the archpriestess of Medaea, but despite that, this caravan looked like it had even more guards, which meant that her chances of eliminating the high priestess weren't good.

"Not that I'd be doing it in person, anyway," Umira murmured, studying the three carriages, one of which appeared to be filled with luggage and supplies. Two dozen guards were more than she'd planned for, but she wasn't the one taking the risk.

She shrugged and collapsed the spyglass, stowing it as she watched the caravan approach still closer to the forest, then pulled out her whistle. While the situation might not be ideal, she didn't have time to adjust plans. Instead she blew on the whistle, and a warbling sound rose from it.

A moment later, just as a couple of the guards were starting to react, an orb of fire erupted from the forest and launched at the lead carriage. Umira paused for a moment to watch the ball of fire detonate and the horses began screaming in panic as the carriage caught on fire. An instant later the raiders erupted from their hiding places.

"Good enough. Now it's time to leave," Umira said, smiling as she slid backward before standing, making sure not to silhouette herself against the sky. Glancing up, she added, "Good luck, Feldan. You're going to need it."

Then she headed toward her horse to make her own exit, whistling softly as she went. The attack either would or wouldn't work, and she honestly didn't care which. Either way, it would help accomplish their goals.

FELDAN SOARLIK CURSED under his breath, wondering why he'd thought that attacking the caravan was such a good idea. He quickly wove a spell, hastily twisting his fingers through the gestures and speaking the incantation to send several bolts of fire streaking out toward the guards clashing with his men and women.

"Damn it!" Feldan swore angrily as two of the targets dodged his attacks, and the third took the brunt of a blast, but the bolt splashed uselessly off the man's enchanted armor.

The attack had seemed to go well to begin with, and the carriage that Feldan had hit with the fireball was still burning, the flames rising higher despite the attempts of several guards to put them out. Their attempts were complicated by the distraction of Feldan's people, as the thirty attackers were fighting ferociously in their attempt to finish off the high priestess.

Unfortunately for Feldan, he'd far underestimated the skill of the guards, and at least a third of his people were down, and only one of the guards had fallen so far. The problem was how long the locals had been fighting for, he realized belatedly. Kelvanis, Sifaren, and Yisara had been in a state of war for over a decade, so they had far more experience than his people did. It meant that they didn't have the best of odds of winning the battle, which made him consider calling for a hasty retreat. If the high priestess was dead, that'd be enough anyway, he decided, and Feldan opened his mouth to order a retreat, then froze in shock.

The door of the burning carriage opened, and a woman stepped out, holding the scorched body of a man in her arms. The woman was only five feet tall and almost delicate looking, but managed to carry the man easily, and she was wearing a gown of white fabric. Her hair was raven-black, and her eyes were a striking electric blue that he could see even from dozens of feet away. She was smudged with soot, but otherwise unhurt, unlike the man she handed to a nearby guard.

"Shit, archers, aim at that—" Feldan began, but at that moment the woman raised her hands and wove a spell quickly and almost effortlessly, with a speed that Feldan couldn't have matched.

"*On your knees.*" The woman's voice echoed across the forest, her tone like iron, and it struck Feldan's mind like a hammer blow. The next moment he was on his knees, and they were aching from the force of hitting the ground. All around Feldan his men and women followed suit, and he realized a moment later that he couldn't do anything.

The woman looked across the clearing coldly, then spoke, her voice barely audible now. "Have the healers tend to your injured and Ollie, Lieutenant. Then take these miscreants into custody. I believe we need to deliver them to Beacon and find out just who tried to kill us."

"Yes, High Priestess," the guard said, bowing his head.

Looking at the woman, Feldan felt his fear grow, and once again he had to wonder just *what* had made him think this was a good idea.

CHAPTER 6

"Phynis, what happened?" Diamond asked, frowning as she stepped into the queen's office. "I left the temple a bit ago and ever since I've seen people running around everywhere."

"Oh, nothing too big… just an assassination attempt on High Priestess Elissa, apparently by followers of Medaea," Phynis replied as she looked up, her tone deadpan.

"*What*?" Diamond demanded, her eyes going huge in shock. "But that's ridiculous! She's coming here to speak with the archpriestess herself! Why would that—"

Phynis interrupted quickly, an apologetic look on her face. "Sorry, Diamond, I shouldn't have used that tone with you, I'm just a little… frazzled, I suppose. This isn't something I wanted to hear about, not when the two haven't even *met*, yet. Also, there's no confirmation of the attacker's identities; we're going off the initial message Elissa's people sent us."

"I…" Diamond paused and took a deep breath, then let it out and shook her head to clear it and regain her poise. Then she spoke again. "No, it's fine, Phynis. I don't blame you, not with as much of a surprise as this must have been for you. I'm just wondering what's going on."

"You aren't the only one. According to initial reports, there were no deaths among Elissa's party, though it was a near thing in three cases, and they'll reach town in about half an hour or so," Phynis explained, shaking her head slowly, her unhappiness obvious. "They also have the attackers in custody, those who weren't killed in the attack. Apparently, the high priestess is skilled with mind magic and disabled them fairly quickly."

"Is that so? That's... surprising. I hadn't realized she was skilled in that type of magic," Diamond replied, frowning in some concern. Mind magic was generally aligned with the element of darkness, which made it a little surprising for a follower of a goddess of light and the sun to use, but there was nothing that truly *prevented* someone from learning whichever form of magic they preferred. After a moment she set the thought aside and looked at Phynis. "Would you like me to meet her at the gates? If some of her company are injured, getting them care quickly seems rather important."

"Would you? That'd be a relief for me," Phynis said, smiling thankfully at the offer. "Desa is arranging for Helia and Evrial to go out, Helia to investigate the ambush site, and Evrial to escort the priesthood into the city, but I'd appreciate someone who *isn't* the guard greeting her."

"I offered, didn't I?" Diamond replied, taking a few steps forward and leaning down to give Phynis a kiss. The queen raised her head to return the kiss, then Diamond continued. "I'll ask if any of the other Jewels want to go with me as well. I want to find out just what is going on."

"You and me both," Phynis agreed, scowling slightly. "I really don't like that someone dared attack her in Everium."

"Agreed. Have you told archpriestess Nadis about the reports yet?" Diamond asked, the thought of Nadis's reaction making her distinctly unhappy. It'd been interesting to meet her after such a long time the previous night, but Diamond had noticed the careful distance that Nadis had kept in her conversation. It made Diamond wonder how much fruit their discussions with her would bear, but it also made her a little less worried about how Nadis would react.

"I haven't, at least not yet. I want more reliable information before potentially making her angry with us," Phynis said, and shrugged. "Besides, it isn't like she *needs* to know, yet. All we have is an initial report."

"True enough. I'll go speak with the others and go meet our guests at the gates," Diamond said, and sighed as she added plaintively, "Is it wrong that I wish that Sistina would figure out her plans for quicker transit through the city a *little* faster?"

"Not at all. Be safe," Phynis said in an amused tone.

"I will," Diamond agreed, and she turned to head for the door, moving briskly.

~

SEEING THE APPROACHING CARAVAN, Diamond grew more worried. One of the carriages had obviously been set on fire, and the upper sections were fragile-looking enough that it made the carriage essentially unusable, though a drover was driving it toward the city anyway, and the other two carriages looked like they were overloaded.

Also with them were twenty humans and elves, none of the latter looking like native dawn or dusk elves, and the sight of them made Diamond's eyes narrow in suspicion. She didn't know for certain how far Medaea's worship spread, but as the former archpriestess, she knew that they had only a handful of temples in the countries where other types of elves lived, and that made her skepticism that they were worshipers grow stronger.

Lieutenant Evrial was leading the guards from Everium in escorting the caravan closer, and Diamond waited as patiently as she could. Finally she headed for the courtyard once the first horses reached the bottom of the ramp leading up to the gate.

As she finished descending, Sapphire spoke, the other woman's voice steady. "Is it as bad as the reports suggested?"

Diamond sighed, looking at the blue-tressed woman and shrugging. "There's no way to know for sure, but it looks like one of the carriages was on fire, so... yes?"

"How wonderful," Amethyst said, sighing unhappily. "This isn't going to make Phynis happy."

"It isn't going to make *anyone* happy, I don't think," Opal retorted, looking quite unhappy as she huddled in her coat. "Plus, it just *has* to be freezing out here."

"In which case I believe it's best to make sure that our guests are healed and into secure, *warm* lodgings quickly," Sapphire said, looking at Opal with a slight smile on her face. "Besides, I told you to dress warmly."

"I didn't have time to change," Opal replied, frowning. "Besides, it didn't look like it'd be this cold from inside."

"It rarely does, and it's only the start of fall. You'd best get used to it," Diamond said, smiling in amusement. It was almost enough to overcome her concern about the attack on their guests. Diamond continued after a moment. "In any case, Sapphire is right. The sooner we help them, the sooner we can get back—"

"Am I too late?" Jaine's voice interrupted, and Diamond stopped, turning and blinking in surprise as she saw the former princess rushing across the courtyard, breathing hard.

"Lady Jaine? What are you doing here?" Amethyst asked, frowning as she added, "You look like you ran all the way down the mountain!"

"I… I did…" Jaine huffed, coming to a stop and leaning over, putting her hands on her knees as she gulped down air. "I h-heard… that Elissa's caravan was… attacked, and had to…"

"Save your breath, Lady Jaine," Sapphire said gently, stepping over to rest a hand on Jaine's shoulder. "While they were attacked, no one in the caravan was killed and High Priestess Elissa is safe. They're just approaching the gate now."

"Oh. Oh good," Jaine said, looking much more at ease as she slowly breathed in and out.

"I'm startled you managed to even make it down the mountainside that quickly, Lady Jaine," Diamond said, examining the city between them and the palace. It was over two miles from the manor where Jaine had been housed to the gates, and there wasn't a direct route, which didn't even consider that it was a descent of close to two thousand feet. She focused on Jaine and frowned. "In fact, I'd say that you had to have left within half an hour of us finding out."

"I was in the gardens, talking to Lily," Jaine replied, gesturing up at the palace breathlessly. "She was worried about the possibility of Wenris showing up again and taking advantage of her gardens, or something like that. I was trying to reassure her, especially after she nearly panicked when she met the Archpriestess, and then I heard about Elissa, and..."

Jaine's voice trailed off as the caravan came through the gates, and Diamond could see the look of horror on her face as she took in the sight of the lead carriage just behind the guards. A moment later the second carriage followed, but it didn't stop Jaine from speaking.

"Goddess, what happened? I heard there was an attack, but they didn't say someone set a carriage on fire!" Jaine exclaimed, looking horrified.

"Well, *that* is a familiar voice, isn't it?" a woman said, her voice surprisingly clear in the open air, and Diamond looked over in some surprise.

Diamond had heard descriptions of High Priestess Elissa before, but seeing the short, attractive woman in normal traveling clothing, complete with breeches and jacket, and her hair drawn back in a ponytail as she rode a horse was *not* how she'd expected to meet her. Diamond would have thought the woman was a guard from a distance, which made the encounter a bit of a shock.

"Lady Elissa! You're safe!" Jaine said, looking relieved as she rushed forward. "When I heard that there was an attack, I was worried sick about you!"

"I was just fine, Jaine. A little smoky around the edges, which required me to change, but just fine," Elissa said, the short woman dismounting and smiling as she hugged the much taller elf, then her smile faded as she continued. "I can't say the same for the driver or Ollie, though. They're both stable, but the other priests and priestesses are tending to them in the other carriage."

"I'm sorry to hear that, High Priestess," Diamond said, frowning slightly as she took a step forward and bowed her head marginally. "I'm Diamond, and with me are Amethyst, Opal, and Sapphire, all of Queen Phynis Constella's court. We're here to provide what assistance we can to your injured and to escort you to safe lodging."

"Indeed? Well, I see why you were said to be unmistakable,

Lady Diamond," Elissa said, smiling again, even as her bright gaze flicked over Diamond and her companions before nodding in approval. "Your offer of assistance is *very* much appreciated after the troubles of the day. While I have some skill with healing, there are limits to what my art can manage, and I'd far rather leave it to specialists. What of the prisoners? I'm fairly certain that they were trying to frame the church of Medaea for the attack, but we haven't had the luxury of time to properly interrogate them."

"They what?" Jaine yelped, her eyes going even wider, if that was possible.

Diamond frowned, but spoke after a moment. "The prisoners are to be taken to secure lodging for incarceration and questioning, and rest assured we intend to do everything we can to ensure they're kept secure. My question is, what do you mean by them trying to frame Medaea's church for the attack? Our preliminary reports weren't detailed, I'm afraid."

"Ah, of course. They all had holy symbols of Medaea, which is odd enough, but the symbols… they're too new. None of them have the well-loved appearance I'd expect from ardent worshipers or zealots. One of them even had a burr on the edge which hadn't been smoothed out," Elissa said, her nose wrinkling as she added, "Additionally, most followers of Medaea aren't known for their warlike ways, so that sets them apart as well. I sincerely doubt that the Archpriestess would have anything to do with something like this, not with Tyria in the city."

"That's rather disturbing, though it makes more sense than Her worshipers attacking you," Diamond said, a whisper of relief rushing through her, but she stepped on the feeling firmly as she continued. "On the other hand, it *is* possible that these really are zealots of Medaea. We can't let ourselves come to conclusions until we have evidence."

"Precisely. Now, why don't we get my people to these lodgings you mentioned?" Elissa asked, her tone brisk as she smiled at Diamond. "I'd like to get under cover so that we can get things sorted out properly."

"As you like," Diamond agreed, and gestured the others forward.

She didn't like the look of the prisoners, but there wasn't much Diamond could do about that part.

"WELL, that's unfortunate. Looks like the lady in charge of Tyria's church got out without a scratch," Bane said, looking over the balcony idly, trying to look like a casual gawker as the guards and priestesses swarmed in the town square. There were plenty of people doing the same, Alexander noted, making the chances of someone taking particular note of Bane or Alexander slim.

"Drat. I'd hoped that she'd have arrived in a coffin," Erin replied, sighing as she tuned her lute carefully. "I knew it wasn't likely, but I really did hope."

"The favored of the gods tend to be very survivable. Moreso when their deity is nearby," Alexander replied, glancing back at her in annoyance. "We knew this wouldn't be easy from the beginning, you know. Hells, it's only really possible because of how many immigrants are in Beacon."

"True enough. Speaking of which, don't you have to head in for your job, Maestro?" Erin asked, looking up at him with a neutral expression. "You don't want to lose it, after all."

"Is it that time already?" Alexander asked, glancing up at the sun, then sighed and shook his head. "Damn, you're right. I'd best get moving."

"Good luck!" Bane called after Alexander, then chuckled as Alexander gestured rudely at him.

He'd have to get ready quickly, but Alexander really didn't mind his job. Most people ignored the pianist in an upper-class tavern, and he *did* like playing the piano.

CHAPTER 7

Elissa adjusted her dress, frowning as she looked in the mirror. The dress was one of her spares, since the one she'd been wearing earlier smelled like smoke, and it didn't feel like it fit quite as well as she'd expected it to. Nothing was visibly out of place, but that didn't mean much, and her gaze drifted down to the semi-transparent section over the brand-like marking on her lower body.

"Maybe I shouldn't wear this dress… we *are* in Beacon," Elissa murmured to herself.

"We are," another woman agreed, her voice somewhat resonant, and Elissa stiffened slightly at the sound of it since no one else was in the room. She thought she recognized the voice, but wasn't entirely sure of herself. Besides, if it was who she thought it was, the owner might not be in a mood to be polite. Not that Elissa could blame her.

A woman stepped through the wall of the room, causing Elissa's breath to catch in her throat. The woman was an angel with violet wings and a glowing lavender halo, along with bright scarlet hair and flawless pale skin. Her purple eyes were fixed on Elissa, and the woman was wearing silver full plate with a sword sheathed at her side. The sight of Zenith made Elissa nervous since she'd been largely responsible for helping adjust the angel's memories. She also wasn't sure what had happened to her since Zenith had vanished after Diane and Jaine's escape the previous summer.

Clearing her throat, something that was unusual for Elissa, she spoke as calmly as she could manage. "Hello, Zenith. I hadn't expected to see you here."

"I'm not surprised. Considering our relationship before this, I'd have been surprised if My Lady told you what had become of me," Zenith agreed, taking a few steps closer and reaching out to gently pluck a pin from the back of the robe, causing it to fall into place correctly, and the angel nodded. "You should be more careful about pins, Elissa. What if you'd stabbed yourself with it? You are many things, but you are not immune to poison."

"No, I'm not. Was it poisoned, then?" Elissa asked, her heartbeat quickening suddenly. The possibility of more than one assassination attempt in a day had occurred to her, but not like *that*.

"Of course not. Your assistant merely wanted to make sure it didn't move out of position when traveling and missed removing one of the pins when she unpacked your clothing," Zenith replied, carefully setting the pin on the vanity. "Now, then. I believe that you owe me an apology, Elissa. You lied to me."

"I did," Elissa agreed, turning to face the angel and barely resisting the urge to frown. Only the heat of Tyria's flame inside her was enough to keep Elissa from kneeling before the angel, and instead she slowly bowed her head. "I lied not only to you, but also to Tyria herself, Zenith. For that you have my sincere apologies… what was done to you was unforgivable, and I make no excuses for it."

"Even if the decision to do it to me was not your own?" Zenith asked, and the skeptical tone of her voice startled Elissa into looking up slightly, and the smile on Zenith's face widened as she continued. "Yes, I'm aware of that as well, Elissa. It took a great deal of work by both Sistina and Tyria, but they unlocked most of my memories, while the others have returned bit by bit. You may have guided the fine points of my memories and attitude in the end, but you did *not* begin the process. You came upon the scene quite late, after all."

"True, but I could have told you, if I hadn't been so afraid. Much as I could have told Tyria what had been done to her," Elissa said, slowly straightening. "As such, you deserve my apology for what I did. It was something that could have been avoided."

"I have my doubts about that," Zenith said, shaking her head. "Sorvos would have acted himself if you hadn't, and to much worse ends, I'm certain. I've been changed and defiled, and yet... I still live. I've been granted my freedom once more, and I've learned from what has happened. Such is the way of life. Now, then. You're right, this is Beacon, and your garb is not quite appropriate to the occasion. I've come to fix that issue."

Elissa opened her mouth to speak, but Zenith didn't wait for her permission or agreement. Instead the angel waved her hand, and a mist of violet light washed out over Elissa. The dress shimmered, then vanished, reappearing on the bed a moment later as another garment slowly faded into existence around Elissa.

The robes weren't very elaborate, though they were incredibly soft as their weight settled onto Elissa's shoulders, and they were modest and warm. Much like what she'd worn before, the clothing was white, but with a pair of purple lines that ran from the collar down along seams all the way to the floor, following the curves of Elissa's body. Another set of lines ran down her shoulders to her wrists, and Elissa blinked, looking in the mirror to see that a final set went down her back as well, giving the outfit an odd symmetry. Another moment passed and a fur-trimmed cloak appeared on her shoulders, one of deep purple while the fur was white. It was different than what Elissa had expected, that was for certain, and she looked at Zenith in surprise.

"This... is not what I expected. Why would you come here simply to give me different clothing?" Elissa asked, gesturing at the wardrobe where her assistant had hung her other sets of robes and dresses. "I *do* have other clothing, after all."

"You do, but My Lady wishes to make a statement. It's already obvious that any followers of Medaea will have to change after everything has been dealt with. However, it is *also* true that you and the followers of Tyria will have to change as well," Zenith said, pausing for a long moment as she looked Elissa in the eyes. "You must have known this from the beginning, Elissa. What has happened to My Lady is without precedent. In the near future, there will be many questions by gods and mortals alike, and it's time to decide how to answer. Tyria cannot simply throw away the beliefs of those who followed Medaea, even if she wanted to. Likewise, she cannot simply throw away all that she was made into, for that is now part of her nature. A compromise must be made, and while it must be something that mortals can deal with, it also must be something that she herself can tolerate."

"So, you're saying that the clothing itself is a message, simply because it is different than anything else which I've worn before this," Elissa said, slowly nodding as she took in the angel's words. "I do wonder how it might be taken, when coupled with the attempt on my life."

"That's a legitimate question, and one which I don't have an answer for," Zenith admitted, shrugging slightly as she did so. "My Lady has been distancing herself for the time being, as she doesn't wish to show favor on one faction or another at this time. Even your clothing could be seen as too much, so you're expected to be clear as to *why* it is different. It isn't a sign of favor, but a sign that you're expected to change, not just those who view themselves as your opponents."

"As you say, Zenith," Elissa said, bowing deeply before the angel. "If you would please convey my understanding, and my acknowledgement of Our Lady's desires? I will do I all can to ensure that the conference goes without difficulties."

"Difficulties are to be expected. No matter who we turn to, you are *all* mortal," Zenith replied, smiling ever so slightly. "The day that an event such as this goes perfectly smoothly is likely the day before the world ends. For now, I will take your message to My Lady. Remember, Elissa, She is watching over all this."

With the gentle warning, Zenith stepped through the wall, becoming immaterial once more. Elissa looked where the angel had vanished for several seconds, then down at her clothing and smiled thinly, murmuring, "I see I'm going to need a new wardrobe again. Ah, well… at least I have enough funds hidden away to deal with that without touching the church coffers. There's enough draw on them as it is."

Smiling a little more, Elissa chose to enjoy how well the new robes fit, and the incredibly soft cloth, then headed for the door. She had a meeting with the local authorities, and Elissa was a touch nervous about meeting Queen Phynis. It wasn't as though the church of Tyria had started on the right foot where Beacon was concerned, what with Tyria having attacked the city. Still, Tyria all but lived here, so Elissa dared to hope that she might be welcomed.

Now, if the archpriestess was there, it might make things a little more strained, but Elissa was determined to take things one step at a time. Her goddess had told Elissa what she desired, and Elissa was going to do her best to fulfill that desire. Even if it *did* make her a little nervous.

"HELLO, High Priestess Elissa, and welcome to Beacon," Queen Phynis said, rising from her chair and prompting everyone in the room who wasn't standing to rise as well. The pink-haired monarch had a steady gaze, Elissa noticed, though there was some worry in it as well as she continued. "I must ask, are you sure that you're well? I know that the reports said that you were unscathed, but I wish to be certain for myself. This attack has upset me."

Also in the room were all the Jewels, who Elissa found fascinating, and not just because of their exotic hair styles, the dryad-like figure of Sistina, a dangerous being if there ever was one by all reports, the captain of Beacon's guard… and a woman that Elissa felt *had* to be Archpriestess Nadis. The cold gaze from the woman was to be expected, and Elissa couldn't help a smile as she nodded to Phynis, feeling like she was surrounded by giants, even if that was normal for her. The closest person to her height was one of the shorter Jewels, Emerald, and the woman was still over six inches taller than Elissa was.

"I'm quite certain, thank you. Lady Tyria has granted me a

blessing which makes me virtually impossible to burn, and they set the carriage on fire. Compared to her own flame, what is a simple mortal fire?" Elissa replied, reaching up to lay a hand on her chest, amused at the concern for her. "I also was an adventurer, a long, long time ago, so I'm not completely unused to danger. I'm out of practice, perhaps, but a little danger doesn't faze me."

"Indeed?" Diamond asked, the woman's eyebrows rising as Phynis settled back into her chair, the door of the small conference room closing behind Elissa. "I wasn't aware that you were an adventurer. You also don't appear that old, for a human."

"I don't speak about it much, but I intended to explain fully once I was here regardless. Someone will dig up the past, I'm certain, and it's best to be up-front about such things," Elissa said, considering the chairs around the table for a moment, then smiling again as Topaz gently pulled out a chair for her, one across from Nadis. "I'm certain it will cause even more problems, but not as much as hiding it would."

"And what, pray tell, would that be?" Nadis asked softly, watching intently as Elissa took her seat.

"Archpriestess Nadis, please… we have only just met Elissa, and we're dealing with a situation that's of concern to *everyone* in this room. With the possible exception of Sistina," Phynis said, glancing over her shoulder at the dryad, whose eyes were half-closed. Nadis paused, then sat back and nodded. Phynis waited for a moment, then looked at Elissa and spoke calmly. "Now, the matter at hand is largely regarding you, High Priestess. Your caravan was attacked by people in Everium's territory, and though none of your company were slain, I'm very displeased that you were in danger. I have trackers trying to determine where they came from, and we'll be working to question the captives, but such isn't guaranteed to produce results. You have my deepest apologies that you were attacked; I'd hoped you'd be safe here."

"Thank you for your concern, Your Majesty, but I do not blame you. Just as I do not blame the church of Medaea for the attack, no matter what holy symbols the attackers might have worn," Elissa replied, nodding and looking at Nadis, whose eyebrows rose slightly.

"Indeed? I thought that you might believe us behind it, or at least to blame," Nadis replied, meeting Elissa's gaze fearlessly.

"Ah, but such would be out of character for you, Archpriestess. I've gone over all the information I could gather about you in the last several months, and I cannot see you authorizing such an attack. Additionally, while it might be possible that zealots might act without your permission, I sincerely doubt that," Elissa said, nodding to Diamond as she continued calmly. "None of them shouted battle cries to Medaea, which would be most curious for zealots, and as I told Lady Diamond, there were too many minor signs of it being set up to draw suspicion on Medaea's church. It is *possible* that I'm wrong, but I refuse to assign guilt when I do not know who is truly at fault. Tyria would disapprove of such."

"That's interesting. I haven't gotten much information from my investigators yet, but if what you're saying is true, that doesn't sound like any sort of religious zealots I've heard of. They usually are quick to cry out the name of their deity," Desa said, her eyebrows rising. "It'll take some time to gather all the clues we can, and Helia is doing her best to track down where they came from. Her initial report doesn't look promising, though. Apparently, they settled in *before* the snowfall, which isn't going to make it easy."

"Unfortunate," Phynis murmured, frowning unhappily. "It's really too bad, since tracking down where they came from would make things much easier."

"Very true," Nadis said, and paused for a moment before continuing, looking at Elissa. "I should also thank you, High Priestess. I would entirely understand if you *were* to blame my faith for the attack. I didn't have anything to do with it, but the chances of a zealot being involved are... unpleasantly high."

"There's no need to thank me. I'm simply trying to look at things logically," Elissa said, looking around the room for a moment before continuing. "In fact, all of you have good reasons to despise me, though you may not be aware of such. All except perhaps Sistina herself."

That brought a round of raised eyebrows from everyone else around the table, and Sistina's eyes opened to look at Elissa. When they did, Elissa found herself unable to breathe for an instant. The power and age in those eyes was… incredible. Not the same as Tyria's, but powerful nonetheless, and it distracted her for a moment. Long enough for Sapphire to speak, in fact.

"What do you mean? You *are* the high priestess of Tyria's faith, but…" the blue-haired woman said, looking at Elissa with an oddly measured gaze.

"Ah, my apologies. I was… distracted. I've rarely seen those with as much power as Sistina, and it was startling," Elissa said, pulling her gaze away from the dryad. "I said that because it's unfortunately true. Yes, I'm the one who shaped Tyria's faith to begin with, which is why I'm the high priestess, or originally was. Things have changed, however. I'm no longer merely Elissa of Silence. I'm also no longer the woman I was when I accompanied Ivan Hall, Ulvian Sorvos, and three of our friends into the Road to Hell, and from there were dragged into the presence of Irethiel."

"You *what*?" Desa demanded, suddenly standing as she glared at Elissa, her voice sharp. "You associated with that *monster*?"

The others were reacting as well, and Elissa suddenly feared that she was going to be attacked as several more people stood. Then Sistina spoke.

"*Silence*." The dryad's voice echoed through the room almost like thunder, and everyone froze, even Phynis as she half stood. Elissa saw the expression of shock on Nadis's face as she looked at the dryad, but Sistina had not finished and was looking around the room with an oddly disappointed expression on her face. "Tyria allowed her to live. *After* she was freed. Withhold judgment for facts. Not anger."

The room was quiet, and after a moment Diamond nodded. She'd been one of the few who hadn't overreacted instantly, Elissa noted, and the woman spoke in a measured voice. "I agree. You might have noticed that she said *dragged* in front of Irethiel. It makes me wonder about the precise nature of the relationship between Elissa and Sorvos."

"I agree. I'll admit to having… acted on impulse for a moment," Phynis said sheepishly, then looked back at Sistina and smiled. "At least I have someone to call me out when I do so. Everyone, please sit and allow the high priestess to continue."

It took a few moments more, but Elissa felt herself relax as the others obeyed Phynis's request, though the looks she was receiving were considerably less kind now. She took a deep breath, then let it out and shrugged.

"If I thought it was possible, I likely would have chosen to hide that Ulvian and I were acquainted, but such would have been impossible in the end, and Tyria would not have approved. Instead, I believed it was best to bring into the light as soon as was reasonable, and not via the cowardice of a letter," Elissa said, looking around the table calmly. "Yes, we were part of the same group of adventurers, but that was before I was aware of his ambitions. Each of us had our own goals. Ulvian wished to master magic, Ivan wished to be wealthy and powerful, and I… I was a vain young woman who wished to find the secret to eternal youth. So we dared try to kill the Road to Hell, and half our group was slaughtered. We were all on the verge of death when Ulvian offered a risky escape route. We said yes, for we didn't have any other choice.

"Ulvian took us straight into Irethiel's throne room with a planar jump. I only then learned that he was in *love* with the demonic bitch," Elissa continued, ignoring the choking sound from at least one of the Jewels. Instead she studied her hand as she continued. "He spoke quickly, and that's all that kept us alive. He had already hatched the plot to take over Kelvanis and give Irethiel slaves, and she was interested. Interested enough that while she branded all of us, she promised not to control us as long as Ulvian's plots pleased her."

"Goddess… when was this?" Desa asked, much of the anger in her voice turned to shock by this point.

"Approximately eighty years ago," Elissa replied, glancing over at Desa and smiling unpleasantly. "I can't claim to have felt the same as you all did, since I was never actively controlled, but I didn't appreciate the threat hanging over my head. I was angry enough that I left him, continuing my search alone. I didn't find it, though I did find a way to restore my youth some three years ago. Then he asked me to come to Kelvanis, and I felt I had little choice but to agree. Of course, that's just an excuse... he also offered me eternal youth, and I *was* still enraptured by the idea. So I came to Kelvanis, and when he made his offer I decided to enact his grand plan and to create the faith of Tyria, the Goddess in Chains."

"You *dared* do something like that to a *goddess*?" Nadis demanded, anger smoldering in her eyes. "For something as simple as eternal youth?"

"As simple as eternal youth? I don't believe you have any idea what you're talking about," Elissa replied, her eyes narrowing. "I've had an explanation from Tyria's own lips about it, and it's something that even gods don't bestow lightly. Did I dare? Yes. Then, as I interacted with others, it reminded me of who I'd once been, before I became a self-absorbed, pigheaded adventurer. I've *enjoyed* being high priestess and helping others. So, when Tyria asked my absolute allegiance in return for the gift of immortality... I took it. I am *her* faithful servant, and should I ever stray from the path, Her flames will reduce me to ashes before anyone has a chance to realize what I've done. I accepted that willingly."

"What do you mean, her flames?" Phynis asked, her voice soft now.

"I walked into Tyria's flames of my own accord at the time. If I had been uncertain about my allegiance, or if I was lying about it, I would have died there. Instead, I'm now a vessel for Her power," Elissa explained, smiling slightly as she saw the faintest hint of understanding dawn on several faces. "That fire is within me. Should I stray from her service, even the tiniest amount... it will consume me. There are no second chances, especially once I told her what I did to her. Tyria will not allow it."

No one spoke for a minute. Elissa took a certain amount of pleasure in that, after the uproar from before. She didn't like it when people implied that she'd been lying, not after everything that she'd been through already.

"I sense Tyria's power within her," Sistina said simply, then half-closed her eyes and leaned against the wall again.

"That settles it, at least enough for me," Diamond murmured, sitting back and looking around the table. "I'm not going to claim that your revelation makes me happy, High Priestess. In fact, it makes me *quite* unhappy about your presence here… but I'm willing to reserve judgment and have faith in Tyria."

"Thank you," Elissa replied, looking at Diamond calmly. "What I've done… there's no way to *properly* make amends, even if it was relatively minor compared to what Ulvian did. However, I intend to do whatever I can to make up for it."

"You don't expect forgiveness, do you," Ruby murmured, her tone indicating that it wasn't a question.

"No, I don't. I might get it from some, but I don't expect it," Elissa said, smiling slightly as she nodded down at her clothing. "Zenith surprised me with her lack of anger, earlier, when she delivered my new clothing. She said that it was a message that I, and the church of Tyria, would be required to change. On the other hand, she *did* require an apology."

Opal snorted softly at that, shaking her head as she tried and failed to suppress a laugh. "An apology? After everything we went through with her… she decided to require an *apology*?"

"I'll remind you that she apologized to *us*," Sapphire said, glancing at Opal and clicking her tongue. "A lot of people were controlled. A lot of people did terrible things out of fear. I don't believe that anyone in this room could have changed what happened without knowledge we didn't possess. After all, if Elissa had tried to stop Ulvian, all that would have resulted was someone else in her place, or her being forced to cooperate with her brand."

"A definite point," Desa admitted, shivering visibly. "I remember some of the things he could do, and they chill my blood."

Elissa's attention turned back to Nadis, and she could see the barely suppressed distrust in the woman's eyes. Not that it surprised her, considering their differences. The question was, how would she react?

"I'll give you a chance," Nadis said at last, her voice calmer than it had been before. "I am going to keep your origin in mind when it comes to our discussions, though. I'll also warn, I won't tolerate a situation where *you* are in charge of any resulting church to my goddess."

"You won't be in charge either," Elissa replied, and felt a surge of satisfaction at the sharp look from Nadis, and she headed off the angry protest by continuing. "Or do you think that with Tyria here in the city with us that she's going to tolerate us making a church that doesn't suit *her* needs? She has two incredibly divergent faiths dedicated to her, and she has to not only merge them, but who she was with who she was made into. Neither of us are truly in control."

"I suppose that is true," Nadis said, obviously dissatisfied, but her glance at the rest of the room made it obvious that she wasn't willing to argue in the presence of everyone else.

"It also runs rather far afield of why we came here," Desa said, clearing her throat. "At the moment we don't have enough information to properly make decisions on what to do about the attack. It appears that everyone is willing to wait for additional information to be acquired, so with that I suggest we adjourn for the moment. I will ensure that each of you are kept informed of any additional information that comes to light."

"That seems quite reasonable," Elissa agreed, nodding politely.

Phynis smiled and stood, prompting most of the others to stand as well as she spoke. "I believe we are best served by following the captain's suggestion. I look forward to speaking with you further, and hopefully under better circumstances. Welcome to Beacon, High Priestess, and I believe that an invitation to dinner will be forthcoming."

"I look forward to the invitation," Elissa replied, bowing her head slightly and nodding to the others as well. "Now, as much as I would like to speak with all of you further, I believe I need to check on my companions and ensure that all of them are settled in. It was an eventful day."

"Of course," Phynis said, her smile fading. "Let us know if there is anything we can do to make you more comfortable."

Elissa inclined her head slightly and turned to leave. As she did so, she could feel Nadis's gaze follow her to the door. She ignored it, knowing that the archpriestess wouldn't do anything more here.

Tomorrow was another story, once they were discussing the fates of their churches. But Elissa had been expecting that much.

CHAPTER 8

Tyria sensed Diamond's presence and opened her eyes, smiling as she looked down from where she was hovering.

Sistina's caverns were incredibly peaceful for Tyria. They were lush with vegetation even in the middle of winter, and contained many plants that had died out in the world outside, but that wasn't what drew Tyria to them. It wasn't that she was linked to Sistina, though that helped, instead it was the soft, peaceful power Tyria still felt imbued into the ground after Irethiel's defeat.

The damage that Irethiel had dealt to the gardens had long since been restored, and that reassured Tyria, as well as accentuating the sense of peace it provided. Paths meandered their way through groves of trees, bushes, and fields of mystical flowers, many of which had been rare even before the Godsrage. Now they were practically unique, save for those which were being grown in the palace gardens above. Mana slowly flowed through the cavern, channeled by the subtle designs that Sistina had created to make the power move in an ideal stream without ripples. To most it would be imperceptible, which was truly remarkable to those who could sense it.

That Sistina had channeled the remainder of Demasa's power

still startled the goddess, as doing so had shown that the dungeon was far more than she appeared to be. At the same time, it had also been both terrifying and wonderful, for while the dungeon had also channeled the power of Kylrius, the touch of Demasa's magic had been comforting, a last touch of her old friend. Or she'd thought it'd be the last touch, if there weren't some tiny remnant of that power imbued into Sistina herself.

The thought caused Tyria's gaze to turn toward Sistina's tree, and her feelings grew even more complicated at the sight of it. Sistina looked like nothing more than a weeping willow with white bark, tiny fruit-like ruby beads, and bright green leaves, though motes of gold light drifted around the tree. Sometimes Tyria wondered why she hadn't initially recognized the tree as the world tree itself, but she knew better. The old world tree she'd seen before had been truly immense, over a mile tall rather than merely two hundred feet, so she could forgive herself for the mistake. Yet at the same time, the old world tree had been far more alien, almost aloof in its own way, not so... so *aware*, as Sistina was.

"Your Eminence?" Diamond's voice wasn't loud, but it carried clearly to Tyria's ears and drew her gaze down to the edge of the pond, where the priestess was kneeling, looking up at Tyria.

Considering for a moment, Tyria chose to descend, her wings beating slowly as she drifted down toward the priestess, still over the pond. It amused her that she liked the spot where she'd been trapped by Sistina so much, but the crystal shaft that provided sunlight from the mountaintop above made her feel even better than if she was elsewhere in the cavern. Besides, Sistina didn't object to her presence.

"Hello, Diamond," Tyria said, keeping her voice soft as she looked down to meet the woman's gaze. Technically Diamond was one of her priestesses, Tyria knew, but the situation had grown less certain when Diamond had wed Sistina and Phynis, especially with Sistina able to control Tyria. Diamond may not think she was Tyria's equal, but the goddess tried to treat the woman that way.

Diamond blushed, looking down at the pond as she cleared her throat, then spoke. "Are you well, Your Eminence?"

"As well as I can be. I've been meditating a great deal of late, and this is an ideal place for it," Tyria replied gently, considering the elf for a moment, then continued. "You appear disconcerted. Is there something that I can help you with?"

"That's the question, isn't it? I'm certain you know of the attack on Elissa's caravan, so I won't go over that. I was..." Diamond began, then paused again, looking torn as she licked her lips and hesitated. She seemed to debate for a long moment, then continued softly, almost nervously. "I was startled when she told us that she was responsible for the changes to you, and even more surprised that you forgave her. May I ask why?"

"Why? Why indeed," Tyria said, slowly smiling as she considered, then stepped onto solid ground rather than hovering over the pond. She extended a hand to Diamond and waited for her to take it before drawing the woman to her feet, which relaxed a little of Diamond's tension. The goddess started down the path, drawing the flushed elf with her as she continued. "I approached her after Irethiel was dead, to ask her if what I'd learned was true. She chose to confirm it, and I asked her why she hadn't told me. Do you know what she said?"

"I... don't. She didn't talk about that, but there were a rather large number of people present, and most of them were hostile to Elissa," Diamond admitted, shaking her head unhappily. "I tried not to overreact, but the archpriestess wasn't happy. I can't really blame her."

"Of course she wouldn't be. Would that I hadn't slept for so long, but... even deities can make mistakes, Diamond. One of mine was believing that I'd be forgotten, and that my power would fade until I vanished entirely. I wished to sleep until that occurred," Tyria explained, pausing to brush a glowing pink blossom on one of the trees, a flower she'd never seen before. At her touch a shower of glittering silver dust puffed out of it, some adhering to her hand, but most of it floated away on the gentle breeze flowing through the cavern. Tyria watched it, then continued on her way. "Either way, Elissa told me she was afraid. Afraid of the consequences, from me, from Irethiel… and that she'd decided to tell me if I asked, but no more. She was telling the truth, of course. She cannot successfully lie to me, and *that* is why I forgave her. She regrets what she's done, and between her deeds in Kelvanis and what's come before, Elissa may spend every year she lives trying to atone for her misdeeds. Thanks to my gift to her, that will be many, many years indeed."

"Ah. I think I understand," Diamond said, relaxing ever so slightly. She fell silent almost immediately, and Tyria suppressed the urge to sigh as they continued along the path.

They moved through the cavern slowly, and Tyria allowed Diamond time to think and work herself up to speaking about whatever else it was she wanted to say. As they moved, Tyria paused, a little surprised as she saw an elf near the edge of the cavern. She hadn't sensed Lily enter the cavern, which was a touch disconcerting, and it took her a moment to realize that the young elf's mana was so thoroughly attuned to that of the caves that she practically blended in, even as the blonde woman industriously weeded a row of peas. After a moment Tyria continued on her way, not wanting to make the shy gardener nervous, and she was a touch amused at the presence of the tiny vegetable garden in the corner of the cavern.

"I'm not sure what to do. I don't know that the archpriestess trusts me, and I don't know what it is that you want, Your Eminence. I don't know that the churches can reconcile at this point, even with you there to help mediate, not with the attack, the news about Elissa, and everything else that's going on," Diamond said at last, her worry palpable.

"You can only do what you can do. No more, and no less," Tyria replied, her mood calming still more, though even she felt an undercurrent of anxiety about the situation. The conflicting prayers she received were disconcerting at times, after all, so she continued gently. "What is coming is necessary, unfortunately. I will lose faithful, of that I have no doubt. Some will find other deities, and others may attempt to found new faiths that are based on what they wish I was. I do not blame them, for faith is the refuge of many from the cruelties of the world. However, I cannot in good conscience allow others to turn me into something which I'm not, and never was. Not even if they have the best of intentions."

"I... what do you mean, Your Eminence? It almost sounds like you're saying that the church of Medaea had things wrong," Diamond said, looking at Tyria with steadily mounting confusion. "I know you've changed, but... is that what you meant?"

"Yes, it is. I don't blame you, for the Godsrage destroyed a great deal, and then I was sleeping, and wasn't there to correct many of the mistakes that were made. Six millennia is a long time even for elves, more than sufficient for teachings to diverge from the truth," Tyria replied, letting out a soft, sad sigh as she shook her head. "Had I woken, I might have changed to suit the faith of your church, truthfully... but then Kelvanis changed everything."

"Oh," Diamond said, swallowing audibly. After a moment she asked hesitantly, "What did we get wrong?"

"That is a discussion for tomorrow, once the meeting between churches is underway. I can't have them believing that I'm showing favoritism... even if I am, to some extent," Tyria said, a smile flickering across her face. "Not for either of the churches, mind you, but I favor Beacon over them, in all honesty. Sistina was the one who helped me free myself of Irethiel's shackles, and she couldn't have done that without the belief of you and your sister priestesses here. Is it any wonder that I favor you?"

Diamond blushed, looking away quickly as she rolled her shoulders uncomfortably. After a moment she spoke, changing the subject. "What of the attack, though?"

"That is an entirely different matter, and unfortunately... I am not sure what I dare do about it," Tyria said, her smile fading at the change of subject, anger swelling inside her, though she kept her voice calm. "I am no longer controlled by a mortal, so acting against mortals who are acting on faith is risky, verging on violating the agreements that ended the Godsrage. Sistina could force me to act, which would allow me to intervene safely, but she won't. No, as the acts of mortals, it's up to all of you to decide your path and deal with it. Too many acts of divine intervention would be as bad for mortal destiny as it would be for me to ignore you entirely."

"I see. I just… I'd hoped that you would be able to shed some light on the situation," Diamond said, looking more downcast now. As the former priestess looked away, Tyria resisted the urge to sigh, instead smiling helplessly as she shook her head.

"I know that's what you wanted, but… would it really be that much better if I made the decisions for you? Gave you all the information you asked for?" Tyria asked, her voice gentle as she looked at Diamond, waiting for the woman to meet her gaze reluctantly, and then finished, her voice soft. "If I did, it would be just another way of controlling you, and that isn't something I want. It would make me little different than Irethiel, after all."

"What? That isn't what I meant, Your Eminence!" Diamond exclaimed, paling as she looked at Tyria in horror. "I didn't think you were like… like *her*!"

"I know you didn't, and I wasn't saying you did," Tyria reassured Diamond, her smile growing a little warmer as she did so, shaking her head gently. "I'm just telling you why deities *don't* give too much information. Knowledge has its price, and even if I know what's going on, which I don't fully, not in this case, it's best that I refrain from speaking idly."

"Ah, I… I think I understand," Diamond said, slowly looking like she was relaxing, and after a moment she nodded, swallowing visibly as she continued. "I'll do my best to respect your choice, Your Eminence, even if I wish that you could help more."

"Thank you," Tyria replied, and she continued along the path, finding herself slightly more content with the company of another.

Perhaps it was that she'd slept for so long, the goddess reflected, but she found herself treasuring the company of others more, even if she had difficulties relating to them. It had nothing to do with the heat that had continuously pulsed through her body ever since her confrontation with Irethiel. She had to keep telling herself that.

~

SISTINA CURIOUSLY WATCHED Diamond and Tyria continue walking. For the most part they were silent, yet at the same time there was far more to their relationship than an outsider might realize, at least at first glance. Sistina's memories had been slowly unlocking over time, though, and Avendrial had been an expert at reading the desires of others, even if she'd been betrayed in the end. The problem there had been that Irethiel had been expected to be ambitious. If she hadn't been ambitious, she'd never have achieved the position she'd been given.

Not that such applied to either of the women Sistina was watching, though. At the same time as she watched them, she was also slowly, carefully opening the shafts for her new lifts, which fortunately didn't take so much concentration that she couldn't speculate.

Diamond had been watching over Tyria for so long that her faith had changed, Sistina finally decided, looking at the priestess's attitude. She was subservient to the goddess, yes, but at the same time, she was one of the ones who'd helped restore Tyria, and she'd watched over the sleeping goddess's body. Coupled with Tyria's relative ignorance of the modern world, it meant that Diamond was almost a mentor in some ways, though she'd never dare think of herself that way.

On the other hand, Tyria knew how much she'd failed her people and was guilt-ridden over it, especially with how Diamond and the other priestesses had been captured and enslaved because she'd been asleep under their feet. It didn't help that she was constantly distracted by low-level arousal which had been inflicted on her by Kelvanis's changes. That was what gave Sistina several clues of what was going on, though, with how Tyria seemed to be trying to clumsily grow closer to the Jewels.

After a bit Sistina mentally shrugged and turned her attention away from the two women to straighten out part of one of the shafts instead. Whether Tyria was trying to woo Diamond consciously or not wasn't her business, and she didn't want to pry. Far more concerning was the attack on Elissa, but Sistina couldn't do much about that. She was a tree, and the city guard was better equipped to investigate outside the city.

A straightforward invasion, Sistina could deal with. Not so much a covert infiltration, not after retracting her domain from the city. The most she could do was make transportation easier, which was why she was fighting with the damned foundries to make *straight* rails.

It was harder than she'd thought it'd be, but she *was* a tree, not a mountain.

CHAPTER 9

Aldem felt a headache coming on, and he wondered, ever so briefly, what had possessed him to come to Beacon. It was a silly question, though, since being chosen to head the temple of Vanir in Beacon had been an incredible honor.

The dawn elf priest had been ecstatic on reaching the temple, for Vanir herself had shielded the Temple of Pure Waters from harm, and it was the first fully intact temple they'd found that had existed before the Godsrage. Even better than seeing the ancient prayers and tales engraved on the walls had been perusing the holy texts that had survived as well, no matter how difficult it was to read them. The powerful water elemental guardian had been helpful with translating the texts and explaining many of the odd phrases that were within them. At times context made all the difference in the world, and Aldem had been both fascinated and horrified to learn that Vanir had been widowed in the Godsrage. How *that* had never been recorded since then was something that he couldn't quite understand.

All the pleasure of learning so much had prompted him to readily agree to Diamond's request that he mediate between Medaea and Tyria's faiths, but now… now he wondered if that had been a poor decision.

They were in a larger building adjacent to the Temple of Pure

Waters, one which Sistina had kindly erected since the temple itself was too small to hold much in the way of priesthood, and the first pilgrims of the faith had already shown up, some of them from much farther afield than either Sifaren or Yisara.

On one side of the conference room was the archpriestess of Medaea, her gaze cool as she looked around, a pair of priestesses on either side of her, and two fully armed knights of Medaea flanked the door on that side of the room, one male, the other female. Opposite Medaea's party was the high priestess of Tyria, who looked far more serene than anyone else in the room, and a pair of human priests, including a rather tired-looking man and a pretty redheaded priestess. Their guards were a dawn and dusk elf, though the two men were less heavily armed than their counterparts. The two sides were eying each other in suspicion, which was prompting a large part of Aldem's regret.

Also in the room were the Jewels, all seven of them, and while Aldem usually liked admiring the beautiful women, he was mostly relieved that none of them seemed to be causing the tension to increase, though he found himself faintly amused that they outnumbered the priests on each side of the table in the center of the room. Regardless of how much he regretted getting himself into this situation, Aldem cleared his throat and spoke loudly.

"If you'd take seats, please? I'd like to get started for the day, before we lose any more daylight," Aldem said, looking at each party in turn.

"If I may, I would have one request," Elissa said, the woman glancing toward Nadis as she smiled.

"What might that be?" Nadis asked, the archpriestess watching her counterpart warily.

"The more people who are present, the longer this is likely to take," Elissa explained, then raised a finger as Nadis inhaled, continuing smoothly. "I'm not asking you to reduce your numbers, Archpriestess. Your guards and assistants make perfect sense, and I'm certain that one of them will be taking minutes of the meeting for later. No, I'm curious if perhaps the Jewels might be willing to reduce their numbers."

"Ah, that does make a degree of sense. Priestess Visna?"

Nadis asked, turning to Diamond, whose smile dimmed at Nadis's words.

"That may have once been my name, but it no longer is *mine,*" Diamond said, looking back at Nadis, her voice surprisingly calm as she continued. "Nor am I a priestess, at least not in the way that you and the others are."

Nadis paused, looking back at Diamond for a moment, and Aldem almost swore under his breath, growing unhappier. They hadn't even started, and things were getting off on the wrong foot. He opened his mouth to speak, but at that moment Nadis spoke softly. "I see, my apologies, Diamond. However, what of the High Priestess's request?"

"Your apology is accepted. As for your request, we discussed it earlier, and the intention has been for Ruby and myself to do the talking. If necessary, the others will leave the room, but I'd prefer that they were able to hear the discussions for themselves," Diamond replied, glancing at the others as she raised an eyebrow and asked, "Would you like them to leave, then?"

At the nods from Elissa and Nadis, the other Jewels began to stir, and Opal stepped forward to hug Ruby, speaking just loud enough that Aldem could hear her. "I think we'll go to the garden for lunch, if you two can make it. Don't enjoy yourself too much, hm?"

"Why, thank you for the ringing endorsement," Ruby replied dryly, and a chorus of laughter rang through the room as the five women filed out. In short order the room was mostly empty, and the priestesses were taking their seats, to Aldem's relief.

Beside the archpriestess and high priestess, their assistants began setting up paper and ink pens as if to take notes, and Aldem blinked as he saw Ruby set a small device made of brass and copper on the table, a quartz gem glittering on top of it. He hesitated, just about to sit, but was uncertain what the device was.

Noticing the attention she'd garnered, Ruby spoke up brightly. "This is to record the meeting. Albert made it, and he explained that it allows another device he has to project an illusion of what it records. If things go on for long enough we'll have to get more crystals, but I thought it'd be easier than writing things down as we went. I'm not a scribe, after all."

"Ah, interesting! We're starting to see a few more devices made by artificers around the city, but not many," Aldem said, looking at the device curiously. "It doesn't help that he's the only artificer in the city, to my knowledge, and he's a Guildmaster."

Ruby nodded, smiling wryly as she exchanged looks with Diamond before replying. "Very true. Sistina is learning a lot from him, and probably will build lots of devices, but I suspect she'll never do things this small."

"She thinks too big," Diamond added, shrugging. "I'm hoping that we'll attract artificers from abroad, but time will tell."

"Indeed," Nadis said, her eyes narrowing slightly. "However, I believe it is time to begin."

Aldem nodded, tensing as he took a deep breath, then spoke. "Agreed. Now then, I am Aldem Corwight, High Priest of Vanir in Beacon, and I will be presiding over this conference between the churches of Medaea and Tyria. While recent events have made the presence of your guards necessary, I must firmly remind you that violence within these walls will *not* be allowed, except in self-defense. Any transgressor will be removed from the city."

"As you say. May I ask how we're to address you, High Priest?" Nadis asked, inclining her head respectfully, which helped improve Aldem's mood.

"Well, considering how many members of the priesthood are here, I was going to ask that you dispense with my title entirely, and simply call me Aldem," he replied, cracking a smile as he looked around, adding, "The situation we're in is rather new to me, but I'd rather that you were polite throughout than on overly formal terms."

"As you like. In that case, you may call me Elissa," the high priestess said, then nodded to her companions, continuing. "These are Ollie and Roxanne. Ollie is the first male priest to be ordained in Tyria's church, while Roxanne has been overseeing the temple in Westgate."

"I'm certain everyone here knows who I am. I'm Diamond,

and this is Ruby. The two of us represent Queen Phynis and Sistina in this meeting," Diamond said calmly, and her gaze drifted to Nadis as she continued softly. "Sistina has directed me to let all of you know that she has not and will not attempt to influence Tyria, unless she desires for Sistina to do so, or if she attempts to harm the city or its residents."

"An interesting claim," Nadis murmured, looking at them for a long moment, then let out a breath and continued. "However, it would be rude of me to insist on a title when all of you are forgoing them as well. You may call me Nadis while in the meeting, and I am accompanied by Felicia and Miriselle."

"Excellent, now then—" Aldem began, hoping that the unsteady peace would hold as they continued, but a sudden heat from behind him interrupted, along with purple radiance that played along the walls and ceiling. He stopped, then slowly turned, hoping that there'd be an angel behind him, but an instant later his hopes were dashed.

Tyria stood there in full armor, her sword in its sheath as she glowed, looking over the people in the room. Her gaze stopped on Aldem, and he swallowed hard, once again wishing he hadn't agreed to host this meeting. He was completely out of his element here.

"Thank you for your aid, Aldem Corwight. While I would have preferred to keep the peace myself, my current circumstances make that impossible. Not when my very nature is part of the discussion," Tyria said, her voice gentle as a flowing brook, and her gaze made Aldem's pulse race.

"I… well, you're welcome, Your… Your Eminence," Aldem replied, swallowing hard.

Tyria looked up at the others, and her voice was just as gentle as she continued. "Now then. I am Tyria, the Eminent Flame. I *was* Medaea until this past year as well, but such is no longer the core of my identity.

"All of you, save for Aldem, have worshipped me at some point in your lives. I have heard your prayers, even if I have not always been conscious of them, and to some extent I know each of you," Tyria said, her gaze slowly playing over the crowd, and as it did her smile faded, and she spoke softly. "Unfortunately, what you've worshipped and believed, each and every one of you… was incorrect."

"What?" Nadis snapped, and Aldem felt like he'd been kicked in the stomach.

This was *not* how he'd hoped for the first day to start.

NADIS COULDN'T HELP her angry exclamation, and she immediately regretted it as the goddess looked at her, and despite every effort she could *feel* herself almost shrink under Tyria's gaze. The presence of the goddess shook her faith, hard, and despite everything it felt like she had on those days when she'd been closest to the divine. Even so, Tyria's claim angered her, and she opened her mouth to speak further, only for the goddess to pull a chair out of thin air and sit as she spoke.

"I'm not saying that your faith was misplaced, or that you were entirely wrong, Nadis. I'm saying that over the millennia, and especially after the Godsrage destroyed so much, that your church's beliefs diverged from the tenets of Medaea," Tyria explained, her calm, reasonable tone soothing much of Nadis's anger. The goddess looked at Aldem, and the gold-haired dawn elf did *not* look happy, Nadis noticed. In fact, he looked more like he'd been tossed in a pit of lions, but it didn't stop the goddess from asking, "Aldem, have you found that the church of Vanir from before the Godsrage is different than what exists now?"

"Well… yes, I suppose so," the man admitted reluctantly, glancing back and forth as he did so, then continued. "There are a fair number of things we didn't know about, like her having once been wed to another deity, and that she used to only be a goddess of fresh water, not of the oceans or seas. There are other things, too, but most of them are relatively subtle on the whole."

"Precisely. However, the difference is that she was available to correct the course of any mistaken beliefs, or to explicitly allow them when they diverged," Tyria said, her smile sad as she shook her head. "I… in my role as Medaea, I was not. My angels would not dare speak for me in such a manner, so the faith was allowed to change without my guidance. It turned into something that, while accurate in some ways, was inaccurate in others. I'm more surprised that no one has looked up the scriptures of mine which are still in Everium's library. As you didn't, I took the liberty of having a copy made."

The goddess pulled a book out of the air and set it on the table, smiling as she looked at Nadis, adding softly as she continued, "Feel free to check it against the original; I made certain that it was an accurate copy. However, this is for you, Nadis."

"I… see," Nadis said, frowning at the book as she heard Felicia's ink pen scraping paper as she rapidly tried to catch up with recording notes. Some of Nadis's frustration had cooled, but she wasn't sure what to say, and instead nodded to Miriselle, who reached over and picked up the book.

"If I may, Your Eminence… may I ask what sort of things have changed? Since you obviously know what Medaea's faith originally was," Diamond asked, and a tiny amount of Nadis's tension eased at the worry she saw on the other woman's face. If Diamond didn't know either, it… well, it might not help, but at least Nadis wasn't alone in her discomfort.

"Certainly. Based on what I've heard in prayers, read in tomes, and been told, your faith holds that Medaea was an elven goddess of healing, the sun, and repentance. A goddess of peace, who tried to comfort those who'd lost others, or who'd try to aid others in finding redemption," Tyria said, glancing at Diamond and smiling ever so slightly as she shook her head. "That is… not entirely inaccurate. I *was* the goddess of healing and the sun, but repentance? No, that isn't quite right."

"What is right, then?" Elissa asked curiously, causing Nadis's abused temper to flare.

"Why do *you* care?" Nadis asked incredulously, looking at the other priestess skeptically, annoyed despite herself. She was fascinated by Tyria's claims, yet at the same time somewhat outraged.

"I may have made many of the decisions that changed her into Tyria, but in the process I had to read about her and understand who she was," Elissa said, looking back as calmly as could be, and yet there was something about the woman's eyes that unnerved Nadis. She was too calm, Nadis realized, and it made her shiver slightly. A moment later Elissa continued. "I learned about her, and yet after the changes she was someone different than I expected. If her faith had changed… that may explain why Tyria is who she is *now*, rather than what she was intended to be."

"That seems likely," Tyria agreed, her smile drawing everyone's gazes back to her. "I was not a goddess of peace, Nadis. I was originally a warrior-angel who tended to the fallen on the battlefield and sent them on their way to the next life if necessary. I was not one of Death's servants, but I was… close, in some ways. In Demasa's court, I was the final arbiter of justice, and when no one could speak for the dead, that role was mine. The sun reveals all truths, purifies the dead that they may rest, and is the pyre upon which evil will burn. I healed those whom I could, I brought light where it was needed… and when necessary, I would take vengeance for those who could not."

"You were what?" Nadis asked numbly, ignoring the inhalation of surprise from Miriselle as part of her reeled in shock.

"I was a goddess of justice and vengeance, not just of the sun and healing," Tyria said patiently, looking back at Nadis with a level gaze. "What you've believed… it might have caused my nature to shift, had I not been captured and changed further. Instead, Elissa and Irethiel attempted to change my core values. Their attempts were… effective, I must say. If they'd chosen a different approach, or known what my nature was, it might have even succeeded more fully. Instead… I believe that a number of nobles in Kelvanath were rather horrified by my actions once I woke."

"What happened?" Felicia asked softly, almost startling Nadis out of her silence, and the archpriestess swallowed, trying to gather her thoughts again.

"Her Eminence woke and examined Kelvanath. In her role as the goddess of slaves, I had expected her to leave things as they were. Instead, she killed the cruelest slave owners in the city, then announced to everyone that if they wished to be the masters of others, they had to be worthy of those who served them," Elissa said, prompting another wave of shock to ripple through Nadis. The human pursed her lips for a moment, then continued. "I must say, the look of shock on Ulvian's face was priceless. He asked me what she was doing, which I obviously couldn't answer. However… the nature of who you were before explains it, Your Eminence. If you often avenged those who died unjustly, it makes sense that you'd do the same for those who'd been abused in your new role."

"Precisely. Now, then, I believe it's time to focus on something else," Tyria said, her expression darkening as she looked at everyone, then continued. "Each of your faiths was incorrect in many ways, and that means some adaptations are necessary. I refuse to be a goddess of slavery, but likewise, I'm not a goddess of peace. If I need to become Medaea again, or if I must take *another* new name, so be it, but for now… you must discuss the situation and attempt to come to terms with a faith which each church can accept."

"Yes, Your Eminence," Elissa said promptly, and the two priests by her side murmured their own agreements.

Nadis noticed that Diamond and Ruby had been silent, and neither of them looked too surprised, though they *did* look concerned. Nadis took a breath and looked at her companions, considering as she met their worried gazes. If they'd been the type to collapse into hysterics, she wouldn't have brought them to begin with, but they obviously weren't taking the goddess's revelations well.

A part of Nadis still wanted to hold out hope that all of this was a lie, that Tyria wasn't Medaea, and that the explanations she'd given weren't true. However, looking at the book in Miriselle's hands, along with the strange sense of… of resonance she felt when in Tyria's presence, she couldn't hold out much hope for that. Instead, she changed her approach slightly, taking a deep breath, then let it out.

"I… would like some time to think on your words," Nadis said, looking at the goddess as her pulse quickened from anxiety. "What you've said is an immense shock, and many people among the church would have difficulties accepting it. *I* have difficulties accepting it. May we retire for the morning, at the least, so that I and my companions can look at this book and compare it to the one in the library?"

Tyria didn't immediately answer, instead looking at Diamond and Elissa. The two looked at each other, then Diamond shrugged and sat back, speaking calmly. "I'm fine with a delay, as I live here. The two of you are the ones who might wish to move more quickly, so I will leave it to you."

"In which case I'm happy to allow a delay. My church is likely to adapt much more easily, since it isn't well-established, so if the information in the book helps us to come to an accord more easily, I'm happy to let you examine it," Elissa said, looking back at Nadis with a slight smile.

"If that's the case, I'll happily adjourn our meeting for the day," Aldem said, more than a hint of relief in his smile as he stood.

"Thank you," Nadis said, and looked at her companions, as well as her knights, adding, "I believe we have an appointment in the library."

They nodded in agreement, and Nadis quickly moved toward the door, leaving behind the discomforting sight of Tyria.

CHAPTER 10

"That's... unexpected," Bane murmured, pulling the spyglass away from his eye and frowning thoughtfully. He was in a tower a fair distance from the building where the churches of Medaea and Tyria were meeting, and he hadn't really expected to see anything for hours. In fact, he'd almost missed it when someone *did* leave.

The sight of the archpriestess of Medaea leaving the building hadn't surprised him; instead it was the pensive look on her face, and that of her companions, that was confusing. If she'd left in a rage he'd have understood, but instead the meeting with the other church had lasted barely an hour at most.

"Well, nothing to be done about that," Bane said, shrugging and smiling to himself. "At least it means I can head back early."

Putting away his spyglass, Bane turned to descend from the tower. He really appreciated how many empty buildings there were in Beacon, though that was slowly changing. It gave plenty of potential hideouts for now, though.

DIANE PAUSED AND SMILED, calling out gently. "Hello, Lily!"

"Huh, what?" Lily asked in confusion as she spun around. The blonde dawn elf had a scattering of freckles across her face, and was paler than most dawn elves were, Diane noticed. It was probably due to how much time she'd spent indoors, when the former queen thought about it, and her smile grew as the young elf exclaimed. "Your Majesty! And His Grace! My apologies, I didn't realize you were there!"

Lily bowed deeply, one hand holding her broad brimmed hat on her head, while the other held the trowel she'd been using. The young woman had a simple outfit on, one suited for the gardens, and behind her was a tree resting in a hole, its roots halfway buried. With Lily distracted, a lion-sized panther cautiously poked its nose into the hole and sniffed curiously.

"You really don't have to call us that, you know," Torkal said, smiling warmly as he exchanged looks of amusement with Diane. That was because they'd told Lily that at least six times that the former monarch could think of, and Lily refused to act like they were normal people. Personally, Diane found it comforting with how honest Lily could be. Besides, not many other people would be willing to tell off a demon lord in person, like Lily had Wenris.

"Be that as it may, it isn't right to disrespect you," Lily replied, still bowing.

"It isn't disrespect, not when we tell you that don't need to. Rise, please," Diane told her, suppressing a smile as she shook her head.

The gardens in Beacon were a marvel to her, as even with the snow the other day the flowers and grass were flourishing as though it was spring. A few magi had told her that it was largely because of Sistina's domain, but it was also due to the work Lily put in as well. The young woman straightened, a nervous expression on her face, and she fidgeted with the trowel, glancing to the side, where a bush with blazing red flowers radiated warmth.

"Thank you for understanding, Your Majesty, but I—Kitten! Get your nose out of there *now*!" Lily exclaimed, and the black-furred feline recoiled just as a paw was about to dig at the dirt, looking supremely guilty as it backed away from the hole. The elf looked outraged, and the panther cowered, looking as guilty as only kittens or children could, in Diane's opinion. She'd heard that Kitten was still growing, and didn't really want to know how big the panther would get.

Diane giggled despite herself, asking, "Does Kitten do things like this often?"

"No, just when she wants attention," Lily said, glowering at the cat for a long moment, then brandished the trowel at Kitten as she continued. "I cleaned your litter box this morning, so don't you *dare* tear up the garden just to get me to play with you. If you do, I'll take away your treats, see if I don't! And I won't let Ilmas give them to you, either."

Kitten's ears went back, letting out a piteous growl as she closed her eyes, and this time Torkal chuckled.

"Does she really understand you, then?" Torkal asked, patting Diane's hand as he focused on Lily and Kitten.

"For the most part, though she tries to pretend she doesn't on occasion. Sometimes I think of Kitten as an oversized housecat," Lily said, the distraction having helped her calm down, Diane noticed. The young woman continued, sounding wryly amused. "Sistina's domain certainly can lead to intelligent animals when she wants it to, but I'm not sure if that's a blessing or curse where Kitten is concerned. Though I have to admit, she certainly adds warmth across the foot of the bed!"

"I believe that," Diane agreed, eying Kitten as the feline took advantage of the distraction to creep away, and took pity on her as she nodded toward the bush, asking, "Speaking of warmth, may I ask what plant that is, Lily? I saw it when I was here before, but it wasn't radiating heat at the time."

"Oh, these?" Lily exclaimed, her eyes lighting up with enthusiasm as she stepped over to the plant, reaching down and stroking a flower, which had a long, trumpet-like funnel around glittering stamen. "This is a fireberry bush, according to Kassandra. I've talked with a few visiting druids, and they claim it died out in the Godsrage, but it wasn't incredibly common before that. They only grow in areas with lots of mana, like nodes or dungeons, as the case may be, and they gather fire mana, which is why they shed heat. I've planted them around the gardens to make the winter more bearable, and supposedly sometime around midwinter it'll fruit. Isana is planning to have a vintner make cordial from the berries, which is supposedly a delicacy. Sistina got a distant look when I asked her about it, but encouraged the idea."

"Ah, interesting," Torkal murmured, taking a step closer to the bush, drawing Diane along with in the process. "I hadn't realized that. It's fascinating… do you know why it's alive here, then?"

"I guess Sistina just sort of… *revitalized* the seeds. From what she's indicated, even if a seed is old and dead, as long as it's reasonably intact she can bring it back," Lily said, frowning. "I did wonder if it was something like resurrection, but she said it wasn't. Just that it was a new plant, or something like that."

"Hmm… interesting," Torkal said, and Diane relaxed as the warmth of the fireberry bush enveloped her.

They stood there for a moment before Diane spoke, her voice soft. "How have things been going here, Lily? You seem pretty happy."

"Oh, they've been great! Aside from a couple of so-called nobles who think that tumbling the help would be fun," Lily said, snorting and grinning as she added, "I told Kitten she could play with them, and they thought better of the idea. Word seems to have gotten around, and I don't get nearly as many requests to show people around the garden anymore."

Torkal laughed, a hint of mingled disbelief and mirth in his voice that brought a smile to Diane's face, even if Lily's words stunned her. "They did *what*? I don't blame you for your reaction, but I can't believe that anyone would make requests like that, not considering what happened with Kelvanis! Don't they realize that a lot of the people here would take offense?"

"Yeah, well… *apparently* some people decided that since Beacon is newly founded, and a huge portion of the current high-ranking nobles are women, it's an ideal place to send their second, third, and fourth sons," Lily said, her smile fading slightly, a finger twirling a lock of hair as she glanced to the side, adding, almost as an afterthought, "Daughters, too, but they're not as common. A couple have been after the queen or her spouses, which has made things a little awkward lately. It eats a lot of their time to deal with, especially since I've heard something about not wanting to ruin foreign relations, or something along those lines."

"Ah, much is explained," Diane murmured, sighing softly as she realized that even with Everium's new foundation, it couldn't avoid politics. At least Phynis wasn't new to the arena, which reassured her. It probably helped that she had a goddess and Sistina backing her up, too.

"Agreed. Well, we probably should get back to our walk and let you work. May I ask what type of tree that is? I'm surprised you're planting it when there's been snow on the ground," Torkal asked, nodding at the tree.

"Oh, this? It's an apple tree! One which I think produces the tastiest apples ever!" Lily explained, her eyes lighting up as she grinned widely. "They have a lovely tartness that perfectly offsets the sweet, and I really, *really* want to try a cider made from them. Sure, it won't be ready this year, but next year… anyway, Sistina's domain will keep it alive, so I can keep working all winter, except if the ground freezes solid. I intend to make this the best garden outside Sistina's ever! Assuming the gods of destruction don't decide to visit, anyway."

"Ah, I understand. Well, I hope the tree and garden grows well for you," Torkal replied, smiling as he added, "Good day to you."

"And you as well, Your Grace, Your Majesty!" Lily said, trying to curtsey, though when she realized she wasn't in a dress the young woman blushed brightly, prompting a chuckle from Torkal.

They stepped away from her, and Diane glanced back to see the gardener breathe out deeply, then turn back to her tree. Diane looked away after a moment, smiling as they continued on their walk through the snowy gardens. Not that there was much snow on the ground, just enough to obscure the grass where it hadn't melted.

"You really seem to enjoy talking to Lily, and I sometimes wonder why," Torkal said, his voice quiet as they lingered near another fireberry bush.

"She's… pure, I think," Diane replied, a surge of affection washing through her as she looked back at him, smiling gently.

"Despite everything Lily went through in Kelvanis's hands, she's… well, she lacks any deceit. Plus, I think one of my favorite memories was when she told off Wenris. You know *that* story, of course."

Torkal laughed, smiling broadly as he murmured, "Yes, I certainly do! You've told me a few times, after all. I just wish…"

"I know," Diane agreed, her smile fading as she patted his hand gently. She did know, after all. Her being essentially the possession of a demon lord bothered him, even if Wenris had left her alone for the past several months. Not that Diane had faith that would last much longer.

They continued walking in silence, and as they did so, Diane's mind drifted to Wenris, and her former superior, Emonael. She often wondered what they were up to, since neither seemed much like most demons to her. Not that she had any way of really knowing.

~

"You aren't any fun these days," Wenris said, her wings slightly drooping as she moped over her teacup. "Before, I could do all sorts of things for fun, but now you keep telling me that if I do something for fun, I'm likely to be smote."

"Yes, I'm aware. Welcome to the price of not only becoming a fairly powerful demon lord, but also to having roused the ire of Fate," Emonael answered, her voice an eerie mirror of Wenris's, though there was something subtly off about the tone of her voice.

The goddess flicked her fingers through the air effortlessly, drawing sigils of a spell as she spoke, and Wenris watched in envy. No one else she knew could cast spells while speaking to another, even if they used the correct tones to invoke magic. It was just too difficult to carry out a conversation and cast a spell at the same time, as far as Wenris knew. It was almost worse that Emonael was a reflection of Wenris, though with her coloration reversed, dark skin instead of pale, and silver-white hair. It made Wenris wish she could cast magic the way Emonael did, even if it wasn't possible.

"You helped me carry out a grand deception over Fate which changed the course of the future, and all without him realizing what was going on. I may not have *broken* the rules, but that isn't enough to assuage his ire. No, that will take at least… a century or five more. As such, we must act more demurely," Emonael continued, a star flickering to life in her hand, one which contained so much mana it made Wenris shiver. The goddess tossed the star upward gently, and it drifted up to join the thousands of others on the ceiling and walls of her observatory. The amount of power in the room always filled Wenris with both awe and fear, since she didn't know what the replica of the mortal sky was meant for.

"I suppose, but it doesn't necessarily make me *happy*, you know," Wenris conceded, taking a sip of her tea, the wonderful flavor barely breaking through her unhappy mood. "I haven't visited Diane in months! I have every right to, but you said that it wouldn't be wise!"

"Because it wouldn't. She needed the time to re-center herself, so your presence would have been counterproductive," Emonael said, and glanced over as she smiled, adding, "Note the word *needed*, if you would? Things have changed."

"Oh?" Wenris asked, perking up suddenly, much of her dismay vanishing. "Why do you say that?"

"Mm… despite Fate focusing his attention on us, we aren't the only ones who he's needed to watch. More the fool him. I play the long game, and am very patient," Emonael said, her voice serene as she looked up at the sky above them, then shook her head. "Others… are shortsighted. Tyria's re-emergence is like a stone tossed into a still pond, as is Sistina's existence. Others won't leave them alone, and their plans are already in motion.

"As such, those with more freedom than I can interfere as well." Emonael's smile widened as she glanced at Wenris, adding wickedly, "Not that they *need* the help, mind you. Anyone who takes Sistina lightly is liable to lose their hand and arm if they aren't careful, if not their head. With every week that passes, she regains more of who she was, and more of who she will *be*. One day… well, I cannot tell you that. Act if you wish to,

Wenris, but don't do too much. You are no longer below the notice of the greater gods."

"Yes!" Wenris exclaimed, almost jumping out of her chair in excitement, a grin flashing across her face as she stood. "I was starting to get so *bored* just managing my domain! Sure, the first couple of months crushing rebellions was a bit amusing, but it gets stale fast."

"Welcome to the joy of power. At least when you don't have a goal for it," Emonael said, murmuring another spell as she created another glowing star to cast into the sky with a languid gesture, smiling broadly as she added, "It's your greatest weakness, Wenris, in its own way. I do like that you enjoy the present so much, however. It's why we're still allies, however loosely."

"Well, at least I'm not your enemy," Wenris said, her joy faltering for a moment. The idea of being Emonael's enemy terrified her, with what little she knew about her former Lady's patient focus. Instead she took a deep breath, then spoke simply, a note of nervousness in her voice. "I promise I won't try to interfere with Sistina. Now that I know that she was Marin, I know how much you care about her."

"You know nothing," Emonael said simply, looking at Wenris without any reproach, but with a twinkle in her eye as she added, "You may think that you do, but you do not. Harm her, and nothing in this universe will spare you from my wrath. Now, go and play, hm? Just play wisely. I'd hate to have to destroy you."

Wenris swallowed hard at the lighthearted warning, her heart almost stopping for a moment, as she knew it wasn't an idle threat. Instead she bowed deeply, her voice steady despite her worry. "Thank you for your guidance, Queen in Mirrors. Without it, I would not have achieved my current position of power. I'll bid you a good day, and will keep your words in mind."

"You are welcome," the goddess replied simply, the dismissal in her voice obvious.

Wenris straightened and walked toward the exit, glancing down through the transparent floor at the lower half of the observatory and the countless motes of light above and below. She did wonder what the lights were for, but Wenris knew better than to ask. She was no longer one of Emonael's servants, so the chances of her getting an answer were even less than they had been before.

Instead she turned her attention to seeing Diane again, and her tail began flicking happily behind her. First, Wenris would have to figure out what these other plots were, but then… *then* she could have some fun.

Assuming Sistina didn't kick her out of the city, at least.

EMONAEL TOSSED the artificial soul into the rest of the array, smiling as she did so. No one else understood what she was doing, outside the primal gods, and that was just as it should be. Wenris was on her way, and that was *also* as it should be. She rather enjoyed thinking about the demon queen's future, and none of it would be directly Emonael's fault. If Emonael was being forced to act, everything would have gone wrong. However, she could feel Fate's watchful gaze on her, and her smile grew a little more.

"I'm not going to act myself, you can see that as well as I can," Emonael said, glancing up to meet his gaze, which she knew would unnerve the other deity. She smiled, adding calmly, "*I* have no need to do so. I don't care about Tyria, after all."

Fate didn't reply, not that she expected him to. Instead he retracted his gaze, and Emonael laughed softly to herself, her smile widening as she murmured, "He *does* amuse me. Even if he holds grudges."

CHAPTER 11

"Gods damn it," Erin said, her tone baleful as she gripped her dagger hilt, and Alexander watched her warily. The woman had a hell of a temper, and she looked riled up to him. Fortunately, Umira seemed to think the same thing, and she spoke up instead.

"Calm down, Erin. We all knew that Feldan's attack wasn't guaranteed to work out how we wanted it to," the elf said calmly, her brown eyes flickering with irritation. "I'd hoped that he'd either have opened his mouth by this point or had the truth pried out of him, but we can't have everything."

"No, but I can curse when everything goes wrong, can't I?" Erin shot back, but her hand came off the dagger hilt. "I'm just angry at how this is going. Nothing's gone according to plan so far!"

"Then we'll just have to change plans," Alexander told her, leaning his chair backward until it was propped against the wall. He wasn't as calm as he sounded, but he didn't want to set Erin off again. While she wasn't really a threat to him, he didn't enjoy pain, either. "We'd hoped to set Elissa and Nadis against each other, and it could still happen, even with a goddess keeping an eye on them. We need more information to judge, really."

"True," Bane said, glancing at Erin as he asked, "How've your attempts to get included into the staff of the houses go?"

"That's part of why I'm so *angry,*" Erin snapped, her eyes flashing with frustration. "The attack caused the lady in charge of everything to clamp down *hard* on who she chooses to take care of the guests. It was bad enough with how she gives former slaves preference, but it only got harder. Now they're bringing all their food from those damnable underground farms, *and* checking them for poisons before feeding the priests. We're not getting at them that way."

"Hell, I thought poisoning was at least an option, but if that's out, it's out," Alexander murmured, his mood souring slightly. He'd rather have started with the poisoning, but had been overruled. He considered, then looked at Bane. "What about the library? That's where you said that Nadis and her assistants went, right?"

"Yeah, it is, and its security is almost as heavy as the palace's," Bane said unhappily, shaking his head as he frowned. "I asked why it was so heavy, since I'm supposed to be a newcomer, and one of the servants explained that since so much knowledge was lost in the Godsrage, the tomes inside are priceless. That being the case, they're guarding it heavily while the books are copied. It'll only take, oh, a century or two… damned elves."

"I resemble that remark," Umira told him, her eyes narrowing slightly as she pointedly brushed a lock of black hair behind an ear.

"I know," Bane replied unrepentantly.

Alexander rubbed his eyes as he suppressed the urge to sigh, wishing he hadn't been assigned to be in charge of the group. After a moment he asked, "So, is there anything we *do* know that we didn't before?"

"Elissa is a potent mind mage, and apparently immune to fire. Possibly cold as well, but I'm not sure on that," Bane said promptly, frowning more heavily. "That makes me uneasy, honestly, but there isn't much we can do about her. Mind magic… it means we have to take more precautions."

"As if we weren't already," Erin retorted, crossing her arms and adding unhappily, "We also know they aren't going to jump to conclusions, which makes them harder to deceive."

"I don't know about that. Elissa put herself in harm's way for others, so I think that if we go for a sufficiently enticing trap, they might just walk into it," Umira disagreed, shaking her head. "No, I think we need to focus on drawing them out of Beacon. It's just too dangerous to act directly here, with Tyria and the dungeon involved. You've seen the golems, too, and those are worse. I can't mentally control them, and the guards here have tough mental shields, for some reason."

"It's almost as though the neighbors had been using magical slavery for years," Bane muttered, earning another glare from the elf, and Alexander couldn't help a sigh this time.

"Enough. If we have to change plans, we change plans," Alexander said, considering for a moment before adding, "I think Westgate is our best bet. From what I've heard, they can use a node here to teleport to Westgate, but not the reverse. That means that if we can draw them to Westgate, they won't have an easy line of retreat. Thoughts?"

"Um, perhaps? There *is* the old temple of Medaea that was dedicated to Tyria there... if we had a priest or two killed, or maybe kidnapped some of them, using the same strategy as before... but like Bane, I don't like the idea of moving too directly," Erin said, tugging at her upper lip.

"Perhaps not, but we do have other people who we can use, and maybe even embroil another country in the process," Alexander said, smiling a little more as he added, "It seems that the new ruler of Kelvanis has put a bit of a crimp in the style of some of our allies."

"Oh?" Bane asked, sitting up suddenly as his eyes lit up.

"Yes, a certain assassin's guild has been rather put out by the new regulations, and they have some... *interesting* allies," Alexander confirmed, glancing around the room as he raised an eyebrow and asked, "What do you think? Shall we see if we can't get someone else to do the dirty work for us?"

"That seems like an *excellent* idea to me," Umira said, slowly smiling, as he'd known she would. The woman never liked putting herself in danger, and both of the others nodded in agreement.

"In that case, I'll send a letter to our superiors, and they'll let Kevin know," Alexander said, relaxing even more as he did so.

The plans might have changed, but he wasn't one to get stuck on a single approach. That was a good way to get killed, after all.

CHAPTER 12

"This is... could it be a trick, Archpriestess?" Felicia asked, her voice trembling. The priestess was obviously holding onto the threadbare hope that Tyria was trying to deceive them, which Nadis understood.

"I'm afraid not... unless this isn't the original copy of *Medaea's Illuminations*?" Nadis said, looking over at the librarian hovering nearby, prompting a sniff from Zarenya, and the dusk elf gave her an annoyed look.

"That tome was here when the city was unearthed and even before," the head librarian replied, her voice a bit testy. "We went through the index to ensure that it was accurate, then looked at all the tomes which might have held information on breaking the slave brands. A cursory overview of that tome revealed no applicable information, so we set it aside. Tyria didn't touch it, I'll have you know."

Zarenya had been a wonderful help, Nadis admitted privately. She'd thought that she knew how to read ancient elven script, but the tomes had been written in an even more archaic form than she was used to, and they'd needed Zarenya's help to translate several words here and there, as well as making sense of some idioms.

That was why the other priestesses were so numb, Nadis knew. They'd expected at least a few untruths among what Tyria had said about Medaea, but if anything she'd been understating things. The tales of who Medaea had been... it was shocking in the extreme, and it shook the foundations of Nadis's faith.

No, not the foundations, Nadis corrected herself firmly as she shook her head. It changed some of the details of who Medaea had been, but it didn't truly *contradict* most of the oldest tales about her. If anything, the information added additional context to her faith, but under the circumstances it was shocking.

"I didn't mean to cast doubt on your management of the library, Madam. I simply wished to be certain, as what we've learned here is... troubling," Nadis said, gently nodding at Zarenya as she conceded the point. After a moment she let out a soft sigh, shaking her head as she murmured, "This will cause difficulties back home."

"Perhaps, Your Holiness, but if I may... perhaps it would be best to send the copy we were given home and begin spreading its contents?" Miriselle suggested, raising the copy of the book which Tyria had given them. She looked a little nervous, swallowing as she admitted, "As much as I hate to admit it, I think... I think this is real, and that Tyria is being honest with us. If we're going to have to change... well, if the faithful find out that we found an *original* copy of Medaea's holy texts, and that we'd diverged from what our ancestors believed..."

"You're saying that it might convince them to accept some degree of changes in another direction," Nadis concluded, sighing again as she sat back. For a minute she sat there, then chuckled darkly. "Ah, how I wish that we weren't in this situation... but we can only work with what we have. I don't want a schism in the church, but no matter what we do, we're going to lose some of the faithful."

"We already have," Felicia said, standing up suddenly, then starting to pace back and forth in the small room. They could have met in the main hall of the library, but there were enough scholars and scribes that it would have been distracting. Nadis also rather liked the reading room, as she'd never seen one with a magical lantern in the shape of a crystal orb before, and the furniture was surprisingly comfortable for lacking cushions.

"Oh? Ah, let me guess, the word that Medaea was captured

and changed by Kelvanis shook the faith of many," Zarenya murmured, and Nadis suppressed the urge to wince as the woman unerringly singled out the problem.

"That's right," Nadis confirmed, looking back at her calmly. "It has been a difficult year, and Tyria's demand that we reconcile our faiths has made it even more difficult."

"Would it be better to have her still serving Kelvanis?" Zarenya asked bluntly, and this time Nadis couldn't suppress her flinch.

For a long moment the room was quiet, and even Felicia froze in place, staring at the dusk elf. For her part, Zarenya just looked back at them, the light in her eyes almost challenging. She didn't care that she was challenging Nadis, the archpriestess realized, and a tiny part of her shivered. What was going on with the natives of Beacon, she had to wonder? They all seemed so different than she expected.

"No, it wouldn't," Nadis said at last, studying the librarian carefully. She debated, then picked her words carefully as she asked, "You seem to be quite... opinionated where this is concerned. May I ask why?"

"Of course you may," Zarenya replied, sitting back in her chair and watching all of them carefully, tilting her head as she considered for a moment. "My assistant, Ellis, is the one who's been tasked with recording the events of the war with Kelvanis, but particularly where they regard Beacon, Phynis, and Sistina. However, even he couldn't gather all the information necessary on his own, so I helped. In the process I grew closer to the priestesses who were guarding Medaea than I had before, including the Jewels, and above all, I was told precisely what happened in the final battle between Sistina, Tyria, and Irethiel."

Nadis's breath caught in her throat, because *that* battle was one where no one knew exactly what had happened. Rumors had raced through the kingdoms, but only the fact that every slave brand had shattered at once had proven that Irethiel had died. No one *knew* what had happened, and the bards had created increasingly outlandish tales. After a moment she swallowed and asked softly. "Why haven't they told anyone what occurred there? If *you* know..."

"Because they're uncertain of what impact it might have, and whether it might draw foreign powers down on us. Despite all Sistina's power, she's far weaker than she was before the final battle with Kelvanis. Tyria makes up for much of that, *if* she can act. I believe she can, but… there's been some discussion of the limitations on divinities," Zarenya said bluntly, frowning as she looked between them, her lips pursed, then she continued. "I will not tell you everything. However, I *will* tell you of Tyria's decision, and how Irethiel perished."

Miriselle had gone entirely still, Nadis saw. Felicia hesitated, then took a seat again, her gaze fixed on the librarian. Nadis was fascinated as well, but she refrained from comment as she considered. At last she nodded, her voice soft. "That… would be interesting to learn. Though I wonder why you're telling us this."

"Because of how Tyria was imprisoned by Sistina. She formed a cage of *faith*, Archpriestess. Empowered by the prayers and belief of every follower of Medaea in Beacon, Sistina trapped her and used that very faith to remind Tyria of who she once was, to unearth the memories of who she was as Medaea. If Irethiel had not come, it would have succeeded relatively easily, without the need for battle." Zarenya's voice was soft, and her eyes grew distant as she murmured, "I wish I could have seen it in person, rather than through the flawed illusions which the Jewels wove for me. Memory is so imperfect, especially when divinities are involved. However, Irethiel *did* arrive, and she tore Tyria away from them, destroying the prison as she ordered her to stay out of the fight. And Tyria obeyed, at least at first."

Nadis's breath caught in her throat at the description, shuddering at the thought of a demon lord ordering a goddess to do something. It was terrifying and caused bile to rise in her throat. A part of her wanted to doubt Zarenya, but she remained silent, instead watching the woman as she judged her attitude, looking for deceit.

"Irethiel would have killed Sistina and possibly everyone else there, but Tyria managed to rebel at last. She *chose* to serve Sistina, as she knew that Sistina would not control her, and cut the link between her and Irethiel. She chose to battle Irethiel, but she wasn't at her best, not with all the attempts to corrupt her the demon queen had made," Zarenya continued, shaking her head as she added in amusement, "I don't think I'll explain her plans. In any case, Tyria would have lost. She *was* losing, when Sistina finally took the ultimate risk."

"Ultimate risk?" Felicia asked, looking confused. "Under those circumstances, what could be that risky?"

"From what little I've been able to understand of the power levels involved, it could have destroyed the mountain and everything in it," Zarenya replied, her smile widening as Nadis paled. The woman didn't continue, as if waiting for a response.

"That… is disturbing," Nadis said at last, shivering, then asked, "May I ask what happened?"

"Of course you may. Sistina's gamble was extraordinarily simple. From what I've learned, Demasa and Kylrius killed each other simultaneously in the event that buried Everium, but for *them*, the clash of their power was… too equal. Around them their power was a constant, self-sustaining clash that froze time itself. Sistina was desperate enough that she tapped into their power," Zarenya said, her smile vanishing at last as she shivered. "I always wondered why the mountain shuddered at that moment. She used the last echoes of their power to destroy Irethiel, Archpriestess, and if she truly had wanted to, I suspect she could have destroyed Tyria as well. She didn't, though, and Tyria… it was then that she was free to determine her fate. *That* is what you're dealing with, Nadis. Tyria isn't just telling you that you need to heed her demands or you'll suffer. She's trying to come to terms with who *she* is. You aren't the only ones whose faith is in crisis, Archpriestess. The goddess *herself* is trying to find her path. She wants to find her own future, and Sistina is giving her the time to decide."

Nadis simply stared for a little while, utterly incredulous. She heard the others breathing hard, and she couldn't blame them. The idea of tapping into the power of not one, but *two* gods and trying to use it… the idea was completely ridiculous. Even if Zarenya was right, the possibility was ludicrous, and yet… and yet it would explain so *much*, about how Irethiel was killed when few would have believed that they'd have a chance against a demon queen in person. It was just the idea of a goddess having difficulties determining who she was that truly made her hesitant to believe Zarenya.

"How do *you* know all this?" Miriselle demanded, her voice trembling. "You're just a librarian!"

"Just a librarian? Tell me, how often have you held conversations near a librarian when you weren't really thinking about it? I hear all *sorts* of things when the Jewels and Her Majesty visit," Zarenya replied, shaking her head and smiling. "Besides, I won't share things which are truly dangerous for them, hm? That might lose me my position here, and there's *nothing* that's worth that."

"Ah," Nadis murmured, trying to calm herself, which was difficult. The roiling waves of emotions within her were difficult to quantify, and she took a deep breath, then looked at Miriselle as she nodded. "I believe that your suggestion is for the best, Miriselle. Have the tome sent to the capital, and they're to make copies as well as send out the relevant information to the different prefectures. I'm not certain what is going to happen from here, but it appears that things have changed."

"Of course, Your Holiness," Miriselle said, bowing her head deeply. "It shall be done."

Turning to Zarenya, Nadis hesitated before speaking softly, thankful that the woman had shared what she had. "Thank you for telling us, Zarenya. What you've said is... illuminating beyond measure. I never would have believed such was possible."

"Nor would I, if I hadn't had the opportunity to see the aftermath myself," Zarenya said, her smile growing a little warmer. "As it is, most of the damage has been repaired, though I doubt everything has gone back to what it was. I'm just glad that Her Majesty agreed that even if it isn't released now, the truth needs to be recorded. The city's safety comes first, though. Perhaps in a few years, once the situation has stabilized."

"That seems reasonable to me," Nadis said, relaxing slightly. Looking at the others, she continued. "Now we have a great deal to think on, though. If you'll excuse us? I believe we need dinner and a chance to digest what we've been told."

"Go right ahead. You aren't the only ones in need of food, after all," Zarenya said, smoothly rising from her chair. "It was quite interesting to help you, Archpriestess, ladies. I will keep what we've discussed to myself."

"Thank you," Nadis said, taking Felicia's hand as the priestess helped her stand.

Thinking about what they'd discussed, Nadis thought that sleep would be a long time coming that evening.

CHAPTER 13

"Do you think the faiths are going to come to terms?" Ruby asked, twiddling her thumbs as she waited.

Diamond smiled, reaching out to pull her friend into a hug, prompting a giggle from Ruby. No, maybe she was her wife now… though that seemed like a rather odd way to consider Ruby. Diamond shook off the thought after a moment, as she knew she was deliberately distracting herself. The relationship between her and the rest of the Jewels was complex, as all of them were romantically involved with Phynis and Sistina, but most of them weren't involved with each other in a similar way. Yet, at least.

They were already in the meeting room, and Diamond was glad that the chairs had been replaced with something more comfortable than the previous day. Neither of the two churches had arrived, which was why Ruby was likely so nervous. And open with her comments, for that matter.

"I have no idea," Diamond said at last, shaking her head slightly. "Nadis was far calmer than I feared she might be, but the revelations of Medaea's past… those likely were surprising for her. They were for *me*, for that matter, even if her change to Tyria was more dramatic."

"Very true. I think she's reluctantly accepting of the need to change. Miriselle seems to be as well, though I'm not sure about

Felicia," Ruby agreed, tapping the table thoughtfully. "As for Elissa… she's hard to read."

"You're right about that. She seems like the type of person who only shows what she *wants* you to see," Diamond agreed, frowning as she thought about the human woman. It was rare that she ran into someone so… opaque, for lack of a better term. Yet at the same time she seemed sincere enough, and Tyria trusted her, so Diamond continued. "I think she's sincerely doing her best to cooperate with Tyria's directives, but I don't know much of what she thinks of it."

"Fair. Given what she said about the consequences of straying, I suspect you're right," Ruby said, then frowned as she obviously considered, then added reluctantly, "Assuming she's telling the truth about that, of course."

"Sistina believed her, and I have faith in her judgment," Diamond replied calmly, then tilted her head as she heard footsteps. "I do believe we have company."

"Which means it's time to get ready," Ruby murmured, taking out Albert's device and fiddling with it as she started getting it ready for the day.

A moment later the door opened and Aldem stepped inside, the priest looking a touch harried as he let out a deep breath, adjusting the armful of books he was carrying. Diamond's eyebrows rose a bit at the sight of them, as all the books looked rather new, and the priest paused as he realized they were there.

"Ah, uh, Lady Diamond, Lady Ruby! I hadn't realized you were here yet," Aldem said flushing slightly as he straightened. "I thought you wouldn't be here for another half hour or so."

"I'd rather be here early than arrive and find that the archpriestess and high priestess had tried to strangle one another," Diamond said, smiling as she nodded to him politely. "That said, you somewhat surprised me as well. Might I ask what all the books are for?"

"Oh, these? They're texts on My Lady, as well as some of her more traditional allies from before the Godsrage. After the discussion yesterday…" Aldem paused, looking a little embarrassed, then continued. "Well, after Her Eminence's explanation, I thought it might be good to look and see what *other* mistakes had been made over the centuries. I honestly don't know if I'll find anything, but I am rather curious. There's enough lost knowledge just in the shrine to keep me busy for decades, I'm afraid."

"Very, very true. From what I've seen of the various libraries, I doubt that we'll have more than a cursory understanding of what Everium was like before the Godsrage for a century or more. Less if Zarenya and the others find assistants they trust, of course, but..." Diamond let her voice trail off and shook her head, deciding not to voice the last part of what she was saying. It wouldn't do to tell people that Phynis and the others were finding it a little harder to truly trust people with valuable information these days. There were too many people trying to take advantage of them as it was.

"Mm, I do understand. I imagine that it's difficult to find anyone truly conversant in such ancient writing. We've had to consult the guardian of the temple quite a bit, and while you have the three survivors of old Everium, I suspect they aren't exactly willing to spend all their time translating for you," Aldem said, smiling wryly as he walked over to his chair and stacked his books on the table. "As much as I'd love to learn, I can hardly imagine how boring it would be to be constantly explaining what it was like growing up."

Diamond laughed softly, and Ruby smiled, nodding in agreement. "Agreed! Cortin, Kassandra, and Nora each have their own lives to live. As it is, I've heard that Kassandra has made progress on a potential cure to her... vampiric ailment, and is just trying to get the academy in order before she goes into deep research. She's even consulted Sistina about it."

"Huh, that's... interesting. I'd almost forgotten she was a vampire, honestly, though mostly because I've only met the woman once," Aldem said, sitting down slowly, then let out a sigh as he looked at Diamond nervously. "That aside... do you know if Tyria is planning to say anything else quite so... disruptive today? I'd like to be able to plan out my day, when I can. I'd honestly prefer to be done and go back to my studies and greeting pilgrims, but I agreed to this, and I won't shirk my duties."

"That you agreed at all has been a great boon, Aldem. Thank you for everything you've done," Diamond told him sincerely, slightly amused by the man's barely concealed anxiety. "As for Her Eminence, I have no idea if something like that will come up again. Either way, the only thing we can do is deal with it if she does, no?"

"I suppose so. I just wish that I had some idea if it was coming, but…" Aldem shrugged, smiling a little now as he straightened. "At least the two churches haven't actively resorted to insulting one another, or heavens forbid, actually *attacking* each other. It hasn't been quite as bad as what I worried about, even if it isn't ideal."

"Agreed. Both Elissa and Nadis are wise women, and with any luck things will continue in a civil manner," Diamond said, looking at Ruby with a grin.

The other priestess nodded in agreement, opening her mouth, then paused. Diamond heard the footsteps a moment later, and her eyebrows rose. While Diamond wasn't annoyed that other people were arriving early, based on Aldem's comments she hadn't expected them to arrive quite this soon.

There was a knock at the door, then it opened and a guard stepped inside, immediately followed by Elissa, whose gaze played across the room for a moment before the human smiled, stepping out of the way of her companions. Ollie and Roxanne stepped inside, followed by the other guard, and they approached the table with respectful nods.

"Bright morning to all of you, Lady Diamond, Lady Ruby, and Your Holiness," Elissa said, her voice almost flawless as she nodded to Diamond, Ruby, and Aldem in sequence. She carefully shut the door and approached at a sedate pace, which was rather slow due to the woman's height. "I hope each of you had a good day yesterday, despite the… unexpected revelations."

"I did, thank you," Diamond replied, and beside her Ruby nodded.

"For the most part, yes, though I *had* cleared my schedule for the conference, so how brief it was turned out to be a shock," Aldem said, nodding politely. "What about yourself?"

"Oh, I had a lovely day. What Tyria told us was the subject of a great deal of discussion once we got back to our lodging, but after a few hours... well, it isn't like we had a lot of information to go off of," Elissa replied, pulling her chair out, and at the same time Diamond heard *more* footsteps. It appeared that everyone had decided to arrive early. While Diamond was distracted, Elissa had continued speaking, though. "Instead I spent the latter half of the day exploring Beacon. None of the descriptions can do the city justice, if I'm being honest, and even if it's largely empty, the sights are breathtaking."

"I agree there. I remember the first day after Sistina built the city, when we emerged from the mountaintop..." Ruby said, her voice soft and her eyes distant with the memory. The other door opened to admit Nadis's delegation as Ruby spoke. "My legs were burning from the effort of the climb, but I'll never forget the sight, as the city appeared before us. The walls looked invincible to me, and I'd never even *imagined* a city like this. I knew she was going to be building a city, since she'd asked the priestesses to donate mana for the ritual, but she never explained the full extent of it. I don't think anything could have prepared me for that."

"I don't doubt you, there. Unlike you, I *have* seen larger cities, as well as mountain fortresses of the dwarves, but none of them are as... fully formed as this one is. Most of them grew gradually over time, which leads to inconsistencies in the city. I wouldn't say that Beacon is flawless, far from it, but it's obvious that there aren't going to be any slums for a long time to come," Elissa said, then nodded to Nadis. "Bright morning, Archpriestess."

"And to you," Nadis said, examining Elissa critically, then murmured, "You're more well-traveled than I anticipated."

"I was born in the south, on Istan. That's where Silence is, after all," Elissa said, shrugging as she smiled a bit more. "Adventurers tend to travel a lot, so it doesn't seem unusual to me."

"Mm, well, that explains why your surname is 'of Silence.' I'd been wondering about it," Diamond said, sitting back and relaxing at the polite interaction between the two.

"Ah, Silence... such a *strange* town," Elissa said, smiling wistfully as she paused, thinking for a moment, then shrugged. "It bore the brunt of the effects of the Godsrage itself, if in a very different manner than the mountains here. Much less directly destructive."

"Oh?" This time, to Diamond's surprise, it was Elissa's fellow priestess who spoke, as Roxanne looked up from the papers she had been preparing for the day. "What do you mean?"

Diamond focused on Elissa as well, honestly curious as to what she meant. She knew a bit about how much damage had been done during the Godsrage, from the Sandsea in the south to the Whirling Abyss of the eastern isles, but she'd never heard of Silence. The subject fascinated her, though she supposed that it was nice to be distant from the horror of experiencing the Godsrage itself. The survivors of old Everium often changed the subject when asked about it, as none of them were terribly comfortable talking about it.

"Well… do we have a few minutes before we begin, Aldem?" Elissa asked, and the priest nodded, looking oddly fascinated as well. In fact, Diamond realized, everyone had stopped talking or moving to listen. The human looked around, then smiled wryly as she murmured, "I see that I have a proper audience for this, hm? So, how to explain Silence?"

The woman was quiet for a minute, then finally spoke softly. "In Silence, you will never hear a word spoken. No dogs will bark, no birds will sing, no cocks will crow. No creature can speak there, nor can magic project the illusions of voices. The only sounds are those created by daily labors or that occur naturally. Those of us who were born there grew up without ever hearing the voices of one another, and for ten miles in every direction the effect is constant. The town has tried moving before, but for whatever reason the zone of silence travels with it. I grew up learning to 'talk' by using sticks that we tapped together, some of them textured to make more complex sounds. In any case, the effect was created by the death of a god of music who can no longer be named. According to legends, he was killed by four other deities above the town during the Godsrage, and with his death the town was plunged into silence, as were his murderers. No, the town is in a near-continual hush, as if in mourning for his death. *That* is Silence."

For a moment everyone was quiet, and Diamond almost felt her breath catch in her throat, trying to even *imagine* a town where no one could speak, where no one could sing. It was… difficult.

"If that's the case, how is it that you can speak so well? I would think that you'd have difficulty speaking, if you grew up someplace like that," Aldem asked, tilting his head as he looked at Elissa with wide eyes.

"Through a *lot* of practice. It took a few years, to be frank, but not growing up with speech allowed me to learn to control my voice a bit more clearly, from what my teachers said," Elissa told him, grinning and shrugging. "It's one of those things that natives of Silence have to deal with, and why a lot of them don't leave. A few of those of us who do leave become merchants, traveling back and forth since we're fluent in both languages. I was tempted to do the same for a time but decided against it."

"Interesting," Diamond murmured, considering the subject, then smiled wryly. "The deaths of the gods did have an outsized impact on the world, didn't it? I wonder if there are other lands we've never heard of who had the same sort of things happen to them."

"Most likely, as unfortunate as it may be," Nadis said, sitting down and examining Elissa closely. It took a moment for Diamond to realize that some of her distrust toward the human seemed like it had eased, which was a good sign. "Now, then… shall we go ahead and start for the day? I know it's early, but as we're all here, I don't see any reason *not* to start."

"Nor do I, but first… are there any objections?" Aldem asked, looking around the table. Diamond shook her head, and the scribes pulled out their pens while Ruby activated the recording device. After a moment Aldem nodded. "In that case, I'm calling this session of the conference between the churches of Medaea and Tyria to order."

"Thank you, Aldem. Now, my first question for you is, did you have a chance to go over the book in sufficient detail, Nadis?" Elissa asked promptly, leaning forward in her chair as she continued. "I'll admit that I found Tyria's explanations yesterday fascinating, but unlike you I wasn't able to go over the evidence."

"We did. With some assistance in translating a few phrases from the head librarian, we were able to examine the books, and Tyria's explanation of Medaea's original nature was... accurate. Possibly even understated," Nadis said, her tone obviously reluctant. "Considering that, we decided to send the copy we were given back to Yisara, with the explanation it was an original copy of *Medaea's Illuminations* that was found. That should allow any... *adjustments* that are decided upon to be made more easily."

"Ahh, not a bad thought," Diamond murmured, nodding in understanding as she sat back in her chair. She did admire how Nadis was handling things, considering the unpleasant situation. Part of her wondered if the decision to sequester the true archpriestess of Medaea's church in the hidden temple had been wise... but what was done was done.

"Indeed? That makes a great deal of sense. Fortunately, our church is young enough that we can handle changes easier, though I'm sure some of the faithful won't necessarily be quite as pleased," Elissa said, glancing at her companions as Ollie cleared his throat.

"If I may, High Priestess? While that's true, I think that the majority of our faith are former slaves at the moment, and they... well, they don't want to *be* slaves anymore. They chose to follow Tyria because she was the first person who truly seemed to *care* about what happened to them," Ollie said, shifting nervously as everyone looked at him. "It's why I followed her, after all, and it's something that has come up again and again. Many of the slave owners in Kelvanath thought they were above the law, right up until Tyria destroyed some of the most powerful men and women in the city. That was the turning point, as far as I'm concerned, and so long as she retains that sense of... of *justice*, I think that many of our people will follow her."

"Well, doesn't that give us some common ground," Nadis said, slowly smiling and nodding. "In that case, let's talk about just what Medaea once meant, and what she means to the people of Yisara now."

Diamond leaned forward at that, happy that things were starting to move forward. Perhaps Tyria's interruption had been for the best, in the end, as neither side seemed to be resisting moving forward now.

TYRIA WATCHED and listened as the three groups spoke with one another, a slight smile on her face. The goddess was present, but she'd masked her power from their senses, and had also turned invisible and almost intangible, as far as mortals were concerned. A sufficiently powerful mage could bypass that, of course, but none of those present were quite capable of that.

Diamond wasn't interjecting much, Tyria noted, but that was mostly because Elissa and Nadis were speaking in reasonable tones, as each discussed the major tenets of their faiths, and in particular what they believed was the most important aspects to their faithful.

Just listening was teaching Tyria a great deal about those who worshipped her, which was incredibly important to her. She might be a goddess, but she wasn't all-powerful or all-knowing. No deities were, to Tyria's knowledge, though the primal gods might come close.

So Tyria watched and listened, learning what she could from her faithful. They wouldn't be so open if she was visible, after all. But as they spoke, she smiled, murmuring softly to herself. "Medaea? Tyria? Or possibly someone else entirely? I suppose I shall have to decide."

CHAPTER 14

The bell's tinkle echoed through the shop, and as it did, Arise Ennarra resisted the urge to swear, nearly stabbing herself with the needle as she worked quickly on the tunic. The last thing she needed right now was more work, and unfortunately she hadn't found any assistants she could trust of late. The last man who she'd *thought* was going to be helpful had been a disappointment after she'd learned he was actually just after her and Iris.

"One moment, I'll be right there!" Arise called out, and glanced over at her sister as she asked, "Are you alright if I go up front?"

"Just *go*!" Iris replied with a laugh, smiling warmly as she worked the loom with the grace Arise remembered. "I'm fine, there's no need to hover."

Iris had recovered startlingly well from her time in captivity, and Arise couldn't even express how grateful she was to see Iris smiling and whole. She'd been surprised that the court mage had been able to heal all the scars and mutilations that'd been inflicted on her sister, and while Iris was far more cautious around people she didn't know, she was practically back to her old self.

After a moment Arise set the tunic aside and pulled off her

thimble as she stood, shrugging as she replied sheepishly. "As you like, I just... I worry about you."

"I'm not going to vanish the second you turn your back. I've learned *that* lesson long ago, and it's why we've replaced all the doors, locks, and windows," Iris said tartly, pausing and setting the shuttle aside, barely giving Arise enough warning to dodge as the other elf tried to kick her. "Now go! We have a customer."

"Alright, if you insist," Arise said, unable to suppress a grin as she quickly stepped out of the room.

Arise loved her new shop, as it was far more spacious than any other shop she'd been in, and running water delivered straight to her home was an incredible luxury. The only thing that would be better was if it was heated, but that was apparently too much for even the dungeon to have built into all the buildings in the city, so instead Arise and Iris were making do with heating the water on the stove, at least for now. Arise had heard that the magi and artificers had devices for heating water, and she hoped to buy one in the near future. If she had one complaint, it was that the building was made of too much stone, but that was why they'd paid for carpenters to line the floors and walls with stained wood.

Stepping into the shop's foyer, Arise began speaking brightly. "Hello! How may I help..."

Her voice trailed off as she caught sight of her guests, and a brief impulse to dart right back through the door and bar it ran through Arise, though she quickly forced it down.

The foyer was a relatively simple room, with samples of the fabric Arise and Iris made as well as several tunics, dresses, and, particularly, coats on display. She'd emerged from behind the counter, and four people were waiting for Arise, only one of which was someone she recognized. If it hadn't been for Isana's presence, Arise *would* have retreated, in any case.

Three humans and an elf were waiting for her, one of them a short woman with pale skin and black hair, in clothing of such a fine weave it made Arise curious where she'd gotten the warm-looking white and purple robes, while beside her were two humans who looked like natives of Kelvanis, with their usual olive skin tone. One was a woman with red hair, while the other was a tall, thin man, and they looked over at her and smiled slightly.

Isana Dayrest cleared her throat, nodding to Arise politely as she smiled. The woman was in charge of keeping the palace running smoothly, and was a thin, icily beautiful dusk elf with long, straight silver hair, and her light blue eyes settled on Arise. To be honest, it somewhat amused Arise that the seemingly cold, primly proper woman had ended up in a relationship with Captain Desa, whose surname was Iceheart.

"Good afternoon, Mistress Ennarra," Isana said politely, gesturing to the others as she continued calmly. "These are members of the delegation from Tyria's church, High Priestess Elissa of Silence, and the priests Ollie and Roxanne. They were looking for excellent tailors, and I believed that you would fit their requirements, in addition to being trustworthy."

"I... see," Arise said, trying to force herself to relax a little, though it was hard. Ever since the end of the war with Kelvanis she'd found herself tense whenever she saw human natives. The stories that she'd heard from Iris caused most of that, even if her sister tried not to burden her with them. Still, she knew enough about the church of Tyria that she knew she could trust them, or at least probably could trust them. After a moment Arise took a deep breath and straightened slightly, looking at the guests. "While more business is welcome, I will say that my sister and I are currently buried in work. I currently have a large backlog of orders, and with winter the demand has only increased, so I'm not certain how quickly I can help you."

"You're truly that busy?" Elissa asked, her eyebrows rising as the woman looked at Arise with her vivid electric blue eyes. "I wouldn't have expected that, even with Beacon being relatively newly settled."

"It's... well, I was going to say complicated, but that isn't entirely true," Arise said, changing her mind on what she was going to say, and took a deep breath before continuing calmly. "The problem is that Beacon has been exploding in population so *quickly*. There are four other tailors, seamstresses, and dressmakers that I'm aware of, and I'm sure more are coming, but we already have well over ten thousand people in the city.

Now, consider that a huge number of those people are former slaves who didn't have much in the way of clothing, and only *five* shops to provide it with winter coming…"

Arise's voice trailed off, and as it did she shrugged helplessly, thinking about the jobs ahead of her. Even with half her profits going to helping former slaves, she was making almost as much as she had back in Galthor, and that was without the inflated prices she'd often charged for dresses for the nobility.

Elissa nodded in understanding, murmuring, "Ahh. That *would* be an issue, wouldn't it? I thought that there were more people who'd be interested in such here, particularly since I've heard a lot of artisans were enslaved."

"To be more accurate, many people were forced to become artisans, and I've noticed a preponderance of former slaves have deliberately abandoned skills they were forced to take up for other professions," Arise explained, shrugging as she continued. "Many of them have applied to the mage academy, joined the city guard, or become adventurers, mostly so they can defend themselves. Not even half, of course, but it does leave us in an… interesting position. Now, all of that said, if you aren't looking for anything *too* complex, I might be able to squeeze you into our schedule in a reasonable amount of time…"

"I suppose I shouldn't be surprised by their reactions, and that lends some weight to the discussions," Ollie murmured softly, rubbing his chin, only to be shushed by Roxanne.

Elissa looked at him in amusement as she opened her mouth to speak, only to have Isana interject smoothly. "Actually, Her Majesty asked me to tell you that you can displace her orders for Elissa and her companions, as well as if Archpriestess Nadis or Lady Diane Yisara choose to visit as well. She pointed out that while Sistina may not have your artistry, she makes perfectly good clothing for most purposes."

"Ah, well *that* changes things… though I really wish I could get my hands on a bolt or two of the cloth the dungeon makes. I've found its properties fascinating," Arise said, cheering up a little at the information, since the queen's orders were a surprisingly large part of her business as well, since they included uniforms for the palace staff among other things. "In that case, I should be able to manage a couple of outfits within a week, if they aren't too complex."

"Excellent," Elissa said, nodding to Isana, then adding, "Roxanne? Would you please remind me to thank Her Majesty when we next see her?"

"Of course," Roxanne murmured, bobbing her head.

"Good. Now, we're primarily looking for warm, comfortable robes. It appears that the style of our clothing is going to shift to primarily white, with simple purple trim, along with possibly a touch of red or gold..." Elissa began explaining, and Arise quickly snatched up a slate to take notes.

She was already getting ideas on what to do, but that would have to wait until after she'd gotten proper measurements of the high priestess and her companions, if necessary. Arise did hope this wouldn't take too long, however, since she still needed to finish the tunic in her workroom.

CHAPTER 15

Wenris slipped through the gates of Beacon without attracting a second glance, which pleased her. Well, that wasn't true, she got *plenty* of second glances, but that was purely because she appeared to be an attractive dawn elf, and nothing more.

To be honest, Wenris was somewhat impressed by the defenses that Beacon had in place, as it was only the power she could put into her shapeshifting that kept the guards from being able to see through her disguise since they had spectacles that helped them see through illusions and shapeshifting. She did rather approve of the precautions, even if it made her life more difficult.

The succubus paused once she was clear of the gates, looking around in interest at the bustling city around her, which was so different than the last time she'd visited. Previously, Beacon had been a cross between a refugee camp and a military outpost, with very few people who she would consider normal city folk around. Beyond that, there had been so few people in the city that much of it had seemed deserted.

Now the city felt much more lived in, and she could see far more people in decent clothing about, more open shops, and fewer soldiers around. There were still adventurers near the dungeon, along with the odd sign she'd seen giving the rules of the dungeon at its entrance. Vendors were hawking their wares, common folk looked more relaxed, and it was… well, *perfect* for a succubus stalking their prey.

Sadly, that wasn't something on the menu, not if Wenris wanted to stay in the city, so she let out a soft sigh and started down the street, heading toward the nearest set of stairs that led toward the palace.

As Wenris moved, she did have to wonder why she felt so much mana flowing below the surface of the mountainside. It felt odd, but she didn't dare touch it, not with Emonael's warning still ringing in her mind.

SISTINA PAUSED and frowned as she felt a powerful presence within the city. Her domain no longer encompassed the city proper, but even so she could sense when sufficiently powerful individuals moved across the surface, and every footstep of the intruder sent a ripple through the aether that she could sense. Perhaps most beings wouldn't sense the presence, as subtle as it was, but she'd worked hard to make the aether as calm as possible throughout her domain, which made disruptions readily apparent.

The presence was making its way toward the palace, Sistina noted, frowning thoughtfully, but at least it didn't appear to be using its power for anything. It also wasn't as powerful as Tyria, though it was closer than Sistina was entirely comfortable with. Even so, it would take the presence at least another hour to reach the palace gates at its current rate, so Sistina decided to leave it be for the moment, instead turning her attention back to positioning the rails in her new tunnels.

Overall her project was coming along well, which made Sistina much happier on the whole. She'd installed the steam engines that would power the lifts the previous day, and had spent most of the day testing them, which meant all that was left was putting in the rails and building the lift carriages, though that would take a good deal longer than she preferred, especially with testing the brakes as well, and then she'd need to build the doors… but either way, it was taking time and patience. At least she had both in abundance, considering how long she'd spent growing as a tree.

The dryad spent about half an hour carefully adjusting the rails according to the designs she'd made with Albert, then examined them critically for a few minutes before deciding to leave them be. After that she opened her eyes and let out a faint sigh as she realized that she'd been sitting still for too long *again*, and her body had grown stiff.

"Frustrating," Sistina murmured to herself, wincing as she moved, getting the flesh and blood body working properly again. It was taking a lot more time than she liked to get used to having a body that could grow sore.

No one was in the room, she noted idly, which wasn't unusual. The others had grown used to her sitting in a room seemingly unaware for hours at a time, so the study was empty. She allowed her attention to shift back to her domain briefly to check where the presence was and nodded, standing up slowly and internally reshaping her domain slightly to encase herself in a bubble of warm air, then headed out of the room and toward the front of the palace, considering as she moved. It didn't seem likely that a deity had come to visit, though such was possible. If they were hostile, they'd get a *very* rude surprise, since Sistina had spent a good part of the summer working on better defenses in the case of another demon lord invasion.

Either way, she wasn't that worried, as the presence didn't seem to be causing problems. Far more important were the negotiations between the churches, as Sistina knew that Tyria was concerned about them, and what the results might be.

"Sistina? Where are you going?" Amethyst interrupted, and Sistina paused, looking over at the door to the library.

"Palace gates," Sistina replied succinctly, smiling at her wife as she shrugged. Amethyst looked like she was tired, though that wasn't too surprising, since she'd been up late the night before, combing through the records of how old Everium had dealt with inheritance.

"Oh? Why are you doing that?" Amethyst asked, her

expression brightening as she took a couple of steps toward Sistina. "Are you testing your… lift, was it?"

"No. More work left," Sistina replied, considering, then shrugged. "Felt… presence. Approaching palace, want to check."

"Oh. That doesn't sound good… do you want me to get the others together? I know we're not as powerful as Tyria, but if we have time we could help a bit," Amethyst said, frowning deeply. "I also haven't heard the alarm go up."

"No, is fine. Presence is… subtle. Not problematic," Sistina replied, then tilted her head. "Company? I built defenses."

"You built defenses. More of them, without telling us?" Amethyst asked, arching her eyebrows again.

"Yes," the dryad replied unrepentantly. If she told them about everything she did, she'd never get *anything* done.

Amethyst stared at her for a moment, then laughed, shaking her head as she grinned, murmuring, "I suppose I should've expected that. Well, if you're sure it'll be safe, I'll come with you. Just let me grab a cloak when we reach the doors, alright?"

"Yes," Sistina agreed, offering her arm, and Amethyst took it and started walking alongside her.

They moved in companionable silence, passing several servants on the way, most of whom paused to curtsey or bow, though Sistina only inclined her head to each of them marginally. They didn't expect anything more from her, which was a relief, considering how a lot of people treated Sistina. The worst incident for Sistina so far was when a woman asked if Sistina would bless her child when they were born, and Sistina had been forced to firmly say no. She wasn't a goddess, and she hated the idea of being roped into giving out blessings for centuries on end. Even if elves weren't as numerous as humans, the amount of time it would take would be horrifying.

"What do you think of Elissa?" Amethyst asked suddenly, and Sistina looked at her curiously. The elf blushed and cleared her throat, continuing. "I… well, the others were saying that she's hard to read, and I just wondered what your opinion of her was. I trust your opinion, and I know they do, too."

Sistina nodded, considering the question for a moment, then took a bit longer to formulate a proper response, even if she wasn't going to be giving an answer that Amethyst liked. When she spoke, she did so in the more fluid manner that her wives preferred, even if Sistina didn't like using it most of the time. It simply took so much concentration she couldn't do much else, though it grew easier over time. "Elissa is an odd woman, very controlled and focused on letting others see what she wants them to see. However, at the same time she is also tied to Tyria deeply. I do not doubt her claim of loyalty to Tyria, and as such I believe you can rely on her to do what is best for her goddess. Whether that is beneficial to the conference or not is an entirely different question, and one I have no answer for."

"Drat," Amethyst said, letting out a faint sigh of annoyance, but she patted Sistina's arm and smiled as she added, "Thank you for humoring me, though. I might wish that you had all the answers, but that would be boring, I suppose."

"Tree, not seer," Sistina muttered under her breath, prompting laughter from Amethyst.

The elf detached as they reached the front doors, and Sistina paused while she darted into the cloakroom, giving the guards a polite nod, and the man and woman smiled in return. Sistina did appreciate that most of the people in the palace weren't afraid of her or overly formal, though she suspected that wouldn't last. She waited patiently for Amethyst, keeping track of the presence with occasional shifts of focus back to her domain. Soon enough Amethyst emerged with a cloak, though, one that would easily ward off the chill, from Sistina's point of view.

"You don't need warmer clothing?" Amethyst said questioningly, glancing down at Sistina's relatively thin dress. "It's fairly cold out there."

"Is fine. Magic," Sistina replied with a shrug, offering her arm again, and Amethyst laughed.

"Of course, why did I even ask? Well, let's go," Amethyst said, her eyes glittering with mirth as they stepped through the doors, which the guards had opened for them.

The courtyard of the palace looked cold, Sistina noticed instantly, with a few bits of snow here and there where the servants hadn't cleared it away, while a thin layer had adhered to some of the roofs. Most of the snow had been carried off by the wind, though she knew that just meant it was likely building up on the sides of buildings. A couple of carriages were nearby, and from the look of them Sistina suspected that Phynis was entertaining guests. The thought caused her to pause and turn her attention to her domain so she could look in the throne room, and when she did Sistina internally winced, returning to her body again.

"Is something wrong? You did that thing where you were distant again," Amethyst said in concern, pulling closer to Sistina as she added, "That usually means you were checking your domain."

"Lord Nocris," Sistina said, a hint of distaste to her voice, though internally she was *much* less pleased.

Lord Allen Nocris was the second prince of Idris, a human nation to Sifaren's north. The prince had been officially sent to Everium as an ambassador along with his sister, Lady Ryn Nocris, but Sistina had noticed that Idris had never interfered when Kelvanis was at war with Sifaren, nor had they done anything to help quell the chaos after Irethiel's defeat. No, the handsome, arrogant man and his sister had been doing everything they could to seduce Phynis, which was the main reason that Sistina disliked them. Besides, he'd *also* tried to order around Lily and other servants, which made her impression of him even worse.

"Ah, yes." Amethyst's expression could have curdled milk, and she looked at the carriage in distaste as she added, "Sapphire is backing Phynis up in the audience, but I doubt that will stop him from making any advances, unfortunately. I wish he'd take the hint that the marriage isn't for show."

"Think he knows. Does not care," Sistina replied, sniffing disdainfully. She considered for a moment, then sighed, muttering, "Politics. Never liked them."

"Never? Does that mean that you have a few more memories of your previous lives?" Amethyst asked, practically pouncing on the word, much of her unhappiness vanishing.

"Some," Sistina replied, waffling a little, then shrugged as she answered. "Not *trying* to remember. Original was… apolitical."

"Oh, well… I wish you'd try to remember. I really would love to hear about what it was like when you were young," Amethyst murmured, looking disappointed. On the other hand, Sistina noticed that the woman was trying to keep close to Sistina in order to stay inside the bubble of warm air.

"First, was seed. Then tree. Took decades to grow," Sistina replied, her tone deadpan, then squeaked as Amethyst pinched her.

"You know what I meant, so none of that!" Amethyst scolded.

Sistina sniffed slightly, heading over to the gates, and one of the guards there blinked, looking at her partner. When Sistina stopped there, looking out at the road expectantly, the other guard shifted. It took a minute for them to build up the nerve to say anything, and Sistina waited patiently.

"Ah, Lady Amethyst, Lady Sistina... is there something we can do for you?" one of the guards asked nervously, the woman looking uncomfortable.

"Sistina sensed someone approaching, and wanted to come out to meet them," Amethyst explained, smiling warmly at them as she shrugged. "She didn't think it was too dangerous, since she let me come with her, so it shouldn't be anything that concerns you."

Sistina internally sighed at Amethyst's explanation, since that wasn't what she'd said at all. The thought of correcting her briefly crossed Sistina's mind, but after a moment she decided that it wasn't worth the effort. Instead she looked at the city and thought about it, particularly about how the roads circled the city going downward, as well as sensing the people on the streets.

There were certainly more people at the bottom or top of the city, Sistina admitted, mostly at the bottom, but there was a fair amount of activity around the temple district and the academy. The in-between areas, though... those didn't have nearly as many people on the roads, which was evidence of the need for easier transport through the city. It was just as well she'd decided to work on the lifts, but a tiny part of Sistina was irritated that she'd never thought about the problems building a mountain city would create. Of course, it *did* help with defending the city, but it didn't make it any less of a mistake.

Sistina's attention snapped to the side as a woman turned the corner, though. The woman was a dawn elf with golden hair and had bright blue eyes, and she was markedly beautiful, drawing many gazes to her as she climbed the streets at a steady pace. The woman wore attractive, warm clothing in deep blue, something that Sistina normally would associate with wealth, but it was the hidden power around her that drew Sistina's attention. The sight of *that* power was something she'd seen before, and she instantly identified the woman, regardless of her current shape.

"Wenris," Sistina murmured, and beside her Amethyst stiffened.

"What?" the elven priestess demanded.

CHAPTER 16

"What are you doing here?" Amethyst demanded, and Wenris resisted the urge to sigh. She'd hoped that she might be able to get through this without a whole lot of indignant rage, but obviously Sistina had seen through Wenris's disguise. That was disappointing, but not particularly surprising.

The guards on either side of the gate were keeping an eye on Wenris, but obviously they didn't realize her true nature or they wouldn't be standing in the open like that. On the other hand, Sistina was just looking at Wenris calmly, without even the faintest flicker of fear in her eyes, unlike Amethyst... and *that* sent a shiver down Wenris's spine.

She was a demon queen, one of the most powerful beings in existence short of the greater gods, so nothing mortal should have been that fearless on sensing her new nature, yet Sistina didn't fear her. Certainly, the dungeon had destroyed Irethiel, but the information Wenris had gathered indicated that had been an exceptional circumstance, not something she could do easily.

Still, it wouldn't do to be impolite, and Wenris let out a soft sigh, raising an eyebrow as she looked at Amethyst, speaking warmly. "Really, *must* you be so unwelcoming, in the middle of the street? Is that appropriate for the dignity of one of Her Majesty's consorts?"

Amethyst flushed at that, opening her mouth to retort, but Wenris wasn't quite done yet, as she continued speaking simply, trying not to upset her further. "That said, I'm *here* to inform Sistina of my presence, and ask her to allow me to visit. See, Diane and I are tied together on a fundamental level, and that allows me to visit her whenever I like. I've chosen to let her life stabilize until now, rather than disrupting it, but there's only so long I can allow that to continue."

"Then you should release her from the bargain," Amethyst shot back, and Wenris couldn't help another sigh.

"That's impossible, like I told you *last* time," Wenris replied patiently, shaking her head. "What I did was create a bargain that entwined our souls. I'll be perfectly honest with you, I did it to give myself ready access to the mortal world, but it's something that *cannot* be undone by any method which I'm aware of. If I perish, so too will Diane. The reverse is not true, of course… but that was the nature of the bond I created."

"Unfortunate," Sistina murmured, her tone filled with multiple meanings that Wenris couldn't quite decipher. The dungeon fascinated Wenris, since she'd started finding records of Avendrial in the libraries she'd inherited from Irethiel, and those told her a great deal about who the woman had once been. Sistina's brilliant green eyes were fixed on Wenris for a long moment, as the dryad considered, ignoring the cold air around her despite wearing a simple dress. Finally, Sistina asked, "Your intentions here?"

"I intend to visit with Diane on the designated dates I set for her, starting the day after tomorrow, and to explore the mortal world a bit. I've been dealing with rebellions and getting my realm in order, so I thought a vacation might be enjoyable," Wenris replied, shrugging lazily as she smiled at the two of them. "Don't worry, I have no intention of causing trouble for your little kingdom. I'm afraid that Sistina's… *friend* already made sufficient threats, thank you very much."

"Friend?" Amethyst asked, a hint of trepidation starting to appear on her face.

"Yes, friend. You know, my former mistress? She of the

mirrors?" Wenris said pointedly, shivering. "She is *very* protective of Sistina, even if she prefers to act indirectly."

"Mm," Sistina murmured, letting out a faint sigh as she shook her head. "She is… persistent."

Amethyst stared at Sistina for a moment, then at Wenris. It was obvious that she was debating what to do, and Wenris crossed her arms in front of her, raising an eyebrow skeptically.

"What? It isn't like I'm going to be trying to seduce you and the others, is it? I'm not even trying to control all of Diane's life," Wenris told the priestess pointedly. "I'm asking politely to come into the city rather than trying to hide it."

"I suppose… but I still don't trust you. Not after everything else you've done," Amethyst murmured, causing Wenris to sigh and look at the sky for a moment. Or, to be more accurate, at the spire with the giant glowing ruby in it.

"She can stay," Sistina said at last, somewhat surprising Wenris, and when she looked down she saw Amethyst staring at Sistina in shock.

"What? Why?" Amethyst asked, pulling her cloak closer.

"Better here than not. Can watch," Sistina said, her words sparking a bit of grudging approval in Wenris, then she went still as the dryad smiled wryly, adding softly, "Might chase off Lord Nocris and sister. Worth it."

"Wait, what? What's this about chasing anyone off?" Wenris asked, confusion and just a hint of anticipation rushing through her. "I thought you'd make me leave everyone else alone!"

"Chase off, not hurt," Sistina corrected, then looked at Amethyst curiously, and it took her a moment to realize that the elf looked torn.

"That… is surprisingly tempting, yes," Amethyst admitted, and after a moment she explained. "Lord Nocris is from Idris, the nation north of Sifaren. He's been making a nuisance of himself, and particularly has been hinting that he thinks our marriage isn't serious, and that Her Majesty should marry him instead."

That made Wenris stop and stare for a moment. While she was a succubus, and as such had encountered an enormous variety of mortals over her life, sometimes she had to wonder why some mortals were so ignorant. Certainly, she'd seen sham marriages before. In fact, she recalled a powerful lord in the east who'd acquired an entire harem he never touched just for the reputation, while keeping a male lover in private, but that was rare. Now, someone trying to break up a marriage to take advantage of it she could believe, but even so, trying something like that with *Tyria* in the palace was just plain stupid.

"Is he an imbecile?" Wenris asked, honestly curious.

"What?" Amethyst asked, looking taken aback, while Sistina's lips curved in a smile.

"I asked if he's an imbecile. Phynis married all of you and Sistina, who is a dungeon who created this city in the space of a single night with magic that's been lost for millennia. You *also* have Tyria in residence, a goddess who looks favorably on Phynis and Beacon on the whole, and *she* wasn't shy about incinerating a large number of overly arrogant nobles in Kelvanis," Wenris explained, gesturing to the east. "Given that, is he really so *stupid* as to think that he's somehow invulnerable?"

"You know... that's a good point. I didn't think about it in quite those terms, but we've been trying to avoid a diplomatic incident between us and them, since they *could* take it out on Sifaren," Amethyst murmured softly, and Wenris couldn't help a snort.

"Could it possibly be even half as bad as what Kelvanis did? You have golems, battle-hardened soldiers, and a lot of people who won't allow any risk of *that* happening again," Wenris pointed out, shaking her head in dismay. "Really, you need to stand up for yourselves, rather than letting Sistina deal with your problems."

"Diplomacy is important. Even if I dislike it," Sistina interjected calmly, narrowing her eyes a little, then gestured. "Come in. Must introduce you."

Wenris's eyebrows rose at the gesture, as it also meant that Sistina was telling her to enter the dungeon's domain. She could sense the edge of it right in front of the gates, which was enough to put her slightly on edge... yet at the same time, Wenris wasn't foolish enough to think she was safe with Sistina right there. So after a moment she took a step forward and inhaled as she felt the presence of a dungeon's domain wash over her.

It was different than the handful of other domains she'd ever felt, Wenris noted, though that wasn't a surprise after her visit earlier in the year. What was surprising to her was the strength of the domain, considering how much mana she'd thought that Sistina must have expended fighting Irethiel. The smooth, ocean-like surface of mana was shocking because it contained so much power already, which made her revise her guess of Sistina's power sharply upward.

"How have you recovered this much in such a short period? I would have thought you'd pushed yourself to the limit during the battle with my predecessor," Wenris said carefully, watching the guards idly as she passed them. Amethyst hesitated, then quickly stepped up to Sistina, taking her arm. It was only when the elf's breath stopped steaming that Wenris realized that Sistina was surrounded by a convenient bubble of warm air.

"Took up artificing. It is useful," Sistina replied, glancing back and smiling more as she added, "Other dungeons are... primitive. Inefficient."

Sistina's smile sent a chill down Wenris's spine, one which she didn't quite understand for a long moment, until she finally placed it. It was the same sort of smile *Emonael* had on her face when she was plotting something terrifying that no one else knew about.

"I see," Wenris said, watching the dungeon warily.

She suddenly decided that Emonael was right. Sistina could defend herself just fine, and Wenris was *not* going to do anything to get on her bad side.

SISTINA WAS TRYING to decide what to make of Wenris now that she had the chance to examine her more closely inside her domain. The new Demon Queen of Chains was good at hiding her power, that much Sistina had to admit, but even so, she couldn't hide from Sistina, not here.

The succubus had an immense amount of dark magic bound

up in her being, along with fire magic as well, which only made sense to Sistina. Irethiel had used darkness and fire as well, so it was only reasonable that her successor would have similar elements… and as she recalled, Emonael had possessed similar affinities, though those memories were incredibly distant.

What intrigued her was the *other* spark of mana deep inside the demon's soul, a spark of light mana that was guttering with every passing moment, yet it burned brightly in her mental vision. If it had been a few months ago, Sistina might not have recognized what that spark was, but Wenris's own words had explained what it was, in the end.

That tiny spark of energy was where Wenris had tied her soul to Diane, Sistina realized, and it provided an opportunity as well. The only question was how to take advantage of that opportunity, and whether Diane would want to.

Regardless, Sistina kept her knowledge to herself, not paying too much attention to the nervous demon queen, and instead she smiled reassuringly at Amethyst and patted her hand. The elf looked a little confused, but her tension eased as well at Sistina's confidence.

Her goal accomplished, Sistina headed for the throne room, intent on rescuing Phynis from her unwelcome guests. Even if Diane didn't appreciate her presence, at least Wenris might be of *some* use.

CHAPTER 17

Looking around the camp, Kevin Sailor resisted the urge to spit on the ground since that would probably be taken the wrong way. Not that he suspected most of those present would disagree with his opinion on the quality of their camp, but he didn't want to ruin his chances of getting the Adjudicator's help.

The camp was in the foothills of the Serpentspine Mountains, in a spot that Kevin's guild had used as a hideout multiple times, the main reason he'd offered it to Adjudicator Bran when the man had asked for advice. It wasn't as good as Kevin's hideout, of course, but after losing their headquarters, Kevin's guild needed almost all of its hideouts.

For the most part the area had dozens of filthy tents, many of which contained haggard men and women who had scraps of former finery on them. At the center of the camp was the hideout itself, a couple of hunting lodges that concealed the entrance to the underground chambers Kevin's guild had built.

These were most of the people who remained of Ulvian Sorvos's kingdom, Kevin knew. There was another Adjudicator at large, but from whispers his agents had heard, Kevin suspected that the man had fled the country entirely. On the other hand, Bran had been trying to keep the country from falling into Slaid Damrung's hands, though he suspected that he and his allies had about given up at this point. Those who were sticking with him now would all be facing a death sentence if they were captured, after all.

Shaking off his wandering thoughts, Kevin headed toward the primary lodge, nodding to a couple of the guards as he went. None of them stopped him, since he visited fairly often, which didn't strike him as the best of ideas, but they weren't his subordinates in the end.

"Master Sailor," a soldier said at last as Kevin almost reached the lodge door, the gaunt man by the door resting a hand on the hilt of his sword casually. "What brings you here this time? Hopefully not bad news."

The man left the word 'again' unspoken, Kevin noticed, and he couldn't help a barking laugh as he shook his head.

"Bad news? Have we had much that isn't bad in the last few months?" Kevin asked rhetorically, pausing so the man didn't try attacking him. "I don't think so. In any case, I wouldn't call what I've come about *bad*, but I also can't say it's good, either. A mixed bag, really."

"Well, that has to be better than last time. Bran was growling at everyone for a week," the guard said, sighing and gesturing at the door. "Go ahead, then. He's probably staring at maps, trying to figure out what to do."

"Unsurprisingly," Kevin said, nodding and turning the door handle, his nose wrinkling at the smell that wafted out. Obviously, the officers hadn't been bathing as much lately, which he didn't approve of, and only made him more thankful that he wasn't lodging with the refugees here.

The interior of the lodge wasn't much different than the last time he'd been there, as it was filled with scattered weapons, maps, and other belongings that had been put wherever the residents could find room for them. On the large table in the middle of the room was a stained map, held in place by rocks, and a couple of men looked up from the map at Kevin's entrance.

One man was a bit shorter, with greasy black hair and a somewhat unkempt appearance, and he was wearing leathers that showed he'd been out in the forests earlier in the day. The blue-eyed man didn't seem happy to see Kevin, given how his expression tightened at the sight of him.

On the other hand, Bran was a different proposition. He was of middling height, with a lean figure that Kevin knew concealed a good deal of muscle. Bran's eyes were brown, while his hair was nearly black, and he wore black plate armor that was in good repair and he had a rapier at his side. When Kevin had first met Bran the man had kept clean-shaven, but now he'd let his beard grow out somewhat.

"Kevin, I didn't expect to see you today," Bran said, straightening and looking at Kevin for a moment, then smiled unhappily. "I see you seem to be doing better than us. Certainly better fed, for that matter."

"An assassin's guild is used to gathering supplies without drawing notice, which gives us some advantages, but there's only so much we can purchase without drawing attention. I get you what I can and charge fairly for it," Kevin replied calmly, stepping inside and closing the door as he nodded to Bran's companion. "Hello, Ruthan."

"Kevin," Ruthan replied shortly, his voice rough.

"What brings you here, Kevin? You're the one who doesn't like visiting often, so there has to be a reason for it," Bran said, glancing down at the map sardonically as he almost sneered. "Are you cutting ties with us? I honestly couldn't blame you, with as sorry of a lot as we are now."

"Of course not. You know enough about us to make life painful, and you paid me so much that would be dishonorable," Kevin replied, anger welling up inside him as he glared at Bran. "In fact, I'm somewhat insulted you'd think that of me. I even warned Ulvian when we distanced ourselves from him, I'll have you know."

"A fat lot of good that did us," Ruthan muttered, and Bran gave him a sharp look.

"None of that! We can't change the past, just our future," Bran barked out, straightening and growling. "Not that we *have* much of a future at this rate. Damrung's army is slowly trawling through the region, and it's only a matter of time before they find us."

"Indeed. They've already found a couple of cells of my people, with predictable results," Kevin said, his anger changing targets as he grimaced unhappily. "They didn't want to be put on trial, so they fought. I know that a couple of them escaped, but the captives will be put to death once the trials are over."

"Unless they give us away," Bran said flatly.

"An unfortunate possibility. That's the only reason I'm seriously considering the offer that came through an intermediary," Kevin said, and his words drew the attention of both men.

"An offer? Would this offer involve us as well?" Bran asked, his eyes narrowing.

"Yes, it would. I will say that the offer was… strange, so I did some investigating into who was behind it. In the end I determined that it's a church dedicated to a deity opposed to Medaea," Kevin said carefully, not completely showing his hand yet. "The offer is fairly simple in the end. They're offering to help us leave Kelvanis and travel to Halstad, where they can guarantee that we'd both become barons at a minimum. Given Halstad, that would allow a good deal of potential for upward mobility."

Bran's eyebrows rose, then fell as he frowned, then spoke. "That… is a generous offer, and instantly makes me suspicious. Why would they offer something like that, and what are they asking for? For that matter, how can they even deliver a reward of that nature?"

"Let's start with how they'd be able to deliver, shall we?" Kevin said, approaching the table and folding his arms. "Leaving would be easy enough, there's plenty of ships that dock in Sirshif, so that isn't an issue. Halstad… well, you know how wealthy it is, along with all the factions in the country, so getting *to* it is easy. The issue is that King Corin was robbed about three years ago. Apparently, someone stole a phoenix egg from his treasury, and he's been offering the title of a baron to anyone who brings him her head, along with a good deal of wealth. Or them, if it's a group, he's not particular.

"Based on that, the people I've talked to tracked down the woman responsible, and her description is striking. A petite, short woman with long black hair and eyes that are an unusual purple-blue hue. Does that sound familiar to you?" Kevin asked, tilting his head slightly.

"Elissa, the woman who's heading Tyria's church," Bran said instantly, his eyes narrowing. "Still, how do you know it's true?"

"Because I gathered information on her when she appeared in Kelvanath and was so close to Ulvian. While investigating, I found a painting that startled me, one from almost ninety years ago," Kevin said, and he pulled open the enchanted sack hanging on his belt and reached in to pull out the painting, then set it on the table.

The painting wasn't large, and it depicted six people, three of whom Kevin recognized, while the others weren't known to him. Ivan Hall, a dead Justicar, Ulvian Sorvos, and Elissa of Silence were all in the picture, and both men looked far younger, while they were each equipped like adventurers. The others were two more men and a woman, one male dwarf, a male elf, and a grinning human woman who had a hand on Elissa's shoulder. The truly unusual thing was that Elissa looked like she hadn't aged a day.

"This... is this Justicar Hall?" Bran asked cautiously, frowning. "That's the Archon, I know it is."

"Yes, it is. Elissa of Silence was an adventuring companion of theirs, and they attempted to breach the dungeon called The Road to Hell. The three of them survived, but only just, and she went her separate way. My investigations since then show that she aged slowly, much as Ulvian did, and her description matched that of Halstad's thief, at least until just a few months before she came to Kelvanis," Kevin explained, smiling as he saw Bran nodding in understanding.

"Interesting. The problem is, what do they *want* for that?" Ruthan asked suspiciously, which Kevin heartily approved of, since it was one of the things that'd he'd wondered instantly. "Last I heard, she was in Beacon, which is a damn deathtrap."

"That's the problem. Their goal is to hurt Medaea, and Tyria, as much as they can. They're not talking about attacking the goddess or Beacon, to be clear," Kevin quickly assured them, taking a deep breath, then let it out again more calmly. "What they *want* is for us to attack the temple in Westgate. The only direct node connections to Westgate are Kelvanath and Beacon, which means that if they're going to call for reinforcements, it'll have to come from those places. If we can draw some of the troops out of Kelvanath with a distraction beforehand, what do you think the odds of either the archpriestess of Medaea or Elissa coming to try to rescue the goddess's faithful are?"

"Huh. While it's a dandy idea, what's to stop Tyria from flying over to Westgate and incinerating us? She has the power to do that, and you know it," Bran said, looking at the map unhappily.

"Mm, apparently that isn't as much of a risk as you might think. See, when she acted on behalf of Kelvanis, it was *because* she was being controlled that she could get away with it, from the explanations I was getting. Apparently, if she starts doing too much, other deities will step in, and that would be bad, considering the Godsrage," Kevin said, and before either man could speak he added, "I'll point out that I wasn't entirely convinced by that explanation myself, at least not initially. Then they pointed out that she hasn't done *anything* since the battle at Beacon, not even when you managed to take out one of Damrung's armies, or when the slaves in Teleth were executed. If she didn't act then, when some of her priesthood were among the dead, why would she act now?"

"Maybe not, but you're talking about the leaders of her church! That's an *enormously* different situation than a couple of minor priests," Ruthan retorted, scowling. "I don't know about you, but if I were a god I wouldn't take that laying down, rules or no rules."

"Maybe so, but let's look at this a different way," Kevin said, deciding to abandon subtlety. "We, and I *do* mean we in this case, have three choices. We can stay here and die when Slaid Damrung manages to hunt us down, we can flee the nation with what wealth we can carry with us, or we can give this a shot, inflict some pain and agony on our enemies, *and* get a solid start as nobility in another country. Which do *you* want?"

For a long moment the room was quiet, and Ruthan crossed his arms, glaring at Kevin wordlessly. Bran sighed, gripping the edge of the table tight, and Kevin stood there, looking back at the two of them fearlessly.

"That *does* put it into perspective, doesn't it?" Bran said softly. He seemed to consider, then continued. "In that case, I don't think I can just make the decision for everyone else. I want to present the options to them and see what they want to do. If we're going to do this, I only want those who *want* to do it involved."

"I entirely understand. If we do it, I'm not dragging any of my people with who aren't willing, either," Kevin agreed, nodding and keeping an eye on Ruthan as he added, "If you want to gather your people and make a decision, I'll wait. That said, I'm not sure how much time we have to act. Winter's coming, after all."

"True enough. Ruthan, would you go get the others?" Bran asked, and the other man nodded.

"Right away, sir," the man said, giving Kevin a distrustful look as he headed toward the back door.

Kevin ignored the look, instead finding a spot where he could lean against the wall. He was sure that the discussion would be interesting, especially after the arguments that'd ensued when *he'd* gotten word.

In the end, he'd decided that the risk was worth it, even if he wasn't happy about it. What he wouldn't give to plant a dagger in Slaid Damrung's *other* eye.

CHAPTER 18

Diamond paused as she came around the corner, a book in hand, and nearly ran into Nadis. The archpriestess stiffened slightly as well, pausing as she'd been speaking to Nora. It was a bit interesting seeing the pale-skinned elf alongside Nadis, as Nora looked younger than Nadis, yet had been born millennia before.

"Ah, hello, Lady Diamond! It's good to see you again," Nora said in her strangely accented manner, not seeming to notice Nadis's reaction. "How are your studies coming?"

"Studies?" Nadis asked, blinking a couple of times as she looked at Diamond in surprise. "Is that why you're here?"

"Yes, as a matter of fact," Diamond replied, relaxing ever so slightly as she smiled at Nora. "The changes to my magic, along with the links to the other Jewels, necessitated some additional experiments when it came to my magic, and when the academy was recovered... well, Kassandra thought that we were wasting our potential. Besides, it'd been so long since I made significant advances in spellcasting that this is... restful, I suppose. As for my studies, I *think* they're going well, Nora."

"Good! I was just explaining a few things to Nadis, since she came across a few interesting references in a holy text," Nora said, looking between them as she added, "I didn't realize you two knew each other."

"Ah, she was the archpriestess of Medaea before me, prior to being captured," Nadis explained, her voice a touch wary as she looked at Diamond, considering before she continued. "It seems there were a number of rituals that were never mentioned in our records, only in her holy text. Worse, many of the methods to *perform* the rituals weren't detailed. Apparently they were considered common knowledge before the Godsrage."

"Oh. *Oh*, one of *those*," Diamond said, wincing a little as she shook her head. "Yes, we've run into a few of those ourselves, I'm afraid. Did she show you one of the new copies of *Marin's Codex*? Volume... four, was it, that dealt with rituals?"

"Five, actually, and no, I'm afraid that Cortin is currently using the volume, and we don't have another copy yet," Nora said, grimacing as she added, "The last attempt at copying it didn't go well. Sistina was displeased enough by the mistakes she burned it."

Diamond flinched at that, inhaling sharply as she asked, "Did she say *why*, at least?"

"Only that 'details matter', as she watched it burn," Nora said, sighing softly, and Nadis looked between them in confusion.

"Um, may I ask what you're talking about? I do remember *Marin's Codex* was considered a definitive resource on magic, but I don't know much more since Yisara has never owned a copy," Nadis replied slowly, frowning a little.

"*Marin's Codex* isn't a single volume, it's nine, as a matter of fact. Also, calling it the *definitive* resource on magic would be giving it a bit too much credit. It was the foundation of a great deal of research, yes, but not definitive. Other magi made advances over what it contained," Nora explained patiently. "That said, it's an amazing work for building a proper foundation. Better yet, Sistina translated it accurately into modern elvish, which removes an enormous barrier for those who wish to use ancient magic."

"As to why she's so upset at inaccurate translations, Sistina is... personally invested in the content of the books," Diamond said delicately, clearing her throat as she added, "Apparently, before she died originally, she *was* Marin. She wrote the books, became an angel, was kidnapped and turned into a demon, then ended up being turned into a tree by happenstance. Her memories are fragmented, but some of her original nature persists even now."

Nadis opened her mouth, then shut it again, blinking at Diamond, then asked incredulously, "An angel, really?"

"Yes. From what was said, she was an angel of Balvess, a god of magic who died in the Godsrage. Unfortunately, Irethiel's predecessor decided that she'd make an excellent subordinate and stole her," Diamond said wryly. "That's why she knew so much about the brands to begin with. She'd had one, once upon a time."

"I… see. I wasn't aware of that," Nadis said, looking like she was digesting the information, and not entirely sure how she should react. After a moment she murmured, "I do wonder why you kept it quiet, though… it seems like important information."

"Queen Calath and Beryl were both informed, as were their agents. If you weren't told, either it was an oversight or, more likely, they didn't think it was important," Diamond said, shrugging calmly.

"Ah, well, it certainly clears up a few questions that I'd had in the back of my mind. I *do* find it a little disturbing that Sistina was a demon, but…" Nadis's voice trailed off and she shook her head. "No, that doesn't really matter. I'm just surprised, I suppose."

"I can't say as I blame you," Diamond said, thinking back and smiling. "I probably wouldn't have reacted well when I heard about it if it hadn't been for Sistina rescuing us from Jared. That was… well, many tears of relief were shed at the time, I can tell you that much."

"Um, would the two of you like some privacy?" Nora interjected, looking at Diamond. "It feels like this is something private."

Diamond looked at Nadis and quirked an eyebrow, though suddenly she found herself hopeful. This was the first time they hadn't met in a formal manner, and she realized they hadn't really had a chance to *talk* about what had happened. It was up to Nadis, though, and Diamond didn't want to push, not after things had been going reasonably well during the meetings.

"I… think I'd like that. Thank you for your time, Nora. It's been a fascinating experience talking to you," Nadis said, nodding graciously to the woman, who smiled happily in return.

"It isn't a problem at all! I'll be over there when you're done," Nora replied, gesturing at a nook with numerous brightly colored tomes on a table, as well as a frustrated-looking human man studying a book. "It looks like Anthony needs some help, anyway."

Diamond and Nadis watched her go, then Diamond gestured at a nearby table. "How about there? I'm not sure there's many other places in the city with more privacy… except maybe Sistina's cavern, but the trip there is punishing."

"How so?" Nadis asked, stepping over to the table in a wordless agreement to Diamond's suggestion, and she followed, taking a seat across from Nadis, setting her books on the table gently.

"It's at the center of the mountain, down at about the same level as the base. So your choices are to trek through dozens of levels of the dungeon, as Sistina doesn't believe in giving shortcuts to her heart, or taking a stairwell from the palace," Diamond said, shaking her head. "It's… a painful climb. If my body hadn't been strengthened by my time here, I probably couldn't manage it."

"Ah, yes… that *would* be problematic, wouldn't it? I was a touch incredulous about the difficulty of the climb to the palace, so that would likely be far, far worse," Nadis murmured, pausing for a moment before asking, "Why have you retained the name they forced on you? I was told that the mind control was undone."

"It was. I'm no longer forced to forget that my name was Visna, or that Ruby was Antessa. However…" Diamond paused, then sighed softly, looking down at her hands as she explained. "My memories were *altered*, Nadis. I don't remember being called Visna in any of the memories of my childhood, growing up, or even on my ascent to becoming the archpriestess. As far as I'm concerned, everyone called me Diamond for all that time. I know that isn't true, but it doesn't change what my memory claims."

"O-oh," Nadis said, blinking a few times, and obviously debating on what to say, but after a moment Diamond smiled slightly.

"That said, truthfully I rather *like* the name. Diamond is... pretty. It suits me," Diamond said, reaching up to stroke a glittering strand of her hair. "Besides, I love the way that Sistina and Phynis smile when they say it."

"Love... well, of course. You *did* marry them, after all," Nadis said, regaining her poise as she smiled, though there was an uncomfortable edge to it. She paused, then spoke softly. "I don't understand you, Diamond. I don't... know how to relate to you anymore."

"I don't think we ever could relate to one another," Diamond replied calmly.

Nadis looked up sharply at that, anger on her face for just an instant. "Why would you say that? We got along well before Kelvanis invaded!"

"No, we didn't," Diamond disagreed, shaking her head gently as she spoke in the same level voice. "You and I barely interacted. We exchanged letters, and I made decisions from the depths of Our Lady's temple. You were in the middle of Yisara, speaking with the faithful day after day. It's easy to seem to get along from a distance like that, but we were in such different positions that I don't think we could ever *truly* relate to one another."

Nadis's eyes narrowed, but the archpriestess didn't say anything immediately, instead simply staring at Diamond. Eventually she asked, "What are you getting at? I thought you wanted to talk to get along better, not to antagonize me."

"Antagonize you? Oh no, of course not!" Diamond said, smiling suddenly as she chuckled softly. "No, what I'm saying is that I think that me being the archpriestess and staying there was a mistake. I had *no concept* of what the faithful were truly dealing with. I got reports of the war with Kelvanis, but do you truly believe that I understood them? Do you think that I could honestly understand the gravity of the situation without speaking with some of the victims personally?"

Diamond paused, looking at Nadis as the archpriestess inhaled, then exhaled, obviously considering what she'd said. At least she didn't look angry, which was a good sign.

"I've been thinking about it frequently for a long, long time. I don't think that I should have been the archpriestess. I may have been a good spiritual leader… but I didn't lead. I wasn't there when people needed me the most," Diamond continued at last, letting out her breath as she sat back. "You should have been truly in charge… but we were following traditions. Traditions that *now* feel uncomfortably out of place, if you ask me. The revelations about Medaea startled me."

"You didn't seem startled at the time," Nadis murmured, looking at Diamond oddly, now. Diamond wasn't quite sure what she was thinking, but it was a good sign, she hoped.

"That's because I knew a little, if not the details. I'd gone to speak with Tyria the previous day, and she told me that both sides were wrong about her," Diamond said, thinking back on the encounter and smiling, recalling her own shock in sardonic amusement. "I asked her what we were wrong about, and she told me I'd have to wait and hear at the same time as you, as she wasn't going to show favoritism. It gave me a chance to at least brace myself, which helped when things turned out to be… well, even more shocking than I expected. I never thought that we'd been following a goddess of the dead."

"Ah. As for her nature, that much was a shock, even if she didn't explain the differences fully. It was… well, fascinating to read about some of them, and they also explain some of the oldest tales of the faith," Nadis said, visibly relaxing as she shrugged. "Still, I don't think that calling her a goddess of the dead is exactly right, either. Ensuring those who die are honored feels a little different to me, as does her former focus on ensuring that they're avenged when necessary. I'm not entirely *comfortable* with it, but I feel I can understand it."

"A fair point, I suppose. How are your people dealing with the discussions, anyway? I know I've been worried about them, and how they might react," Diamond said, leaning forward again, relief rushing through her at Nadis's reasonable response. "While I might not feel suited to being a member of the priesthood anymore, I find that I'm rather heavily invested in trying to prevent you and Elissa from coming to blows."

"As much as I may dislike her, I have to admit that seems... unlikely. She's kept calm and reasonable even when I've provoked her. I haven't done it consciously for the most part, but I have," Nadis admitted, taking a deep breath. "The others are... reluctantly dealing with the issue, even when they aren't happy about it. Honestly, I suspect an enormous part of the problem is how different Tyria's appearance and name are from what we've been taught."

"Oh?" Diamond asked, blinking in surprise, not having expected *that* aspect of the discussion. She remembered Tyria stating she might take a new name early on, but she hadn't anticipated her *appearance* being the problem.

"The faithful have followed Medaea for decades if not centuries, you know that. The name is ingrained in their minds, and as such it's something which the people are comfortable with. Conversely, *Tyria* was introduced to them initially as a goddess of slaves, something which they've despised with every fiber of their beings," Nadis explained, hesitating for a moment, then continued. "As for her appearance... well, I suspect it comes back to the same issue. Our statues were all patterned off an early sculpture based on Medaea's actual appearance, so people know it and are comfortable with it. Tyria doesn't fit that image, and instead was made into something to suit Kelvanis. Don't you think that the faithful would be reluctant to see a constant reminder that she was hurt by them? Controlled like that? It's also why I'm so leery about her connection to Sistina."

"That makes far more sense," Diamond said, sitting back as she began thinking, a slight frown on her face. She hesitated for a bit, debating on what to say. Finally, she let out a sigh as she looked at Nadis. "I... well, on a personal level I feel that she shouldn't need to change if she's comfortable as she is, but that's partially selfish, due to what happened to me. You make some excellent points, really. The problem is... I don't know what's fair.

"As for her connection to Sistina, I think that's a much more difficult subject. You see—" Diamond began, but at that moment the doors opened and Desa stepped into the chamber, a grim look on her face as she glanced around and spotted the two of them.

"Diamond, Archpriestess, there you are! I'm glad you're together," Desa exclaimed, ignoring a couple of annoyed looks thrown her way by people who were studying. "If possible, please come with me. The prisoners finally talked, so we have a *little* more information. *Finally.*"

Diamond blinked in surprise, then relief rushed through her. She'd begun to wonder if they'd ever learn who Elissa's assailants truly were, which made the news a relief. But then she looked at Nadis in concern, opening her mouth just as the other woman stood.

"It appears that we'll have to continue this discussion later, Diamond," Nadis said, her voice firm, and a slight glitter in her eyes. "As useful as it is, I believe it's best to find out who tried to frame my church *now.*"

"As you like. We're coming, Desa," Diamond agreed, standing as well. She did hesitate, before regretfully leaving her books behind.

She could always pick up her studies later, in the end.

CHAPTER 19

The room was rather full, which was part of why Tyria was keeping herself concealed. Elissa, her guards, the priest Ollie, a couple of the city's guards, a golem, and the prisoner were there, along with Albert Windgale. Even more importantly, Tyria knew that Diamond and Nadis would be there any moment, which would make the room even more heavily crowded than it already was.

The prisoner was the leader of the people who'd attacked Elissa, Tyria knew. Feldan Soarlik was a normal-looking human, with brown hair, brown eyes, and had a fair amount of stubble from his stay in the jail so far. He also had a hint of power around him that Tyria recognized, though she wasn't going to act on her knowledge. Like she'd told Diamond before, acting in the mortal world capriciously was dangerous, and she wasn't about to do anything that would cause the greater gods to come after her.

Her gaze flicked to the side as the door opened to reveal a guard, followed by Nadis, another guard, Diamond, and finally Desa. Diamond and Nadis looked a little more at ease in each other's company than they had that morning, which improved Tyria's mood slightly, though it was minor compared to the worries currently plaguing her.

"My apologies for the delay, we were at the academy when

we received word," Nadis said, nodding to the others, then looked at the prisoner, her eyes narrowing slightly. "So this is the man who led the attackers?"

"That's right. From what was said, he's the one who threw the fireball at me, and injured Ollie," Elissa confirmed evenly, glancing at Ollie as she added, "Are you sure you're fine being here, for that matter?"

"Of course I am. I'd rather look the man who almost killed me in the eyes and decide what I think than hide from it," Ollie said, his gaze unwavering as he stared at Feldan. Tyria could sense the truth of his words, and slowly she smiled more, pleased with the young man. Few people could truly reserve judgment for one another, and she doubted that Elissa and Nadis would ever get along on a personal level. On the other hand, Ollie would make an excellent high priest one day, Tyria thought. That was one of the opportunities that needed to be opened in Medaea's church, in fact.

"I… see. That's generous of you," Nadis said, looking more than a little taken aback by how calm the two clergy were, but she focused instead on the prisoner, who was separated from their chairs by prison bars. "Now, then. What is all of this?"

Albert cleared his throat and explained. "As I don't believe we've met, I'm Albert Windgale, the head of the local branch of the Western Adventurer's Guild, Archpriestess. As an alchemist, I was called upon to help interrogate the prisoners, and I learned early on that they were rendered immune to all of the common elixirs for compelling truthful speech. That's unfortunately common among secret agents, so I wasn't able to do much. However, they *aren't* immune to most of the simple truth elixirs, so when Feldan decided he was willing to talk, I was called in to ensure he was speaking the truth."

"Not that you were damned well needed. I was willing to talk, so would you get out of my face?" Feldan demanded, his words clipped short as he wrinkled his nose in distaste. "You smell terrible."

"Ah," Nadis said, nodding and smoothing her dress as she took a seat. "That would explain it."

"Additionally, I can tell you that Feldan isn't native to this continent, either. While it's faint, I detect the accent of one of the natives of the Great Labyrinth to his speech," Albert added, looking down at the man with a slight smile. "I hadn't expected him to be from there, considering how far away we are."

Tyria tilted her head slightly in interest at that, since it was new information to her. She *did* know that the city around the Great Labyrinth was rather far to their east across the ocean, after all. She didn't know what the northern continent was named these days, as there was a good deal to re-learn about the world.

"I'm afraid that we already realized that the attackers were foreigners, Albert. Unlike you, we're well aware how few non-dawn or dusk elves follow Tyria, so seeing the attackers was rather… telling," Diamond said, her voice calm, and a smile flickering across her face. "Would you please let Feldan speak? I'd like to get this over with, if possible."

"As you wish, Lady Diamond. I'm just glad the jail is at the base of the city," Albert said, glancing at Feldan as he took a couple of steps back.

"Unfortunately," Tyria heard Desa mutter under her breath.

"Fine, fine… so, I'm Feldan Soarlik. Yes, I attacked the caravan, and I don't regret it, either," Feldan said, spitting on the floor as he looked around the room and scowled. "Now that that's out of the way, just execute me and be done with it."

"Why?" Elissa asked calmly.

"Why what? Isn't that what you do with prisoners?" Feldan retorted angrily.

"Don't give me that. We both know you're just being difficult; you wouldn't have called us all here for *this*," Elissa replied politely, looking at him closely. "You're a powerful man, even I can tell that. Why did you attack me? You aren't a zealot of Medaea, you don't have the attitude of an assassin or mercenary… no, you're something else. So I have to ask *why*."

"Ha! And why should I tell you?" Feldan asked, his voice almost taunting as he looked around the room. "I could just have been trying to waste your time."

"I suspect because you don't want to spend the rest of your life in prison cells, and neither do your people. Maybe you had a message to send, but I'm not sure," Desa said, looking at the man pointedly. "Besides, you were under the effects of the elixir when you told us you were ready to talk to everyone, so spit it out already."

For a minute Feldan didn't speak, instead looking around the room angrily. He didn't look at Tyria, of course, his gaze passing right over her, but he obviously wasn't a happy man. Instead he took a breath like he was about to yell at Desa, then let it pass.

"Yes, I *did* that, didn't I? Damn, I would've rather yanked your chain more, like I am now," Feldan said at last. He looked at them for a moment, then continued. "We're followers of Baldwin, if you absolutely have to know, and we were trying to sow chaos between your two little factions."

"What? Baldwin? Isn't he the Forge God?" Desa asked, blinking in confusion as she looked around the room. "Why would his followers be interfering here?"

For a moment the room was quiet, no one seeming to want to speak.

"Ah… Baldwin and Medaea had an… unfortunate relationship, from what legends have to say," Diamond began, her tone slightly delicate.

"What she *means* is that they were enemies," Feldan interrupted impatiently. "She took his eye and a hand during the Godsrage, and he was forced to create a new hand from metal to make do. When we heard about what happened here, we thought it only fair to create a little chaos, though…"

Feldan's voice trailed off as his gaze settled on Tyria as she let the concealment lapse, also drawing the attention Albert and the guards. It took a moment more for the others to react and turn to face her, which she understood. Her gaze was fixed on Feldan's, though.

"What you claim is interesting, since I have no recollection of those events," Tyria said, prompting the man to color briefly, but she clarified as she continued speaking. "I'm not saying we didn't fight. I remember battling Baldwin during the Godsrage and our battle did immense damage to our surroundings, as I could barely scratch him, and he couldn't prevent me from healing myself. The part that surprises me is that I also remember us calling a truce, just after what I suspect was the world tree's destruction. My memories end there, so I do not know what happened afterward… but I find it *very* difficult to believe myself capable of taking his eye or hand."

"You… you can't be…" Feldan began haltingly, swallowing several times as he stared at her in mingled fascination and horror.

"My Lady," Elissa said, standing and gracefully curtseying.

Almost as if prompted by her words, the others quickly stood and bowed or curtseyed, though Albert's was relatively shallow, as was those of Nadis's guards. Tyria resisted the urge to sigh, waving them down.

"Go ahead and take your seats. I've been keeping an eye on how the conference has progressed, but also have been endeavoring not to interfere as long as it is going well. This, however, is slightly more curious to me, as I've wondered about the gaps in my memories, particularly how fragmented things are immediately before my slumber," Tyria said, shaking her head slowly. "I know *why* I slept. However, these… issues aren't the fault of Irethiel or Ulvian Sorvos, as much as I might wish to blame them. No… and more curious is that Feldan isn't entirely certain that his decision to cause trouble was his own idea."

"How do you know that?" Feldan demanded, his scowl fading to be replaced by shock.

"I can sense the truth of things, and it was obvious," Tyria said simply, letting her gaze play across the others as she considered, then added, "As to Baldwin, I should stress that we were not truly *enemies*, even if we were opponents in the Godsrage. There was no significant bad blood between us, but we each had different allies. That was what set us in conflict, I'm afraid."

"I… think I understand, Your Eminence," Diamond murmured, nodding slightly, then turned back toward Feldan as she arched an eyebrow, then spoke. "So why is it that you're unsure that it was your own idea? I trust Tyria's ability to sense the truth, so I believe it's worth asking."

Feldan's jaw tightened slightly, and for a moment the man was silent, staring at Tyria with mingled anger and fear in his eyes. She could practically see him trying to decide what to do or say, but Tyria wasn't about to do anything to force him to speak.

"The moment I cast my spell to attack, I wondered what in all the hells I was doing," Feldan said at last, his tone grating. "I don't know about anyone else, but that is a jarring moment to have second thoughts. If it'd been a little later, sure, but then? It's odd. Worse, I shouldn't have called for an attack on the caravan to begin with. There were twice as many guards as I counted on, and I'm not so much of an idiot that I'd expect to beat them with only thirty people. It doesn't make sense the more I think about it, which makes me think I was being manipulated. By who or what, I don't know, but if I was, they left just after I attacked."

"That is interesting. And even if you'd informed us immediately, my own use of mental control likely destroyed any clues that were left behind," Elissa said, frowning a little. "I'm not going to apologize for it, as it reduced the number of injured and dead, but it makes this more complicated."

"Assuming it's true," Desa said bluntly.

"The elixir is still working," Feldan spat out, glaring at Desa angrily.

"Yes, it is. However, enough strange things have happened in the last year that I refuse to take everything at face value. I *think* you're telling the truth. Whether or not you're right is an entirely different subject," Desa replied calmly, looking directly back at him. "Oh, I'm sure that Tyria knows more than she's telling us, likely because the arcane rules of the gods require it, but that isn't information *I* have. What I know for certain is that you attacked one of Her Majesty's guests in Everium's territory, and banditry is punishable by imprisonment or death. As we do not have evidence you were acting of your own free will, you'll be kept imprisoned for now."

"Fine," Feldan replied, scowling back at her. "Will your investigators at least quit badgering me about why we did it?"

Desa inclined her head slightly, smiling as she said. "Yes, unless they have something they need clarified. Even if *you* didn't act of your own volition, I somehow doubt all of your people were controlled as well. In any case…"

"I believe it is time for me to go. I've not met with any other deities since I woke, and I believe that it's time for that to change," Tyria interjected, nodding to those in the room graciously as she added, "Please keep up the good work. I'm afraid the skies are cloudy, however, so watch for danger."

Before they could say anything more, Tyria concealed herself and left the room, mentally shifting slightly out of phase with the world again so she could move through the walls. Extending her wings, she took flight in an instant, shooting upward into a sky that was lit by the colors created by the setting sun.

As she ascended, Tyria considered, a tiny part of her growing a little reluctant as she thought about the consequences of speaking to other deities. She'd been gone for so long that even those she'd thought of as allies might not look on her favorably, and yet... yet it was time and past for her to make contact with them.

"Zenith," Tyria murmured, mentally reaching out for her angel, and an instant later she felt her magic link to the mind of the woman.

"Yes, my goddess?" Zenith asked eagerly, her mental voice echoing in Tyria's head. *"How may I serve you?"*

"I would like you to seek an audience with Baldwin. I wish to meet with him as soon as is reasonable," Tyria told her, closing her eyes and waiting.

For a moment Zenith was silent, then she spoke softly. *"If that is your will, it shall be done, but... you fought him during the war, my lady."*

"I know. However, he's the one who can explain things, and I need to speak with him. Please take him the message," Tyria said, letting out her breath unhappily, then opened her eyes to look to the west.

"As you wish, my goddess," Zenith agreed, not arguing further. Almost regretfully Tyria cut off the link, staring at the sky.

The sunlight was beautiful on the mountains, particularly with the way the colors radiated across the sky. Tyria simply hoped she wasn't making a mistake.

CHAPTER 20

"Hello, Lily!" The warm, pleasant voice should have been comforting. Instead it sent a chill down Lily's spine, and she spun around, brandishing her shears like they were a dagger.

Behind her was a succubus, one with an over-exaggerated figure, a jaw-droppingly gorgeous face only marred slightly by the crimson eyes with their vertical slit pupils, and who was grinning widely. Unlike the last time she'd seen the succubus, the woman was wearing what might almost be considered normal clothing, but even that set Lily's nerves on edge.

"W-what are *you* doing here, Wenris?" Lily demanded, taking a couple of steps back until she bumped into a tree that she'd forgotten was there in her shock. "I thought you went back to the hells!"

"I did! There were a few rebellions to stamp out, and you wouldn't *believe* the mess that had been made of the palace, so it took a while to get everything in order. At least the palace here was uninhabited before you took up residence," Wenris replied, her eyes glittering with mirth as she looked down at the shears in Lily's hands. "Do you really need those? I'm not going to attack you. Though if your panther attacks me, I *will* defend myself."

Lily belatedly noticed that Kitten was silently preparing to pounce on Wenris from the bushes behind the woman, all the play gone from the feline's eyes. Instead Kitten looked like the predator she was… but *Lily* knew that would be a terrible idea, from everything she'd heard about Wenris.

"Kitten, stop," Lily said, her heart pounding loudly in her chest, and she swallowed hard as Kitten gave her a confused look, then slowly settled back on her haunches, obviously ready to pounce at a moment's notice. Then Lily took a deep breath, trying to keep her voice from trembling as she spoke. "What… what are you doing here? What do you want from me?"

"Want from you? Oh, Lily… while I'd *adore* it if you chose to become one of my followers, I truly don't think you have the constitution for that. No, you're a pretty young elf, and innocent enough that your soul is tempting… but not worth me coming in person for you. Besides which, Sistina would be annoyed if I tried, and *that* isn't worth it at all. No, I'm not here for you at all," Wenris replied, laughing and grinning as she reached out to pat Lily's cheek gently, her grin widening still more. "No, I came over to say hello! I'm going to be meeting Diane and Torkal here a little bit later, and I wanted to assure you that I remembered your instructions from earlier this year. I won't be doing the sort of things succubi are notorious for in your garden."

"Err…" Lily murmured, caught off guard and confused.

"I'll *behave*," Wenris said, taking a couple of careful steps forward, bypassing Lily's shears effortlessly, then whispered in Lily's ear, her voice heady with unspoken desire. "I *promise*."

Lily managed to retain control for all of an instant, mostly until Wenris leaned back and she saw an avenue of escape. Then her control broke, and she ran for safety, her face and ears burning with embarrassment. Behind her, Wenris's laughter echoed through the garden, only heightening her embarrassment.

Wenris laughed as Lily fled, amazed despite everything at the speed of the young elf. The succubus was fairly certain that if Lily was in a footrace with adventurers, she'd leave the majority of them in her dust. Either way, Wenris did enjoy letting the young woman's embarrassment get her out of the way.

Looking back at the panther, Wenris raised an eyebrow at the feline, asking, "Are you going to join your mistress? Or would you rather play with me? I'm afraid I play rough, though."

The panther looked at Wenris for a moment, obviously not impressed at all, then raised a paw so it could calmly lick it and rub behind an ear. With that done, the panther slowly got up, stretched, and ambled off after Lily, as if making a point of the fact that it wasn't following Wenris's directions. That caused another burble of laughter to escape Wenris, and she looked around the garden now that she had a moment to herself.

It truly was a lovely place, she had to admit, and while she'd seen some gardens that were more beautiful, only a couple of them were in the mortal world, and none of those had been created in less than a few months. In fact, most of them had been carefully cultivated by empires over the course of decades.

"An ideal neutral ground, I think," Wenris murmured, idly circling the garden and reaching out to touch a few of the plants. The magic infused into them was incredible, and she had to wonder what most magi would think of the gardens. They'd probably try to ransack them for magical components for enchanting, most likely... but she suspected that wouldn't happen for a long, *long* time.

The succubus ignored the elf who poked his head into the garden, then saw her and rapidly retreated. If she remembered right, he was the beloved of Lily, and he wasn't particularly attractive to her. No, instead she looked through the garden and finally decided to take a nice position in a gazebo near a pond. It mirrored the location where she and Diane had first met rather nicely, in her opinion, and while it was cool, that could be easily changed.

Wenris cast a spell casually, delighting in how much larger her reserves of mana were, as well as the increased potency of her spells. She still had to speak the words of the spells, but she was almost on the verge of being able to form the gestures purely mentally, and *that* would have been unimaginable a year before.

Her spell completed, and as it did the temperature quickly rose from cold to a nice, even heat like the interior of the palace, and the handful of flakes of snow around the gazebo melted. Wenris nodded in satisfaction, wishing that she had a tea set to make the similarities even stronger, but… it probably was best she didn't. Diane probably wouldn't trust something like that.

Instead she settled into a chair and waited, smiling as she hummed softly to herself. Soon would be the time she'd chosen to demand for herself with Diane, though that wasn't today. This was her way of being polite.

The first sign of her guests arriving was the soft crunch of shoes breaking the snow, and Wenris casually glanced over to ensure it was Diane, and when she did she couldn't help a warm smile.

Diane was as beautiful as Wenris remembered her being, though the former monarch was bundled up in warm clothing and had a wary expression on her face. Beside her was a taller blond dawn elf, and Wenris's eyes lit up a bit brighter at the sight of the handsome man. She immediately placed him as Torkal, and inwardly she had to admit that Diane had good taste. Even so, she didn't let herself react openly.

"Ah, Diane! How are you doing? Please, take a seat. I warmed up the gazebo, so there isn't a need to remain cold," Wenris said, gesturing to the other three chairs set around the table. "As for your companion… is that your husband, then?"

"Hello, Wenris," Diane replied, her voice calm, though Wenris could see how nervous she was. "And yes, he is. What are you doing here?"

Wenris's smile faded a fraction, especially as her gaze settled on Torkal's hand, which was resting on the hilt of his sword. Obviously, he wasn't happy to see her, and she sighed internally, wishing that mortals would learn what they could and couldn't challenge.

"You know better than that, Diane. I'm going to forgive you using the wrong form of address where I'm concerned during this meeting, but not afterward," Wenris said, steel creeping into her voice as she said, "Sit. Down. And if that sword leaves its sheath, Torkal will regret it. While I promised Sistina not to attack anyone during my visit, I will *not* allow anyone to attack me without responding appropriately."

"You can just—" Torkal began snarling, only to stop as Diane laid a hand on his shoulder. When he met her gaze, the elven woman shook her head gently.

"Please don't, dear. She's not one to make idle threats, I know that much," Diane said, her voice almost a whisper.

"Precisely right," Wenris said, and gestured at the chairs again. "I would have provided tea, but I knew you wouldn't trust it, Diane."

"For good reason," Torkal said, his voice seething with rage.

"Yes, but there's no need to be overly rude," Diane said, and Wenris's mood improved slightly as Diane approached, moving the chairs so that she and Torkal could sit directly across from the succubus. Torkal followed unhappily, watching Wenris carefully.

"Good girl. Diane knows what sort of things I do when she's rude, so you might want to follow her advice, Torkal," Wenris said, sitting back in her chair comfortably, flicking her tail around so it could lash next to her ankles.

Torkal just glared, and Diane let out a soft sigh, then murmured, "If I may… may I ask why you're here, Wenris?"

"Much better," Wenris said in approval, nodding as she added, "First of all… thank you for following my directions on the new moon. I checked each time, even if I didn't come visit, and if you hadn't… well, I would have been *unhappy* with you."

The instructions for Diane to sleep alone on the new moon had been something Wenris had given on a whim, originally, mostly because she wanted to prove she had some power over the woman, and to create a persistent reminder. From the way Diane's face colored, Wenris suspected that she hadn't realized that Wenris was checking on her.

"I… will admit I have considered disobeying a time or two. I almost forgot once, but I decided to be safe," Diane said, looking at Torkal uncomfortably. "I've been surprised that you *haven't* visited."

"If you think the wards your magi put up could stop me, I'm afraid you're overly optimistic," Wenris said dryly, and Torkal's face paled a little as she continued. "No, I listened to the advice of my former superior, and she recommended I give you time to settle back into your life before intervening again. That's why you were left alone for all this time, Diane, but I'm afraid that's at an end. Tomorrow is the new moon, and I *will* be visiting."

For an instant the other two were quiet, and Diane paled slightly, then a slight flush rose in her cheeks, accompanied by pheromones that Wenris rather enjoyed, while Torkal's face flushed as well, but his was the flush of anger.

"Why can't you leave her damned well alone?!" Torkal snarled, leaning forward as he grabbed Diane's hand. "Hasn't she suffered enough already? I—"

"Enough," Wenris replied coldly, infusing power into her gaze and voice that brought the man to a strangled halt. He gasped, and Diane paled, but she didn't say anything. Wenris stared at Torkal for a few moments more, then spoke, her tone as cold as ice. "You seem to be under a mistaken impression, Torkal. Diane is *mine*."

"But—" Torkal began, but Wenris cut him off again.

"No, you will *listen,* and come to understand your place in this. Which is that you have *no choice* in what happens to Diane," Wenris said implacably, staring the man down in annoyance. "She sold herself to me to ensure Jaine's escape with her mind intact. Her soul is now entwined with my own, and of all the gods, the only ones with a *chance* of undoing such would be the primal gods, who rarely pay attention to mortal concerns. I could drag her into my realm today without causing any of the deities to so much as blink, save possibly in pity. I *choose* to allow Diane freedom, both to associate with you and her family, as well as to live a life of relative ease. I could take that away in an instant… and you *cannot stop me*. Is that clear?"

Torkal's breath hissed out, and Wenris could *see* the rage in his eyes, but before he could speak Diane's fingers tightened around his hand, her worry obvious. He glanced at Diane, then visibly forced himself to back down as he let out a breath, speaking angrily. "Yes, you're *clear*."

"Good. I'm trying not to cause too many issues while I'm here, but if it comes to protecting that which is mine by right, I will do so without hesitation," Wenris said, allowing a smile of satisfaction to reveal itself, and she let her voice relax. "Now, then. Diane… do you have any questions about just what the freedom I grant you allows you to do? I'd rather be clear about things than spring them on you suddenly."

"Well…" Diane hesitated, looking a little torn as she looked at Wenris.

A tiny part of Wenris couldn't help her amusement at how Torkal was glaring and grinding his teeth, though. She also knew that he couldn't help his attraction toward her… but she *was* a succubus, after all. If he'd been immune, she'd have been far more concerned.

SISTINA LOOKED at the three in the garden and nodded internally, satisfied with her examinations at last. Torkal wasn't a happy man, and Sistina didn't blame him, not really. It didn't help that she remembered being on the other side of things, though, as her memories of being a succubus were… similarly possessive and overbearing, even if she hadn't been as bad as Wenris was. That made Sistina want to laugh, as she knew that Wenris was being positively *benign* by demonic standards. Still, she wasn't going to upset them with a comment to that effect.

Instead Sistina looked at the three thoughtfully again. Torkal's mana was much like that of any other elf she'd seen over the years, if a little stronger than most. Like with most mortals, it was a swirling mixture of all six elements, reasonably well in balance, though not as orderly as the mana of a mage.

Conversely, Wenris's mana was almost entirely darkness and fire, though air, earth, and water did thread through it here and there. The only source of light mana was that pinprick she'd noticed before, which didn't surprise Sistina. Demons were like that, Sistina suspected, even if she'd never had the chance to look at any of them except Irethiel, Serel, and Wenris in her domain before.

Diane was intriguing, though. Unlike any mortal Sistina had seen save for a couple of priestesses and Jaine, the woman had an overabundance of light mana. In fact, it was stronger in her and Jaine than even any of the priestesses possessed, save for Elissa. Since she'd heard that both had been changed using some of Tyria's blood, that made sense to Sistina. Still, for the most part Diane's mana was normal, save for a tiny core of darkness at the center of her soul, and tendrils of darkness that were slowly extending outward from it.

The sight confirmed Sistina's suspicions where the connection between Diane and Wenris was concerned, and at last she nodded internally and shifted to her body.

Sistina was in Phynis's office, and her wife was busy reading reports and doing paperwork, as she often did these days. Considering for a moment, Sistina fluidly stood, drawing Phynis's attention as she stepped over and leaned down to give her beloved a gentle kiss. Phynis blinked but returned the kiss eagerly.

After a long moment she broke it off and Phynis caught her breath, then smiled and asked, "What was that all about, hm? I thought you were going to be busy most of the day."

"I will be," Sistina replied, taking care to speak properly this time. She wanted to be clear, and Phynis deserved a proper explanation. "However, I have something I wish to address. Diane and Wenris."

Phynis's eyebrows rose, and after a moment the queen bled her ink pen and set it aside, looking at Sistina speculatively as she spoke. "Coupled with how you're speaking, *that* makes me wonder what you're thinking. For you to interrupt your work on your projects… well, it isn't something you usually would consider. What's going on, dear one?"

"Diane is bound to Wenris. You know this," Sistina said and paused for the queen to nod before she continued softly. "It is not fair to her. She does not deserve to be pulled to the lower planes when she dies. I *know* what it is like there."

"No, it isn't. However, you're the one who agreed that the bond wasn't something that could be broken, even if Wenris agreed," Phynis said, looking at Sistina even more curiously. "Unless you've found a way to do that?"

"No. However, I believe I have found a possible solution. A

difficult one, but possible," Sistina replied, and she smiled. "The link does not go in a single direction. It is the privilege of mortals to shape the future, and they can make changes that even the gods are not allowed."

"Sistina… you're being cryptic," Phynis said patiently, her own smile wry now.

"My apologies. If we cannot break the bond, I see one solution to prevent Diane from being dragged into the hells," Sistina said, shrugging and glancing in the direction of the gazebo, even if there were numerous walls in her way. "We give Diane the means to drag Wenris to the light."

Phynis stared at Sistina for a moment, her mouth hanging slightly open. Sistina waited patiently, knowing Phynis would get over her surprise soon enough, and braced herself for the inevitable incredulity. Of course it just figured that Phynis would surprise her.

"I see. You don't think small on *anything*, do you?" Phynis murmured, a smile slowly growing on her face. "You truly believe it is possible?"

"Yes. Not *easy*, but possible," Sistina confirmed, then glanced away as she added, "However, I need to speak with her and others *tonight* if we are to have a chance. May I go have messages sent?"

"Go ahead. And if I'm not there when you explain everything, I expect you to tell me how the conversation goes!" Phynis said firmly.

"Yes," Sistina said, grinning a little as she leaned down and gave Phynis another kiss, then stepped away as Phynis laughed.

Sistina was already making a list of people she wanted present, and she hoped that Diane wouldn't be annoyed with her interference.

CHAPTER 21

Diane looked up and blinked, confusion rushing through her as the door to the sitting room opened and four women stepped in. Diamond, Elissa, Lirisel, and Nadis stepped inside, and each of the women looked at her and Torkal in confusion as well.

"Ah, did we come to the right place?" Lirisel asked, looking perplexed as she looked at Diane. "Sistina sent a message asking us to meet her here."

"Ah, that explains why you're here, then. I did wonder… she didn't say that she was going to be inviting other people as well," Diane said, relief rushing through her, even as her confusion grew deeper. "She asked me to stay for a meeting this afternoon, along with Torkal."

"Hm… odd, that," Diamond said, tilting her head as she looked at Diane speculatively. "Do you know why she asked you to stay? Her message to us was quite vague."

Nadis sniffed derisively, muttering, "Vague is putting it mildly. No sooner had we finished with the conference for the day than she sent us a message. 'Meet with me for a matter of grave import' indeed."

"I… can't say that I know, not for sure. I suppose it *might* have something to do with my meeting with Wenris earlier," Diane said, shying away from her mixed feelings where the succubus was concerned. As much as she hated to admit it, Wenris had her thoroughly wrapped around her little finger, and it was essentially impossible for Diane to deny the succubus. Beside her, Torkal's expression darkened, but it was Elissa who looked up abruptly, as did Diamond and Lirisel.

"Wenris? Didn't she inherit Irethiel's demonic mantle?" Elissa asked sharply, the intensity of her gaze startling as she focused on Diane. At Diane's nod she asked, "What is she doing *here*?"

"Making demands of Diane, of course," Torkal grated unhappily, the venom dripping from his voice. "She couldn't leave her alone."

"What? Why would she be making demands of you? For that matter, how is she even in this world?" Elissa asked, stepping toward a chair as she frowned, watching the others sit. "Demon lords or queens cannot enter our world unless they're summoned, at least not under any normal circumstance."

"Ah... hadn't you heard that Diane made a bargain with Wenris in order to protect Jaine's mind?" Diamond asked delicately.

Elissa's head whipped around to stare at Diamond for a moment, then she looked at Diane, and what startled Diane more than anything else was the sudden guilt that she saw in Elissa's gaze. The woman didn't speak immediately as she sank into her chair, letting out a soft sigh.

"No, I wasn't aware of that. If I had been... oh, Goddess... I'm sorry, Diane," Elissa said, her voice filled with pain. "I know we didn't exactly get off on the right foot, but I never wanted something like that for you. What price did you have to pay?"

"It isn't your fault. I... well, belong to her. It's something that can't be undone, I'm afraid, and apparently she can visit *me* whenever she pleases. Though at least she's wary of coming onto the palace grounds, which makes me even happier we came to Beacon for the winter," Diane explained, sighing softly. "This is the first visit she's made since taking her new position, and I'm... worried."

"For good reason," Sistina's voice wasn't too audible through the door, but that changed after a moment.

The door opened again and Sistina stepped in, accompanied by a confused-looking Jaine, and Diane blinked in surprise, looking at the gathering of women in even more confusion. The gathering was an odd group, she realized slowly, but she could see the pattern thus far. Aside from Diane, Sistina, and Torkal, all of those present were priestesses. Well, she supposed that Jaine wasn't a priestess yet, but that was liable to change in the near future.

"Sistina? What's this all about?" Diamond asked, far more forthrightly than Diane suspected anyone else would be. "It's been a long day, and you're talking... well, you aren't dropping words."

"This is important enough that misunderstandings are something I wish to avoid," Sistina said, and Diane's jaw almost dropped, as the sentence was likely the single longest thing she'd heard the dryad say in the time she'd known her, but Sistina wasn't finished. "I should not have called everyone here without speaking with Diane first, but time is in short supply."

"If time is in short supply, might we get started, then?" Nadis asked, looking at Sistina warily. "As Diamond said, what *is* this about?"

"We are still waiting on Tyria. Possibly on Zenith as well, but I'm uncertain if Tyria will be bringing her," Sistina said, politely pulling out a chair for Jaine, who took a seat, looking around the room with wide eyes, but she didn't say anything, which was only appropriate, as Diane almost choked.

"Tyria?" Torkal's eyes went wide as he almost spluttered. "You invited a *goddess*?"

"Yes. I did not command her to come, I simply asked," Sistina said, shrugging as she added, "I could command, but I will not. It is up to *her* to break the bond between us. She has declined, thus far."

"She what? How could she break the link?" Nadis asked, and most of the room was looking at Sistina incredulously, Diane included.

Warmth suddenly radiated through the room, and from above a figure slipped through the ceiling and directly behind Sistina. The dryad didn't so much as twitch as Tyria landed behind her, her hands coming to rest on Sistina's shoulders as the goddess gave a gentle smile.

"I'm the one who chose to sever the link between myself and Irethiel, and to forge it with Sistina. If she chose to grip the link tightly, I wouldn't be able to sever it, however. She is powerful, in some ways more powerful than Irethiel was, yet she hasn't," Tyria said, breaking the sudden silence as she looked around the room more. "Yes, I could sever that link. However, some of the changes Irethiel made have had… side effects. If I severed it, I would suffer the full consequences of those changes, and I'm not ready to risk that, not yet. I'd far rather let Sistina be in a position to stop me should I lose control of myself."

Diane's eyebrows rose at the explanation, and her mouth opened as she inhaled, then paused before she spoke, considering whether or not she dared ask what Tyria meant. In the end, she decided to let the comment pass.

"Ah, since you're here, Your Eminence… may I ask what this is about?" Diane asked, her voice a bit unsteady.

"That is an excellent question, and one I have no answer for. I am as in the dark as you are, and Sistina will have to illuminate us," Tyria said, looking at Sistina as she added, "Zenith will not be joining us, I'm afraid. She is on a task for me, and I'm afraid Baldwin is making her wait."

"Very well. As we are all here, I will begin," Sistina said, looking around the room calmly, her hands folded in her lap. "All of you are now aware of the bond between Diane and Wenris. It had not occurred to me that you might not know, but fortunately it came up beforehand. I called you all here because I have a partial solution."

"What?" Diane asked, her eyes widening slightly as shock rippled through her. "B-but… I thought it couldn't be broken. That it was impossible to break!"

"Impossible is simply a term for something which we currently do not know how to do," Sistina corrected, shaking her head. "I do not know how to break the link between the two of you. It's a fundamental link between your souls, but *that* is precisely what gives an opportunity."

"What sort of opportunity?" Torkal asked, his voice

trembling with just a hint of hope, which Diane desperately hoped wasn't about to be dashed. Her fingers tightened in his grip, hoping that it would comfort him.

"First, I must explain a few things. Can you see souls, Tyria?" Sistina asked, looking up at the goddess curiously.

"Not in the same way that you can, but yes, once they leave the body. To me, a soul looks like a faded outline of the person, made of light or darkness, or a shade in between," Tyria replied, a hint of curiosity in her tone.

"Interesting. However, souls are made up of mana, a combination of all six types. Demons are somewhat different, as are those of deities. Allow me to show you," Sistina said, and the dryad lazily gestured at the center of the room. "This is Torkal."

The outline of Torkal appeared in the center of the room instantly, mostly as a thin line of shadow around what appeared as a riot of colors, and Diane's jaw dropped at the sight. Within it swirled air, earth, fire, and water, as well as darkness and light. It was strange and beautiful in its own way, and she couldn't help being fascinated.

"Oh my. I always knew dungeons could see the world differently, but this is… intriguing," Tyria murmured, her words heightening Diane's amazement.

"Torkal is a normal mortal, where the composition of his mana is concerned. Angels, demons, and gods are not as well-balanced," Sistina said calmly, looking around the room. "Tyria is composed primarily of light and fire mana, in overwhelming amounts. Demons are primarily darkness, along with whichever elements are most aligned with them, commonly fire as well. Water elementals are composed primarily of water. This is the information you need for the opportunity I see. Now, here are Diane and Wenris."

With another flick of a finger, Sistina added two more images, and at the sight of them Diane blanched.

On the left was an outline of Wenris, and the demon was composed almost entirely of writhing shadows and fire, the other elements almost nonexistent within her figure. On the other hand, the only sign of light was a tiny, flickering pinprick of white at the demon's very core.

To the right was an outline of Diane, though, and it confused and worried Diane in turn, partly because it was so different than Torkal's image. She had a fairly normal balance of most elements, but when it came to light or darkness her soul was… different. Light seemed to gently suffuse almost all of her being, and it was certainly in much greater abundance than she might have expected. However, there was a tiny orb of darkness at her core, and veins of darkness were radiating outward from it.

"What… is that?" Lirisel asked, sounding perplexed as she tilted her head. "With Diane, I mean. She has a lot of light within her, and the darkness… it's like it's spreading."

"The darkness is. That is the connection between Diane and Wenris, connecting your souls. There are two reasons your soul hasn't been overwhelmed, Diane," Sistina said, meeting Diane's gaze sympathetically as she shrugged. "You have not been touched by her since she became a demon queen, for one. The change was unnoticeable the previous time you visited, I believe because she had not been a demon queen for long, but that has changed. When she touches you, I believe the effects will accelerate dramatically. The other reason is the drop of Tyria's blood which was infused into you and Jaine."

Diane's heart almost stopped at the explanation, her blood chilling as she felt Torkal's grip tighten. She opened her mouth just as Tyria spoke.

"Hm? My blood helped? But… how? I'd think that with how Irethiel infused some demon blood into me…" Tyria began, frowning.

"Insignificant," Sistina interrupted succinctly, prompting an outraged gasp from Nadis. "It may be enough to have an effect on you, but it's too minor when compared to the light mana you contain. A single drop contains so little demonic essence that mortals can ignore it. If you attempted to infuse enough blood into a mortal that it would affect them, they would explode."

Everyone in the room flinched at that, but Diane quickly spoke, her mouth dry at this point. "Um, if I might ask… what will happen if the darkness spreads through me entirely?"

Sistina paused, looking at Diane closely, seeming to consider her words, then spoke, slowly and levelly. "Cravings will assault you, usually bloodlust, lust, or hunger. Sometimes you will grow more prideful, envious, or temperamental. At first you will resist, but the darkness will grow stronger. You will come to revel in those sensations and will not want to change back. It is a horrifying experience to look back on, now that my soul is largely in balance again."

The sound of a pin dropping could be heard in the room, and Diane shuddered, chills running down her spine as terror almost overwhelmed her, looking at the image of her soul.

"You have a solution, though," Elissa said at last, looking at Sistina with narrowed eyes. "There's no other reason you would have called us here, so… what is it?"

"The connection goes both ways. The problem is that Wenris has a far stronger soul than Diane does. It would be like trying to fight a snowstorm with a torch," Sistina said, looking at the image again, her expression oddly thoughtful. "That doesn't mean it cannot be done, however. If Diane can be fortified, *purified* of the darkness encroaching upon her… perhaps I should simply show you."

Sistina gestured, and everyone's gazes were drawn back to the images as Torkal's image faded away. The light within Diane's soul grew stronger, and the darkness spreading through her was forced back. It made several surges, trying to expand, but each time the light was reinforced to defeat it. At the same time, the flickering light within Wenris grew steadier and stronger, then began to spread through the demon slowly, carefully infiltrating the body as the darkness had been trying to do to Diane. It spread more and more… until finally it began to overwhelm the darkness and expanded even more rapidly, and the shadows within Diane faded to almost nothing.

"It would not be easy," Sistina said simply, looking at Diane calmly as she explained. "Aiding you without eliminating the natural darkness in your soul would be difficult, as that is a necessary part of you. If done, however, you could slowly redeem her… and in the process destroy her mantle. Another would claim a similar mantle eventually, but it would be far weaker, without the millennia of accumulation that hers has had."

Diane looked at the images for a long, long moment, hope growing within her, along with some concern. The images faded away after a few moments, and she looked at Sistina, hesitating, then asked softly, "What would I have to do?"

"Combination of… a combination of things," Sistina corrected herself, scowling. "My apologies, focusing enough to keep a normal conversation is… draining. I am getting better, but it is difficult. First reinforcing your soul. You can safely be infused with two more drops of Tyria's blood, if she allows it. You would have to *request* them, however."

"I'm glad you've been paying enough attention to realize that," Tyria murmured, but Sistina ignored her as her gaze drifted to the clergy in the room.

"You would need to spend a great deal of time in holy places, such as temples. I would recommend sleeping on blessed ground as well. During her visits would be best, but that might make her wary. If she chooses to remove you, all is lost, so I do not recommend it," Sistina continued, taking a deep breath and letting it out. "Wish I had a light node. Would be *much* easier. Take baths with blessed water frequently. Receive holy blessings daily. All of it *should* work."

"Should work? You're recommending all of that without any guarantee of success?" Nadis asked, her eyebrows rising quickly. "I thought you said you had a solution!"

"It *is* a solution. The theory is sound," Sistina replied, her voice steadily growing more curt, almost staccato-like. "Souls are *difficult,* though. They fight. They defy expectations. Cannot guarantee that it will work, no. Chances are… good. Eight tenths? Nine tenths? But good."

"Sistina, shh," Diamond interrupted at last, looking at the dryad in concern. Sistina opened her mouth, then shut it and tried to shrug. After a few moments Diamond looked away, a faint smile on her face as she looked at Diane. "My apologies, everyone, but when she gets like that it can lead to… problems, shall we say? Regardless, no matter what else happens, the choice isn't in our hands. Diane? Do *you* wish to attempt this?"

"Is there any question?" Torkal demanded, glancing over at

Diane, then flushed as he apologized. "Sorry, dear, it's just... I don't want her to... to..."

"It's alright, dear. You're just trying to protect me in the only way you can," Diane said, letting out a soft sigh as she looked at the others and nodded, nervousness making her almost jittery. "And yes, he's right. If there's a way to draw a silver lining out of all the dark clouds around me, I will take it. Happily, even. I'd resigned myself to the knowledge I'd be the plaything of a demon after I died, but... well, will you help me, then? I obviously can't do it alone."

"Mother, if you think I'm going to abandon you, then obviously Father has been hitting you when no one else was looking," Jaine said tartly, prompting a ripple of laughter through the room, and the young woman grinned as she added, "Besides, it just means that us coming here was the *best* choice we could have made, unlike what Beryl might have thought."

"A fair point," Diane admitted, then looked toward the others.

"I can confidently speak for Her Majesty and for the other Jewels, when I say that you'll have our full support, such as it may be," Diamond said calmly, looking at Diane as she hesitated, then continued. "The art of magic we were forced to learn is... ideal for this, odd as it may seem. It allows us to combine our power and convert it to light magic, so it may be useful. Or it may not, I cannot be certain."

"As if I would leave you alone in this, Lady Diane. Your sacrifice was great, for Yisara and its people, so if you wish to risk this, I will aid you as I can," Nadis said, and her gaze drifted to the side as she asked, "Lirisel? Do you agree?"

"Of course, Archpriestess! You won't be here forever, but the church will do everything we can to assist in this matter," Lirisel said, almost jumping as attention turned to her, her cheeks coloring a little. "I'm just trying to figure out if quarters in the temple would be better, or blessing a room outside the temple."

"I'd recommend the latter, if you don't wish to alert Wenris of what you have in mind," Elissa replied, her arms crossed in front of her as she looked at Diane, then nodded. "And yes, Diane, I am willing to help as I'm able. Much like Archpriestess Nadis, I cannot be here indefinitely, but I'm more than willing to do what I can. While my influence on you when you were captured wasn't as great as that of Wenris, I regret that I pushed you as much as I did."

"Thank you. All of you," Diane said, relief rushing through her. At last, quite hesitantly, she looked over at Tyria and swallowed, realizing the goddess was looking at her, a tiny smile on the deity's face. It was obvious what Tyria was waiting for, but that didn't make it any easier for Diane. It took a minute to screw up her courage, then she asked, "Ah... Lady Tyria... might I ask for a couple of drops of your blood?"

"Of course you may. I won't grant them right this moment, but when you're ready for the infusion... yes," Tyria said, and her gaze drifted to Elissa as she added, "I expect Elissa to take care of that for you, since she did it once already. Perhaps you can even get yourself changed back to your old self, if that's what you desire."

"As you wish, Your Eminence," Elissa acquiesced.

For her part, Diane was simply glad that no one was looking at her as she blushed. No one but Torkal, at least, and she saw his smile.

"Done?" Sistina asked, looking around the room with a raised eyebrow. After how eloquent she'd been earlier, the change was somewhat jarring to Diane, but she wasn't going to argue.

"I believe so," Diane said after a moment, and she smiled as she climbed to her feet, adding, "Thank you, Sistina. You didn't have to do this."

"Did not have to. Was *right,*" Sistina said, nodding slightly as she tried to stand and failed. Then she looked up at Tyria, whose hands were on her shoulders. "Yes?"

"I think you need to relax a little, Sistina," Tyria said calmly, smiling as she added, "You truly *are* troublesome, you know that?"

"Am not," Sistina retorted, glowering at the goddess, her tone almost threatening. "Could make you let go."

Most of the others had stood at this point, including Diane, and she couldn't help staring incredulously at the two women.

Diamond giggled under her breath, to Diane's surprise, but neither the dungeon nor the goddess seemed to mind.

"Then do it," Tyria retorted, her hands not moving.

"Spoilsport," Sistina muttered, folding her arms in front of her, then closed her eyes.

"Come on, they do things like this from time to time," Diamond said, gesturing at the door. "Would anyone like dinner in the palace? If we're all here anyway..."

Diane looked at Torkal, asking softly, "Dear? Your opinion?"

"Why not?" Torkal said, smiling a little more as he looked around at the others, adding, "I mean, I haven't felt this hopeful in *months*."

"Agreed," Diane told him, and she glanced back as she stepped out of the meeting room, seeing that the goddess and dryad were still in the same spot.

The interesting thing was the hint of affection she thought she saw on Tyria's face... but Diane was sure her eyes were playing tricks on her. They had to be.

CHAPTER 22

"Do we really have to go to Westgate? It just snowed!" Bane protested, gesturing at the door.

The window had the filigree of frost around its edges, and Alexander still couldn't believe that almost every building in the city had glass windows. At least he thought it was glass. Regardless, he suspected that wouldn't last in the long term, not with as expensive as glass was. More importantly, beyond the window was a layer of snow about three inches thick, and as Alexander watched a horse walked by pulling a wide, plow-like attachment to shove the snow toward the side of the street. It didn't get rid of all the snow, but Alexander supposed it was better than nothing.

"Yes, it did snow. That means the trip is going to be even *less* pleasant than it would've been yesterday," Alexander retorted, turning back to his pack and examining his things again to make sure everything was in it. He was having to abandon a few minor knickknacks, but nothing important was staying behind. "We already know that the rebels are moving to Westgate to act, but do you *really* want to risk them bungling it? What would Mazina say?"

Bane paused, then shivered as he murmured, "You have a point, I guess. I just didn't want to have to go out into that."

"You aren't the only one. You should've heard what Erin had

to say about it," Alexander said, wincing at the memory of the curses she'd spat.

"What I had to say about what?" Erin asked suspiciously, pushing open the door of their room. "We're both packed and ready to go."

Alexander straightened and nodded to Erin, gratified by her efficiency. Behind her was Umira, who looked oddly bored by everything. On the other hand, the elf *was* from the far north, so she tended to ignore the weather most of the time.

"I was just saying you were *quite* unhappy with the need to go to Westgate," Alexander explained, not even trying to pretend he hadn't said anything. That'd just make her angrier, and she usually didn't care as long as other people were being accurate.

"Gods, yes. Having to go out into that mess is absolutely terrible. It isn't what we were told was going to happen when they asked for volunteers for all this," Erin said, her gaze darkening as she scowled out the window. "I'm from the south, damn it!"

"You'll live," Umira replied lazily, glancing outside as she added, "This isn't even bad for the area, from all I've heard. The snows get really deep in this region, and having several feet of snow on the ground is common by midwinter."

"Ugh, the sooner we get out of here the better, then," Erin said, shuddering.

"That means you need to finish packing, Bane," Alexander said pointedly. "They're leaving separately from us, so the sooner you're ready, the sooner we can catch up."

"Fine, fine... I hope to see you two tonight," Bane said, grumbling under his breath as he moved to his half-full pack.

"Don't get eaten by wolves!" Umira replied, her tone bright and friendly, and the two women headed for the front door, Erin muttering something all the way.

"She's far too easygoing about all of this," Bane said, but only after he'd heard the door shut. "Umira, I mean."

"I think it's something to do with mind magi," Alexander replied, deciding to set another pair of socks aside to wear. "They're so used to messing with the minds of other people that they're also willing to adjust their own mood. Who knows if that's just how she made herself feel, or if she's just incapable of getting worried?"

"Seems dangerous to me," Bane said, sighing and looking up as Alexander pulled his boots off. "What if she brings something dangerous down on us?"

"That's why we send her on the risky missions," Alexander said, grinning a little wider at the big man. "She doesn't seem to care, and it keeps *us* safer. A winning situation, if you know what I mean."

"True enough, I suppose. I just wonder if we're going to be able to pull all this off. Like you said, Mazina is set on everything, but... both churches seem more stable than first reports implied, you know?" Bane asked, looking up at Alexander, a hint of nervousness in his voice. "I'm not afraid of destroying things, or even of death in the process... but I want to make a *difference* in the end."

Alexander shrugged, pulling on the other pair of socks as well, ignoring his own concerns as he focused on what mattered. "True, and I don't blame you, but... here's the thing. She claims that our Lord and Lady want this, and do you want to disappoint *them*?"

"Err, no, of course not!" Bane said, blanching at the very thought, and Alexander smiled, unable to blame him. *No one* wanted to upset their Lord and Lady, not if they liked living.

"That's what I thought. Now, then... let's get moving, shall we? We've got a ways to go, and not a lot of time to do it in," Alexander said, putting his boots back on so he could do up the laces again.

Hopefully his feet wouldn't freeze, that way.

CHAPTER 23

The room they were in had a large tub, and the sight of it was amusing to Tyria, largely because it was so unlike the pool she remembered Elissa had used in Kelvanath. This one was deep enough that Diane would be able to immerse herself, though, which was good. Better, the water had been anointed with a variety of herbs as well as a good deal of holy water, which should make Sistina's mad scheme work better.

Tyria couldn't help a ripple of surprise, even now, at the sheer arrogance of the dungeon's plan. Dragging a demon to the light, kicking and screaming all the way… that wasn't something that she'd ever heard of happening. Oh, demons could be redeemed, but it was a long accepted fact that it was far easier to corrupt an angel or the like than it was to redeem a demon. Of course, the plan wouldn't be possible if Wenris hadn't connected herself so deeply to Diane, but it was still shocking to Tyria. Not that she was going to tell the *mortals* that.

"Your Eminence? Do you think this will suffice?" Elissa asked, a thread of anxiety in her voice. "It isn't as large of a pool as the other was, so I'm afraid that the concentration might hurt Diane…"

"That isn't an issue, Elissa. If anything, it will allow her to absorb the power more easily than in a larger pool. If she hadn't done this before… well, then things might be different," Tyria replied, dragging her attention back to the present as she smiled at the priestess. "No, it should be fine. Did she decide to make any changes to herself? I know she could change herself back entirely."

"She did, though not much, compared to the first time. She wants her old eye color back, as well as removing the symbol on her forehead," Elissa said, frowning slightly as she added, a bit hesitantly, "I'm not sure if she realizes that she's young again, though. She'll likely outlive her husband… do you think I should tell her?"

Tyria paused, considering the issue seriously for a long moment, though there really wasn't any question in her mind. What she was really considering was how it would be best to go about telling Diane, since it was a rather delicate subject.

"You should. However, I believe that you'd best inform her in private, and let her decide what she wishes to tell Torkal," Tyria said at last, pulling off a gauntlet as she spoke, her mood darkening slightly. "I suspect he was older than her to begin with, so it will lead to an earlier parting than she might have expected."

"True enough. Though they *are* elves, and aren't much past two hundred, or he isn't, at least. That gives them a lot of time together either way," Elissa murmured, her gaze slightly distant, then she frowned. "On the other hand, that could go… poorly, I imagine. Plenty of people I've met have had problems after only a few decades together, let alone centuries."

Tyria couldn't help laughing at that, shaking her head in amusement. She pulled out a needle, one she'd gotten from Sistina and which she suspected was sharper than it had any right to be. For good reason, since it was difficult to make a goddess bleed. She tightened her jaw and carefully pricked a finger, having to use far more force than she'd have preferred to break the skin, then pulled the needle away as a brilliant scarlet dot welled up from the wound, radiating some of her internal fire.

She quickly extended her finger over the tub, and watched as the drop grew, trembled, and finally fell into the water. It was like a tiny red star, and as it hit the water it spread rapidly, tinting the water purple rather than red. It took several more moments for another drop to form, and Tyria had to consciously restrain her healing abilities to keep them from closing the wound, however small it might be.

The second drop finally fell into the tub, and Tyria let out a soft sigh as she relaxed, allowing her finger to heal virtually instantly, and at the same time she concentrated her power into the needle, which began to glow, smoke, then it vaporized entirely. She did *not* want an item which had injured her around, not after the trouble sympathetic magic had already caused her.

"There. Now, as to their relationship… that's one of the things about elves, Elissa. They tend to be far more deliberate about entering relationships, and as such they're far more stable, generally speaking," Tyria said, turning to the priestess and smiling as she put her gauntlet back on. "That isn't to say they don't have divorces, but when they do they tend to be relatively amicable. Other couples will just… take some years away from each other on occasion, to have some freedom to do what they will. I honestly have no idea what Diane and Torkal will do, but I'm sure they'll come to a solution."

"As you say, Your Eminence," Elissa said, looking at the tub for a long moment, then smiled wryly. "I will admit… I sometimes wish that *I'd* gotten a bit more height after your blessing. I've been somewhat envious of Diane and Jaine, there."

"You gained immortality, after a fashion. That is *quite* enough of a blessing, Elissa," Tyria gently scolded the priestess. "Now, if you want to get taller, you can just find a sufficiently skilled transmuter and—"

Tyria stopped as the world rippled, and Zenith stepped into the room, immediately kneeling before her as the angel spoke. "My apologies for the interruption, my goddess."

"It isn't anything to apologize for, Zenith. As you're here, I presume this is regarding Baldwin?" Tyria asked, a hint of anticipation rising up within her.

"Yes, My Lady. He agreed to meet with you, and told me to inform you that he would be waiting at the center of the mountains until sunset," Zenith reported, hesitating before she admitted, "He didn't seem very pleased to hear about you, My Lady. Not *upset*, precisely, but… not happy, either."

"I'm not surprised," Tyria said, frowning slightly as she glanced in the direction of the center of the Godsrage Mountains. She hadn't gone there yet, and from everything she'd heard it was a dangerous place… but those she'd heard from were mortals. After a moment she mentally shrugged and looked at Elissa. "Please don't inform the others about where I'm going. Doubtlessly Sistina is aware, but there's no need for anyone else to know."

"As you wish, Your Eminence," Elissa said, bowing deeply.

"Good. Take care of Diane, and make sure she's kept safe," Tyria added, heading for the wall as she slipped out of phase with reality again, thankful that Sistina wasn't trying to stop her. If she was, the wall would have been distressingly solid.

The next moment Tyria was moving through the walls, then emerged from the palace as well. Clouds were overhead, and Tyria glanced back to see that the sun was a decent distance above the horizon, but that still didn't give her time to dawdle.

It was a long flight to the center of the mountains, especially with how she knew space had once folded there. The question was if that was still the case, or if it'd gotten worse.

"Nothing to be done but figure it out for myself," Tyria murmured, and she took flight, drawing on her full speed as she shot toward the center of the mountains.

A tiny part of Tyria worried that she might be flying into a trap, but at the same time she didn't see what other choice she had.

DIANE SWALLOWED HARD, then knocked on the door, almost timidly. The door was solid, yet the knock sounded unusually loud. That was probably due to how nervous she was, since Tyria might be present.

"Come in!" Elissa's voice was pleasant, and Diane glanced over at Torkal, who grinned.

"Well, go on. I doubt she's going to bite," he said, his voice far more hopeful than it'd been the previous evening. "You're sure you're not going to change anything else?"

"I like my new nose *much* better, thank you," Diane replied tartly, opening the door and stepping inside. "If nothing else came of what happened, at least I don't need to wonder who in all the hells the bards were composing songs about!"

Stepping into the room, Diane paused at the faint, familiar fragrance filling the air, along with a large marble tub in the middle of the room. Elissa was standing next to the tub, her hands folded as she glanced over at Nadis in amusement, even as the archpriestess glared back at her. Zenith's presence was a bit of a surprise, but a thread of relief rushed through Diane as she realized that Tyria wasn't present. She wasn't sure she'd *ever* get used to the company of a goddess. Still, she was rather surprised by Nadis's presence.

"Archpriestess Nadis, I wasn't expecting to see you here!" Torkal spoke first, pausing and bowing before her. "I thought it was just going to be the high priestess and possibly Tyria."

"Her Eminence had something else come up, and left Zenith in her place for the time being. As for the archpriestess, she still doesn't trust me, so she wished to witness this herself," Elissa said, and as Nadis inhaled the human smiled and added, "Not that I blame her for that. If she was in charge, I know I'd want to be here as well, to see how this was done if nothing else."

"It wasn't because I don't trust you," Nadis said, then paused and added, "Mostly, at least. I want to ensure that Diane comes out of this as intact as possible, is all… though I'll admit that the magic radiating from the tub makes me doubt anything I could do would have any effect."

"My Lady's blessing is not something which should be trifled with, let alone her blood," Zenith said calmly, looking at the pool for a moment, then up at Diane as she smiled sadly. "Hello again, Diane. I don't believe we ever met, but I watched you for a time, before your first baptism. I… apologize for acting under misconceptions."

"Ah, hello, Zenith. And no, we haven't, not directly at least," Diane replied, blinking quickly as she looked into the angel's eyes, a hint of her worry thawing at the remorse she saw there.

"As to that, even if you'd known there wouldn't have been anything you could have done. We both had little choice in what we could do, in the end."

"Perhaps, but even so… it was dismaying when My Lady and the priestesses here finally managed to crack the barriers hiding my old memories. They were forced to keep me imprisoned for a time while I came to terms with it, else I might have taken drastic actions," the angel said, letting out a sigh, then laid a hand on the edge of the tub. "Still, here we are once more. Be aware, the power within the tub is immense. You may feel a burning sensation, which will likely be Her power searing away the darkness trying to spread through your body, Diane. I just wish to warn you, lest you panic."

"Thank you," Diane said, hesitating as she looked at the priestesses. Torkal closed the door behind her, and after a moment Diane asked, "Is there anything specific I need to do this time?"

"I'm afraid I don't know how this worked before. I seem to recall Jaine talking about it once before, but I don't recall the particulars," Nadis said, looking at Elissa.

"Unsurprising, really. As for that, no, Diane, there isn't anything in particular this time. Just disrobe, submerge yourself for as long as possible, then you can come out and we'll dry you off," Elissa said, gesturing to a towel on a nearby chair, one Diane had neglected to notice until then. The human's smile was infectious as she added, "I'd say we'd need an invocation to Tyria, but when the goddess herself blessed the water, that feels just a *touch* silly."

"True," Diane agreed happily, looking over the water, which had been dyed purple, and she took a breath, then let it out. "That being the case… no need to wait."

She blushed a little as she started disrobing, handing her clothing to Torkal as she did. Since she'd known that this was coming, Diane hadn't done up her hair like she usually did. The thought relaxed her a little, even if she wasn't entirely comfortable being watched by the priestesses. Elissa had the good grace to look away, but Nadis was watching closely, her gaze intense enough to make Diane hesitate.

"Ah... is there a reason you're staring, archpriestess?" Diane asked, heat rising in her cheeks as she hesitated, still in her underclothes.

"Oh, my apologies. I'm just looking at you because I want to be able to identify what changes occur," Nadis said, her gaze jerking upward as the woman blushed, clearing her throat. "I... didn't realize how it might make you feel. Would you like me to look away?"

"No, if that's why, I suppose it makes sense. I was just a bit uncomfortable," Diane said, relaxing ever so slightly at the explanation. It made sense, and Torkal was studiously avoiding looking at Nadis, with a smile on his face that made Diane ever so slightly suspicious. Regardless, she quickly finished undressing, thankful that the palace was such a mild temperature. Even in Yisara it would've been brisk at this time of year.

Diane handed the last of her clothing to Torkal, and he rearranged things so he could hold it more easily. Stepping over to the tub, Diane carefully put a foot inside, and shivered as she felt intense heat radiating through the water. She found herself hesitating for just a moment, then gritted her teeth and slid fully into the pool. Just like the last time, the water didn't splash or ripple as she entered it, instead accepting her like she was meant to be there.

A gasp escaped her lips, for the water was much, *much* warmer than the last time. It was a raging furnace that penetrated deep into her body, and sweat began forming almost instantly, just as a searing heat seemed to almost *burn* in Diane's chest.

"Dear, are you alright?" Torkal asked, stepping forward as he looked at her in sudden concern. "You don't look good."

"I'm... I'm fine, it's just... that sensation Zenith warned me about. The water is also m-much hotter than it was last time," Diane replied, waving him off. She inhaled, then added, "Is that... r-right?"

"Yes. My Lady is now a goddess of fire, not just the sun, and instead of a broad pool with a drop of her blood, you're in a small tub with two. That is enough to make its heat dangerous,"

Zenith said, hesitating for a moment before she admitted, "I would be wary of allowing you contact with so much power, but My Lady and Sistina are much better versed in such things than I am."

The explanation didn't exactly soothe Diane's fears, and from the look on Torkal's face, Diane suspected he wasn't happy with it either. Even Elissa and Nadis looked at one another in concern, and anything that could make *them* agree wasn't reassuring at all. On the other hand, since she hadn't burst into flames yet, Diane suspected she was probably safe.

"In that case… here I go," Diane said, taking a deep breath, then paused to let it out before taking a shallower breath. She'd learned that taking a deep breath oddly made it harder for her to stay down for longer. Then she submerged herself.

The moment her head slipped below the water, everything changed. The heat didn't vanish or become any cooler, but it was almost like someone had taken Diane into their arms and cradled her. The *effects* of the heat dimmed, and it was almost like she could hear soothing words being whispered in her ear as the heat penetrated deep into her body, searing away something dark, leaving her mind more at ease.

Heat tingled across her skin, and holding her breath felt almost effortless as the moments rolled by. The biggest problem was holding herself underwater, but Diane managed, keeping her eyes closed. It almost felt like she could stay there forever, and Diane let her mind drift for long moments as she relaxed. Right up until that same welcoming sensation gave her a gentle push toward the surface.

Diane broke the surface suddenly, letting out her breath and spluttering a little from the water that'd been in her nostrils. She wiped away the water from her eyes, blinking rapidly as the water seemed to steam off her, then looked up hopefully, standing up as she asked, "Did it work?"

When Diane glanced down, she noticed that the water was clear as crystal now, and that her body seemed unchanged from before, which felt promising. On the other hand, the slow smile from Torkal and the way Nadis seemed to be relaxing gave her hope.

"It appears so, dear," Torkal said, nodding slightly. "Your hair is back to pure gold, and your eyes are a lovely blue and green again."

"You even lost the mark on your forehead, so I would call that a success," Elissa added, stepping to the side and picking up the towel, which she spread as she asked, "How do you feel?"

"I feel..." Diane paused and took stock of herself for a moment.

Her body didn't feel much different than it had before, to be perfectly honest. Yet at the same time, the air felt a little clearer, her mood a little brighter, and some of the unspoken tensions had faded away. It was... lovely, and even the prospect of what was coming that evening didn't worry her. So she smiled as she stepped out of the pool and into the towel.

"I feel just fine. Better than before, in fact," Diane said simply.

"I'm glad to hear that," Nadis said and smiled as she added, "In the meantime, I believe that a few blessings are in order."

"Agreed," Torkal said and sighed as he added, "I wish we could eliminate her and be done with it, but... we do what we must."

Diane nodded, but refrained from comment, as she didn't entirely agree with him.

No matter what Wenris had done, the succubus had kept her promises to Diane, and a part of her was almost giddy at the idea of turning the tables to redeem the succubus. Not that she'd tell Torkal that.

CHAPTER 24

Traveling into the Godsrage Mountains wasn't easy, not even for a goddess. Tyria had been forced to kill half a flight of a strange, frost-breathing eagles, then she'd dodged an ice-aligned mana storm only by the barest of margins. While her inner fire would have allowed her to survive the raging torrent of snow and bitter cold, it would have injured even her, and she was quickly coming to understand why the mortals considered the area to be impassible.

Now she was dealing with a pair of vicious, *stupid* frost drakes, and the dragons roared loudly as they lunged at her, spitting orbs of frost between snaps of their jaws. Tyria dodged past a swipe of one of their claws, drawing her sword fluidly as she glared at them, speaking coldly. "I'd suggest backing off… if you have enough of a mind to realize the pair of you will die, otherwise."

The only response were a hiss and a roar from the two as they spun around, pure savagery in their gazes, and Tyria sighed as she shot forward at them, her blade flashing ruthlessly. The next moment she was past them, and the drakes fell from the sky as their heads detached. Mere drakes weren't a threat to Tyria, not when she was able to deal with entire armies on her own, but they were still annoying and delayed her.

She took a moment to ensure her sword was clean before

sheathing it again, and as she flew toward the center of the mountains Tyria looked down and shivered, sorrow rippling through her.

The immense mountain range was craggy and sharp-edged, obviously younger than most mountains elsewhere across the world, and they were covered in thick layers of snow and ice, with mist obscuring much of them. Yet even that mist and snow couldn't obscure the past entirely.

Here she saw the fallen trunks of immense trees poking from the ice. There she saw what looked like a lake that had flash-frozen instantly, then been pushed into the sky like a glacier. And in yet another spot she saw the ruins of an ancient building, one large enough to be a palace. One by one, she flitted by the wreckage of the Eternal Wood, and as she passed Tyria couldn't help a shiver. For her, the vibrant fey nation had been lush with life only a few years before, and now… now it was gone.

The folding of space wasn't gone, though, and the only saving grace was that it hadn't gotten worse over the passing millennia. Tyria ripped through the sky like a meteor, the cold here biting at her skin even through her fire, and she shivered, then dodged as a glowing blue phoenix lunged up out of the mists at her. The creature missed, and it wasn't as fast as Tyria, so she didn't even slow down, leaving the frozen creature in her wake.

As the sun passed its height, barely visible through the clouds, Tyria came into sight of the center of the mountains, and she came to a sudden, almost jarring stop as she stared, murmuring in shock, "What… in all the heavens?"

In front of her was a massive crater, the location where the world tree had once grown, but she couldn't see into it. Within the circle of mountains was a vast, swirling funnel of seething white clouds, sparks of lightning crackling in its upper reaches. It wasn't a tornado, nor even a hurricane, though the winds were obviously powerful, and she couldn't help being taken aback by the sight.

For a long minute Tyria just hovered there, her wings beating to keep her aloft, then she shivered and shook her head, murmuring, "No, I don't have time for this."

She moved toward the funnel, and as she did she felt the temperature dropping even further, riming her armor in frost, though her internal fire kept it from getting too far. She held her breath as she hit the funnel, and was instantly thankful that she had.

Frozen wind ripped at Tyria, almost howling in her ears, and immense amounts of mana seethed through it, clawing at her body. Tyria shuddered and called on her power, sheathing herself in a barrier of violet flames to repel the assault, plunging through the wall of wind as rapidly as she could. The mana ate away at her barrier, but before more than a tithe of her defense had degraded, Tyria reached the center of the mountains, and everything went silent instantly.

Inside the funnel it was as quiet as a grave, and a shiver ran down Tyria's spine as she looked down and realized just how right the term was. Like she'd told Sistina and the others, she *could* see souls, as part of who she'd been as Medaea, and what she saw was terrible.

The souls of thousands of the unquiet dead were scattered about inside the vortex, though they weren't truly undead. Most of the bodies she could see were frozen husks on the ground or buried in the depths of a lake of ice, and all of them were around the base of the funnel of a vast volcano, dull crimson light still flickering within it. Then Tyria had to look again, and her eyes widened still more.

The volcano's exterior was sheathed in ice, which was why she didn't recognize what it was at first, but at a second glance she realized the truth. The ice was covering a layer of bark, not stone, which meant she wasn't looking at a volcano… no, it was the stump of the world tree itself. As a chill rippled through her, Tyria looked up, and she could see a figure in metal armor hovering over the caldera, a huge hammer slung across his back.

"Baldwin," Tyria murmured, looking down at the battlefield where so many fey had died again, hesitating for a moment before she asked herself, "Why did he want to meet me *here*?"

Tyria paused in the odd hush, and after a moment she realized that while everything was frozen around the ruin of the tree, the air wasn't nearly as cold here as it was outside. Mana pervaded the air in densities far greater than even in Sistina's domain, with a surprising amount of fire mana as well. She shook off her curiosity, though, and instead flew toward Baldwin, along with the heat rippling up from the stump below him.

Baldwin half-turned as she approached but didn't do anything else, which gave Tyria a moment to look down, and the sight caused her stomach to clench hard. The interior of the trunk was charred, most of the tree a massive shell containing nothing. Far below them was a massive bed of coals, where the wood slowly popped and seethed, motes of mana boiling off bit by bit, and creating a wave of heat above the stump proper.

"Amazing, isn't it? Over six millennia later, and the fires *still* haven't killed the tree," Baldwin's deep voice broke the hush, with a note of weariness in it that startled Tyria. "Not that anyone can stop it. It's been tried, and nothing we can do can so much as touch those fires. No, in a few more millennia the fire will sever the roots, and the world tree will die in truth. And with *it* will go magic itself. I wonder what will become of us, with as much mana is invested in our bodies?"

Tyria looked up at Baldwin and pursed her lips slightly, seeing a scar crossing his right eyelid, though there was now a golden orb where his eye had been. He'd changed, now with a narrow dagger-like beard, and she couldn't tell if one of his arms had been replaced or not, with how his armor covered his body. A part of her was startled that he was being so fatalistic, but a moment later she realized that he had no way of knowing about Sistina, or that she was the new world tree. After a few moments she shrugged, setting the thought aside.

"I have no idea what will happen, being honest. I suppose we'll deal with it when it happens, no more and no less," Tyria said, examining Baldwin carefully, then added, "You've changed, I must say."

"Not as much as you have. If I hadn't been told you were Medaea, I wouldn't have believed it on first sight," Baldwin said, and he sneered slightly as his gaze drifted across her body. "Your armor also isn't what I'd consider the most functional, either."

"You can blame both of those on Irethiel," Tyria replied,

shrugging as she looked down at her armor. "It's partly my own, for going to sleep for so long, but I certainly didn't choose my new appearance, name, or armor. It… works, I suppose, but I'm not thrilled with the openings."

"Succubi," Baldwin muttered, his tone baleful as he shook his head slowly. After a moment his expression cleared and he focused on her. "Well? Why did you want to meet me?"

"Some of your worshipers attacked mine a short time ago, though there are doubts that they were acting of their own volition," Tyria said bluntly, folding her arms as she looked at Baldwin levelly. "They claimed I cut off your arm and took your eye during the Godsrage."

"Good grief, they're *still* going on with that story?" Baldwin muttered, reaching up to rub his helmet in irritation. "You know as well as I do that—"

The deity stopped as he looked at Tyria, frowning deeply as he tilted his head. "You know the truth as well as I do, so why are you looking at me like that? You were *here* when it happened, and it isn't like we've been lifelong enemies."

"As a matter of fact, I *don't* remember," Tyria replied, her tone a touch tarter than she intended as she glared at him. "I remember our fight, and right up until the moment we called a truce, then headed south. After that everything is hazy, though, and I only remember that the world tree was destroyed, and my grief at finding that Demasa and the others had all died while I was fighting you."

"That's ridiculous. Why would you forget *that*?" Baldwin asked, looking confused now as he tugged on his beard gently. "We fought side by side, until we realized we were outmatched!"

"Fought *who*?" Tyria demanded, her patience growing thin at last.

"Us, of course," another voice interjected at that point, though, that of a young man who was amused, yet with a vindictive edge to his words.

"Yes, and if it hadn't been for interference, neither of you would have gotten away," an eerily similar female voice added.

Tyria spun around, her sword clearing its sheath as Baldwin swore and unlimbered his hammer.

Behind them were a pair of deities, and the sight of them made Tyria's sense of worry spike hard. Each of them looked human, with tanned skin and athletic bodies beneath their armor, as well as glowing red eyes and long black hair. They were twins, and just similar enough that it was hard to tell that one was male and the other female. The man had a rapier loosely held in one hand, while the woman was easily spinning a massive black axe. They were Erethor and Eretha, the twin deities of destruction.

They were also ancient enemies of Medaea, as she'd clashed with them dozens of times over the millennia in her attempts to gain justice for the fallen. Seeing them here wasn't good, and the power she could feel radiating off them... *that* worried Tyria, since they felt even more powerful than they were before.

"Don't worry, Medaea, there won't be a need to hurt your church after this," Erethor said, a broad grin on his face.

"Not since you won't be escaping this time," Eretha added, her tone unpleasantly cheerful.

CHAPTER 25

In the frozen snows below the hollow shell of the world tree, a pair of amber eyes opened as she stirred for the first time in decades. Not much snow had drifted down to cover her body, fortunately, which meant that she didn't have to put in much effort to move as cognizance returned to her.

A searing sensation burned near her heart, like it had for countless years, but it was colder now, more embers than a raging fire. That was what had happened to her rage as well, and it was a cold thing, seething beneath the surface... but now its targets had come at last.

At the same time, though, she felt something else. A faint breath of fresh air, of flowers that had been dead for so long she'd almost forgotten their scent, and she smiled. The seed had taken root at last, and *that* was more important than even vengeance.

Still, vengeance had its place as well. As the sounds of metal clashing on metal began, she mentally reached out for the spells she'd laid years before... and slowly, the magic came at her command.

"HEAVEN'S DAMN IT, NOT *AGAIN*!" Baldwin spat out, and the ring of metal on metal split the air as Eretha's axe hit his hammer, sending him flying backward into a section of the stump's rim.

The ancient wood cracked as he slammed into and through it, but the deity recovered before hitting the ground, growling loudly.

Tyria didn't have time to help him, though. Erethor was far too close for comfort, his rapier rippling with black energy as he tried to skewer her, and it was all she could do to keep up with him. She unleashed a wave of fire at the deity, but he dodged, a sardonic smile on his face.

"Come on, Baldy, I just want to take your other eye too. And maybe your head…" Eretha said excitedly, her voice almost sickly sweet as she rushed forward with her axe.

"I *thought* that this sort of thing was forbidden after the Godsrage!" Tyria snarled, beating her wings hard as she tried to open the distance between her and Erethor. Unfortunately, she didn't have much success.

"Oh, it has been," Erethor agreed, grinning widely as he added, "On the other hand, since when have *we* cared about the rules? As long as you were moping in your little prison, we were content to let you destroy yourself."

The deity shot at her, and Tyria hissed as she dodged a hair too slowly, and he managed to clip her left ear. Dark magic tried to rip into her body, but she managed to overwhelm it, mostly due to how the blow barely hit her.

"And if you were corrupted by Irethiel, that would've just been delicious!" his sister added brightly, hammering Baldwin back surprisingly easily. "Destroying who you were entirely… mm, such a lovely thought. Then you broke free, and it fell to us to finish you off."

"We'll be punished, of course. But it won't lead to our deaths, which means it'll be *completely* worth it," Erethor said, and with a smile he flickered forward faster than he'd been moving so far. Tyria only had an instant to realize that his hand was pressed against her midsection and it was wreathed in black energy. The god grinned, and the light exploded against her.

Tyria's internal organs shuddered as it felt like she'd been hit by Sistina's Siegebreaker Array again, and her ribs creaked like they were about to shatter, but that was only the beginning, as the force of the blow sent her flying downward like a meteor. Ice and stone shattered as she hit the ground, and she coughed blood as several organs were pulverized by the impact combined with shadow magic.

Instinctively she channeled healing magic through her body, rebuilding the organs rapidly, and she spread her wings. Or to be accurate, she *tried* to spread her wings, only to find that she couldn't move.

"What…?" Looking down, Tyria's eyes widened as she saw the net of darkness that'd wrapped around her body and wings, and she quickly began struggling, forcing her body to ignite with flames in the process. The flames began eating away at the net, but it was terribly slow.

"After last time, we didn't want you to be able to run. How can we kill you if you escaped again?" Erethor asked.

"You damned, destructive, id—" Baldwin began, only to get sent flying backward as Eretha landed a hit on his left arm, denting the armor so deeply that his arm bent unnaturally, and when he hit the ice it shattered in over a hundred feet in every direction.

Eretha looked like she was about to speak, but a different female voice interrupted, her words oddly archaic. "You are quite right about one thing. How *can* I kill you if you escape?"

The snap of a pair of fingers echoed through the crater, and the vortex *stopped*. At the same time a green-gold aura erupted from around the edge of the crater, immense magic vibrating the very air as pillars of the light snapped into existence, forming a vast, net-like dome in the sky. It seethed with power, and Tyria couldn't help a flinch since the power within that net was enough to threaten even a deity. That was *high magic*, and Tyria had no idea where it had come from.

"Who's there?" Eretha demanded, spinning around, her axe at the ready, and Erethor turned as well, looking around cautiously.

Their distraction gave Tyria a little hope, and she surged power into her fires, trying to strengthen the flames to consume the net faster. It worked, but the problem was that the shadowy net was oddly resistant to her power, a fact which worried her still more. The twins had obviously been planning this for a long time. Across the crater, Tyria saw Baldwin drag himself out of the ice, panting as he propped himself up with his hammer.

It was the *other* figure who pulled herself out of a snowbank that drew all of their attention, though. The woman was tall, curvaceous, and beautiful, and with a single, elegant flick she removed crusts of snow and ice from her skin. For an instant Tyria thought the woman was a ghost, but then she realized the truth, that she was still alive.

The woman had amber eyes and pale green skin, along with a heart-shaped, stunning face and ruby-red lips, though there was nothing pleasant in her gaze as she stared at Eretha and Erethor. The woman was wearing armor made of some type of pale white wood, scarred by the countless passing years, and her hair was long, pale lavender that almost matched some of the ice around them.

"What, you don't remember me?" the woman asked, glancing around the crater with a slow, angry smile. "I would have thought you would, after you left me for dead."

"I don't know who you are, but you can die now, you mortal —" Eretha snarled, lunging toward the woman, swinging her axe with enough force to topple a mountain.

The nymph made a simple gesture, like she was shoving something aside. An instant later the net above her rippled, and a massive hand formed of pure magic erupted from the web and slammed into Eretha with such force that the goddess bounced off the ground and into the net opposite the hand. The woman screamed in agony as the magic wrapped around her, searing blackened lines into her armor.

"Unhand her!" Erethor snapped, raising a hand which was wreathed in black fire, but before he could do anything the nymph smiled even more, flicking a finger, and a bolt of energy descended from above like lightning.

This bolt was shimmering orange, and it slammed Erethor into the ground. The impact shook the entire crater as a circle thirty feet across was crushed into powder, and the ground itself descended over a dozen feet where it'd hit, causing Tyria to bounce. Erethor had been forced to his hands and knees, and Tyria could see blood dripping from his lips, to her utter shock.

"Did you really think that I would challenge the two of you without certainty that I could face you? That I would face a pair of gods of *destruction* without preparations?" the nymph asked, her words soft and angry. "Oh, *last* time you struck from the shadows, taking us by surprise. Even so, we fought. We even managed to injure you, if only a little."

The words caused Tyria to freeze as inspiration struck her at last, her memory stirring, and she murmured, "The Eternal Empress."

The nymph's smile widened as she glanced at Tyria and spoke pleasantly. "Ah, I see that *someone* recalls who I am. It is nice to be remembered."

Tyria could hardly believe what she was seeing, after all the dead she'd seen around the crater. The Eternal Empress had been the nymph ruler of the Eternal Wood, and the guardian of the world tree. She'd only seen the woman once from a distance, but the nymph had struck her as one of the most powerful mortal beings in existence. That she was still alive, *here,* seemed impossible, though.

"You… how can you be doing… this…!" Erethor gasped, trying to force himself to his feet.

"Have you never heard of high magic? I assure you, *I* certainly have," the Eternal Empress said, her voice cooling again as she looked down at him, the glowing red-orange magic still weighing him down. "I spent a few centuries making preparations for if you returned, since I didn't wish to leave this place. Every few decades I made certain that the circles were intact and didn't need repairs, *all* so I could destroy the two of you if you returned. Assuming you were alive, of course."

"Impossible! Nothing could survive that!" Eretha protested, struggling violently against the massive net, which only made it dig deeper into her body.

On the other hand, the black fire trapping Tyria was weakening even more rapidly, and any moment she hoped to free herself. Baldwin looked like he was just trying to avoid notice as he watched the Eternal Empress warily, and Tyria couldn't say that she blamed him. There were legends about what happened to those who offended the fey, and even deities tended to leave them alone.

"Impossible? I am tied to the world tree, you ignorant godling," the Empress retorted, the fire in her eyes flashing brightly. "So long as it lives, so too shall I, and you did not kill it. Have you never heard the phrase *do not a small harm*? You did a small harm, and did not finish the job. And so, I believe it is time to nail you to the sky."

Tyria broke the net at that moment, gasping as the dark magic stopped searing her body, but when the Empress raised her hand to the sky, she froze. The nymph's voice rose in song, but it wasn't the beautiful songs of the fey that were spoken of around campfires. No, this was the type of song whispered of in tales of horror and dread, of the baying of hounds and war cries of the deadly wilds.

The net directly above her opened and a meteor descended, blazing with fire like the sun itself, fire which even Tyria would beware, and the goddess staggered backward, shielding herself with her wings as it descended on the Eternal Empress… yet no explosion came, and when Tyria's wings lowered, the nymph was holding a glowing, molten stone in her hand as magic shaped it into a spear a dozen feet long, seething and shimmering with starfire. The Eternal Empress smiled as her song came to an end, cocked her arm as she took aim at Eretha, and threw the spear, which left her hand as a mere streak of light.

"No!" Erethor cried out in panic, but he could do nothing from the spot where he was trapped. Nothing but watch, that was.

The streak of the spear was unstoppable and unerring, and for an instant Tyria's heart almost stopped, wondering what would happen if yet *another* deity died in the heart of the mountains. In that instant, someone stepped into the way.

A man with silver hair and eyes stepped into the path of the spear, wearing white robes that gave him a distinguished look. Fate raised a hand, and a bubble of silver light flashed into existence, just in time for the spear to hit it. Tyria *heard* the deity grunt as the spear drilled into his barrier, then the shield shattered and the spear slammed into his palm. That stopped the spear, but her eyes widened as she saw that a black mark was in the middle of Fate's hand.

"*Enough*!" Fate snarled, his words echoing through the crater loudly, and a ridge of ice shuddered, then collapsed with a rumble at the echo.

"Fate," the Eternal Empress said flatly, looking at him with narrowed eyes. "You're going to interfere with my vengeance?"

"Only because I have no *choice*," Fate spat, glaring at Eretha angrily enough that the goddess recoiled slightly. "If I had my way, you'd get to kill these two and good riddance to them! Unfortunately, the rules about not allowing gods to fight in the mortal world were decided upon for a reason, and I can't allow them to be killed here."

Tyria took a breath, wondering if she should say something, but before she could Fate added, "Also, *this* was decided by Time herself. She saw this event coming millennia ago and left a message that I was to interfere. So if you want to take it up with anyone, argue with *her*."

Everyone fell silent at that, and after a moment the Eternal Empress folded her arms and spoke, her voice cold as ice. "Fine. If it were any but a primal god, I would not set aside my vengeance for now, but I know better than to argue with *them*. This isn't the end of it, however."

"I'm well aware of that," Fate said, growling under his breath. "Now, release them."

"Thank you, Fate, I—" Erethor began, but Fate cut him off with a snarl.

"Shut up! You think I don't know just what you idiots were up to?" Fate said, anger seething in his voice. "I've already called for a trial of gods, and there's no question of what the verdict is going to be. If you so much as set a *toe* in the mortal world for a century, you're going to be stripped of your powers and thrown to the lower planes, mark my words."

"As to that, ah..." Baldwin began, but hesitated as Fate glowered at him, then at Tyria.

"Fine, perhaps I need to lay down the law. None of you are allowed to interfere in your churches unless they *ask for assistance*. You cannot fight on their behalf. Let them damned well figure out their problems for themselves, because that's what we all agreed to do," Fate said, looking around at them, and his eyes narrowed as he looked at Tyria. "*You* are a special case, but you'd better tread carefully as well. I don't *care* if you have a direct connection to the mortal world, you're still treading on thin ice."

"Mortals were the ones who bound me. I simply shifted the bond to another mortal," Tyria replied, folding her arms as she tried to retain a sense of poise, her eyes narrowing as she looked at the twins, neither of which had been released yet. "Unlike them, I've been trying not to step out of bounds."

"Yes, but speaking of them—" Fate began, only to have the Empress interrupt.

"I'll let them go when I'm ready to, Fate. You are a powerful deity, powerful enough that you might be able to kill me, but I think I could do more damage than even *you* would expect if you push me," the Empress said, looking at him coldly. To Tyria's surprise, he seemed to back down rather than meet her glare, and the nymph smiled and continued. "Now, I just have one thing to say to you two utter *fools*.

"I know you're alive, now. Before you came here, I knew you might be, but you'd attacked other deities, and I wasn't sure. I was dying by inches anyway, and didn't have the time to find out, since it would have taken me away from my grief," the Eternal Empress explained, and her smile turned almost cruel as she tilted her head at them. "I'm afraid that has changed, though. *Now* I know you live. Now the hunt shall begin, and no matter how long it takes, no matter what roads I may have to walk, I *will* find you. And when I do… you will die. *That* I promise, by the world tree itself."

"Really? You think *you* will last long enough to catch us? Your precious tree is dying, and when it does, so will you," Erethor sneered, looking up with a good deal of effort. "You caught us by surprise, but—"

"Erethor, shut up," Fate interrupted, a flicker of worry

crossing his face. "As soon as we're done with the trial, I *suggest* you two find a good hiding spot. You'll need it."

"What? You... you can't be serious! She's a mortal!" Eretha protested in disbelief.

"Yes, and if I hadn't intervened, she'd have killed both of you," Fate said, and looked at the Empress. "Now, would you please let them go? I don't want this to take any longer than it has to."

"Very well. But if they attack me after I release them, they *will* die," the Empress replied and snapped her fingers.

All around them the spells faded away, and the vortex began spinning once more. The moment it did, the twins quickly jumped away, grabbing their weapons and looking at the nymph warily. Thunder cracked all around them, and Tyria blinked as lightning suddenly wreathed the entire vortex, startled by the change.

"And there was your backup plan, if they somehow managed to pierce your barrier," Fate said, eyeing the vortex warily. "You put a lot of work into this trap."

"Yes, I did. Now, take them away. My anger may be cold now, but it's everything I can do to keep from finishing them off here and now," the Empress replied, her voice seemingly calm.

"You'll be destroyed," Eretha said, glaring at both the nymph and Tyria. "If it's the last thing I do, it'll happen."

"After you," Tyria said, deciding to keep her reply as brief as possible.

"I hate all of you," Fate muttered, and with a gesture he snapped out of existence along with the twins.

Tyria let out a breath of relief as they vanished, and glanced over at Baldwin, who was still cradling his shattered arm. He looked back at her dourly, and she shrugged.

"Would you like me to heal your arm?" Tyria offered, figuring that an olive branch was in order. "I wish we hadn't been ambushed, but I suppose this is better than the alternative."

"If you wouldn't mind," Baldwin said, grimacing as he shrugged carefully. "If you want, I could even fix your armor."

"I believe the two of you are forgetting something," the

Eternal Empress said, her voice cool as she looked at them calmly.

"Yes, of course. My apologies," Baldwin said, bowing his head slightly. "Thank you for the timely rescue, Eternal Empress. I... was not aware you still lived."

"Nor was I. It took me a surprisingly long time to realize who you were," Tyria added, nodding as she spoke. "You also have my thanks, as I feared I was about to die."

"Were it not for my bond to the world tree, I would have long since perished," the Eternal Empress said, glancing at Tyria as she smiled. "A bond which you and I share, if not quite in the same manner. How *is* the sapling doing?"

CHAPTER 26

"The *what*?" Baldwin demanded, the man doing a double take as he stared at both of them, and Tyria couldn't help an instant of surprise either.

"How… how do you know about that?" Tyria asked after a brief moment of shock, looking at the Eternal Empress in disbelief. If the woman had been *here* for the last six millennia, there was no way she should have known about Sistina.

"Oh, come now. Do you *really* think a seed from the world tree could leave the Eternal Wood without my permission?" the nymph asked, almost scolding as she shook her head. "No, I personally handed over the one seed which ever left the forest, to a lovely young lady from Everium. Not that she knew what she'd been given, just that she was supposed to keep it close. And she did, even after her death."

Tyria's breath caught in her throat, feeling almost strangled by the information. Baldwin wasn't taking it well, she didn't think, as the man flushed bright red for a moment, then spoke, his voice unsteady. "You're… you're saying there's a *new* world tree? And that Medaea is bound to it?"

"Of course I am. So you're Medaea?" the Eternal Empress murmured, studying Tyria for a moment, then smiled as she added, "My, you've changed. As for that, yes. Weak and immature, but its growing nicely. I look forward to feeling it come into its full power at last."

"Ah… I'm afraid something *odd* happened to the tree," Tyria eventually managed to speak, taking a deep breath, and when the Empress gave her a sharp look she flinched, remembering that spear. Still, she forged onward. "I don't know *how* it happened, but somehow the soul of a demon merged with the seed, and they became a dungeon."

"Beacon. You're talking about *Beacon*," Baldwin muttered softly, his expression becoming more complicated.

"Yes, that's right," Tyria admitted, shrugging and deciding that hiding it at this point didn't make any sense. "Sistina said that she was trapped in a gemstone, and just as her soul was going to be snuffed out, she ended up merging with the seed. She's… an odd woman."

"Sistina? Not Sistina Constella, I presume," the Empress said thoughtfully, reaching up to tap her chin. "She died of old age, after all… and I'm fairly confident went on to her afterlife. I do recall she had a ruby pendant she valued a great deal, on the other hand. It gave me an odd feeling, though it possessed no aura of magic."

"No, it wasn't her. *That* much I can guarantee, since we know exactly who Sistina was when she was mortal, ages past," Tyria quickly said, shaking her head. "Once she served Balvess, and before that, as a mortal… well, you've heard of Marin, I'm certain."

Both of them fell silent at that, the nymph looking thoughtful, while Baldwin stared at Tyria in disbelief. Neither spoke for a moment, which made Tyria distinctly uncomfortable.

"What in all the stars *have* you gotten yourself embroiled in, Medaea?" Baldwin demanded at last, looking a bit outraged.

"I didn't do anything! I was *asleep*, I'll have you know," Tyria retorted, and after a moment she reached for his broken arm and took a deep breath before calling on her power to heal.

It took a few moments and she was a bit out of practice, but she felt his flesh begin to knit as his bones started moving back into place. Baldwin hissed under his breath, then tapped his armor, which creaked as it slowly returned to its normal shape.

Then the Empress spoke, and Tyria almost lost her concentration.

"Marin. *That* is a name I have not thought about in a long, long time," the Empress murmured softly. "I remember her visit… not long after I was bound to the tree. It's been a long time. Yet why am I not surprised?"

"You met her?" Tyria asked, blinking in surprise.

"Yes, of course. She was middle-aged at the time, and still working on her research. From us she learned about the world tree and the ley lines," the Empress explained, glancing back at the ruins of the tree as her smile dimmed. "We hoped she would join us and take the risks of becoming fey at the time. If nothing else, she was a passionate woman, relentless in her pursuit of knowledge, and that is something we appreciate. She left, though, and never returned. I… it has been a *long* time."

The tears she saw in the nymph's eyes startled Tyria, then she shook herself, looking back at Baldwin as she sensed his injuries fully heal. He met her gaze with a nod, looking troubled as he shifted a little.

"I don't remember her from before she completed her research," Tyria admitted after a moment. "I think that most deities considered her… insignificant. By the time I'd heard of her, she'd already died."

"You aren't the only one. Only a handful of deities had taken note of her, and almost all of them were aligned with magic," Baldwin rumbled, shaking his head slowly. "The idea of her being reincarnated as the world tree, though… that terrifies me a bit."

"It shouldn't," Tyria said, and the god's head rose to meet her gaze.

"Oh? Why not? She has immortality, immense knowledge of magic, and the passion to become even more skilled with it than before. While it may render my worries about losing all magic moot, she could be *incredibly* dangerous," Baldwin said, his tone challenging.

"Because that isn't who she is. Think about it, Baldwin. Marin *never* tried to rule over others, in her first life or in her time in Balvess's service. Even in her time as Sistina, she has functioned as a guardian and builder, not as an overlord," Tyria replied bluntly, looking at him a touch more coldly. "You're thinking about her the way most would regard someone with great ambition. She doesn't have that. She just wants to protect those she cares about, and possibly research magic even more."

"Ah, then she has not changed much. Good," the Empress said, slowly smiling. "I will admit, *I* wondered somewhat. Even if she was a good woman when I knew her, time can change anyone. Look at yourself for an example."

"I fell victim to a demon lord's machinations and was something of a fool after the Godsrage," Tyria admitted, wincing internally at the thought of her own actions. "Speaking of which… I assume that we arrived after those two had destroyed the tree? I'm afraid my memories of the time aren't clear."

The Empress's eyebrows rose, but she nodded slightly in response. "Yes, that is right. The twins came from nowhere, severing the tree's trunk in their opening strike, and while magic rebelled they slaughtered most of my people. I arrived and fought, but it was too late, and they had prepared. You two arrived, but they struck hard, heavily injuring both of you as you were forced to flee. I seem to recall seeing you struck in the head by a blast of their magic, but then a boulder landed on me. By the time I freed myself, you were all gone."

"I see. That likely was what caused my memories to be so fragmented, then," Tyria murmured, scowling. "I *really* dislike those two."

"I don't think anyone *likes* gods of destruction. They don't give a damn about anyone," Baldwin said, scowling. "I *thought* they were supposed to be aligned with Kylrius, but they tried to kill both of us. I don't think they were even supposed to attack the world tree, for that matter."

"As you said, they do not care about others," the Empress replied, then smiled coldly. "On the *other* hand, they had better take Fate's advice. I'm going to hunt them down and *end* them, even if it takes until the end of the world."

The smile on the nymph's face sent a chill down Tyria's spine, and she swallowed hard. She didn't really *pity* the two deities, but Tyria was quite glad that she wasn't the one being targeted.

"I wish you luck with that. Now, then… was there something else you wanted to talk about, Medaea?" Baldwin asked, glancing around as he grimaced. "I'd like to get away from here. I thought it made sense before, but I've only had bad luck every time I've come here."

"I can't say that I blame you. As to that… no, there's nothing else. Erethor and Eretha told me what I needed to know, which explains the problems that have been occurring," Tyria said and let out a sigh as she added, "That said, with Fate's warning, I'm not sure what I can *tell* my faithful."

"I do believe that is your own problem to work out. *Do* give Marin my regards when you see her," the Empress said firmly, folding her arms.

"Fair. Do you want me to work on your armor, though?" Baldwin asked, grimacing as he added, "Personally, I just want to let bygones be bygones. We weren't really enemies, after all."

"I'd like that, I think. Would you mind adjusting my sword as well? I'm afraid that Irethiel altered both of them, and it doesn't… quite *suit* me, if that makes any sense," Tyria replied, warming up a little to him.

"Sure," Baldwin nodded, straightening. "Now, what exactly do you want?"

CHAPTER 27

Wenris swirled the dress's skirt and frowned unhappily, turning to look at her back in the mirror, and particularly at how it almost reached her wings. While the dress was pretty enough, on the whole, she didn't exactly like it. The problem was that she didn't dare go overboard in Beacon.

"Why do I have to be so modest?" the succubus muttered under her breath, a touch irritated.

No one answered, of course, mostly because she was alone in the small apartment that had been set aside for Wenris's use. It wasn't on the palace grounds, sadly, but Wenris suspected that was because Sistina didn't want to have her constantly leeching mana from the dungeon, even if she was giving mana to the residents of the palace.

The thought of the mana the people within the palace were absorbing sent a shiver down the demon queen's spine. No matter how powerful she was, the ability of mortals to grow was something she couldn't underestimate, and no one had seen what heights they could achieve if allowed to live within the confines of a dungeon, and *that* made her wary, even if Sistina hadn't on her own.

A ripple in the aether caused Wenris to pause, though, and she frowned, trying to localize it. The source was distant, that much she could tell, but without being outside she'd have a hard time localizing it. It also was powerful, which concerned her a little more… but after a moment she shrugged, resolving to investigate if she had the chance to do so. For now, she was going to be reclaiming Diane. The elven woman wasn't as much of a reward for her centuries in hiding, compared to the mantle of the Queen of Chains, but the elven woman was rather delightful in her own right.

"Ah, well… it isn't like I'll have to wear the dress all night," Wenris said, grinning at her reflection, then turned to leave, humming to herself.

She didn't see how the image in the mirror didn't turn like it should have, but instead watched her leave, then smiled as though it'd seen something amusing.

"ARE YOU READY, DEAR?" Torkal asked, his voice taut as he looked at her.

"Ready? For something which could lead to me losing who I am entirely, despite everything that's been done?" Diane asked in a trembling voice, raising her eyebrows as she looked up at him. "I'll never be *ready* for that."

That wasn't entirely true, of course. A part of Diane was eagerly looking forward to being with Wenris, so *that* foolish part of her mind was ready, but a large part of her would have liked a few more centuries of time to distance herself from the succubus, if at all possible.

"Well, true enough, but… well, I care about you. And what if she decides—" Torkal began, but Diane decided she'd had enough, and went up on her toes as she silenced him with an insistent kiss.

The man responded after a moment of hesitation, returning the kiss fervently, which she appreciated, letting her eyes half-close as she held on to her beloved. Torkal had always tried to protect her, she knew, and she hated that he couldn't do anything now, but… there wasn't a choice. After a little while she broke away, meeting his gaze warmly.

"We cannot change what *she* does, dear. We can only control ourselves, and do the best we can. I'm not going to lose you to Calath, hm?" Diane said, her eyes twinkling.

"Dear! Have I ever even looked at her that way since I proposed to you?" Torkal protested, sounding a bit exasperated, which was rather the point of her comment, in truth.

"No, but I want to be sure," Diane teased, then looked at the door. "Still, she'll likely be here any minute, so I'd best be ready."

"True enough. Just... be safe, please?" Torkal requested, looking even more nervous somehow.

"Of course," Diane said simply, glancing down at her dress, not entirely happy with how Wenris might react to it. The succubus had a way of reading things that Diane hadn't expected from outfits or body language. It was frustrating at times, but fortunately it wasn't mind reading.

Her dress was simpler than many Diane owned, as it was made of soft wool that had been bleached a pure white. It clung close to her body for the most part, and the interior was lined with satin to keep her from itching, but it was a very nice dress, especially with how cold it was outside. The question was how Wenris would react to it.

The knock at the door distracted Diane, though, and she cleared her throat, then called out. "Yes?"

"Your guest has arrived, Lady Diane," Maria said, the woman's voice trembling slightly.

Diane couldn't blame her, since Wenris likely reminded her of her time in Kelvanis. Neither Maria or her sister, Meredith, had left Beacon after being freed from their slave brands, and they'd been chosen to serve Diane and Jaine when they'd returned. From a few things Diane had heard, their one complaint was that one of Phynis's maids was *also* named Maria, which occasionally caused some confusion.

"Thank you, Maria," Diane said, opening the door to look at the beautiful, dark-haired human. Maria returned her smile nervously, giving a gentle bob of a curtsey, and Diane added, "If you'd like to find something to do while she's here, that's perfectly fine. I entirely understand if you want to avoid her."

Maria flushed a little at the offer, looking at the ground as she spoke. "Is… is it that obvious, Lady Diane? I was trying not to show how she makes me feel, but I'm just so… so *skittish* around her. I remember what she did to you, too."

"Oh, I feel… similarly. We've had a lot to work through," Diane said, leaving unsaid her own attraction to Maria, which she knew the human felt as well. Ulvian and Wenris had deliberately pushed Diane into Maria's arms during captivity, and the feelings that had formed didn't fade easily. For that matter, Diane knew that Jaine and Meredith had been spending a *lot* of time together, but she wasn't going to pry. Their lives were their own to live. After a few moments she shook off the distraction and focused, though. "Still, I'm going to meet with her. We don't want her getting upset, do we?"

"Of course not!" Maria said, looking a touch horrified. She hesitated, though, then asked, "Is there anything you'd like prepared for your return in the morning?"

"A nice, warm bath would be nice," Diane replied wryly, and glanced back at Torkal, adding, "And ensuring that my husband is available, hm?"

He snorted, smiling as he replied. "As if you could keep me away!"

"If that's what you want, I'll make sure it's ready for you," Maria said, smiling as she added, sounding a little amused. "If nothing else, hot water is easy to come by in Beacon!"

"True enough," Diane said, giving her and Torkal each a last, nervous smile before heading for the stairs into the foyer. It felt like there were butterflies in her stomach, and she couldn't honestly say whether she was afraid of Wenris or excited to see her.

The question continued until she reached the top of the stairs, and Diane stopped instantly, her eyes widening as she saw the succubus below her, even as Wenris looked up in return.

Wenris was in her natural form, or at least what Diane *thought* was her natural form, though her figure wasn't quite as exaggerated as it had been before. The succubus's bat-like wings were on full display, as was the silken length of her tail, and her horns were barely visible against the demon's curly, raven-black hair which spilled down to her waist. Wenris's eyes glowed a dull red, their slit pupils betraying her nature as she smiled, but it was her dress that caught Diane's attention, as the succubus's attempt at modesty drew even more attention than if she'd been naked, in Diane's opinion.

There was a narrow black bodice that covered the succubus's breasts, as well as another across her hips, and both were attached to each other by fabric that ran up her sides, and she also wore long sleeves that each hooked over her middle finger. The dress was filled out by an elaborate, sheer black lace that was almost translucent, and it covered everything from Wenris's neck down, save for the plunging back that allowed her wings to extend. It was beautiful, and revealed just enough of Wenris's body to make someone want to see more, as did the onyx gems sewn into the dress, and one glittering from the demon's navel. It *also* made Diane wonder if her dress might not have been something of a poor choice.

"Diane, you've changed your eyes back!" Wenris said, slowly smiling as she looked up at Diane and took a deep breath, then paused, tilting her head as she added, a note of delight to her voice. "And… what's this? Do I smell Tyria's blood on you? You've remade your body anew once more!"

"Ah… yes, I have," Diane said, taken aback by Wenris instantly identifying the changes. It took her a moment, then she continued, trying to ignore the way her body was heating up. "I didn't want to look like Ulvian wanted me to, so I asked her to change me back, and she agreed."

"I see. Mm… but you *do* smell lovely, I must say. And your outfit suits you," Wenris said, her smile widening even more as she took a deep breath. "White as newly fallen snow… it fits, in my opinion. Now, then, shall we go?"

"Is that wise? You're…" Diane began, but her voice trailed off as Wenris's body rippled and changed. In a few moments the demon's horns, wings, and tail vanished, and her eyes instead were a bright sapphire blue, making her appear like a beautiful human foreigner.

"Yes, walking around the city in demonic form *would* be a poor idea. However, I wanted to show you who I truly was to begin with, Diane," Wenris purred, then made a beckoning gesture. "Now, come here, my queen."

"I'm not a queen," Diane replied automatically, but she didn't even realize she'd started moving until a few seconds later, and she flushed brightly as she realized what she was doing, as well as how Wenris was looking at her. She wasn't going to be able to resist at all, even after several months away from Wenris, Diane realized.

"Yes, you are. You are *my* queen," Wenris replied with a particular emphasis on the possessive term, extending a hand to Diane confidently. "I am the new Queen of Chains, and you are mine. That makes you my queen if I say you are, even if you've lost Yisara. A pity, but there wasn't any chance of your people giving it back to you with our link. Well, that and your pesky contract with Kelvanis, I suppose."

"O-oh," Diane said, her eyes widening still more as a thread of fear rippled through her. She laid her hand in Wenris's, and gasped as the succubus pulled her in close and kissed her.

It was like an electric shock ran from Diane's lips to her toes, causing them to curl in her shoes as her entire body tensed, then melted in the demon's embrace. Wenris was warm, almost *blazing* with heat, and Diane realized belatedly exactly what Sistina had meant about Wenris's touch being dangerous. Not that the thought lasted long, as the heat spilled into her body, and she found herself returning the kiss hungrily, almost like she'd been starving for attention.

The kiss went on and on, until finally Wenris pulled away, leaving Diane feeling dizzy as the succubus held her, trying to catch her breath as Wenris chuckled softly, then spoke. "Oh, you *did* miss me, didn't you? Mm… I missed you too, though I'll admit to having some fun when crushing several upstarts. Not that they could compare to you."

"Um, what?" Diane asked, trying to regain some semblance of thought, but Wenris's presence seemed to just be destroying any ability to concentrate, as her eyes kept drifting downward.

"You're mortal, and you have a strong soul. *That* is something which would attract any demon. It's the reason I was willing to give up Jaine, because you were far, *far* more valuable to someone like me," Wenris replied, her gaze drifting up the staircase, then she turned, pulling Diane toward the door. "Now, come along. We have a nice dinner waiting for us, then a room together. I don't want to waste our time together."

"A-as you wish, Mistress Wenris," Diane stammered, moving with Wenris as the succubus pulled a thick fur cloak off a cloak rack and put it on, then opened the door to reveal the streets and snow-covered roofs of Beacon before them, as well as a carriage waiting in the driveway of the manor. Wenris paused for a moment, looking at Diane speculatively, then smiled.

"Unless, of course, you'd prefer to skip the dinner? You *do* look a touch out of sorts. Perhaps I left you alone for too long?" Wenris teased gently, reaching out to run a finger along Diane's left ear, and the elf blushed brightly, at both the pleasant sensation and the implications of what Wenris was suggesting.

"I'll leave that up to you, Mistress Wenris," Diane whispered in response, trying to fight the way she was feeling, and utterly failing. "Whatever you desire."

"Mm, but of course," Wenris said, her eyes glittering mischievously.

Then she helped Diane into the carriage, and they were on their way to wherever Wenris had in mind.

CHAPTER 28

Nadis stopped short, staring downward as she saw a carriage roll by, her hands tightening suddenly around the back of the chair. She gripped it so tightly she felt pain for a moment before she forced herself to loosen her grip on the chair.

The sight of Diane in the carriage shouldn't have caused such potent feelings, particularly not anger, and it wouldn't have on its own. No, it was the apparently human woman who was in the carriage with Diane that caused rage to well up inside Nadis. The way Diane was blushing, plus the smile she'd seen on the woman's face... *that* was enough for Nadis to identify the woman as the new demon queen who'd replaced Irethiel.

If she was able destroy Wenris that moment, Nadis would have. While she and Diane had never been close, she'd respected the queen's iron will and willingness to do what was right even at the worst of times. That she was bound to a demon due to that just made everything worse. It didn't matter that they were trying to save her by the expedient of redeeming Wenris, though. Nadis wanted Diane freed *now*.

"Whatever did that chair do to you, Nadis?" Tyria's voice distracted Nadis instantly, and she bit back a yelp as she spun around to face the goddess.

Tyria looked much like she had before, with one exception

that took Nadis aback, blinking as she looked at the goddess. Unlike every other time she'd seen Tyria, the goddess wasn't in her armor, and there was no sword by her side. Instead she was wearing an elaborate toga, one of white, purple, and gold. The goddess was also smiling gently at Nadis, and the priestess quickly gathered herself, bowing her head slightly before her goddess.

"Nothing, of course. I simply… I saw Diane and who I believe to be Wenris passing by," Nadis replied, a shadow flickering across her face as she thought about the woman in the carriage. "I'm frustrated."

"You're angry there's nothing more you can do," Tyria corrected, shaking her head as she glanced out the window. "I do not blame you. We are simply doing what we can."

"It's… well, don't *you* hate demons, My Lady? After everything they've done, particularly Irethiel?" Nadis asked, waving at the window.

"Hate demons? No, of course not," Tyria replied, looking at Nadis with obvious surprise. "I may hate some *individuals*, and given half a chance I'd have beheaded Irethiel myself, but I don't hate them as a whole. If anything, I pity them."

"Pity them?" Nadis asked, shock rippling through her at the goddess's words. "Why would you *pity* them?"

Tyria paused for a long moment, studying Nadis with her lips pursed. Then she carefully walked over to the window beside Nadis, folding her arms behind herself, looking over the city as the sun's light slowly faded.

"Demons are mortal desires made manifest. What many call mortal *sins*, accentuated to the greatest extremes. When a mortal dies and goes to the lower planes, they are tormented for what seems like an eternity, either by individuals or the environment itself. That can happen in the blink of an eye from the point of view of this world, too. Slowly, that which is light is leeched away, leaving only the base desires aligned with the region they're in… and they become demons," Tyria explained softly, sighing heavily as she shook her head. "Even those that didn't deserve to go there, but ended up there due to the actions of others, those who were sacrificed, misled, or even those who were branded in the war… all of them have that happen to them, Nadis. Some are changed more directly, such as what happened to Sistina when she was captured as an angel, but each demon once had the potential for great things. Each had the potential for the greatest heights of good… and they've lost that. Often forever."

"What? But—" Nadis began, then cut herself short as she shook her head, confused by what she was hearing. Many of the lessons she'd heard claimed that demons had always been there, and that they were the source of all ills, them and the dark gods themselves.

Tyria smiled at Nadis gently, shaking her head as she spoke. "I don't blame you for not knowing. Most of those who learn of this don't like speaking of it. Neither do we gods, dark or light. Oh, some demons learn to rise above their natures, at least after a fashion, but it is rare. Most of them desire nothing more than to reduce all others to the same state. *That* is the darkness that I fear will eventually consume us all. If all demons were ever to band together against the gods… well, the results would be catastrophic. Yet I do pity them, and Wenris is one of those demons that I feel was close to rising above her nature, but the mantle she bears, *that* is dangerous. The Demon Queen of Chains… it's a seductive, incredibly corrupting mantle. If Diane and all of you can change her… well, the world would change by that act. I cannot do it, though. Only mortals can."

"Only mortals? But… you're here, and you're far more powerful than we are," Nadis said, yet at the same time her concerns were settling down. It was strange to be standing next to a goddess, speaking so easily, and yet… it also felt oddly right.

"Ah, but we deities are not the ones who choose the path to the future. *That* is forbidden by divine law. It's you mortals that make the choices that truly matter," Tyria replied, reaching out to lay a hand on Nadis's shoulder. "We can interact only when mortals make it possible. By faith, by prayer, or even by capturing us when we're foolishly sleeping… mortals are the ones who *allow* us to help them. If you need my aid, it is up to you to call for it. I will do what I can."

"I…" Nadis paused, blinking and flushing a little at Tyria's gentle touch, embarrassed by the show of affection. Tyria confused her so very often, and she looked out the window, clearing her throat before she continued. "I think I understand. I've often wondered why the gods didn't intervene more, and that would explain it."

Tyria nodded, looking out the window beside Nadis, and neither of them spoke for a long minute, then two. Nadis wasn't sure what to say or how to break the silence, especially since she didn't know why Tyria was there.

"I met Baldwin. His followers may have been behind the attack on Elissa, but they were not acting on his behalf, or the faith as a whole," Tyria said at last, glancing at Nadis and giving a wry smile. "I also learned a fair bit more… but I'm not allowed to talk about it. Fate decided to put his foot down, so aside from when all of you call for divine aid, I'm not allowed to intervene. It's a bit frustrating."

"What? *Fate* showed up?" Nadis exclaimed, almost yelping as her eyes went wide. "I… were you in our world? I thought the greater gods couldn't come here!"

"Yes, we were. As for the greater gods, well, Fate is a special case. He can go where he's needed since he's the one who enforces the agreements," Tyria explained with a shrug and a smile. "Even so, the meeting was… illuminating. I was wondering about a few things, and now I have answers. How did *your* meeting go? Are you making progress with Elissa?"

"I believe so. We're currently feeling things out, but the church of Tyria will likely become a branch of the faith with her in charge of the Kelvanis region. We're still working out a number of things, especially regarding finances and tithes, but I think we've come to at least tentative agreements," Nadis admitted, growing nervous as she spoke, her mind drifting to one subject she'd been dreading bringing up. Still, there wasn't a better time to bring it up than when her goddess was right there, so she took a deep breath and asked, "Would you be willing to become Medaea again?"

"Of course," Tyria replied instantly, glancing at Nadis as her eyes twinkled, sending a rush of pure relief through Nadis. The goddess continued warmly. "I've been expecting this, and I *have* been watching the negotiations from the shadows. As a matter of fact, I left my sword and armor with Baldwin, who offered to reforge them into something more practical again. Irethiel weakened them significantly, which is… annoying. I need to give Sistina a message, then see if she has any idea how to change me physically. While I am a goddess of many things, transformations aren't one of them."

The sense of relief almost overwhelmed Nadis, growing even stronger as the goddess continued speaking. She hadn't realized just how worried she was about how Tyria might react until that moment, but the knowledge she was willing to become something Nadis and the rest of her church would recognize as their goddess, though… that was a huge weight off her shoulders. Then what Tyria said fully registered, and Nadis paused, frowning.

"Ah… not that I want to contradict you, My Lady… but if that's the case, why did your blood change Diane and Jaine?" Nadis asked after a moment, a bit confused.

"My blood didn't change them. My blood was used as a source of power and as a divine blessing," Tyria corrected, shaking her head. "Making a transmutation affect a creature permanently is difficult. Making it so that it's their natural form is harder. Changing the body of a deity in the same way? That takes incredible skill with magical transformations and immense power as well. I might be able to power a spell to change myself, but the magical knowledge… *that* is beyond me. That's why I need Sistina."

"Ah, well, I suppose that makes sense," Nadis said, then paused and frowned. "Though that *does* make me wonder how they managed to change you to begin with."

"Lots of time, mana, and the use of demon blood on a variety of unfortunate mortals which they twisted into becoming demons," Tyria replied, shrugging a little. "From what Elissa said, Ulvian's original plan would have taken a few years to change me, but Zenith's capture allowed him to work far more swiftly. In any case, I had best go see Sistina. I hope your night goes well, Nadis. Dream of dawn."

"Thank you, My Goddess," Nadis replied, and watched as

Tyria vanished briefly, then the glowing figure appeared outside, darting through the air toward the palace.

As much as part of Nadis wanted to worry about Tyria going to Sistina for the chance to become Medaea again, she couldn't really blame her. Short of going to another deity, Nadis couldn't think of another who might fit the requirements Tyria had laid down, and she didn't trust them any more than she trusted Sistina. Possibly less, in fact.

"At least Medaea is coming back to us. We'll lose some people, especially when Elissa and her people join us… but in the end, our goddess is returning, and we will be stronger for her presence," Nadis murmured, bowing her head as she closed her eyes and prayed internally, feeling more at peace than she had in years.

Now they just needed to finish the conference, and things would be much better.

~

"…TRYING to determine how to control the mana. While you make it seem easy to craft golems, all of our attempts have led to them exploding," Farris said, a hint of frustration on the woman's stony face.

Phynis rolled her eyes, a smile playing across her lips despite herself. Farris had once been one of her guards, right up until the healer had been murdered by Jared Falgrave. Sistina had been bonded to the woman's soul, though, and a few months later she'd inserted Farris into her current body, a stone body made to look like an elven woman, and with several intricate carvings across her body and filled with gold, particularly around the glowing green emerald set in her collarbone, and with silver hair atop her head. The golem's faceted green eyes glowed as well, and Farris had taken to wearing nice but durable clothing.

"Practice," Sistina replied calmly, taking a sip of soup carefully, then smiled at Farris. "Simple, not *easy*."

Farris glowered at Sistina, and around the table everyone else laughed, Opal the loudest of all. Phynis opened her mouth to speak, but Ruby beat her to it. "You really should know better than to expect Sistina to give you the answers, Farris. She wants you to figure it out by *doing* it, since that means you learned properly."

"Books explain how. Practice gives precision," Sistina murmured, nodding at Opal as she smiled. "Am good. Others were better. *Can* be better. Practice, and *surpass* me."

"Ah, Sistina? I think that might be just a *bit* ambitious of you. We're starting at a point so far behind where you are that it's hard to fathom," Phynis interjected, both amused and a little horrified by the thought that Sistina wanted them to be *better* than her. "You've been learning for thousands of years, and have more knowledge than most *nations*. I don't know that it's possible for us to catch up with you."

Sistina simply raised an eyebrow at Phynis skeptically, then spoke flawlessly. "Of course you can, if you put in the effort. I forgot a great deal, and I'm learning artificing, now. It did *not* exist when I was an angel or demon. You have all the tools you need to catch up with me. It's up to *you* to put in the time and effort to do so."

Phynis couldn't help a deep sigh, though she was amused despite herself. Sistina protected her and the others, gave them safety and love… but the dryad also was of the opinion that they needed challenges to grow. Once she'd heard Sistina mutter something about wondering how they'd deal with a polluted pond, but no one had understood what she'd meant.

Just as Phynis was raising her glass to take a drink of wine, the wall shimmered and Tyria stepped through it, landing and folding her wings. Phynis blinked, unused to seeing the goddess without her armor, and she *thought* she saw a hint of anxiety in Tyria's eyes. It was particularly a surprise since the goddess was interrupting their dinner, since she normally avoided that, even if Phynis *had* extended a standing invitation for Tyria to join them. She had to admit, though, she was always a little nervous around the goddess. She *knew* that Tyria was attracted to Sistina, after all, and the goddess's beauty… well, it made her a touch insecure. This night it was just Phynis, Sistina, the Jewels, and Farris, though, so it was a fairly quiet night.

Slowly the others fell silent as they caught sight of Tyria, and

Phynis put down her glass, tilting her head as she spoke. "Lady Tyria! I didn't expect you this evening, were you coming to join us?"

"While I do appreciate your invitation, such would be inappropriate of me," Tyria said, looking at Phynis with a slight smile. "No, I've come because I needed to speak to Sistina."

Sistina looked at the goddess and tilted her head, an eyebrow arching. "Baldwin?"

"Yes, I met him. He asked me to meet him at the heart of the mountains, and it was... eventful. He's not responsible for what's going on, however," Tyria replied, smiling nervously as she added, "I'd say more, but Fate was *quite* firm when he told us that we were supposed to leave mortal affairs to mortals."

Phynis opened her mouth at that, then shut it, swallowing uneasily as she digested what Tyria had said. The idea of Fate being involved almost gave her hives, after hearing a little about the deity from Desa. Her guard had encountered Fate while she was Emonael's guest, and it hadn't been something Desa had enjoyed. That incident indicated Fate had a short temper, which wasn't something she wanted to hear about regarding a god who was in charge of people's destinies.

"Interesting," Sistina murmured, sitting back in her chair thoughtfully as she ignored how the others were quietly talking among themselves, listening closely. "Why come here?"

"Because I met someone in the process, someone I thought long dead," Tyria said, pausing as she looked around the room at everyone, obviously thinking, then shrugged. "She said that she met you as Marin once. Do you remember the Eternal Empress?"

Everyone fell silent, and Sistina's eyes widened for an instant, betraying more shock than Phynis could remember seeing on her face. On the other hand, Phynis choked slightly, stunned.

The Eternal Empress was a legend even in the chronicles of Old Everium. She was the ruler of the Eternal Wood, and Phynis had read many accounts of people who'd gone there to meet her, and they'd spoken of the immense power at the nymph's command, as well as her wisdom and beauty. Among nobles, it'd been customary to make a pilgrimage into the Eternal Wood, and there was something about the descriptions that seemed slightly familiar to Phynis. Even so, they'd just been legends, and Phynis assumed that the fey monarch had died with her kingdom.

"The Eternal Empress lives?" Sistina asked, carefully reaching out to pluck a grape from its vine, rolling the sphere between her fingers.

"She does. She also asked me to give you her regards," Tyria said, looking at Sistina closely. "Or, to be more accurate, to give *Marin* her regards. She was glad to hear you lived."

"How… how could she still live? The center of the mountains… *no one* has come back after going there!" Phynis protested, her voice trembling slightly.

"No one but me, perhaps," Tyria said, taking a breath, but Sistina spoke before she could keep going.

"She is tied to the world tree. So long as it lives, it was said she would survive. I would not have thought she would be unkillable… but perhaps she was," Sistina said slowly, her gaze oddly distant. "The tree could not have been fully dead. It is the source of mana, the heart of the ley lines. So it sustained her for all this time, all alone."

"That's terrible!" Emerald said, her eyes widening as she shivered. "I… is she alright?"

"I'm not sure that I could honestly say she's *alright*, but she certainly isn't injured," Tyria replied, her expression growing slightly distant as she winced. "She is… surprisingly cognizant and focused after such a long time alone. I daresay she's one of the few beings that I believe matches or exceeds Sistina's magical knowledge."

"Makes sense. Lived before research finished," Sistina said, and smiled in amusement as a chill ran down Phynis's spine. "Maybe she'll visit."

"Perhaps so," Tyria said, shrugging as she continued. "However, there *is* another matter which I would like to consult you on."

"Oh?" Sistina asked, looking back at the goddess curiously.

"Would it be possible to get your help with changing my appearance back to what it was as Medaea? Or at least most of the way back?" Tyria asked, "Permanently, of course, which I know is more difficult."

Sistina blinked a couple of times, then smiled and nodded. "Yes. Simple."

At that Tyria stopped and stared at Sistina, then asked incredulously, almost sounding a little outraged. "Simple? But... I'm a goddess! Permanently changing the fundamental nature of my appearance is—"

"Simple," Sistina interrupted calmly, to Phynis's shocked amusement. "Takes mana, lots. Still simple. Just need appearance. Never met *you* before."

The near outrage on Tyria's face was incredibly amusing, somehow, and despite herself Phynis couldn't help the impulse to snicker under her breath. Her laugh seemed to break the ice, though, and the others around the table laughed softly as well, even as Tyria looked around for a moment, her expression turning more bemused than anything.

"Farris, I think that it's going to take you a *lot* of practice with the golems," Sapphire said, smiling at the mage as she teased. "If Sistina thinks both changing Tyria's appearance and making golems is simple, well..."

"*Is* simple, though," Sistina protested, looking around the room incredulously. "Precision, power, yes. Simple, but finicky. Has to be just right."

"If you say so, Sistina. I'll look at the books again, promise," Farris replied dryly, obviously giving up on getting more information out of Sistina.

"I... suppose you could say that," Tyria said, still looking a little put out as she folded her arms in front of her. "I guess I just need to try to remember what I looked like."

"Fortunately, while the orders I was given prevented me from speaking about your presence and what happened at the temple, My Lady, they did *not* include removing memories of what you looked like," Diamond spoke up, reaching over to squeeze Phynis's hand as she smiled. "I'm willing to project what I remember as an illusion, if you'd like. For good or ill, it mostly stuck in my memory."

Tyria blinked, then smiled as she nodded, sounding grateful.

"That would be appreciated, Diamond. The problem for me is while I remember what I looked like somewhat, and would recognize myself… I wasn't a goddess of beauty, and didn't admire myself much. I was blonde, I know that much… and had blue eyes."

Phynis nodded slightly, looking at Diamond curiously. Her wife pursed her lips slightly, concentrating for a long moment, then raised her fingers to make short, precise gestures as she began speaking the words of a spell. It took longer than Phynis was used to for the priestess to finish the spell, though, about half a minute in total.

As Diamond finished the last word of the spell, a symbol flickered in the air, then an illusion slowly formed over the table. It was a couple of feet long, and depicted a stone bier with a woman on it, one which caused Phynis's breath to catch in her throat.

The woman wore a simple white robe, and her wings were pure white. Her hair was long and almost like sunlight made into threads, glittering as the woman inhaled and exhaled slowly. She was an elf, but more like one of the foreign ones Phynis had met, pale-skinned and statuesque, while she glowed from within like the sun was embedded in her flesh. Looking at the woman, then at Tyria, Phynis realized that while she *had* been changed, the goddess still looked surprisingly like she had before, just with a different hair color, and a more muted glow to her skin. No, she also had somewhat more accentuated curves, Phynis realized a moment later, but it was a bit subtler of a change. There was also the amethyst gems set into her forehead and chest, of course, but those were obvious additions.

"You're beautiful," Phynis murmured, looking at the illusion, then at Tyria.

"Thank you, Phynis," Tyria said, looking at the illusion thoughtfully, then nodded slightly as she added, "I suspect that Diamond is misremembering how much I glowed, however. That seems a lot brighter than it should be, as I don't recall being on the verge of blinding others with my presence."

At that, Diamond's cheeks turned pink, and Ruby laughed softly as Diamond cleared her throat and replied. "I *did* say it's what I remember. I'll fully admit that I might be idealizing things, or that my memories might have been… changed due to meeting you so many times since then."

"That seems likely, but still, thank you, Diamond. Have you seen enough, Sistina?" Tyria asked, looking at the dryad again.

"Yes. The stones?" Sistina asked, touching her forehead, then the top of her breastbone.

"Ah, if you could remove them, that would be ideal, yes," Tyria blushed a little, reaching up to touch the gem set into her forehead, looking a bit self-conscious. "I forget they're there, much of the time."

"Unsurprising," Sistina murmured, nodding as she considered, then added, "Will prepare. Three days?"

"That would be excellent. Thank you, Sistina," Tyria said, and to Phynis's surprise the goddess bowed deeply, prompting a soft inhalation from Diamond.

"Do not bow," Sistina scolded, shaking her head firmly. "Am supporting you. You choose your path. I will not dictate."

"Believe me, that's something I have noticed and greatly appreciate," Tyria said, straightening again and looked around the room for a moment before adding, "That said, I suppose I had best let you get back to your dinner. I hope all of you have a good evening."

"And you as well, Lady Tyria," Phynis replied, nodding graciously, and with that the goddess went ephemeral again. Phynis sometimes wondered why she could see the goddess phase through the walls when no one else seemed to be able to, but she'd decided it wasn't worth worrying about.

"Well, that was certainly interesting," Sapphire said, looking around the table thoughtfully.

"Mmhm, but… what about dessert? We have one coming, don't we?" Amethyst asked, her tone slightly hopeful as she looked at Phynis, and the queen couldn't help laughing.

"Yes, yes we do. It's just fortunate that it *is* such a long climb down to Sistina's cavern. Obviously, we need it," Phynis replied in a teasing tone.

"Hey!" Amethyst protested loudly, and *that* caused everyone to laugh, even Sistina.

CHAPTER 29

Wenris decided that she rather *liked* how Diane's eyes sparkled in the light, as well as how different they were. A tiny part of her had been annoyed that Diane had chosen to change her eyes back, but that had faded quickly. In truth, the odd purple marking on Diane's forehead and the purple eyes had shown her connection to Tyria more than Wenris, so the change was welcome, after a fashion.

So was the way that Diane kept blushing, Wenris thought, smiling as she licked the cream off her strawberry. For someone so poised and experienced, it was entertaining to see how easily Wenris could embarrass her. Regardless, dinner *was* wrapping up, which meant they were going to be moving to the more enjoyable part of the night soon. With that in mind, Wenris bit into the firm strawberry, shearing it off just short of the stem and savoring its flavor as she chewed, while Diane looked down, focusing on the last bits of her strawberries and sponge cake.

"Well, *that* was scrumptious," Wenris said at last, smiling widely as she murmured, "I must say I do love how the gardens here can produce fruit year-round. Most regions, you only get things like this a handful of times a year, unless you're using magic to get it from somewhere it's currently in season."

"It *is* rather nice," Diane agreed, finishing off another

strawberry as she looked up, hesitating for a moment before she asked, "Can't *you* get it from wherever you want, though?"

"Me? Oh, no… my home is *quite* inhospitable for the most part. Few plants grow there, so the only vegetation is a handful of indoor gardens. Those take quite a bit of care, too," Wenris said, thinking back on her palace, and grinning as she remembered how Ulvian had been running about frantically over the last few months, trying to get things up to her exacting standards. She didn't say anything about that, though. "That said, I do believe it's time to go, my dear. We've finished the meal, and I'm afraid there aren't any good playhouses in Beacon yet, so we'll have to call it a night."

The spike of pheromones from the elf prompted another smile from Wenris, as Diane swallowed hard, admirably hiding her anticipation as she spoke. "Ah, really? Don't we need to pay for the meal?"

"I paid in advance, primarily for privacy. That's why we haven't been disturbed save for when dessert arrived," Wenris said, smiling more widely as she added, "I also paid *quite* generously, so don't worry about them being upset. I suspect the gold will more than suffice to soothe their feelings."

"As you say, Mistress Wenris," Diane acknowledged, the elf sounding and looking torn. She obviously was trying to decide what she really wanted, which was amusing to Wenris, since *she* knew what the elf wanted, and was going to give it to her.

Wenris rose gracefully, taking a couple of steps around the table to offer Diane a hand. The elf took it and stood as well, obviously not sure how to respond, but Wenris didn't do anything more than smile more as she led the way to the cloak rack nearest the door. That wasn't usually in the room, but Wenris had paid the proprietor *very* well for the evening.

She carefully settled Diane's cloak around her shoulders, and the elf's blush grew still brighter as she looked up at Wenris, her lips parted as she inhaled, then froze as she looked into Wenris's eyes. Wenris paused as well, staring at her lovely elven queen, and after a moment her smile widened still more as she leaned in to kiss Diane.

Diane didn't resist at all, instead melting into Wenris's arms, her own arms wrapping around the demon's back, almost making Wenris gloat internally. She doubted that Diane did this for anyone else, and as eagerly as Diane accepted the kiss... well, it was all the succubus could do to keep from taking advantage of her then and there.

At last Wenris broke off the kiss, reveling in the taste of Diane's soul, so pure and bright, lovely to every sense the succubus possessed. It was something that didn't last long with most mortals, and it was absolutely *intoxicating*. So Wenris breathed in deeply, then purred. "Oh, Diane... I would *love* to take you home with me. But you wouldn't last long there, so I have to savor you. Now, do you want to come back to my apartment?"

"I..." Diane paused, catching her breath, her eyes bright with desire, and the elf shivered before she breathed out. "I would *very* much like that, Mistress Wenris."

"Good," Wenris purred, heading for the door.

She almost forgot her cloak in her haste, in fact.

DIANE'S LEGS almost gave out as she reached the door of her manor, and only Maria's quick reaction kept her from falling anyway. The human quickly helped her up, speaking in obvious concern. "Are you alright, Lady Diane?"

"I'll... I'll be fine," Diane replied, her voice slightly raw after the previous night.

It felt like all her muscles had been given an intense workout, and she'd wanted nothing more than to stay in bed that morning, cuddled into Wenris. It'd taken every ounce of control she'd had to force herself to leave, and the succubus had just given Diane a knowing smirk as she'd slipped out the door. *That* had nearly been Diane's undoing, in fact. Fortunately, there'd been a carriage waiting for her or Diane wouldn't have made it back at all.

Worse still was how Diane *felt*, though. The previous night... she shuddered involuntarily as her mind shied away from it. Even the thought of how the moonlight had shone off Wenris's skin, or the wild, triumphant light in the demon's eyes sent a thrill of pleasure through Diane. She didn't want to think about that, not now. Not that she could *stop* thinking about it.

"If you say so, milady," Maria replied, helping her the rest of the way into the foyer and closing the door behind Diane, giving the driver a nod. "You look like you just ran a marathon."

"I think a marathon would have been easier," Diane said, smiling at her as best she could, though she suspected her voice was shaking quite a bit.

"I'm not certain, but I'll take your word for it," another woman said, and Diane looked deeper into the house and blinked. Lirisel was present, as was Torkal. Lirisel had been the one speaking, and the woman looked rather concerned, while Torkal looked like he'd bitten into something foul.

"Ah, Lirisel, dear… sorry, I didn't realize you were here at first," Diane said, looking at them and shrugging as she tried to stand up straighter. "I'm afraid it was… was a long night."

"I can only imagine. If I could do something…" Torkal began, but his voice trailed off as he rushed forward to support Diane. At the same time, though, Diane heard the undertone of his voice, realizing that he was both angry and jealous at the same time. She honestly couldn't blame him, when she thought about it, but it made her… sad, after a fashion.

"You can't. No one really can… though I suppose that's why Lirisel is here, yes?" Diane asked, looking up at the priestess expectantly, her nerves still feeling raw. She was also ignoring the craving in the back of her mind, whispering that she should go back to Wenris's apartment.

"That's right. She came here early this morning with *far* more holy water than I've ever seen before," Torkal said instantly, grinning as he added, "I don't think most temples have that much on hand, in fact."

"You can thank the temple of Vanir for that. We're helping them with a few things in exchange for the blessed water, which they have in abundance," Lirisel said, a slight smile creeping across her face as she added, "They don't have as many priests here as we do, and apparently they weren't expecting as many pilgrims as have arrived."

"Ah. Well, I certainly *need* the help, considering everything," Diane admitted, closing her eyes and fighting with her perceptions, trying to remember what it was like just after her second baptism. It took a few more seconds than she was comfortable with, but eventually she managed to speak, if rather slowly. "It's… I can't even describe this, but it was everything I could do to pull myself away earlier. I don't know how I would've reacted if I hadn't… hadn't gotten help yesterday."

The others had just started moving her toward the back, but Torkal slowed a little as he asked, his tone growing a little more concerned, "It… was really that bad?"

Fortunately for Diane, Maria spoke up at that point, preventing Diane from saying something foolish, even as a part of her mind flickered back to the middle of the previous night, heat surging through her all the while.

"I wouldn't say *bad*, milord, but I spent a little time with Wenris myself. I was under her control when Diane was imprisoned in Kelvanath, and I…" Maria paused, her voice breaking ever so slightly. Then she spoke again, almost breathlessly. "I can't begin to describe it, milord. Succubi aren't dangerous because they're cruel, though they can be that. They're dangerous because they know *exactly* how to target and use your desires. She shaped Lady Diane into what she wanted her to be in a matter of *months,* and could have done far, far more than that if she'd so desired. As powerful as she is now…"

"She could convince me to *beg* her to take me away with her," Diane admitted softly, opening her eyes to see the shock on Torkal's face, and she smiled wanly. "She could do that in a matter of *hours,* dear. The others… they weren't wrong when they said we have to keep from letting her realize what we're trying to do. If she learns what we're up to, I won't have a chance to resist."

"Which is all the more reason to get you into the bath," Lirisel said firmly, folding her arms as she looked at Diane in worry. "The sooner we get started, the less chance her power will have to spread. Now come along, please."

"Of course, priestess," Maria said obediently, and Diane sighed, wishing her legs worked better as she was helped up.

They led the way into one of the downstairs rooms, where a large tub had been set up and filled with water. She was a little too tired to care much beyond that, if she was honest, and sighed as the others hesitated, then began undressing her. Diane tried to help, but after fumbling with a button for several seconds she gave up and let them take care of everything.

Soon enough she slipped into the water, and the touch of it against her skin caused her to hiss, shivering. The water felt cold against her skin, and the chill slowly penetrated deep into her body, quenching some of the embers burning within her flesh. It took a minute, then she murmured, "The water feels so *cold*."

"Well, it *did* have quite some time to cool off after I arrived. My apologies, but we didn't know when you were getting back," Lirisel said gently, though she didn't sound quite as sorry as Diane might have preferred.

"True," Diane admitted, inhaling slowly, then holding the breath for a moment. After she let it out she opened her eyes, looking up at Torkal. She winced at the look in his eyes, and spoke after a brief hesitation. "Are you alright, dear?"

"I… don't think so. I want to pretend that I am, but what she's doing to you… it's all I can do to even pretend to bear it," Torkal admitted, looking downward rather than meeting her gaze. "When you first came back, I was ecstatic. I was willing to put up with anything, because you *were* back, you were safe, or at least I thought I was. I thought I could deal with you having to be alone once a month, and put up with her potential visits. Now, though… it's torture to be faced with it."

The room was quiet, and Diane saw Maria studiously look away, instead folding Diane's clothing as if that was enough to take all of her attention, while Lirisel was watching the wall intensely. It wasn't true privacy, but it was as close as Diane was going to get, she realized, sorrow surging through her as she took a deep breath, then let it out again.

"I'm sorry," Diane said at last, looking down herself, swirling the water anxiously as she began adapting to the cold at last. She wasn't sure what to say, but she spoke anyway, unsure if what she said would be *right*, but at least she'd be honest. "I… don't really blame you. I was afraid of what would happen when I heard her conditions originally, and I wasn't sure how to react, especially with how *you* might react. I just… I didn't know what else to do. I'm sorry, dear, and I wish I had an answer for you. If you want to leave, I won't blame you."

"What? No, no, that isn't what I meant at all!" Torkal exclaimed, his gaze jerking upward and sounding almost panicked as he looked at her. "I didn't mean I wanted to leave you alone, dear, I just… just… I've been *frustrated* that I can't do anything at all to help you. That I just have to sit here and do nothing while she… she…"

Diane's nervousness eased ever so slightly at that, and she nodded slowly, smiling at Torkal as she let out a near-silent breath of relief. For a moment she'd been worried that he'd almost fallen out of love with her, and that… well, she wasn't sure what she'd do. Torkal was an anchor for her, and without him… she feared what Wenris might be able to do to her.

"It isn't your fault, dear. If anyone, I think you should blame Sorvos. He was the one who put me in her hands, and led to all of this," Diane said, shrugging gently. "If he hadn't, we might still be back in Yisara, dealing with the nobility."

"Gods forbid *that*, considering how much trouble they were," Torkal muttered, his affected outrage halfhearted at best as he smiled at her, shifting uncomfortably in his chair. Finally, the man admitted softly, "I'm sorry to drop all of this on you now, love. I didn't mean to… but it just burst out."

"I don't blame you, not in the slightest," Diane replied quickly, shaking her head as she let out a soft sigh. "It's… not a good situation, and you've been dealing with a lot of stress. Both of us have, and I'm just glad that Jaine seems to be avoiding all of it."

"From your lips to the gods' ears," Torkal murmured, closing his eyes and taking a deep breath, then letting it out. "I just… hope we can get through this without any *more* trouble."

"As do I. Unfortunately, there *are* still those people who attacked Elissa, so I'm not going to be holding my breath," Diane said, and her thoughts drifted off as she murmured softly, "I wish we knew what they were up to."

CHAPTER 30

"I *hate* snow," Bane growled, pulling his cloak close as they threaded their way past a couple of parked wagons. Alexander couldn't help a laugh at that, though he couldn't really blame his friend. A couple of their nights on the way to Westgate had been particularly cold, which hadn't made the trip very pleasant.

It didn't help that Erin and Umira had pushed them to move farther each day, not giving as much time to set up camp as Alexander would have preferred. Their desire to get to Westgate had meant the group didn't have nearly as good of a campsite on any night, and Alexander suspected that they'd done it on purpose, as Umira had an enchanted *tent* of all things, one which meant the two women had been comfortable, even if he hadn't been. Still, he wasn't about to stir up trouble with either of them, especially since they'd finally reached Westgate.

The city was certainly different than many in the region that he'd seen, though. When they'd been traveling to Beacon originally, their group had passed through Kelvanath, several other cities of Kelvanis, and Westgate before finally reaching Beacon, and the contrast between the cities had been stunning, especially after he'd seen some of the elven nations across the sea.

Kelvanath had struck Alexander as a primitive human city,

much like you could see in many parts of the world. More prosperous nations had started luring artificers to their cities, and as such steam engines and enchantments were more common, ranging from clock towers and rail lines around the city to magical weapons, like staves that could launch fire bolts, though those were still vanishingly rare. Kelvanath had possessed none of that, instead possessing the blockier, imposing structures of many human or dwarven nations, though most of it had lacked the precision dwarves were renowned for. Most of Kelvanis's cities had been made in the same mold, which was why Westgate and Beacon were both so confusing by comparison.

Westgate, conversely, was largely composed of the typical human buildings from Kelvanis, but it *also* had structures made of stone in a more flowing, natural style somewhat like the elven cities he'd seen, yet somehow more primitive as well, without the delicate enchantments or fragile appearances he was used to, and still other buildings were made of wood that had almost been grown into their final shapes. It was rarely alive, but looked incredibly natural, and often had gardens around the buildings that almost disguised their nature at an initial glance. The three styles were interspersed with one another, though most of the wooden buildings were to the north, while the stone ones were to the south. The old Kelvanis governor's mansion had been destroyed at some point, and Alexander had seen crews clearing the grounds, while he'd wondered what they were going to replace the building with. Still, at the time he'd thought that the city would give him an idea of what Beacon would be like.

That had been a mistake, for Beacon hadn't been *anything* like Westgate, nor like any other city which Alexander had ever visited, even dwarven fortresses. He couldn't even express how imposing Beacon had been, with thousands of perfectly constructed stone homes, each of a quality which Alexander would expect for the nobility elsewhere, running water, often *hot* water, and golems patrolling the roads. The designs were both ancient and modern at the same time, and it was strange to the human, but somehow he was just happy not to be in Beacon anymore. It probably was because, to him, the city had been a manifestation of the alien mind and sheer *power* of the dungeon. Someplace like Westgate was just… comfortable, by comparison. Even if there were far more carts and people along the roads.

"Where are we supposed to stay?" Umira suddenly asked, glancing back at Alexander, and he smiled in response, feeling a touch vindictive.

"Oh? I thought you and Erin knew, since you've been rushing ever since we left Beacon," Alexander replied calmly, taking a bit of satisfaction with how the two women scowled at him.

"No, we don't," Erin replied, her tone biting. "Just because you're slow doesn't mean—"

Erin's voice cut off as Alexander met her gaze, his smile vanishing as anger surged within him, and he *saw* her fear well up. Perhaps he'd been just a bit too accommodating of her attitude, he realized, but this wasn't the place to address something like that.

"We haven't been slow, Erin," Alexander replied, his words deceptively pleasant as he looked at her. "If you want to lead the way, go ahead. Wander around aimlessly, and waste your time. In the meantime, I'm going to find somewhere warm, thank you."

Alexander pushed past the two women, just as a flush rose in Erin's cheeks, and not one brought about by the cold air.

"That isn't fair! You didn't say anything before this!" Erin protested after a moment, only to be interrupted.

"Shh. Don't make things worse, would you?" Umira scolded the other woman, prompting a chuckle from Bane, who Alexander could hear following, while Umira continued. "He's been putting up with your tantrums for weeks, and he didn't have to."

"But—" Erin began, just as Alexander turned a corner which made her words inaudible. He snorted softly, shaking his head as he continued down the street.

"Honestly, I'm amazed at how patient you are. She's been a right pain in the ass since we reached shore," Bane said, and Alexander glanced back to see the big man adjusting his hat, and grinned back at him.

"Oh, it's not a big deal, really. Erin has always been difficult, so I expected something like this from the beginning. The thing is, I *also* have known where my line was," Alexander replied, mentally figuring out which streets would take them to the house he'd been told to go to. "If she goes too far, she gets the boot."

Bane went silent at that, and Alexander understood why. In their faith, one wasn't simply kicked out. That wasn't how they worked at all, so if Erin was to be expelled, it would be as a lifeless corpse in a ditch. Alexander was confident that he could do the job, even if Erin *was* good at what she did. He was just confident he was better.

Some hissing and grumbling came from behind a few moments later, indicating that Erin and Umira had caught up again, and Bane wisely dropped the subject, just as Alexander preferred. It wouldn't do to make open threats, since Erin seemed to have gotten the hint from the look in his eyes.

Instead he wound his way through the city, hoping that the safe house would be reasonably nice here, too. Despite Alexander's misgivings with Beacon, he *did* like the buildings there, and would miss the water in particular. There was nothing quite as refreshing as a hot bath when it was cold outside, in his opinion.

Soon they were close, then Alexander paused, blinking as he saw the house, and he double-checked the address on its gate, just to be sure he hadn't taken the wrong turn somewhere. When he saw he hadn't, he looked up at the house again, murmuring the name on the gate. "The Branching Oaks, hm? Odd name for a house."

The house was in its own yard, with a stone wall around most of the grounds and a wrought-iron fence blocking easy access, along with a tiny house for a gatekeep built against the fence. There were several oak trees scattered around the yard, which he suspected were the source of the name, while the building itself was somewhat larger than he'd expected, but constructed in a human style. There were expensive glass windows in several places, smoke slowly wisped out of the chimney, and it was large enough that he wondered why they'd been instructed to come here, since it didn't look like the best location to avoid notice.

Finally, Alexander shrugged and reached over to where a rope hung from the brick wall and pulled it. He assumed it hooked to a bell inside the gatekeep's home, considering the location. Nothing happened for a minute, and Alexander was seriously considering pulling the rope again when the gatehouse's door opened.

"I'm coming, I'm coming, don't pull the damned rope again," a woman said, and her voice was familiar, though it took Alexander a moment to place it. It was when a woman came around the corner, her cheeks rosy in the cold, that his breath caught in his throat, seeing a few stray strands of blue around her face.

"Lisa?" Alexander asked, and the woman looked up, then her face lit up with a brilliant smile as she saw him, her bright blue eyes twinkling as the light exposed how the pupils were slightly elongated.

"Alex! I knew you were coming, but I didn't expect you today!" Lisa exclaimed, quickly moving to unlock the gate. "How are you? Have you been eating well?"

"Ah, I'm fine, Lisa. As for food, have I ever starved?" Alexander said, heat rising in his cheeks a bit as he grappled with the sight of Lisa, and a thread of worry worked its way through him, which he tried to tamp down on. She opened the gate, and he hesitated before he asked, "Um, why are you here, if you don't mind me asking? I expected to meet someone a bit less important."

"Oh, Alex… you should know better than that," Lisa scolded, and looked across the others as her grin brightened. "Why don't you all come in? It's brisk out here, and I'm sure you'd like some nice, warm tea, and maybe a scone or two."

"That sounds lovely," Umira agreed, not realizing how Alexander's dread was growing stronger. On the other hand, none of them had been raised by Lisa.

Alexander followed Lisa, a touch more reluctant than the others were, though he *did* want to get out of the cold as well. He was just afraid of what was coming.

The door of the house creaked open, and as it did, Lisa tsked at it, murmuring, "I oiled that just yesterday! Ah, well, it's probably the cold."

Alexander stepped into the house after Lisa, finding himself in a short hall with a thick rug, a boot-rack to the side, and what looked to be a reasonably large cloakroom nearby. There were two doors leading deeper into the house, one on the left and the other on the right, but he knew better than to head toward them. He immediately sighed and stepped out of the way before leaning over to start unlacing his boots, glancing at Bane as he stepped inside and explaining. "You'd best take off your boots, Bane. Lisa is insistent on keeping the floors clean."

"Precisely! I won't have you tracking snow and mud across my nice, clean floors," Lisa agreed, smiling as she took off her boots practically effortlessly, then unhooked her cloak and folded it across her arm as she offered a hand. "Your cloak, Alex?"

He bit back a reply, instead unhooking his cloak and offering it to her so she could put it in the cloakroom. The others were giving him odd looks, which he suffered, but they followed directions anyway. It was only when they were almost finished that anyone dared ask the questions he'd been expecting.

"How do you two know one another?" Bane asked, looking between them. "Alexander seemed surprised to see you, Miss Lisa."

"I raised the lad, of course! Someone had to do it, with as much trouble as he was prone to getting into," Lisa replied instantly, hanging the last of the cloaks and coming out, smiling broadly as she continued, obviously amused. "Not that it was bad, mind you. Getting into trouble is the best way to show that a youngling is worth your time, and otherwise I'd have drowned him and been done with it."

Everyone paused at that, and Erin stared at Alexander. He simply sighed and rolled his eyes, murmuring, "Yes, well, I didn't get drowned, for which I thank my lucky stars. I assume that someone is waiting to meet us?"

"You'd be right! This way," Lisa said, grinning again, this time wide enough he saw a flash of her teeth. Alexander wondered if anyone else noticed that they were marginally more pointed than they should be.

They were led to the door on the left, and it opened silently at Lisa's touch. The sound of the fire popping was the first thing Alexander noticed, and he warily took a step inside. The room had a sofa and several chairs, but it was the woman in the chair opposite them that instantly caught his attention and prompted him to bow.

The woman was tall, seemingly human, and oddly androgynous in appearance, closer to handsome than beautiful, though her short brown hair was fine and her hazel eyes were mesmerizing. She was wearing simple, warm clothing that wouldn't have been out of place on any tradesman, and had a throw rug across her lap while she worked on intricate needlepoint. She looked up and smiled slightly as she nodded.

"Ah, Alexander, Bane, Erin, and Umira. I see you've arrived at last," the woman said, her voice far more distinctly female, and there was an edge to it that made Alexander shiver. He really wished that the others knew who she was since they were slower to bow than he'd prefer.

"Lady Mazina, I didn't realize you'd be meeting us here," Alexander said respectfully, holding his bow, and he could *hear* the abrupt inhalation of the others at that, as well as practically sense them growing worried.

"Of course you didn't. I didn't want you to know," Mazina said, her tone as bright as her gaze was cold. "Now, all of you come in here. I want to hear *exactly* what you learned in Beacon, as well as why both the Archpriestess and High Priestess are alive."

Alexander swallowed, straightening again as he tried to put his thoughts in order. This would be an unpleasant experience, of *that* he was certain.

CHAPTER 31

"I see," Mazina murmured, taking a drink from the cup sitting next to her and watching them idly, with Lisa hovering in the background. The others were all sitting as if on pins and needles, and none of them looked happy, which made Alexander feel much better.

The past three hours had been a slow, methodical interrogation by Mazina, as she questioned each of them in turn about what *exactly* they'd been doing in Beacon, as well as what mistakes they'd made in the process. At no point had Mazina chastised any of them, but the look in her eyes was enough to strike fear into the heart of almost anyone, in Alexander's opinion. Not that she'd seemed particularly upset with him or Bane, since no one had expected the full extent of how Beacon would favor women.

"What do you think of the plan with the rebels, Lady Mazina?" Alexander asked, trying to hide his nervousness. "It was the best idea we could come up with that allows better chances for success."

"Mm, your plan isn't bad. Considering what you've encountered so far, it's better than attempting to act in Beacon, certainly," Mazina said calmly, setting her cup down again as she focused on Alexander and smiled. "That isn't to say that it can't be improved, however. *Unfortunately,* I've also received information from our Patrons, informing me that they can no longer intervene directly."

Alexander flinched at that, but nodded. No one in the church of Erethor and Eretha dared mention their names outside of their holiest of sanctums, not since the vast majority of other faiths tried to stomp them out at the slightest rumor of their existence. An enormous part of the reason they'd even come to Everium was because of their deities, so them not being able to intervene was… discomforting, at least to Alexander.

"Ah, forgive me if I'm speaking out of turn, but do we know why?" Bane asked, his voice a touch anxious. "It isn't the dungeon, is it?"

"No, no… I'm told that somehow Fate caught wind of things, and now they're tied up behind divine restrictions," Mazina said, shaking her head slightly as she let out a sigh. "Fools, the lot of them. Regardless, that means that any actions we take need to be carefully planned, and we need to arrange for assistance ourselves. I've brought a few items of my own to help, and I think I can summon some assistance as well. The issue will be ensuring that whoever comes *dies*."

"What would you have us do, Lady Mazina?" Umira asked, sitting forward in her chair as she continued. "While I am skilled, I'm afraid that my magics are… less effective here. The locals are unfortunately wary of mental control magics, and many of them have trained to resist them."

"Indeed. That's why I expect all of you to participate in the raid of these rebels," Mazina said, her smile vanishing as she looked at them with narrowed eyes. "You're not going to be the primary strike force, of course, not until the targets arrive. You'll help with the distractions, though. Once they *have* shown up, however… I expect you to exterminate those that have offended our Patrons. Is that clear?"

"As you wish," Erin spoke up, her voice just a *bit* nervous. That made Alexander want to smile, but instead he nodded calmly in agreement, a little relieved that he wasn't in charge anymore.

"Do you mind if I help them, milady? It's been some time

since I've gotten some proper exercise," Lisa asked, and smiling as Mazina looked at her in surprise.

For a moment the only sound was the fire crackling, and Alexander could practically feel the curious looks that Bane was giving him, but he ignored his friend for the moment. While he understood why Bane wondered about Lisa, he wasn't going to say anything about her, certainly not in front of Mazina.

"If that is what you wish to do, so be it. I will *not* be taking direct action, however. There are too many places to stoke into wars for me to get involved directly here," Mazina said at last, and looked at the group as she grinned again, her eyes glittering. "While Medaea may be one of our Patron's old foes, a war here would be far too small for it to be truly worth our while. Do what you can, then leave. I will not waste too many resources on a backwater."

Alexander nodded in understanding, inhaling slowly, then asked, relieved that he thought the conversation was coming to an end. "In that case, might we get some rest? I'm not sure if the other rebels have arrived yet, but meeting with them sooner than later seems like a good idea."

"All but you, Alexander. Lisa? Show them to their rooms and have dinner served, if you would," Mazina said, focusing on Alexander as she smiled. "Alexander and I need to discuss *exactly* what things I've brought with me, and how they can be used most effectively."

That didn't make Alexander feel any better, but he bit back any impulse to try to beg off, instead simply nodding and looking at the others as they got up. Bane chuckled and patted him on the shoulder, saying. "We'll save you something to eat, you hear? See you in a bit."

"Sure, thanks," Alexander replied dryly, watching Lisa chivy the others out of the room.

As the door closed, his gaze went back to Mazina, who studied him for a moment, a hint of a smile playing across her lips. Then she asked, "Are you still scared of me, Alexander?"

"Always," Alexander replied instantly, without even thinking about it, then paled as he realized what he'd said. Fortunately, his mother didn't seem offended, and Mazina smiled even wider at him.

"Excellent. I always *did* enjoy being feared, and you were wiser than your siblings," Mazina said, sitting forward as she set the needlepoint aside at last. The pattern on it was jagged, and a shudder ran down Alexander's spine as he recognized the symbols as those involved in a particularly nasty curse. The others had no idea just how dangerous Mazina could be, but he still remembered what had happened to his younger brother. The sight would haunt him until the day he died permanently, he suspected.

"I've done my best. It isn't as though I lacked object lessons, between you and Lisa," Alexander admitted, taking a deep breath again, then glanced at the doors, adding, "I don't think any of them realize that, though. They just know you're powerful and unforgiving."

"Quite. That's why they were chosen to come out here, as a matter of fact. I didn't want to risk those who were too useful, if possible," Mazina said lazily, glancing at the door and considering for a moment, then added, "Aside from you, of course. Based on what I've heard, however... Umira is still useful, as is Bane. Erin is expendable, so if you see a chance to push her in front of a sword, feel free."

"As you say," Alexander said, bile rising in his throat, even if he didn't really like Erin. He hoped none of them could hear what was being said. If they *did*, likely as not they'd expire shortly thereafter. Lisa might seem kind at first glance, but looks could be deceiving.

"Of course. Now, then. Based on what I've heard of the local levels of competence, we cannot be sure of these rebels succeeding, and more reinforcements may arrive than they can deal with. That being the case, I'm willing to call forth four ruiners for you, and I brought several liberated projects from artificers," Mazina said briskly, smiling broadly as she added, "You always were fond of those, and I believe the ley line disruptor will be of particular use."

"I... see. Yes, the disruptor will be useful, if we can get it into position," Alexander agreed, his thoughts beginning to whirr at last. "As for the ruiners, they *are* quite powerful, so..."

They began discussing how to use the resources Mazina had brought, and despite his misgivings, Alexander focused on making the best suggestions he could. While he wasn't the most faithful follower of their faith, he *did* prefer the thought of being destroyed last, rather than first. And that was what would happen if he angered Mazina.

CHAPTER 32

Daniel Fisher yawned as he slipped on his cloak, then adjusted his sword belt so the hilt wouldn't let much warm air out. It'd looked cold outside from the window, so he preferred to be comfortable while crossing the courtyard.

"What's taking so long?" Sina asked, poking him from behind, and Daniel yelped, squirming a little as he glanced back at her, then grinned.

Sina was a fairly typical dusk elf, with tanned skin, blue eyes, and gray hair. She also wasn't particularly pretty, which was the only reason they'd met, since attractive elves rarely ended up working with Kelvanis's legions. She hadn't been a slave for some time, though, and the shop she now owned did good business selling produce to adventurers, even if she mostly left the selling to employees these days. She had her armor and cloak on already, which made him a little chagrined.

"Sorry, I just wanted to make sure I wasn't going to lose *too* much heat out there," Daniel said, smiling and leaning in to give her a brief kiss, then opened the door and stepped outside, gasping as the cold air nipped at his ears. "Yeesh, I don't think I'm ever going to get used to how cold it gets here!"

"Suck it up, army boy," Sina replied, stepping outside as if unfazed, and he couldn't help a laugh.

"Hey! I haven't been in the army for over a year," Daniel

protested, starting across the broad square that separated them from the Adventurer's Guild. There wasn't too much snow on the ground since the guard tried to keep the streets clear, but a dusting of snow was slowly drifting down around them. "You've been hanging around Darak too much, haven't you?"

"He's fun, so why not?" Sina replied challengingly, glancing at him with a smile, and her eyes glittering just a *bit* too sharply. "Would you rather I hung out with Sayla, instead? That might make you a happier man, I suppose…"

"No, no! I didn't mean anything like that!" Daniel replied quickly, his eyes widening. "I mean, it's just… what did I do today, anyway?"

"You stole the blankets," Sina said promptly, glaring up at him, and Daniel winced.

"I'm sorry, I didn't realize that," Daniel said, bowing his head in the hopes that she'd let the subject drop. "Maybe I should get another blanket for me, instead just a pile for both of us?"

"Then how would I latch on to you for warmth in the middle of the night?" Sina demanded, pausing to glare at him as she continued. "I swear, sometimes you need…"

Sina's voice trailed off as she looked past him, and Daniel blinked, then looked toward the dungeon. His surprise grew still more as he saw a group of people near the dungeon entrance, and he gawked at them somewhat.

Albert was there, which was enough of a surprise, but beside him were the adventurers who'd mentored Daniel and his friends; Darak, Joseph, Nirath, and Penelope. Beyond them, there were another two adventurers that Daniel only vaguely recognized as some of the guild's enchanters, which startled him, since none of them were dressed like they were going to go on a delve.

"What's going on over there?" Daniel asked aloud, growing even more curious as he saw they were just standing around, looking at the mountainside. They certainly weren't looking at the dungeon entrance, which made him wonder.

"I don't know, but it's worth finding out, I think," Sina said, and a surge of relief rushed through Daniel as he realized that she'd been distracted from her annoyance with him, at least for the moment.

"Sounds good to me!" Daniel said, hurrying after her. As they drew closer, Daniel heard Penelope speak, and her tone set his teeth on edge since he'd been on the receiving end of it more than a few times. The powerfully built woman scared him when she was in a mood, which she appeared to be in now.

"Albert, when is this *event* supposed to happen?" Penelope asked crossly, the brunette's breath coming out in puffs of white as she glared at her brother. "If you're wasting my time out here, I'll shove you down a well, see if I don't."

"Sistina told me that she'd be opening the passage shortly after dawn, so either go inside and leave me alone or wait. *You're* the one who wanted to come out here, when I was just asking Darak for his help," Albert snapped, opening a circular metal device, and as he did Daniel saw a couple of lights appear above its surface. One was along the edge of the device, while the other was a tiny glowing orb that had just risen above the edge. Daniel had only seen the sundial used a couple of times, but he supposed that creating an enchanted device that didn't rely on the sun being visible was far more useful for someone like Albert, who needed to keep track of timing more precisely than he did.

"It should be interesting, and—ah, Sina, Danny! You're up early," Darak said, the dwarf turning and grinning at them as they approached. "Planning on a delve today, then?"

"That's the plan, or it was until we saw all of you," Daniel said, nodding to everyone as he asked, "Mind if I ask what's going on? Is it something that means we should stay out of the dungeon?"

"Stay out of the dungeon? Oh no, nothing like that!" Albert said, looking up and snapping his sundial closed as he grinned. "No, Sistina and I were working on the designs for a way to get up and down the mountain easier, and she's been building it for the last little while. She's supposed to open the entrance for one of them here any minute."

"An easy way to go up the mountain?" Sina asked, looking at Daniel speculatively, but she continued. "What do you mean? I know it's pretty rough for most people, but we've got pretty good endurance..."

"That doesn't help with the time, though. And I don't know about you, but less climbing is something *I* appreciate," Joseph said, running his fingers through his brown hair. "Now, if the entrance would just open so we can get on with things, I'd—"

"She's moving," Nirath interrupted, and Daniel's gaze flicked past the tall, icily beautiful elf to the mountainside.

He didn't see anything at first, aside from the entrance to the dungeon itself. The entrance was different than it'd been a few months prior, as the unassuming cave entrance had been replaced with a hall of pillars, along with a large set of double-doors at the end next to the sign with the dungeon's rules. Seeing adventurers from other regions gawk at the sign often made Daniel laugh, since Sistina was a different dungeon than any other he'd heard about. But that wasn't the point, more important was figuring out where this new entrance would be.

At that point the stone a good distance to the right of the dungeon entrance rippled, drawing Daniel's gaze, and he blinked, slightly disoriented by the sight of stone rippling like water. While he'd seen Beacon created from the mountain, the details had been largely obscured by the brilliant pillar of light at the time, so this was a little new to him. Still, moments later the stone shifted aside to reveal a deep tunnel about thirty feet wide, with several glowing stones set into its walls.

"I don't care what you say, it's always weird to see stone move like that," Darak said, crossing his arms and scowling at the entrance unhappily. "Rock isn't supposed to flow like that. Not unless it's lava, and then it's *rightly* pissed at everything."

"Perhaps, but that shows that she's ready for us. Time to check out Sistina's new lift," Albert said, taking a couple of eager steps forward.

"Lift?" Penelope asked, not moving yet, and Albert paused, looking back at the unmoving group. When he didn't say anything, Penelope spoke, exaggerated patience in her voice. "Al, either pull your head out of the clouds and tell us what to expect, or we're not going *near* that tunnel."

"It isn't—oh, fine!" Albert said, scowling as he looked back and forth between her and the enchanters, then gestured at the tunnel. "It's a steam rail, but with the engine at the top of a shaft. It has several cables attached to a carriage designed to move on the rails, effectively a room, and it *lifts* the carriage up and down, until it reaches several stopping points higher up the mountain. Does that answer the question?"

Murmurs of surprise rippled through the others, and from the way Darak's eyebrows rose, Daniel could tell that he was impressed, and the dwarf unfolded his arms as he peered down the tunnel.

"A steam rail?" Daniel asked, exchanging confused looks with Sina, who looked like she had no better idea of what that was than he did. Fortunately, Nirath took pity on them.

"You've seen or heard of minecarts?" the elven mage asked, looking at them curiously, and when they nodded she smiled and continued. "Good, this will be easy, then. In some cities, they lay tracks like those, but wider, and build steam engines to move the carts around. Think of them like the steam carriages the guild arrived in, but smaller for the most part. They're also a bit more practical, in most cases."

"There's been discussion of building them between cities, but just enough monsters or people are prone to stealing the rails that it hasn't gone anywhere. Not to mention how expensive it is to make enough rails for that," Joseph chimed in, looking at the tunnel curiously. "This sounds interesting, though. I'm not sure what to make of it."

"You won't make *anything* of it if you don't come inside," Albert replied testily, huffing a little as he turned and headed into the tunnel.

"I suppose there's nothing for it," one of the other enchanters said, shrugging as he headed toward the tunnel. "It should be interesting, at least."

"Assuming the 'carriage' doesn't fall on our heads," his companion replied waspishly, the half-elven woman looking a little cross. "I hate being asked to look at things like this."

"Then why'd you come out here?" Penelope asked, heading after her brother with a sigh.

Daniel hesitated, considering for a moment as he frowned at

the tunnel while the others headed forward. Eventually he looked at Sina and tilted his head. "What do you think? Should we make the others wait for a bit?"

"Like Eric will even be down yet; you know how he is about waking up," Sina said, and gestured forward. "Besides, why not take a look? I'm not going to step anywhere that looks dangerous, but I know Sistina well enough. She's not going to build anything she thinks is risky."

Shrugging, Daniel thought about it, then admitted, "Well, you'd know better than I would, considering how much time you spent in there. I don't see any reason not to take a look, anyway."

Sina laughed and followed the others, with Daniel not far behind her. He'd been telling the truth, but he also didn't have quite as much faith in Sistina as Sina did. Oh, she'd killed the demon queen who'd killed him, even if Albert had managed to bring him back from the dead quickly, and she'd saved Sina's life when she could have killed her… but Sistina was a *dungeon*. Daniel had only narrowly escaped death inside the halls enough times that he wasn't about to put much faith in her hands.

Not that the other adventurers seemed to agree with him. Darak and the others were far more experienced than Daniel was, and *they* seemed to think that Sistina was positively welcoming, compared to other dungeons. The one time Daniel had tried to caution them, Penelope had given him a sharp look and asked, with a tone so dry it should have turned their ale to dust, why Sistina hadn't simply dropped a golem on them and killed them outright, if that was the case. At that point he'd decided to drop the subject.

Not that she didn't have impressive structures, though, *that* much Daniel had to admit, looking at the smooth walls of the tunnel, and how the glowing orbs were all precisely embedded in the walls, with delicate carvings surrounding them. The ground was also carefully textured to give a solid grip, he noticed, and as they moved deeper, he saw the carriage that Albert had mentioned, along with a section of the floor that had been cut away and replaced with metal. The carriage really *did* look like a room, too.

The carriage was odd, with a solid steel frame around the edges, along with a steel floor and ceiling, and Daniel could just barely see the rails in the corners. There were fences on three sides, and he'd guess that it could fit three wagons if someone was careful, while in the corner was a box with a series of levers. Odder, from his perspective, was the fencing that was raised above the entrance.

"What's this, Al?" Joseph asked, stomping on the metal section of the floor that Daniel had noticed.

"Oh, that? When the lift is activated, that will lift up to form a fence," Albert replied, nodding over as he added, pointing at the fencing in the air. "That's similar; it'll drop into place to keep anyone from falling out as the cables draw the lift up to the next stop."

"That… is interesting. Hm, excellent metalwork," Darak murmured, studying the floor piece, then glancing up at Daniel as he grinned. "That's what I'm here for, to make sure all of this is solid. Apparently Sistina trusts herself, but prefers other people to double-check things."

"What happens if a cable snaps, or something like that?" Sina asked, looking up as she stepped up to the edge of the carriage. "It's a *long* way down from the top of the mountain."

"There are brakes that will latch onto the rails in that case, which should slow it to a stop if enough cables break. In addition, after Lady Diamond raised some concerns as well, Sistina decided to include enchantments to slow it to a stop if it somehow reaches the bottom third of the shaft," Albert said, and nodded at the enchanters as he added, "I checked the enchantment designs, but since I'm a bit biased, I thought I'd ask a couple of experts to take a look as well."

"And all without pay," the human man muttered.

"I never said we weren't getting paid! We're getting three silvercaps for this, so don't give me any of that," Albert retorted firmly. "You'll each get half of what one sells for, so quit your bellyaching."

Darak's head jerked up at that, and the dwarf protested. "Hey, you never said anything about that kind of payment!"

"No, because you wanted a variety of potions *and* someone to upgrade your armor enchantments. The cost of that would run you more than what they're getting paid, Darak, so we can swap you to a flat fee if you'd like," Albert replied, crouching next to the box with the levers as he studied it.

Daniel whistled softly, considering before he said. "That sounds like it's a lot of gold, considering how much you said the potion you gave me cost."

"Yeah, well, stronger armor means I'm less likely to get pounded into paste the next time I run into one of those danged constructs," Darak said, rubbing his head and frowning, then sighed as he said, "No, I think I'll keep things as they are. Thanks, Albert."

"You're welcome. And I haven't forgotten about your debt, Daniel," Albert said absently, prompting Daniel to wince.

"I've been paying it back!" Daniel protested guiltily.

"One copper at a time, yes, but you're not even halfway there," Sina pointed out, her eyes narrowed as she added, "I *still* can't believe you tried to attack a demon lord who incapacitated most of the guild!"

Before Daniel could protest more, Darak laughed, grinning as he spoke up. "Danny's nothing if not brave! Brave doesn't mean *smart*, though."

Daniel opened his mouth, then froze, trying to decide what to say as laughter rippled around the room, most of the people examining different parts of the lift. Finally, Daniel simply scowled and muttered, "Fair enough. Sina, can we go?"

"Huh? Why?" Sina asked, blinking as she gestured at the carriage. "Don't you want to see if it works?"

"Nah, I don't want to risk getting killed if it drops on us. Besides, I have a debt to pay," Daniel said in resignation, glancing at Albert as he heard the man chuckle softly.

"Have fun, Daniel, and watch your step," Penelope called out cheerfully, and he couldn't help rolling his eyes as he turned to leave.

He wasn't *really* all that upset by what the others had said, but it was a pointed reminder that he had things to do. A few moments later Sina trotted up behind him and slipped one arm through his, grinning at him.

"You really *are* brave. Dumb, sometimes, but brave. Don't let it go to your head, hm? I don't want to lose you," Sina said, her tone slightly teasing, but her eyes sparkled.

"I'll do my best, promise," Daniel said, relaxing a little more.

"Still, I have to say I'm looking forward to the next few days. I've heard there's a group of high-ranking adventurers on their way here who transferred from the Southern Adventuring Guild," Albert said idly to the others, his voice echoing down the tunnel and a note of anticipation in his voice. "They're always thinking they're superior to us, so I'm looking forward to seeing their reactions when—"

Behind Daniel and Sina there was a sudden creaking of metal, and a chorus of cursing from the room. *That* made Daniel chuckle softly.

SISTINA WISHED she could hold her breath as the gears of the lift creaked, then began turning, drawing the cables connected to the lift itself up the shaft. The wheels on each rail turned smoothly, to her relief, but she didn't let her attention waver for even a moment.

She could see inside the lift for now, but only because she hadn't retracted her domain from the lift shaft, something she planned to do once she'd decided the lifts could be used safely. That meant she should see Albert and the other adventurers on the platform, which was a motley group on the whole... but that pretty much described all adventurers, in Sistina's opinion. More importantly, when she retracted her domain, she wasn't going to abandon the rails and other major supports for the lifts, which would help her avoid rust or corrosion leading to failure. Hopefully.

The key was to see if there were any flaws, in the end, and Sistina wasn't happy that Albert had decided to risk a half dozen additional people. Oh, she didn't like him risking *himself,* for that matter, but he'd flatly refused to let her have a golem activate the lift instead. That would have been much safer for everyone but the golem, but he'd said something about not wanting a golem to try something so interesting for the first time.

So instead Sistina was watching the platform with an eagle eye, keeping an eye out for any burrs, weaknesses in the cables, or even bends in the rails. She'd done a lot of work to ensure the rails were straight, but she honestly didn't trust them to stay that way, with how much of a pain it had been for her to make them to begin with. Oh, it'd been worth the effort, as learning to turn out lengths of metal that size and consistency had helped her refine her control, but it didn't mean she wanted to do it more than necessary.

There were a few problems, for that matter, not that she suspected that those on the carriage noticed. One of the wheels was slightly out of alignment, which she fixed, and like she suspected, some of the rail had some burrs that would have increased the amount of wear on the wheels more than she liked. Even more importantly, one of the cables connecting to the platform wasn't *quite* secure enough, and that was something she needed to fix quickly. She'd made sure that there were twice as many cables to support the platform as needed, but she preferred that redundancy not be needed.

Still, in all, the test went even better than Sistina anticipated, as the gearing worked almost flawlessly, the different sections of fences raised and lowered in response to Albert's manipulation of the handles, and the steam engine at the top of the shaft puffed away, not even seeming to strain at the weight it was dealing with. On the other hand, Albert *had* said she'd overbuilt the engine.

It took several minutes for Albert to work the lift up to full speed, though, which wasn't that fast in all truth. It was still much faster than climbing the mountain by foot, of course, but the platform stopped at each of the tunnels Sistina had dug for exits farther up the mountain, though she hadn't actually opened them into the city proper yet. She didn't want people wandering in when it wasn't ready yet, after all.

Eventually they reached the top of the shaft, just a few dozen feet from the palace, and Albert stopped the lift, looking up as he spoke softly. "Alright, *that* worked like a dream. I wish all of my first attempts went that smoothly."

Thinking about the numerous problems she'd fixed, Sistina mentally glared at the man, wishing that she could communicate with others more easily in this state. She couldn't, though, so she settled for impotent fuming instead. She wasn't going to drop a rock or gear on his head just because he annoyed her, no matter *how* satisfying it might be.

"Well, aside from rattling us around a bit, that was impressive," Darak admitted, patting the wall of the carriage gently, then paused and asked, "So, do we at least get to see the top of the mountain? I don't see an exit."

"It's almost like Sistina didn't want someone wandering inside, then tripping over their own feet and falling down the shaft," Penelope said, her gaze resting on Joseph as she smiled, obviously teasing.

"Hey, I resemble that remark!" Joseph replied, pretty much on cue, and prompting a chorus of laughter from the others.

Their reaction did ease Sistina's annoyance, though, so she decided to be nice to them, and carefully eased open a narrow passage, sized for a single person for now. It had a door, but she left it open so that the light would shine down the tunnel.

"Ah! It appears that Sistina heard you, at a guess," Albert said, looking down the passage, then grinned. "Shall we? That was *far* better than climbing the mountain."

"That sounds excellent to me. Maybe I'll visit the academy while we're here," Nirath said, glancing around with the same strange smile on her face that Sistina had seen before, one which made her slightly uncomfortable.

She'd met the elf a couple of times, and she suspected that if it weren't for her having married Phynis and the Jewels, the elf might have tried courting her. Even so, she'd heard from Farris that the woman seemed to have an odd fascination with what it was like to be bound to a dungeon.

Thinking of the Jewels, Sistina decided to pull her attention away once the group started toward the end of the tunnel. She suspected that Albert would come visit soon enough, and *that* meant it was time to get out of bed.

Sistina opened her eyes to find that both of her arms were complaining *loudly* that they lacked blood flow, and she blinked, then looked downward in momentary confusion. The sight of Phynis's metallic pink hair to her right explained some of it, as did Opal's glittering orange hair on her left, each of their heads resting on her shoulders where they could obstruct her blood flow.

"Ow," Sistina said simply, blinking at them again. When she'd first woken that morning, Opal had been *next* to her, as it was the priestess's turn with Sistina, so Phynis's presence was a bit of a surprise.

"Oh, you're back!" Phynis said, looking up and grinning as she adjusted her position, while Sistina noticed she was in a gown for the day already. "What do you mean, ow?"

"Arms need blood," Sistina replied calmly, wincing as she tried to move.

"Oh, sorry! You're just nice and warm," Opal said, pulling away and yawning as she sat up, then stretched. The beautiful elf gave Sistina a satisfied smile, then asked, "Mm, is the test going well?"

"Some problems, fixed them. Minor problems," Sistina said, letting out a tiny breath of relief as Phynis reluctantly sat up, letting blood painfully tingle back into both arms again. She sat up herself as she continued, resisting the urge to rub her arms. "Albert coming to visit. Need to get ready."

"Drat. I'd hoped he'd be busy for a while… but I suppose that was too much to hope for," Phynis said, letting out a faint sigh, and Sistina arched an eyebrow at her for a moment, then smiled.

"I *do* still have to prepare the ritual for Tyria, I feel I need to point out. This was a… *minor* expense where mana was concerned, comparatively," Sistina said, feeling the need to speak more eloquently on that particular subject.

"Mm, how much of a drain will it be?" Phynis asked, frowning as she ran her fingers through her hair, trying to straighten it out. "You said it takes a lot of power, right?"

"Yes, it does. However, with the steam engines and mana condensers…" Sistina paused, considering for a few moments, then shrugged. "Perhaps half my reserve. I am doing much better than last year."

"Mm, considering what we were up against, is it wrong that I wish you'd had all of that last year instead?" Opal asked, and laughed at Sistina's wry smile. Then the priestess paused, considering for a moment before she continued. "Speaking of Tyria, do you think she's going to ask us if—"

"Please don't," Phynis interjected, her eyes widening slightly as the princess sat up quickly. "I really don't want you tempting fate where she's concerned. If she decides… well, we'll figure it out if it comes to that."

Sistina kept her mouth shut, not wanting to say the wrong thing. While she liked Tyria well enough and was *well* aware of the goddess's feelings where she was concerned, Sistina also wasn't going to ask her lovers to accept another person into their relationship. They were in charge of that, and she didn't want to give the impression of pressuring them.

Opal glanced at Sistina and gave a knowing smile, though, which made Sistina want to sigh. While she could hide her nature from most of them, Opal and Sapphire in particular were… difficult. It was hard, as she *had* been a succubus once upon a time.

On the other hand, it was also why she knew how to take advantage of Wenris's weaknesses, such as they were.

"Taking bath," Sistina announced, grabbing a robe and dress from the wardrobe.

"Ooh, I'll join you!" Opal said, and Phynis laughed in response.

"In that case, I suppose I'll go delay your guests, Sistina," Phynis said, sounding slightly amused. "Do hurry, though? I have other things to do today."

"Yes, love," Sistina replied, smiling back at her, then paused for a moment to consider before adding, "Thank you."

"You're welcome. Now *go*," Phynis said, and Sistina laughed, then headed for the door.

CHAPTER 33

"Who the hell are you?" Kevin snarled, his dagger practically appearing in his hand, almost as suddenly as the masked man had appeared in the room.

They'd only reached Westgate the previous night, which was far later than Kevin would have preferred, but it'd been unavoidable with the snows slowing them down. Worse, the snow made it far easier to track Bran's soldiers, and even Kevin's people had been forced to split up as well. During that time a few of his people had vanished, Kevin had noticed, and he was grimly certain that they'd decided to cut their losses, which was... aggravating. Not unexpected, but unfortunate in the extreme. He just hoped the ones who were going to distract Slaid Damrung's soldiers wouldn't do the same.

Of course, most of their troops were hidden in a few encampments outside the city. They couldn't easily smuggle most of them into the city, and only how difficult it was to get guards good descriptions of those wanted in Kelvanis made it possible for any of them to enter.

On the other hand, anyone simply *appearing* in the center of their hideout set Kevin's teeth on edge, as his wards should have stopped them from doing that, or at least warned him that they were coming. Kevin mentally reached for his wards and froze as he realized that they'd been almost completely destroyed without him noticing.

In that moment, Bran had drawn his sword and a half dozen other assassins had their weapons out as well. The man smiled in response, his mask covering the upper half of his face, and he casually looked around before speaking, his voice lazy. "If you really want to draw the city guard down on yourselves, please, go ahead and attack. I'd enjoy killing a few of you before letting you destroy yourselves."

Everyone froze at that, as if unsure of what to do, and the man let out a soft laugh, one that angered Kevin a little. He *hated* people like that, who took pleasure in flaunting their power over others. It was part of why he'd become an assassin to begin with.

"Who are you?" Bran asked, his voice surprisingly calm as he watched the intruder warily.

"Oh, come now. You wouldn't tell me who you were if you intruded, so why would I tell you?" the intruder scolded, shaking his head. "No, I'm sure you have much better questions than *that*."

Kevin growled despite himself, but paused and let Bran speak, since the man seemed to be calmer than Kevin was.

"Fine, then. Why are you here?" Bran asked, his eyes narrowing slightly as he looked at the man.

"That's quite simple! I'm here to offer you a good deal of assistance in your endeavor. You see, the people who contacted you want to be sure of your success, so they decided that other assistance was in order," the man said, grinning at them, the tinted lenses of his mask glittering in the lamplight. "The question is whether or not you're willing to accept it."

"What sort of help?" Kevin asked, trying to get a read on the man in front of him. He could sense magic around the intruder, but the sensation was oddly muddled, as if something was interfering with his senses. That made a certain amount of sense, and the man *was* quite confident in a situation that Kevin considered unfavorable.

"Help blowing open the gates to the city for your allies and dealing with defenders, of course," the man said, smirking in amusement. "We also can ensure that after the target arrives, no one else will be able to teleport in for at least an hour. It's just a matter of whether you're willing to accept our aid or not."

"You expect us to simply take your word for that? How do you expect to deal with the defenders?" Bran asked warily.

"I'm *so* glad you asked!" the man said, and snapped his fingers, at which point Kevin's heart almost stopped.

A creature appeared in the center of the room, and the sight of it struck fear into the heart of *anyone,* in Kevin's opinion. Even hunched over, the monster was eight feet tall, almost brushing the rafters, and instead of a single head it had three serpentine necks with enormous fanged maws on them, each with glittering red eyes. Two hulking arms nearly dragged on the floor, with claws that could easily disembowel a horse, and the entire creature was covered in a thick, sickly green exoskeleton that glistened horribly in the light. Even worse, Kevin knew what the creature was, and knew this was it when it was suppressing its strength.

"What in all—" Bran demanded, taking a step back as a serpentine tongue flicked out of the central mouth, causing a sound almost like a whip cracking which prompted everyone to shrink back slightly.

"Shh, don't upset him. I'd hate for him to eat one of your men to soothe his feelings," the intruder said, grinning even more, now. "*This* is a ruiner. I have four of them in total, and they can destroy virtually anything, though they aren't invulnerable. I'd happily pit them against a set of golems, however, which is why I believe they'll be of use to you."

"That..." Kevin began, then swallowed, suddenly understanding why the man was so confident. Even if they outnumbered the monster by a large margin, Kevin's instincts were finely honed, and even if he didn't recognize the danger, his instincts were telling him to get the hell out of there. He controlled himself as he forced himself to finish. "You're the ones who contacted us to come here, aren't you? *They* are the only ones who create things like that."

He deliberately didn't say Erethor and Eretha's names, as he preferred not to draw the attention of the gods of destruction. Beyond that, what bits and pieces he'd heard of their cult made him wary of interacting with them, or at least inclined him to try to avoid upsetting them.

The man simply laughed, ignoring Kevin as he focused on Bran, smiling as he spoke warmly. "Now, Adjudicator, I believe I've answered your question. These give me the confidence that I require to help you, at a minimum. I'm not going to take care of everything for you, mind, but destroying the gates to let your soldiers in will be *effortless* for him."

Bran glanced at Kevin, still pale, but Kevin could see the man make his decision. Not that Kevin blamed him for it, considering the naked threat standing in the middle of their hideout, and how difficult things were going to be as it was. Any assistance would be incredibly helpful, let alone something as powerful as this ruiner appeared to be.

"I… will accept your offer, then," Bran said, his voice betraying a hint of reluctance. "I don't know why you're offering, but—"

"It doesn't matter *why* we're doing this, just that we are," the man interrupted again, obviously not caring what Bran had to say. "The ruiners will attack at dawn the day after tomorrow. *You* figure out what you're doing when they do. The targets will be the temple of Tyria, the western gate, the garrison, and the city market. At least until reinforcements arrive, then they're going to focus on the teleportation platform."

With that the man swirled his cloak, and he and the ruiner vanished in a pop of imploding air, leaving the room mostly empty. For a moment no one moved, then one of the Kelvanis soldiers collapsed, speaking in an unsteady voice. "What in all the gods was that thing?"

"That's an excellent question," Bran said, slowly relaxing and sheathing his sword as he scowled at Kevin. "For that matter, how did they get in here? I thought you said this place was safe!"

"It *was* safe, but they ripped my wards apart before they could even warn me they were coming," Kevin shot back, glowering at Bran in return. "If you think that *you're* unhappy, you have no idea just how much that upsets me."

"Huh," Bran said, looking around the room for a moment,

then sighed as he spoke to his men. "Come on, clean up already. It isn't like we have anywhere else to go, and they're gone now."

The others hesitated, and Kevin gave his own people a nod, sheathing his dagger as he watched them start moving, a bit more reluctantly than Bran's had. He might lose more people over this, he knew, but there wasn't much to be done about it. Bran approached him after a moment, though, and the man's voice was soft when he spoke.

"Who *were* they, then? You seemed to figure it out, but didn't say anything," Bran said, looking a touch upset at this point. "I'm getting tired of being kept in the dark, Kevin."

"I don't *know* who they are, but..." Kevin hesitated for a moment, then replied, barely loud enough for Bran to hear. "I *think* they're the cult of the Destroyers."

Bran audibly choked, staring at Kevin in a touch of horror, and even more fear. Then he swallowed, closing his eyes as he inhaled deeply, then let the breath out. Eventually he murmured, "I... I see. Well, we don't have any other choices, now do we?"

Kevin considered that briefly, then shook his head. "No, we don't. If they tracked us here so easily, without being noticed... there's nowhere we can go without them being able to track us down."

"Then let's make plans. Two days isn't nearly enough for my peace of mind, but it's what we have," Bran said, letting out a soft sigh as he looked at their people and grimaced. "This had better be worth it."

"Agreed," Kevin said, starting toward the table in the corner. At least their maps of the city were up to date.

LISA SMILED and nodded slightly in approval, the bowl of water rippling in front of her as it showed Bran and Kevin. It had also carried their words to them, which told them enough, and Alexander relaxed a little at the look of approval on Mazina's face.

He'd never gone to their hideout, despite speaking to them; instead Lisa had projected an illusion of him. The ruiner *had* gone there, though, so his threats hadn't been idle, but more importantly, the rebels were going to be cooperating, which was rather important.

"Excellent. It appears things are going to go as planned," Mazina said, nodding in satisfaction, then looked up, considering for a moment, then pointed at Umira. "You are going to help cause chaos in the market. Ensure there's a lot of death and destruction. Bane, your target is the gates. While the ruiner can destroy them easily, it's not the most intelligent creature in the world, and might attack the people we're helping. Erin, you're to assist the one attacking the garrison, and attempt to take out their commanders."

She stopped there, and after a moment Alexander cleared his throat, then asked, "I presume that means I'll be helping with attacking the temple, then?"

"That's right," Mazina said, looking at Lisa as she smiled. "Lisa will keep an eye on the teleportation platform and activate the disruptor once the targets have arrived, then assist in the attack. If you make mistakes, you'll get yourselves killed, and the gods will *not* be pleased with you."

"As you say, Lady Mazina," Bane said, bowing deeply, and after an instant of hesitation, the others followed suit.

"I'll certainly do my best!" Umira said brightly.

"Indeed," Erin murmured, a bright glint to her eyes as she fingered her knife.

Alexander suppressed a sigh, glancing at the bowl as he bowed his head, speaking calmly. "The gods' will be done."

He wasn't looking forward to this.

CHAPTER 34

Deep within Sistina's domain, she could sense the shadows growing, almost seething with power. It was close to the point where the academy had once rested, and she'd been keeping an eye on the spot for some time.

It was probably a darkness-aligned node, she'd realized some time ago, and that pleased her, since at present she only had air, earth, fire, and water nodes inside her domain. Oh, Sistina knew that having more than one node in close proximity to the others was unusual beyond belief, but based on some ancient, fragmented memories, she believed that such was natural for the world tree, and each node gave her significant advantages when it came to using magic.

Still, the shadows hadn't coalesced into a node in the past two months, so she'd given up on actively watching them, and instead focused on things she could control. In particular, Sistina was working on the delicate spell form that Tyria had requested. Looking at each inch of the metal circle carefully, she tweaked the runes slightly as she considered the power levels involved.

Mana was ephemeral, but many people underestimated how destructive it could be, which was why control was paramount, in Sistina's opinion. The amount of mana it would take to alter a goddess was *immense*, and that was why she'd been working so carefully the last couple of days. Getting Tyria's appearance to exactly what she'd been shown... that took a bit more work, but not nearly as much. The simple truth was that the more detailed the desired result, the more complex the spell would be.

The circle she'd made was forged of adamantine, which had been difficult to find, even for Sistina. While she could transmute materials into other types, the greater the change, the more mana it took, so she'd first scrounged through her domain, scavenging ancient weapons that'd been lost, and when that had been insufficient, she'd turned some of the other metals into adamantine as well.

Once formed into a circle, Sistina had started on the runes themselves, and *those* had to be flawless. If she made a mistake, the mana infused into the circle would escape, and she'd *really* prefer avoiding that, since it very well might destroy her cavern. Not that she was telling anyone *else* that. It really was a simple task... just a finicky one.

So Sistina continued with what she was doing, mentally humming softly to herself as she carried out the enjoyable task, occasionally glancing toward the forming node idly. There was little she enjoyed more than performing magical research, in *any* of her lives.

"YOU HAVE *how* much in the treasury?" Nadis demanded, looking up in shock from the document, her jaw almost hanging open.

"You can read the page as well as I can," Elissa replied, frowning down at the document in front of her as she tapped her fingers on the table slowly. "The question is, where did it come from? We didn't have a *tenth* of this when I left Kelvanath."

"Ah, according to what I've seen in some of these documents, it appears that some of the slaves we helped were former nobility," Roxanne said, examining a page from a rather large stack, her eyes almost glazed over. "Um, Ollie? I think you have the one mentioning the bequests."

"Oh, really?" Ollie said, quickly shuffling through them, then paused, whistling under his breath. "That would do it! It appears that the adjudicators claimed the lands of numerous nobles who opposed Ulvian, and used them to make fairly hefty profits. They took some of their wealth with them when they fled, but King Damrung has been trying to return properties to the freed slaves over the past few months. Those we've helped have donated significant amounts, it appears… and most of them have requested that we use the funds to help former slaves as well."

A ripple of relief ran through Nadis at the explanation, because she couldn't fathom how Tyria's church could possibly have come up with a treasury like the one she was seeing legitimately, not in less than a year. While the church of Medaea was somewhat wealthy, they had a great number of expenses as well, and their treasury was only a quarter of the size that Elissa's currently was.

"I understand. I was… a touch shocked, I'll admit. I couldn't guess how you got something like that in less than a year, with all the property that your church has been acquiring and renovating," Nadis admitted, letting out a breath of relief.

"Mm, a large part of that was simply Ulvian handing property over or funding us directly, but donations wouldn't have brought us to this point, not even close," Elissa admitted, her unease fading as Nadis watched. "As for the requests… I think that for the time being, it's best to keep the finances of the churches separate, Nadis. A gradual merger seems to be better. That said, I *do* want to honor these bequests, and I know there are a great number of former slaves who've ended up in poverty or worse. Kelvanis is trying to make reparations, but that takes time and funds, at a time that they're still tracking down Kelvanis's rebels. The least we can do is help them get back on their feet while the king gets his house back in order."

"That seems like a good idea to me, though it *does* bring up another question," Nadis said, frowning as she paused, then corrected herself. "Two questions, really. We can discuss the exact details of the gradual merger in a minute. The problem is Beacon and Sifaren."

"Oh?" Elissa asked, her eyebrows rising as she glanced

toward Diamond and Ruby, and Ruby smiled slightly. "Why would they be problems?"

"It isn't anything personal, Diamond, but Beacon has an enormous number of former slaves at this point, but I don't know that Lirisel is equipped to deal with determining their needs or distributing aid to all of them," Nadis said, looking at Diamond, and the woman laughed in response.

"Oh, I don't blame you in the slightest! The problem is that the only member of the temple who was good with administration is Ruby," Diamond said, nodding to the other woman, who spoke up quickly.

"Also, if you think I want to get sucked back into something *that* big, you'd be wrong," Ruby added, shaking her head. "It's bad enough that Phynis and Isana come to me for advice on some things. No, you're going to need to find someone else to help her."

Elissa raised a finger, drawing Nadis's attention.

"If I may?" Elissa asked, and paused to make sure Nadis agreed before she continued. "A possibility I see is that you could transfer one or more of your priesthood here to assist Lirisel, and specifically to make sure that the needs of former slaves are determined properly. I would be happy to send one of my own, perhaps even leaving Ollie or Roxanne here, who would determine how funds are released. If our representatives have disagreements, they can send letters to us to figure out whether one side is being unreasonable or not."

"Mm… that seems reasonable," Nadis agreed, glancing at Felicia and Miriselle, who were also going through documents.

One of them might work, she imagined, but she also might be better served by drawing from one of the other factions of the church, to help soothe their fears where Tyria's church was concerned.

"What was your other concern, Archpriestess?" Miriselle asked, setting a document aside in one of the piles. Nadis was honestly astounded that Elissa had agreed to let her people go over them as well, but it *did* help foster more trust. "You said something about Sifaren."

"Sifaren, yes," Nadis said, focusing once more as she

hesitated, then admitted, "The faith has never been as strong among the dusk elves. It's always been said that the light is dearer to dawn elves, so Medaea's faith wasn't strong there to begin with. Now... now it's even weaker than it was, and the church doesn't have a single high priestess who oversees the region anymore. The last one we had was before the war with Kelvanis entirely, and I know there are plenty of former slaves in their territory."

"Ah, *that* is a major concern," Elissa said, her expression growing more pensive as she sat back in her chair and tapped her fingers on the table again. "I'm afraid we don't have the best of relations with Sifaren, which is unsurprising. Tyria's attack there didn't help, even if many of those who were freed see us more favorably. It would be significantly more difficult to get aid to those in Sifaren... which is a point I should have realized. Thank you for bringing it up, but do you have any ideas on how it could be addressed?"

"Well, one possibility is with the assistance of the Jewels and Beacon. While neither of us have much influence..." Nadis began, relaxing a little more as she spoke.

Things were going well, and the rumblings of dissatisfaction from Yisara had grown a little quieter, which filled her with hope.

CHAPTER 35

"Damned backwaters. What possessed the dungeon to form all the way out *here*?" Adrian the Black muttered, scowling as he looked around unhappily.

He had to admit that Westgate had a certain rustic charm to it, particularly with the variety of building styles that made up the city, but it was so much less convenient than most of the other cities that he'd traveled through that it chafed, and even more that there wasn't reliable transportation to Beacon yet. He could hardly believe that they'd run out of stagecoaches and were waiting for some of them to come back. It would be faster for them to *walk* to the new city, which was what they were planning to do.

"You know dungeons, though. They're all weird… though the tales about this one are weirder than most," Kaylen replied, the elf chuckling as he smiled. "From the sounds of things, it *might* even prove to be something of a challenge. Possibly even a good way to prepare for the Great Labyrinth."

"I'll believe it when I see it," Harriet muttered, then frowned as she nodded ahead of them. "Hey, you see that, too?"

At the half-elf's gesture, Adrian looked forward, then scowled even more. The city gates were open, but they were also practically blocked by a large caravan, and he could see a lot of people outside. While the gates were wide, squeezing through the mess wouldn't be pleasant in the slightest, and he let out an aggravated sigh, glancing back toward the horizon, where the sun hadn't made its presence known yet.

"Why does everything feel like it's conspiring against us today?" he asked, raising his gaze to the sky. "I just want to get to the damned *dungeon*!"

"Calm down, sometimes things like this happen," Clarissa chimed in softly, the priestess's voice soothing, and the human nodded to the side. "Look, there's a bakery over there. Why don't we grab some fresh bread or something while we wait for the gates to clear?"

"Um, well..." Adrian hesitated, looking toward the bakery, its nature mostly apparent due to the signboard with a stylized bread loaf sketched on it, along with the scent of baked bread wafting into the street. The smell *was* somewhat enticing, after the abject failure that had been their breakfast at the inn.

"I agree with her. I told you that inn didn't look promising to begin with, even if the driver recommended it," Kaylen said, shuddering as he added, "I had no idea anyone could *do* that to flapjacks."

"They probably give the driver a cut for any guests," Adrian said, letting out another sigh, then nodded. "Fine, fine... we may as well get something decent out of this. Though if the mess is still there when we're done, I say we push through."

Harriet nodded in agreement as they headed for the bakery, and as they did so, Adrian took a moment to wonder what the owner would think of four heavily armed adventurers barging in. The thought brought him a moment of amusement, at least, and he grinned, then paused as he sniffed again.

"How in the blazes do they have *cherry tarts* at this time of year?" Adrian demanded, picking up the pace suddenly at the smell of his favorite dessert, to the laughter of his companions.

Beatrice yawned, taking a moment to stretch before she went back to work, sweeping the temple steps vigorously as she tried to ignore how the cold was nipping at her nose, almost like it was teasing her for being out so early. At least her cap was keeping her ears warm, and even if it somewhat muffled sound, that was a small price to pay for the comfort it provided.

A part of Beatrice wondered what would become of the temple, from the comments that the priests and priestesses had made about the negotiations that were occurring in Beacon. They didn't seem *too* worried that something bad would happen to it, but they were concerned that the faithful might not take it well when the churches merged. For her part, Beatrice doubted that would cause many problems, after speaking with many of the people who came to the temple.

The priests often dealt with the major injuries or diseases that the faithful had contracted, but they didn't listen to all the concerns the way that Beatrice did. The faithful tended to confide about their problems to the acolytes in a huge amount of detail, which was why she knew that most of them had been somewhat relieved to know that Tyria and Medaea were the same person. Oh, some of them had been worried, but the idea that Tyria was more benevolent than they might have feared comforted many, while the fact she was willing to defend them made most of the people she'd spoken with happier.

Looking up at the horizon slowly brightening, Beatrice smiled and murmured, "It's going to be a good day."

"ARE YOU SURE ABOUT THIS, SIR?" Ryan asked, his voice almost inaudible, and Kevin resisted the urge to sigh.

"Of course not. I just don't see much of a choice, aside from abandoning any chance of rebuilding our guild in another country. If we just go somewhere else, I doubt the locals are going to take kindly to us setting up shop," Kevin replied, his gaze fixed on the garrison's gates. "They'd rip us apart, or force us to join *their* organization, and I really don't feel like being at the bottom of the heap again."

"True enough," Ryan admitted, and fell silent, which Kevin appreciated.

It'd been hard to find a good vantage point where they

wouldn't be spotted, but Kevin had learned that the owner of this shop was out of town, so they'd taken up residence in the upper floor. Still, that also meant that any movement would likely be easier for the guards to spot, which was why he didn't want to talk.

The sun was about to rise, Kevin knew, and his jaw tightened slightly, wondering if the ruiners would actually show up. He expected they would, but there was always the chance that they'd been lied to. Bran was waiting near the gates to rendezvous with his soldiers, while those who'd entered the city already were near the old manor grounds, ready to ambush the priestesses when they hopefully arrived.

Now the only thing to do was wait, and worry. Kevin *hated* not being in control.

One moment everything was calm, as people slowly went about starting their day. The market hadn't really gotten started for the day, with a few merchants open and others just setting up, while the first customers were beginning to browse what they had available, and the handful of outdoor stalls still stubbornly open were huddled in their tents.

The next moment a high-pitched, multitoned screech split the air as the ruiner appeared in the middle of the marketplace, its heads at full extension as they emitted their bone-piercing wail. All around it the air shuddered and warped, as the stones beneath its very feet began to crack and shatter, while a nearby tent began rapidly rotting and decaying.

Umira watched it arrive, feeling completely detached from fear or other emotions as she studied the creature for an instant. Normally she'd be somewhat afraid of the creature, that much she admitted to herself, but after spending a couple of days in the same building with them, she'd decided to adjust her mind a little further. It meant she couldn't really take pleasure in watching the destruction that they were causing, but it also meant she wouldn't be going catatonic, either. That was rather important, in her opinion.

Instead she watched in fascination as the ruiner ripped a sign off a nearby building, post and all, and threw it at a screaming, panicked horse. Then a tongue shot out of its left head, snagging an unfortunate elf, and dragged the screaming woman back to it. When it started swallowing the woman whole, though, Umira decided that it was quite enough, as somehow that was making her queasy even after all her adjustments to her mind.

Shrugging, Umira focused instead on casting a spell, deciding to take the simplest, easiest route she could manage. As she spoke the final words, she smiled and whispered. "Panic and run."

The spell rippled outward from her hands, carrying her suggestion with it. Considering what the people in the streets had just seen, it didn't surprise her when the magic took effect almost effortlessly.

People screamed, panicked, and began running every direction, just as the ruiner began ripping through the nearest buildings, letting out more of its screeches.

Umira considered briefly, then realized that *not* fleeing might be obvious, so she calmly turned and started down the alleyway, humming to herself as she heard the front of one shop begin creaking, then collapsed.

"What in the—" Alissa demanded, then stopped, barely out of her office as her eyes widened in shock.

As the new commander of Westgate's garrison, Alissa had managed to deal with an immense amount of the neglect and damage throughout the compound over the last several weeks, something that had made her proud, as had the discipline she'd managed to instill into the soldiers in that time.

The sight before her didn't reflect either of those things, though. The gate had shattered along the left side and was hanging half-open, while the left half of the gatehouse was crumbling where something had smashed entirely through it. As Alissa watched a soldier's sword struck the horrific monster standing in the courtyard and *disintegrated*, like it'd rusted away in seconds, and the creature casually backhanded the man into a wall while it finished swallowing another of her soldiers.

"Shit!" Alissa swore, then yelled, "Everyone, keep your distance! Magi, blast it!"

The next moment Alissa darted back into her office, thanking the heavens that she'd asked Sistina to give her something to deal with powerful demons if Kelvanis had gotten too desperate, and her eyes lit on the bow hanging on the wall, along with the five glimmering arrows in the quiver beneath it.

Just as she was about to take the bow, Alissa felt something wrong and dodged to the side. A knife lanced through the air where she'd been an instant before, slamming into the wall and cutting deep into the wood. The next moment the knife slid out of the wall, retracting back into the hand of the woman who'd just thrown it.

Alissa's sword was already in her hand, drawn without her even thinking about it, and she scowled as she took in the appearance of the woman in an instant. The plain, human brunette wouldn't have been out of place anywhere in the city, with simple brown eyes and her hair in a braid down to the middle of her back. The things that were unusual were the dark leather armor with an odd sheen to it, betraying magic to help the wearer blend into the background, the wicked daggers in each of her hands, and the sadistic grin on her face.

"Why'd you dodge? It would have made this *much* quicker," the woman said, grinning as she added, "It's time for you to die, elf!"

"Why do I always seem to get the crazy ones?" Alissa muttered, having a sudden flashback to Ulvian Sorvos, then she snorted derisively. Compared to him, the woman in front of her was like a clown. On the other hand, how she felt must have shown on her face, as the woman's face darkened with anger, then she lunged forward as the sounds of explosions echoed from outside.

Alissa resisted the urge to laugh as she dodged the first stab, brandishing her sword as she focused on her opponent. She needed to deal with her quickly, before the monster killed too many of her soldiers.

CHAPTER 36

The crashing sound and screams distracted Adrian from the utter bliss of the cherry tart, and he blinked, then looked toward the door, which Clarissa was already opening. The high-pitched wail sent a shiver down his spine, though, and it almost ruined the flavor for him, which did *not* make Adrian happy.

The baker had explained that they'd been importing fresh fruit from Beacon over the past few weeks, since the city somehow was able to keep growing produce year-round, something which made Adrian happier than he had been initially, and also made the delay well worth his time. The sound of boots and horses screaming wasn't pleasant, though.

"Ah, we have a problem," Clarissa said, her voice unusually tense. "There's a ruiner attacking the gates."

"A what?" the baker asked, the portly elf paling suddenly.

"Hells, what's one of those doing here?" Kaylen demanded, almost dropping his handkerchief as he fumbled out his staff. "And why is it that *every* time there's a disaster in a city, it's when we're visiting?"

"Damn it all, this day is just getting better and better. Come on, let's deal with the problem," Adrian growled, popping the last of his tart into his mouth, then pulled on his gauntlets as he stepped outside.

All around him people were rushing into the city in a stream away from the gates, and as they passed Adrian frowned, because nowhere *near* all of the people he was seeing looked as panicked as he might have expected, and a lot of them were wearing leather armor... and had weapons. Even stranger, the majority of them were humans, when he'd seen mostly elves in Westgate so far.

Still, he only had a moment for the distraction, and he swallowed a curse as he saw the gates, which had been knocked back when a wagon had been thrown into them. The ruiner was busy tearing into the guards, and Adrian *was* impressed at their bravery, since the majority of guards he'd known would have run at the sight of the beast. Unfortunately, he *also* knew that the vast majority of guards would be completely useless against a ruiner, which rather spoiled the effect.

"Storm, heed my call," Adrian murmured, raising his right hand, and his mana surged in response, a lightning bolt descending from the heavens to land in his hand, taking the shape of a sword, though one formed of pure lighting. Just to be sure, he added, "Harriet, care to get its attention?"

The half-elf didn't respond verbally, instead putting two arrows to her bowstring and firing almost before he finished speaking. The arrows ignited with a dull red flame in midflight, spreading out ever so slightly as they lanced across the street unerringly.

Just as the ruiner opened its left mouth to eat one of the soldiers, the man hacking at it frantically with a rapidly disintegrating sword, Harriet's arrows arrived. One severed its tongue on its way into the creature's gullet, while the other punched straight into one of its tiny eyes on the right head. The monster screamed in pain, ignoring the man who fell to the ground as it spun to face Adrian and the others, its mouths snapping shut and five eyes glaring at them murderously as blue ichor dripped from the arrow, which quickly disintegrated as well.

"...holy light, descend on us and protect us from the shadows," Clarissa murmured, and a soft white glow enveloped

Adrian and the others, shielding them from the worst effects the demon could throw at them.

"Come on, ugly. You're blocking our path, *and* interrupted my breakfast," Adrian said, beckoning the ruiner toward him with his free hand, grinning.

The creature screeched and charged, and as it did Kaylen whispered the words of a spell, his gestures drawing glowing lines in the air. Adrian didn't wait to see it, though, instead rushing forward to meet the monster in battle.

If nothing else, it *would* help him work off some of his frustration, even if he wondered why such a powerful demon was in the area.

~

"THE HELLS?" Bane demanded, flinching backward as a torrent of fire and lightning ripped upward in a pillar, looking on in shock. His mouth was somewhat agape as he watched the quartet attack the ruiner.

The group was an odd one, with a dark-haired human man fighting the ruiner in close combat, his clothing thick, but not quite obscuring the glittering armor beneath its warm folds. More vivid was the longsword of solidified lightning that was cutting gashes in the ruiner's exoskeleton as it was driven backward.

There was a tall, white-robed human woman near the back, but the symbols along the hem of her robes burned with fire that discomforted Bane, while the silver staff in her hand was topped with a glowing sapphire. Next to the blonde woman was a red-haired elven man with a black staff in one hand, who wore light chain beneath his clothing, and he also had a sword at his side. Not that it mattered much, with how the man was creating runes in midair seemingly effortlessly, and he was the one who'd dropped the torrent of magic on the ruiner.

Last was a half-elven woman in leather armor, and whose aim was so good it was unbelievable. The brunette didn't say much, but Bane hadn't seen her miss even *once* in over a dozen shots, which was eerie as hell. The ruiner was taking a *lot* of damage, and Bane considered, then decided against trying to assist it.

"I was told to help the soldiers get into the city, and keep the ruiner from attacking them, that's all," Bane muttered to himself, glancing at the people who'd run into the city after the demon attacked. Sure, it was a little suspicious that they'd run *past* the creature to get into the city, but he doubted that the soldiers on duty had the presence of mind to notice that under the circumstances.

For his part, he hoped that the others were doing better than him, since he had no idea where the four mauling the ruiner had come from.

BEATRICE MUFFLED a scream as the temple rocked again, the doors shuddering and cracking under the impact of the beast against them, causing dust to sift down from the ceiling. Beside her, a half dozen priests and priestesses were standing pale-faced, their arms outstretched as they poured glowing purple flames onto the door, reinforcing it and hopefully damaging the monster that was attacking the temple.

The appearance of the creature in the square outside had shocked Beatrice, and it was only by the grace of Tyria that she'd managed to get through the doors of the temple before it caught her, as it's tongue had glanced off the statue she'd partially been behind, spoiling its aim. Even so, she'd barely managed to bar the doors before it had slammed into them, cracking the enchanted barrier with its first hit. The screams of those who'd been outside had wrenched at her heart, because they'd mostly been just random citizens who'd been in the wrong place at the wrong time. There was nothing Beatrice could do, though. She wasn't a mage, and had no training in battle. Her only skills were at comforting others and mundane healing, nothing more.

She *could* pray, though, and Beatrice closed her eyes, taking a deep breath, then began murmuring, "Goddess, hear my prayer. May thy flame guard us from the evils at the gate, and shelter us if it falls. May I have the courage to face what comes…"

Another impact shook the door while she prayed, but Beatrice ignored it, hoping against all expectations for salvation.

~

TYRIA'S EYES snapped open as the whisper of a prayer reached her, only one of many, but distinct despite that. She'd been contemplating what she'd heard from the Immortal Empress, trying to decide what she should, or *could* do, when the prayers arrived. There weren't a lot, but it was more than enough for her to realize something terrible was happening in Westgate, and that her temple was under attack. For a bare moment Tyria almost took flight, but the warning from Fate stopped her, and she hesitated, her thoughts racing.

"Zenith!" Tyria snapped out, her magic surging as she reached across the worlds for her servant and *pulled* the angel to her. The world rippled in response, and suddenly the angel joined Tyria, looking startled as she appeared over Beacon as well.

"My Lady?" Zenith asked questioningly, a faint tremble to her voice. "Is something wrong?"

"The temple in Westgate is under attack, and the faithful have called for aid," Tyria said, very precisely choosing how she was responding, trying to avoid angering Fate in the process. "I would like you to go try to shelter them. I don't know what you'll face, so I will not require you to go."

Zenith blinked, then smiled and nodded, speaking quickly. "Your will be done, My Lady!"

The angel shot off into the distance, and Tyria smiled as she headed for the horizon and the sun that was beginning to rise. She'd only responded to a prayer, so Fate really couldn't fault her for that. Nor would he be able to blame her if Sistina happened to overhear, which she likely had.

Tyria hoped so, at least.

CHAPTER 37

"Huh?" Diamond murmured, blinking as Sistina sat up abruptly and got out of the bed, racing toward the wardrobe. "'stina?"

"Westgate under attack," Sistina replied shortly, her voice cold and precise. "Overheard Tyria. Need to get help."

"What?" Diamond demanded, shock stripping away any remaining sleepiness, and she shot upward, swaying and a bit light-headed as she asked, "What happened?"

"Don't know. No reports yet," Sistina replied, glancing at Diamond for a moment, then asked, "Wake the others?"

"Of course!" Diamond replied, and she quickly pulled herself out of bed, marshalling her mana as she prepared to send a message to the other Jewels to wake them quickly.

Before she even finished or got out of bed, Sistina was already gone.

~

"What in the world? What's going on?" Torkal asked, standing up and looking out the window, Diane just behind him. They'd gotten up to attend the morning services at the temple, so the distinct pounding sounds were a bit startling, and she looked outside only to blink at the unexpected sight.

Outside were dozens of steel-skinned golems, marching toward the palace. She didn't know what they were doing, but the sight made her nervous, since the last time she'd seen so many of the golems in one place was before Irethiel invaded.

"I'm not sure, but that doesn't look like a good sign. Maybe something happened at the palace?" Diane said, her tone questioning, since she doubted that something would happen there, of all places.

Of course, her curiosity grew still more as a couple of messengers rushed past, heading down the street at a breakneck pace.

~

"THAT'S ODD," Wenris murmured, sitting in her chair idly, a bit curious about what she was seeing.

It'd only been a few minutes since she'd felt Tyria reach across the worlds to summon an angel, who'd streaked across the sky to the east a few moments later. Now she was hearing a lot of movement, and she found herself curious. Not curious enough to get up, but she *was* rather intrigued.

"Ah, well," Wenris said, shrugging as she went back to her schemes. She'd finally figured out where the noble bothering Phynis tended to hang out during the days, and she wanted to deal with young lord Nocris. The better Phynis felt about her, the more freedom she'd have in Beacon, after all.

~

ALISSA SIDESTEPPED ANOTHER THRUST, and *this* time the woman had finally gotten frustrated and overextended herself, something which she wasn't going to let pass, not with the screams she heard from outside.

Slipping under the woman's guard, Alissa took ruthless advantage as her sword cut deep into her opponent's shoulder. The brunette quickly staggered backward, but as she did Alissa whipped her sword around, hamstringing her and cutting the artery in her leg in the same movement, then took a quick step back.

"Wha—no, how can you be so fast?!" the woman demanded angrily, dropping her dagger as she tried to stem the bleeding, though she wasn't having much luck.

Alissa didn't reply, instead lashing out with her blade, the tip cutting the woman's throat, which should lead to her death much more quickly, she hoped. Only then did she comment coldly. "You should try living in a dungeon for about a year, it does wonders for strength and speed alike. Now, to deal with your *friend*."

She wiped her sword clean and sheathed it, hoping not too much residue would build up inside the sheath. She'd clean it properly later, but Alissa quickly grabbed her bow and the arrows, rushing out the door to take a look around the courtyard again, and the sight made her blanch.

Over two dozen soldiers were down, most of them likely dead, and the monster looked barely injured. The barracks was creaking, on the verge of collapse, while there were multiple craters across the ground where spells had landed. Worse, she was fairly sure that several of her magi had vanished, which gave her a good idea of where they'd gone. How the monster had *fit* them into its gullet was another question, but one she didn't really want an answer to.

Some people would have yelled at the creature, Alissa knew, but she wasn't them. She preferred to kill her opponents quickly and ruthlessly, so she nocked an arrow and took aim, murmuring softly, "Sistina, I hope this works."

She loosed the arrow, and as it left the string the arrow lit up, shining bright as a star as energy of all six elements rippled around it. The arrow traveled almost faster than Alissa could see, and her jaw dropped slightly as it slammed into the monster, then detonated in a swirling explosion of the elements.

The wall shook as the monster was launched out of the explosion into it, a spray of blue blood splattering across the wall, then the creature landed on the ground. One of its heads was a mangled mess, there were fractures across its entire exoskeleton, and a gaping hole in its chest, though it didn't go entirely through the creature. For an instant Alissa thought it was dead, but then it began moving again, and she scowled, drawing another of her precious arrows and taking aim again. The other soldiers in the compound were also attacking with their own arrows, and just prior to Alissa loosing her arrow, a mage unleashed a lightning bolt into the monster, causing it to twitch and fall backward again.

This time the arrow didn't surprise her when she fired it, and the missile slammed home with another explosion that scarred the wall… and Alissa's stomach lurched quite suddenly as there was an eruption of blue-green gore from the middle of the explosion. As the smoke cleared, she looked on in horror for a long, *long* moment.

Where the creature had been was an enormous spray of steaming entrails and organs that she couldn't identify, all of it dripping with the same blue ichor that'd come out of the monster when it'd been injured, while the organs themselves were a sickly green. Worse, the bodies of over a dozen soldiers were laying entwined with the gore, many of them with horrific acid burns across their bodies while the ichor sizzled against them. There were far more organs than should fit inside the creature, too.

"Medics!" Alissa exclaimed, rushing down the stairs. "Everyone, get the injured out of that gunk *now*."

The nearest soldier rushed in, and Alissa winced as she saw the ichor sizzling at his boots. Thankfully he didn't stop, as he bodily dragged a man free, while others quickly came to help.

"Get water and rinse them off! We want that acid off as fast as possible," a female healer snapped, and quickly added, "Don't worry about them being cold, we can heat them up indoors!"

Just as Alissa was about to dive in to help, a runner rushed around the corner of the gates, screeching to a halt as he took in the sight of the garrison, his eyes going wide. "Dear gods! Captain, I—"

"Report!" Alissa snapped, glowering at him as worry rushed through her. "We were attacked by a monster, but just killed it. Is there something else?"

"Y-yes! There are multiple attacks from around the city, one at the temple of Tyria, one in the market, and one at the western gate! All of them are from unknown, three-headed creatures. The one at the gate is being fought by adventurers, but—"

"Enough. Edwin! You're in charge here; get the injured treated as quickly as possible!" Alissa snapped out, fear rushing through her as she realized that she was going to have to make hard decisions, and quickly did so. "First squad, with me! We've got the market. Second squad, back up the adventurers. Third squad, try to distract the one attacking the temple until we can get there. We don't have time to dawdle, so *move*."

She paused just long enough for the under-strength first squad to start gathering, then Alissa rushed out the gates.

Kevin cursed under his breath, glad he hadn't stepped in earlier. The ruiner had seemed to have everything well in hand at first, so he hadn't seen the need to interfere. Then the elf had shown up with her bow and destroyed it in two shots, which beggared belief. If he'd been out there… Kevin shuddered to think of what might've happened to him.

"Boss? What're we going to do?" Ryan asked, glancing out the window nervously. "I thought those things were practically unstoppable!"

"Practically, not actually. Which means we need to deal with *her* before she ruins our plans," Kevin said, nodding firmly as his gaze hardened. "We're going after them. She's going to be in the back on her own, so when she stops to use the bow, we deal with her and steal the bow and arrows. In and out like shadows, you hear me?"

"Right, that sounds doable. If we're careful, she'll never even know we're there," Ryan agreed, relaxing slightly.

"That's sure as hell the plan. I've seen enough other people die in these parts that we'd *better* stay unnoticed," Kevin said, and quickly headed for the stairs, willing mana into his clothing to help him move quickly and silently.

"WHAT'S GOING ON?" Nadis demanded, feeling chilled by the sight of dozens of golems marshalled together. There had to be at least fifty of them, and more were arriving as she watched.

The archpriestess had been preparing for the day's meeting when she'd seen the golems marching past, then Elissa had gone racing by, heading for the palace in a carriage just as a messenger came to Nadis's door. She hadn't delayed, instead hurrying to the palace, and now she found herself with Captain Desa, a dozen soldiers, Phynis, Sistina, the Jewels, Elissa, and Elissa's soldiers, all of whom looked worried. All but Sistina, at least.

They were in the palace, in a room Nadis hadn't ever seen before, but a single look at the floor told her what it was. The broad circle carved into the floor, fitted with carefully laid stone blocks and adorned with hundreds of arcane runes, was a teleportation circle, and one that was subtly different than any of the others that Nadis had seen before.

"Westgate is under attack," Desa replied, her voice crisp. "Sistina overheard Tyria ordering an angel to go to the aid of the temple there and started marshalling the golems and the others, which gave us a bit more warning. I received a message from the mayor not long ago, informing me that at least four powerful demons are attacking the city. We don't have many details, but the garrison and temple are under siege, at the least. Additionally, Kelvanis doesn't have soldiers available to help; they left to deal with insurgents yesterday."

"Which means it's likely the same people who tried to assassinate me before," Elissa said, her gaze hard as she tapped her arm impatiently. Rather than her usual robes, the priestess was wearing a set of older blue robes, though these had gold arcane symbols stitched across most of their surface. She also had a gnarled black staff in one hand, which made Nadis a touch uneasy. "As soon as Sistina is ready, I'm going to the aid of the temple there."

"Not until after me and my soldiers, High Priestess," Desa snapped, her eyes narrowing slightly. "They're attacking the garrison, yes, but attacking the temple sounds an awful lot like bait to me, coupled with Kelvanis. They probably *want* you to come there."

"It's certainly an effective trap, then," Elissa said, scowling as she added, "If Zenith was sent, I know she'll do her best to fight any attackers, but she's been bested twice before that I know of. I'd rather not risk her death when I might be able to prevent it, and I *was* a powerful adventurer."

"No arguing," Sistina said, frowning as she looked around the room. "I cannot help. My domain is *here;* can teleport, no more."

"Of course, Lady Sistina," one of Elissa's guards said, the man bowing slightly to her. "Thank you for your assistance."

"You are welcome," Sistina said calmly, then paused. "Ready."

"I'd like to come with you," Nadis said suddenly, almost startling herself with her interjection.

"Archpriestess?" Phynis asked, blinking in surprise. "Are you sure? I don't know how well you'd do in a battle, but—"

"That doesn't matter, not really. If the faithful are in danger, and despite whatever misgivings I may have, Tyria's church follows the same goddess as I do, I cannot abandon them," Nadis said, focusing on Elissa now as she licked her lips, hesitating before she admitted, "It also will do *both* of our churches good to see us cooperating with one another, I think. I may not be a powerful mage when it comes to battle, but I'm a powerful healer."

"I see. Well, I think it may be a bit rash of you, but I'd welcome your company, Archpriestess," Elissa said, slowly smiling, then glanced at her guards as she ordered, "Guard the archpriestess as you would me. I know how to defend myself, so she takes priority."

Several knights saluted, and they quickly surrounded Nadis, which *did* make her a bit anxious since a couple of them were humans from Kelvanis. Nadis stepped on her worry firmly, though, as she knew that many people in Kelvanis were perfectly good individuals.

While they were talking, Desa had quickly taken her soldiers into the circle, and the mage looked around, pulling out a wand of pale wood with a glowing blue gem on the tip. A couple of golems stepped into the circle as well, and Sistina raised her hand. As she did so, the circle began to glow with a soft yellow light and almost looked like it'd begun spinning for a moment. Suddenly the light flashed, and the people within the circle were gone.

"Next," Sistina said calmly, looking over at them.

"Be safe, Nadis, Elissa. I really, *really* wouldn't want the last couple of weeks to have been for nothing," Diamond said, smiling at Nadis, though her worry was obvious.

"You and me both," Nadis replied, though she was startled by the vehemence in her voice, as well as the chuckles it prompted from the others.

"Travel safely," Phynis said, sighing as she added, "Alas, my magical training hasn't progressed enough that I would be any help."

"As if Desa would let you go with," Ruby said, rolling her eyes visibly.

Elissa calmly stepped into the circle, Nadis following her along with the other soldiers. They could still fit four golems in the circle, so more of the steel-skinned giants stepped in, armed with halberds.

Sistina raised her hand again, and the glow rose all around Nadis. As the light began spinning, she took a moment to wonder if this was *really* a good idea. Then the light flashed and she was gone.

CHAPTER 38

"It's about to blow!" Kaylen snapped out, and Adrian responded immediately. He retreated incredibly quickly, dodging a last tongue-lash of the ruiner.

The creature was marred with dozens of gashes that'd cut through its armor, along with burns from spells and Adrian's blade. He'd have done better with a physical weapon, but ruiners tended to destroy any weapon that touched them, so he'd gone with one it *couldn't* destroy. Not that the gate was in good shape at this point either, as long as they'd lingered near it.

That said, Kaylen was right about the ruiner, as its exoskeleton cracked and it began swelling up. Adrian covered his eyes and braced himself, knowing what was coming.

With a horrific squelching sound, the ruiner burst like an overripe tomato, spraying its acidic blood everywhere as its organs spilled across the ground. A few spatters hit Adrian, and he cursed, taking a few steps back.

"Gods above!" an elven man exclaimed from behind him, and Adrian blinked, barely giving the horror on the ground a look as he glanced back at the soldiers who'd just arrived.

The soldiers were in reasonably good armor and had their weapons out while they bore grim looks, some of them even looking like acid had been eating at their gauntlets. They weren't the match of any ruiner, but coming *toward* it took courage, and Adrian let Storm depart, causing his sword to vanish.

"Nice of you to show up. A bit late, I'm afraid, and I doubt any of your friends it ate are alive anymore," Adrian said, nodding toward it with a grimace. "Though I do wonder what ruiners are doing in the region."

"A ruiner, is it? First I've ever seen of them, before the one attacked the garrison," the man replied, scowling at it, then looked at Adrian and added gratefully, "Thank you for dealing with it. I'm afraid the captain went to deal with the one in the market."

"There're more?" Clarissa demanded, turning toward them suddenly. "And you dealt with one?"

"Well, the captain did. She shot it with a heavily enchanted arrow, and it exploded like that one," the guard explained. "There's another at the temple, as well as the one in the market."

"Crap," Kaylen muttered, paling slightly. "They *never* come in groups, unless someone summoned them. We'd better—"

A glowing light streaked across the sky toward the city from the west, causing Adrian to blink, as he could barely make out the sight of an angel in armor, her sword already unsheathed. He couldn't make out much about her, not in the few moments she was in sight.

"Looks like they called for divine aid already. Not sure if it'll be enough, though," Adrian said, grimacing. "I *hate* ruiners. Let's go see if she needs help."

"Why do they, ugh, *explode* like that?" the soldier asked, wrinkling his nose, then starting to follow as the adventurers started into the city, heading in the direction the angel had been flying.

"Ruiners contain a dimensional space that allows them—" Kaylen began, only for Harriet to interrupt.

"They're bigger on the inside than the outside, so they can eat as much as they want," the half-elf said bluntly. "They also will destroy anything in their path. We'd better go."

"Alright," the soldier said, following them as the adventurers began to move more quickly.

Not that they could keep up when Adrian and the others began to run, though.

LISA SMILED from her vantage point in the tower, watching the building where the teleportation circle was located. A few moments before a group had quickly departed, though none of the elves or golems had been the priestesses, to her disappointment. This time, though, another group had come out, and it had *both* of the women they were here to kill, and that improved her mood immensely.

"Oh, joy! That means I can deal with them at the same time!" Lisa said, grinning broadly at the sight of them.

She reached down and tapped the device that Mazina had given her, sending in the surge of mana that would bring it to life. The object was a series of brass and gold cylinders, each etched with complex designs that'd been threaded with silver wire. Lisa wasn't an artificer, it would require her to learn too much about creating things, but she knew enough to enjoy devices of the type. As it whirred to life, vibrating, Lisa turned away and started undressing, humming to herself as she did so.

It wouldn't do to ruin a perfectly good outfit, and it wasn't like the dead guards would notice what she was doing.

SISTINA STOPPED, blinking, then narrowed her eyes as the ley line connecting to Westgate suddenly destabilized. She'd been about to teleport more golems to the other side, but with the disruption she couldn't.

"Sistina? Is something wrong?" Phynis asked, her voice anxious.

"Ley line. Something is... wrong. One moment," Sistina said, and promptly plopped onto the ground before leaving her body to examine the ley line in detail. As she did, Sistina internally growled as she detected a pattern to the interference, something she'd experienced before.

The ley line was being flooded with outside mana, disrupting the aether and making it difficult for anything to easily traverse it, and in a lot of ways it was like the aetheric disruptor that had been used to disable her earlier that year. Unlike that one, however, *this* device was actively creating the disruption, and it was only focused on the ley line itself.

That gave Sistina an idea, since she'd been working on ways to defend herself from the disruptors ever since her brief death. Trying to do it from this end of the ley line would be tricky, since she hadn't intended her solutions to be used from so far away, but it should be possible since the target was 'downstream', as it were. The only question was whether or not she'd have time to do something about the device before the people on the other end ran *out* of time.

Considering that, Sistina immediately got to work weaving her spells and performing calculations as quickly as she could manage.

"HELLS," Alexander swore mildly as the ruiner was thrown across the town square, the impact of the angel hitting it echoing through the city, along with the blast of flame the woman had emitted.

The ruiner had just about broken through the doors of the temple, based on the cracks Alexander was seeing, and he was honestly shocked that the doors had lasted as long as they had, even reinforced by burning magic. He couldn't imagine how many enchantments it would take to do that, since ruiners were specialized in destroying structures. He'd been hoping that he wouldn't have to step in at all, but when an angel arrived… well, that was something that meant he had little choice in the matter, so he sighed unhappily, drawing his sword with one hand as he stepped out from his hiding spot.

Rising from the ground fluidly, its joints moving in ways no mortal would be able to manage, the ruiner hissed, then charged the angel, who raised her sword as she prepared to receive it.

The clash of its claws against her sword was loud enough to

make Alexander wince, and he was impressed that she was able to stand her ground, as well as how her sword survived the ruiner's claws. Not many weapons could do that.

Alexander waited for a couple of moments, then rushed at the angel's back just as the ruiner lashed out with its tongues *and* its claws, forcing the angel back several steps as she blocked them, her sword flashing through the air, while a shield of flames protected her from the other attacks. It didn't protect her back, though, and Alexander smiled, his muscles coiling like springs just before he lunged at her, his sword cutting through the air silently.

The next instant the angel's wings beat, and Alexander's sword cut through empty air as the angel looked down at them, her crimson hair swirling in the cold breeze.

"I thought I felt someone watching us and wasn't about to let my guard down. The last time I did, I was captured by those who wished to destroy everything I was," the angel said, her voice beautiful but as cold as the air around them, at least until an aura of fire began to burn around the angel, heating the air. "I will not allow that to happen again."

"First you'll have to survive," Alexander replied, his heartbeat quickening as she glared down at him, and he resisted the urge to cringe, since he was afraid of what was coming. He *hated* getting burned, as the recovery was always horrible. "You're no match for a ruiner, I can tell that much."

"I don't need to be a match for it. All I have to do is hold the pair of you off," the angel replied, her sword lashing out to knock a tongue of the creature away from her. Her words sent a chill down Alexander's spine, but he shook it off.

"We'll see about that!" Alexander snapped, and he raised his arm, beginning a spell of unravelling as he took aim at the door.

The angel lunged toward him but the ruiner wasn't about to let her get away with ignoring it, and the battle ensued more fiercely, though a blast of fire forced Alexander to hastily abandon his spell for the moment.

Her disadvantage was that she was trying to protect others, Alexander knew. All they had to do was get through her defenses once, though, then the angel would die.

~

ELISSA STEPPED out of the teleportation chamber calmly, and frowned as she did so, her instincts claiming something was wrong. That wasn't a surprise, considering the city was supposedly under attack, but the problem was she didn't know *what* was wrong.

The old manor where the Adjudicators had ruled Westgate was in ruins, though it was still better than just after the destruction, as the elves had been working on clearing it up for the past couple of months, once Everium had solidified their control of the city and finally gotten a makeshift government in place. It probably wouldn't be cleared entirely until the next spring, with how the majority of the building had imploded, but the stables, several outbuildings, the walls, and the teleportation chamber had all survived the destruction.

Captain Desa and her soldiers were already in the courtyard with the golems and some local soldiers, and as she paused the golems that had arrived with her strode forward to join the others. Four of them were armed with halberds, while the other four had gigantic arbalests attached to one hand, which Elissa imagined would be painful to be shot by. Her guards had formed up around her and Nadis, and Elissa looked over the walls, frowning as she did so.

The haze of smoke from fireplaces made it a touch harder to tell where the problems were at first glance, but she heard faint noise even so, with more smoke rising from the direction of the markets. They were too far from the temple to be able to tell more, but Elissa wasn't going to assume it was safe.

"Lady Elissa! There were four creatures attacking the city in total, but we know the one at the garrison was killed. One is in the market and at the gates, and we're—" Desa turned to her and began speaking, the elf's gaze focused, but she never got the chance to finish as a flurry of bolts of fire slammed into the gates, reducing them to splinters that flew across the courtyard, prompting everyone to flinch and shield their faces, even if the gates were far enough away that they weren't in much danger.

"You were right," Nadis said, her voice barely audible as men and women poured through the gate, though mostly men.

There were more than a hundred people rushing through the gates, all of them armed, and Elissa instantly identified a few magi among them, causing her lips to tighten. Worse, she thought she recognized a few of them, particularly the quartet of strong, *fast* men and women in front.

"I hate being right," Elissa replied grimly, and shouted, "Enforcers in front!"

With that she launched into an incantation, her old instincts coming to life at long last, as she found herself in the middle of a battlefield for the first time in ages, and not one where she was trying to keep people alive. Words spilled from Elissa's lips, and the golems and the soldiers began moving as well. Desa's voice was raised, her wand glittering as mana pulsed through it, and her soldiers were rushing to face their opponents. Elissa grew a bit more surprised as she realized those guards were moving nearly as fast as the Enforcers, but she didn't have time to think about it further.

Elissa completed her spell with a sharp, precise gesture, and a wave of rippling light blasted out from the middle of the attackers, almost like an explosive rainbow. The ground was unaffected where it passed, but many opponents were caught in it. A couple of them fell over, twitching and possibly dead, while all but one of them began moving more spastically, as if they'd lost track of what they were doing. Only the one managed to shield himself, but Elissa wasn't going to let them—

A multitoned roar interrupted her, and Elissa paled, spinning around as she muttered, "Oh, shit. A *dragon*? Goddess help us."

An immense, winged shape swooped upward, as if it'd just launched from the watchtower that was behind it, and Elissa wondered where the creature had come from. It was more than seventy feet long, measuring from nose to tail, and it glittered with bright blue scales, its eyes glowing an unearthly blue, and fangs filling its mouth. The dragon inhaled, and that gave Elissa just enough warning to shake off her shock. Her hand darted into a pouch, pulling out a tiny crystal orb, which she threw to the ground hard.

The dragon exhaled suddenly, and a torrent of water like a geyser erupted from its mouth, gushing toward her and Nadis unerringly. The instant before the wave struck them, the crystal orb shattered on the ground and a crystalline barrier snapped to life, forming a magical dome twenty feet across and which covered the majority of her guards.

Water hit the barrier with enough force that the shield trembled, cracking in a few places, but it sprayed off the barrier harmlessly, to Elissa's relief. After a few seconds the torrent ended, and just in time, as the barrier began to shimmer, then faded. A tiny part of her thanked Tyria that she hadn't ever sold off all her adventuring gear, as otherwise she might have died from the sudden attack.

"How unfortunate; I'd hoped to deal with the pair of you painlessly," the dragon said, her voice distinctly female and cold, then she clicked her tongue in an almost motherly tone, a change which sent a shudder down Elissa's spine. "I suppose I'll just have to make it painful, and—"

Eight spears made of ice slammed into the side of the dragon's head at that moment, cutting her off, then a pair of steel bolts hammered into its chest, cracking a couple of scales. Elissa's breath rushed out, a bit shocked as she realized that Desa had turned on the dragon, and didn't waste her breath speaking, just launching into casting a spell.

"Right. I know a couple of shields, I'll use them," Nadis muttered, her voice shaking a little, but the archpriestess started casting her own spell.

"Keep the soldiers off us! We'll try to stop the dragon," Elissa ordered her guards, her heart pounding almost like a drum.

"Yes, Lady Elissa!" one of them said, his eyes wide, but he turned toward the main fight.

The battle was fully joined, and Elissa barely glanced at it, surprised at how the battle was going so far. The Enforcers were tangled with Desa's guards, and while each of them were obviously using magic to enhance their speed and power, the elves almost matched the Enforcers individually, and had split into pairs to deal with them, while the others were helping the golems and soldiers stem the tide of attackers. Not that they'd be able to hold off all of them, Elissa knew. There were just too many attackers, and only the relatively narrow gates kept them from being able to swarm the defenders under.

As she wondered where their additional reinforcements were, the dragon growled, then spoke angrily. "Naughty children, attacking me. Obviously you need to be *punished*."

The dragon swooped down at them, coming in for a landing, and Elissa gritted her teeth, rushing to the side as she ran through her arsenal of spells mentally, cursing as she did so. Dragons were virtually immune to most mental magic, which was *not* good for Elissa.

"I suppose I'll have to go with basic spells," Elissa muttered, and she began chanting the words to cast a fire bolt.

ALISSA SWORE as a fleeing civilian ran through the line of fire, obviously not realizing what he was doing. Unfortunately, that gave plenty of time for the horrible creature to grab and swallow another woman. The sight made her stomach clench, but there wasn't anything she could do to stop it, and she'd already lost a soldier who'd been a bit too brave. Without his head, Chen wasn't going to be getting healed.

The market was on fire, and the sheer amount of destruction shocked Alissa, as she wouldn't have expected this much damage quite so quickly, not even if the monster seemed to decay anything that came near it. The problem was that she only had three more shots, and she didn't want to waste them.

So she prayed for people to clear the line of fire, holding her breath as she drew the arrow back fully.

Then Alissa loosed the arrow, launching the incredibly powerful missile across the market.

CHAPTER 39

"Sistina, what's wrong?" Diamond demanded, her voice impatient enough it actually registered for Sistina, and she paused, then inhabited her body quickly.

"Ley line disrupted, like I was. Preventing reinforcements," Sistina explained precisely, pausing as she considered, then added, "Preparing spell to… *fix*. Ambush must have happened."

"Oh, gods!" Phynis said, her eyes widening. "Do what you need to do! Are the golems going to be enough?"

"Don't know," Sistina replied, turning back to the circle, and transferring her awareness back to her domain. She could still hear the others, but trying to split her awareness was hard, even now.

"We'll go," Diamond said, and *that* almost made Sistina make a mistake with the spell she was hastily crafting.

"What?" Phynis demanded, obviously shocked. "But—"

"We've been going through lessons with Kassandra for a reason, Phynis. If the city's in danger, and the people there deliberately stopped reinforcements… we're the most powerful magi who can help them," Diamond said, her tone determined, and through her domain Sistina could see the determination and worry on the faces of the others, as well as Phynis's fear.

"Sistina can't go, and it's daylight so Kassandra isn't able to help," Sapphire added calmly, her voice controlled as she spoke about the vampire. "We'll take as many golems with us as we can, too."

"I... well, be safe, then. Assuming Sistina's plan works," Phynis said, taking a couple of quick steps forward and hugging Diamond. Sistina wished she could do the same, but she didn't have time, and couldn't risk taking too much of it.

Instead she finished her preparations and returned to the body just long enough to warn them. "About to find out."

Before they could say anything, she channeled mana into her spell recklessly, hoping she hadn't made any mistakes, and the magical diagram surged to life, carved into the stone around where the metaphysical ley line passed through her mountain. The mana surged, and reality warped inside the circle as her spell began manipulating the magical conduit. Sistina's breath would have caught in her breath if she'd been in her body, but the circle held... even if the stone around it cracked, and she had to hastily reinforce it against the raw mana bleeding off.

A precisely targeted *pulse* of mana suddenly rushed down the ley line, forcing the mana flow back into alignment, but that was merely a secondary effect of the spell. The question, in Sistina's mind, was how the pulse would affect the device destabilizing the ley line.

Sistina rather hoped that it would explode in the user's face.

IN THE TOWER Lisa had left not long before, the ley line destabilizer was whirring softly, using its mana to prevent anyone from using the ley lines to reinforce Westgate. Next to it was the neatly folded clothing that the dragon had abandoned before returning to her natural form, along with the bodies of the two guards she'd killed.

Then the pulse hit the device, and there was a grinding sound from it as a high-pitched whine filled the air. The spells carved into it had been designed to deal with some magical feedback, but this was far beyond what they'd been designed for, and the pulse had been very carefully designed.

The whine reached a crescendo, and then the spell

overwhelmed the device. All at once, the pulse turned every bit of mana stored in the destabilizer into fire magic, and it exploded violently.

~

Desa swore as the dragon's tail hit her ice shield, shattering the barrier almost effortlessly, and her curse cut off abruptly as the tail hit her in the side, sending her flying a dozen feet to the right. If it hadn't been for the enchanted armor and the months living inside Sistina's domain, Desa would likely have broken ribs or might even be dead. She certainly wouldn't be conscious.

Even so, she was definitely bruised, and casting a spell wasn't happening for the moment, which was bad with the dragon bearing down on her, its eyes glowing brightly.

That was when the guard tower behind the dragon suddenly exploded, the walls erupting off it in every direction, while the roof launched upward spinning, then fell toward the ground with a tremendous crash.

"What the...?" the dragon asked, pausing in mid-lunge as she swiveled her head to look at the wreckage, and despite her own shock, Desa took advantage of the opening to dive to the side and hide behind one of the halberd-wielding golems.

She did wonder where the other reinforcements were, but Desa had to assume that the attackers had done something to keep Sistina from sending more golems, and the ones she had weren't in the best of shape. Whispering the words of a spell, Desa sighed with relief as a hint of healing magic flowed through her ribs, thankful that she'd spent some time mastering the basics of healing magic through the summer. The academy was an amazing thing.

"No more toying with you; time to die," the dragon said abruptly, spinning around as her claws extended, flashing with glittering blue light.

Desa ducked, but then she realized that the dragon wasn't aiming for her at all, and she yelped. "Elissa!"

The dragon's claws lashed out at the priestess and Nadis behind her, both of whom didn't even look like they were trying to dodge, and Desa's heart almost stopped as Elissa was struck. Her fear turned to surprise as the claws went clean through the woman, leaving trails of white light shimmering in their wake before Elissa shimmered, then popped like a soap bubble.

"You're going to have to do better than that," Elissa said, suddenly appearing only a few feet from Desa, smiling as she did so, and she glanced back before she murmured, "Though if we don't get help soon…"

"Sneaky little thing, aren't you?" the dragon snarled, spinning back toward them, a claw hammering into a golem and sending it flying, the construct's halberd bending, and deep gashes cut into its armor. While it wasn't destroyed, the construct shook the ground when it landed, and wasn't getting up quickly.

The dragon inhaled sharply, and Desa paled, quickly whispering the words of a spell, creating an icy shield shaped like a cone to stop the blast of water she knew was coming, hoping that she'd deflect most of it from hitting them, or the soldiers behind them. Their people had taken several losses already, and the attackers were starting to overwhelm them. That's when a barely audible chant grew louder, and Nadis's voice made itself heard.

"Goddess, may the sun illuminate our enemies and render them powerless!" Nadis cried out, and a shining burst of light erupted from the entrance to the stables, showing that the archpriestess had also been concealed by an illusion, and an orb of glowing golden fire was in her hands.

The orb shot outward from her hands, splitting rapidly into hundreds of tiny orbs, which in turn transformed into the links of glowing golden chains. A loop wrapped itself around the dragon's mouth and tightened, quite abruptly muzzling the monster, while the others quickly took hold of the dragon's limbs and planted themselves in the ground, drawing taut to immobilize the dragon.

"Well done!" Desa's exclaimed, relief rushing through her, and she continued. "Now let's deal with—"

"No!" Nadis quickly interrupted, her voice slightly panicked.

"The spell will break if you attack her, and it'll only last a minute or two at most! We have to help the others."

Almost as if on cue, an arrow slammed into Desa's shoulder from behind, only to be deflected by her armor. Desa cursed and spun around, paling a little.

The two golems with halberds which had been supporting the soldiers were both battered and scarred, while almost half their soldiers were either down or had fallen back with injuries. Only one enemy Enforcer was still up, but the man was fighting like a savage beast, driving back all three of her soldiers attacking him.

Desa barely spared the dragon a glance, then growled as Nadis rushed forward, casting a spell as she moved toward the injured. She was frustrated to leave the dragon be but left it alone as the creature fought its creaking chains, instead turning to try to support the other soldiers.

Of course, that was the moment when one of the enemy magi threw a fireball at her.

THE EXPLOSION LAUNCHED the monster backward, and Alissa hissed in triumph, then ordered, "Hit it while it's down!"

"Yes, sir!" the nearest magi exclaimed and immediately began casting her spell, while the other magi in the squad followed her example.

They weren't the only ones, either, as a few of the city's regular guard were alongside them, though they were fumbling with their crossbows while Alissa's other soldiers began pelting the monster with arrows.

The monster was trying to struggle out of the wreckage of a wagon, with a signpost snapped off in one claw, while its exoskeleton was cracked and had holes in it, much like the other one had after her first shot, though this time she hadn't managed to hit it head-on. Alissa paused as she touched the next arrow in her quiver, unsure of what she should do. If her soldiers could finish it off without the arrow that would be ideal, since there was at least one more of the monsters at the temple, and—

The detonation from the center of the city caused Alissa to flinch and turn, and just in time at that. As she turned, she saw a human man just a few steps away, wearing simple traveler's clothing and wielding a shortsword. The flicker of shock in his eyes, and how they jerked to the side gave her just enough warning for Alissa to finish spinning as she drew her sword. A big man was approaching from her left as well, a dagger in one hand, and Alissa barely had time to defend herself as the two attacked.

The dagger skittered off her bow with a shower of sparks as the man spat a foul oath of frustration, and Alissa couldn't help her own shock at how tough the wood was. She blocked the other man's attack with her sword, and as she did, Alissa spat, "What is it with assassins today? Can't you idiots just *leave us alone* already?"

"Damn it, just shut up, you damned—" the man with the sword began spitting out, just as the other man pulled back. Alissa gritted her teeth and jabbed the tip of the bow into the man's throat, cutting him off violently, kicked one of his knees, and likely broke it, then drove her sword into him before he could recover.

"Damn it!" the other man said, looking shocked at her speed, and he raised his free hand, chanting as his fingers moved in the gestures of a spell, and it barely gave Alissa time to react.

Her initial instinct was to dodge, but with her soldiers behind her, and not knowing what the spell might be, Alissa didn't dare do that. Instead, since he was aiming his hand at her, she saved an instant by releasing her sword and lunged at the big man, spinning her bow to hit the underside of his arm, knocking it upward just as he completed his spell.

As his arm rose, streamers of dark red fire erupted from the man's hand, dozens of snake-like missiles of pure heat. Alissa tried to dodge one that raced toward her, twisting her head to the side, but she just didn't have time. There was a flash of heat, sizzling, and she staggered, falling to a knee as all sensation from her ear vanished, while agony raced through her face. Most of the streamers went racing into the sky though, and an expression of triumph appeared on the man's face.

"Hah! Not so tough now, are you?" the man said, grinning as he flipped his dagger around. "What're you going to do now, girl?"

"This," Alissa said, focusing through the pain, and brought the bow up with all her strength between the man's legs just as he started bringing his dagger down.

The crunch was quiet compared to the clamor of combat, but the man stopped, his eyes almost bulging out of his head. Alissa hissed, tripping him with a leg sweep, then slammed his head against the ground, knocking him unconscious, she hoped.

A moment later she heard one of the soldiers exclaim, "Back, it's bulging, so I think it's going to explode!"

There was a horrific tearing sound, and Alissa barely had time to look, which she ended up regretting. The monster had exploded, and bodies had poured out of it, far more numerous than she'd like to deal with.

"Captain? Captain, are you alright?" the nearest mage asked, his shock obvious. "I'll get you to the healers, just—"

"No," Alissa said, cutting him off and nodding toward her attacker. "Someone get this filth into custody and keep him alive, the others get anyone who might be alive out of that monster. First aid on me only; we need to get to the temple."

"But your face!" the mage protested but took a step back as she glared at him.

"My face can wait. Compared to what I went through in Kelvanath, this is *nothing*," Alissa replied, her voice taut with anger as she thought back on the orders that she'd been given while enslaved.

"Y-yes, sir!" the mage replied, and got moving, while one of the other magi rushed over. If Alissa remembered right, the lady knew some healing spells, which she wasn't going to object to.

Now they just had to get to the temple in time to make a difference there, too. And figure out what the explosion was from, for that matter.

CHAPTER 40

Lisa was... annoyed. She didn't like being annoyed, as it was a mostly alien emotion to her. So was the cheerfulness she normally put on display, for that matter. No, her thoughts were normally cold, and carefully calculated.

That was beneficial as she analyzed her situation instead of acting impatiently. The detonation from the direction of the ley line disruptor concerned Lisa, as it likely meant there was an unknown factor in play, but she wasn't going to let it force her into a foolish decision. Nor was she going to let confidence in the pathetic survivors of Kelvanis's former regime lull her into declining to act.

The handful of mortals defending themselves were in bad shape, Lisa knew. At least half of them were incapacitated entirely, and as she watched one of the golems crumbled under a focused assault by the assassin magi. The others weren't in much better shape, but the assistance of Medaea's priestess was quickly getting some of the defenders back on their feet, while the priestess of Tyria, their target, was doing what she could as well. Unfortunately for her, the attackers had known she specialized in mental magic ahead of time, which kept her from outright incapacitating the lot of them, but it didn't protect them from her using targeted spells to overwhelm their defenses. At least one of them had died from terror already, while a few more of them were unconscious.

All that being considered, she focused instead on her bonds, her eyes narrowing as she focused on the chains muzzling her. That was the primary source of her annoyance, and the magic within the chains… it grated at her, that a mere elf had stopped her, however briefly.

However, the woman *was* a mere elf. Even if she was the archpriestess of her faith, her magic was only that which a mortal could command, and it was obvious that she wasn't practiced at using her spells in times of crisis. The spell which bound Lisa was imperfect and hastily cast, and *that* gave the dragon an advantage. After all, dragons were innately resistant to magic, a fact which the priestess seemed to have forgotten.

Lisa focused her mana into her mouth and claws, channeling it into her scales to enhance her resistance still further. She could feel the chains weakening a little, then a little more, and she waited patiently, rather than providing resistance that might cause the spell to focus on her struggles. Instead, she analyzed the distance between her and the two priestesses, gauging the distance exactly. Her breath hadn't done the job so far, and this time the women weren't hidden by illusions, so if she struck hard and fast, she could deal with them once and for all.

The dragon's muscles slowly coiled as she prepared herself, waiting for the precise moment she needed, when the two women were most distracted. Then, as Nadis focused on a victim, falling to her knees, and Elissa aimed her staff at one of the assassin magi, Lisa struck.

She moved suddenly, throwing every ounce of strength her body possessed into her sudden lunge, and the brittle spell didn't stand a chance. It shattered as if it'd been made of glass, the chains bursting into motes of golden light. None of the mortals had a chance to do much more than start turning in her direction before Lisa was halfway to her targets, though the unnaturally fast elven mage was moving more quickly than most.

It still wouldn't be enough, though.

~

THE TELEPORTATION WAS UNUSUALLY SMOOTH, to Diamond's shock. She was used to feeling like she'd been yanked across a room instantly, and like her stomach had to catch up, but not this time. This time it was more like the floor had dropped a couple of inches… and that was it.

She didn't have time to get her bearings, though, not with the sound of combat coming from ahead of them, and Diamond snapped to the golems. "Forward! Defend those in the livery of Everium, Medaea, or Tyria!"

The golems immediately rumbled to life, moving toward the doors still hanging open before them, and Diamond hoped her orders would suffice. If Desa was still in the area, she'd be able to adjust their orders, though. The problem with golems was how literal they were with orders, and if someone who wasn't in a uniform and attacked them… that would be bad.

"Let's go!" Ruby urged, and Diamond nodded, silently drawing on all their magic.

"Yes, but let's be prepared," Diamond said, spindling power within her as she began chanting the words to a spell, one that all of them knew. Almost as if by instinct, the others joined her in the chant, following the golems as they rushed out to see what was happening, even their strides oddly in sync with one another.

Diamond and the others emerged in a war zone, and her eyes widened in shock as she took in the sight of the immense blue dragon in magical restraints only a dozen yards from them, along with the burning tower and dozens of people locked in raging combat, along with a large number of fallen around them. Even as Diamond took in the sight, she could see a few of the attackers making their way around the buildings where Desa, Elissa, and Nadis were holding the line, which would make a difficult position even more dire.

At that instant the dragon suddenly lunged forward, shattering the bindings seemingly effortlessly, and a deafening roar echoed through the square as it lunged toward Elissa and Nadis, nearly stopping Diamond's heart. However, her spell was already prepared. No, *their* spell, and Diamond did the only thing she could and thrust her hands toward the dragon at the same time as the other Jewels, a star appearing above her hands.

The eruption of light from her hands was as bright as the sun, if not brighter, and it spread into a column almost ten feet across, wide enough it seemed to be coming from all seven of them, and the beam slammed into the dragon in mid-leap. All across the square snow began to sag and melt, while the ice nearest Diamond and the others turned to water which began steaming. A thunderous *boom* echoed through the clearing, and the spell ended, revealing what had just happened.

Across the courtyard from Diamond, the dragon had been thrown into one of the awnings attached to the wall, crushing it, whatever it'd contained, and partially damaging the wall itself. At least the parts that Diamond and the others hadn't almost melted with their spell, at least.

The dragon had held up surprisingly well in the face of a spell that could melt solid stone, though, and Diamond blinked, her mouth falling open slightly. The dragon's wings were scorched and tattered, but largely intact, while its scales along one side were blackened and cracked, but otherwise the dragon appeared to be almost completely fine. *Angry*, perhaps, but fine as it started dragging itself out of the wreckage.

"Wind," Sapphire said, her voice surprisingly calm as she made the suggestion, and Diamond nodded in agreement, starting on the spell she knew the others had in mind. They only had a handful of combat spells that could damage something like a dragon, and letting it take the initiative would be a bad, *bad* idea. No wonder the enemy had been confident in their ambush, though. If Sistina hadn't gotten them here, Diamond shuddered to think of the consequences.

"Good timing, ladies! Golems, Three of you secure each flank, the rest of you take the front line!" Desa called out, her rising spirits obvious as she ordered the golems into position.

By this point the initial arbalest golems were out of ammunition, Diamond realized, and were using their weapons as clubs instead. Fortunately, a moment later they finished their spell, just as the dragon got to its feet.

The air stirred, then exploded into a gale as what looked almost like the beginning of a tornado funnel descended on the dragon. The creature said something, but couldn't be heard over the wind's roar, and the funnel surrounded the dragon, ripping it off the ground even as the dragon attempted to grab hold of the wall or something sturdy. Unfortunately, there simply wasn't time, and the wind was too powerful.

"Come on…" Amethyst whispered, barely audible to Diamond, but it was loud enough to make Opal laugh.

The dragon was drawn into the sky, and the funnel turned into more of a sphere of swirling, raging winds. Then, as the dragon was buffeted about, the spell began creating blades of air that lashed out at the dragon. One after another, and at an ever-increasing rate, blades descended on the dragon, smashing against its scales mercilessly.

At first the attacks had no effect, simply shattering against the scaly hide without leaving a mark, but soon that changed. First some of the scales chipped, particularly where they'd been burned before, and then the blades began to bite into the dragon's flesh, as deep scarlet blood began to fall into the furious wind.

The dragon roared as its injuries mounted, and as it did so, Diamond's eyes widened, feeling mana concentrating in the dragon's direction. Ruby spoke quickly. "Careful, it might be about to—"

A blast of magic erupted from the dragon, as it roared words sibilantly, its claws dancing through the air in gestures despite the buffeting winds… and then it bodily *ripped* the spell apart, to Diamond's shock. She knew that spells could be dispelled, but with as much mana as they'd thrown into the spell, she couldn't believe that their spell could be undone so easily, let alone by someone inside it.

"Crap," Diamond whispered, seeing the dragon stabilize in midair, its wings beating heavily as it dripped blood. "Shield!"

The others started casting a shield with her as Diamond's stomach tied itself in knots, suddenly *far* more afraid of the dragon than she had been.

That was why she froze when the dragon suddenly turned

tail and fled, accidentally interrupting the spell in her shock, and watched the dragon fly into the distance at a high speed, dripping blood as it did so.

"It ran?" Emerald asked, her voice a touch incredulous. "But… it was so powerful!"

"We have no idea how much mana it had, though," Diamond said, her thoughts catching up, and she shook her head, then glanced at the fight, which had slowed a bit due to their display, and she added, "Come on, let's deal with the problem, shall we?"

"Agreed," Ruby said, her gaze hardening as she looked at the attackers.

The people attacking seemed to waver at the sight of them, and Diamond smiled as a few of them followed the dragon's example.

~

Alexander cursed internally, frustrated by how long the battle was taking. Despite his expectations, the angel was making the fight much, *much* harder than it should have been.

The ruiner's claws tore through the air where the angel had been a moment earlier, crushing several paving stones almost effortlessly, but she'd already moved, her sword lashing out at Alexander. That frustrated him, because she'd taken entirely to attacking him instead of the ruiner, except for the one time when Alexander had tried ordering it to destroy the temple doors.

Alexander blocked her attack with a grunt, riposting and drawing a little blood as his sword cut into a gap along the angel's hip, which was at least *something*. Her injuries were starting to mount, but despite that he couldn't see any fear in her eyes, simply unwavering confidence. It was unnerving, and—

The sounds of boots echoed through the now-abandoned courtyard, and Alexander's gaze drifted over, then widened as he saw people coming. Not just people, either, but in the lead were a group that practically gave him hives at the sight of them. A black-haired human man led the way, armor glittering from under his clothing, and was carrying a sword made of lightning in one hand. The others just behind him were obviously adventurers as well, with soldiers just behind them, and with *those* coming, he didn't have time to wear the angel down anymore. And as much as he hated to do it, Alexander only saw a single option.

Instead of trying to stab the angel, Alexander threw himself at her, hissing as her blade cut into his shoulder, but wrapped his arms around her, partly pinning her in place. She looked startled, to say the least, but before she could say anything, Alexander snapped at the ruiner. "Eat, already!"

"What—" the angel began, but it was too late for her to do anything, as the ruiner eagerly obeyed.

Its tongue lashed around the pair of them mercilessly, and as it did so Alexander braced himself for a *very* unpleasant death. It'd probably be one of the worst ones he'd experienced, at that. They were yanked toward the creature as the angel tried to angle her sword to cut the tongue, but Alexander fought her and managed to prevent her from acting before one of the mouths opened wide and came down around them.

Oaths of surprise came from the direction of the adventurers along with the clatter of the angel's sword on the ground, and Alexander's breath hissed out as he was pressed into the angel's armor painfully, and something constricted tight around him. It was like a seething, somewhat acidic vise was pressing against his entire body at once, and it seemed to last a short eternity… and then they fell into a pool of seething, acidic juices.

Pulsing walls of strangely colored flesh surrounded them, and agony seared through Alexander as his clothing and skin began to melt. Hidden in secondary passages, he could see bones… and it took him a moment to realize that the only illumination was from the angel's halo, and the violet light was casting everything in strange hues.

"Are you suicidal?" the angel demanded, her voice angry as she turned on him. "You're going to die here, you know!"

"If this—" Alexander began, only to be interrupted by a cough, pain searing down his throat, while he wondered why the angel was barely showing signs of injury so far, despite the acid around her. Then he continued. "If this was enough to kill me for good, I'd have died permanently *long* ago. I'm just trying to take you with me."

"If you say so. Unfortunately, while this isn't the way I wanted to do this… I suppose it's time to pray," the angel replied, looking around her, then fell to a knee as he watched in confusion, and she began speaking, her voice quiet in the ruiner's stomach. "Lady of Eminent Flame, I call to thee for a shard of thy power…"

For a moment Alexander thought the angel was praying to grant herself solace in her last moments. But then her halo began to burn, and his eyes widened as violet flame wreathed the angel's body with steadily growing intensity.

"SHIT!" Adrian blurted out, his eyes going wide as the man who'd tackled the angel and the beautiful woman were both swallowed by the ruiner. It was still a good distance from them, and he swore again as it turned toward the temple, and the cracked doors wreathed in fire that barred its way.

He'd just seen a beam of light shoot across the city as they'd run, enough mana in it to leave Adrian shaken, which concerned him a bit. *Then* a dragon had fled the area, bleeding from dozens of wounds, and leaving Adrian wondering just what in all the hells was happening in the region to have brought spells and creatures like that into a city in the middle of *nowhere*, along with an angel. Not that he had time to wonder, really.

"Gods above, did that man *let* himself be eaten?" Kaylen asked, sounding like he was in shock.

"Doesn't matter, Kay. We need to kill the beast fast. If we're quick enough, we can save the angel," Clarissa snapped out, her voice unusually intent. It was the fact it *was* an angel, Adrian realized belatedly. Even if the angel wasn't a devotee of her god, Clarissa obviously was concerned about her.

"Right! It takes time for even something like a ruiner to kill an angel," Kaylen said, shaking his head and skidding to a stop as he raised his staff, then began chanting loudly, lightning beginning to flicker along the staff.

Harriet didn't say anything, instead firing an arrow at the ruiner in mid-stride. Unfortunately, this time the ruiner ducked slightly, causing the arrow to glance off its shoulder.

"Damn, I hate having to hurry," Adrian muttered, charging at the ruiner.

Then it paused, and Adrian skidded to a shock, blinking in confusion as threads of smoke seeped from the creature's mouths.

Fire erupted from the ruiner's body, rampaging purple flames that wreathed it entirely, blackening the creature's armor as it let out an unearthly scream of pain. Adrian stepped back, staring in horror as it staggered, clawing at its chest helplessly as the fire surged higher and hotter, cracking the ruiner's exoskeleton.

The creature exploded as suddenly as the flames had appeared, prompting a flinch from Adrian as he braced himself for the shower of gore. Gore which never appeared.

Instead of gore, from within the ruiner appeared the angel once more, though she was resting on one knee, her hands clasped together in prayer. Her armor was pitted from acid, and some of her feathers were the worse for wear, but the angel was surrounded in the same purple flames, and the bodies of several people fell to the ground… some of which were even alive, though the man who'd tackled the angel wasn't among them. The angel paused, opening her eyes, and blinked as the flames around her slowly died. Then she stood up, looking a little stunned.

"Hm. That… was unexpectedly easy. Perhaps I should have let the beast swallow me to begin with," the angel said, her voice musing, then she shook her head. "No, no… if I had, I wouldn't have been worthy to call upon My Lady's flames."

"Er, is that normal?" the guard leader who'd been following Adrian asked, his voice hesitant.

"No, it isn't. That's the first time I've heard of a ruiner being killed from the *inside*," Adrian said, looking at the angel, then belatedly released Storm again. After a moment he spoke up. "Ah… are you alright, Lady Angel?"

"Zenith, if you please. As for me, I'm fine, thank you. I

should also thank you for your aid," the angel replied, smiling radiantly at Adrian in a way that brought a flush to his face. "Now, I'm afraid that I need to check on My Lady's faithful and ensure that they're well after all of that. Would those of you who can please ensure the injured are cared for? I'm sure the priesthood will assist as soon as they're able."

"Um, sure?" Adrian said, blinking. Fortunately, Clarissa had already headed toward the wounded laying on the ground, and the angel turned away, heading for the temple.

Adrian started toward the injured as well, and as he did the sound of more boots came in their direction. He tensed, then relaxed as a group of elves came around the corner. The elf in the front had definitely seen better days, and he winced sympathetically as he took in her face, which was blackened across the left side, and she was missing a good chunk of hair *and* her ear as well. The woman was wielding a bow made of odd white wood, and she had an arrow nocked.

"Captain, what happened to you?" a soldier asked in concern.

"An assassin tried to kill me. We dealt with the one in the market, what about the gates?" the woman replied curtly. "For that matter, where's third squad?"

"I'm not sure, but the one at the gates is dead, killed by the adventurers, and the angel..." the man began, but Adrian quickly turned his attention to the wounded, none of whom were in good shape.

Clarissa nodded at him, smiling slightly as she cast a healing spell on one of them. As Adrian pulled out a healing potion, Clarissa spoke calmly. "The angel's beautiful, isn't she?"

"Oh, shut up," Adrian growled in response, prompting soft laughter from his friend.

"Let go of—mrrph!" Umira began, only to be cut off by the gag as the soldiers hastily shoved it into place. They'd already bound her hands in hard leather gloves, which made using her magic difficult at best, and she couldn't help her anger as she twisted, trying to escape the bonds.

She was regretting running into the soldiers, as it appeared that deciding to play with them had been a mistake. Umira had thought they'd help her get out of the city more easily, but instead, all it'd done was rouse the suspicions of the others.

"Damn, that was close," one of the soldiers said, wiping sweat from her forehead as she nodded to one of the others. "If you hadn't noticed that something was wrong, who knows what she'd have done to us?"

"It wasn't hard to tell something was wrong. There was no reason for the lot of you to be calmly walking toward the east gate under these circumstances," the elven mage replied modestly, though his blue eyes were hard as he glared at Umira. "If you ask me, we've seen enough mind control in the city to last us a century."

"Agreed," one of the others said, nodding firmly, then gestured at Umira. "Let's get her in a cell, then head over to the temple. I hope we aren't too late."

"Sounds like a plan to me," the mage said, and the soldiers picked her up as Umira squirmed, trying to escape.

It wasn't going well.

THE BLAST of light vaporized a couple of the magi in the back, and with them Bran's hopes died at last. Even if they'd taken heavy losses so far, he'd thought that they were going to win, particularly with the support of the dragon. Then the seven magi had shown up, and golems had begun pouring out of the teleportation platform, proving that reinforcements *hadn't* been cut off. Worse, the four Enforcers he'd managed to hold onto had all fallen, though he wasn't sure if they were simply injured or dead. Now everything was lost, though, and he decided to cut his losses at last, and hoped they could get out of the city in time.

"Damn it, everyone fall back! Fall back!" Bran exclaimed, gesturing at Ruthan. "We've got to get out of here!"

"Right! Everyone, fall back in sequence!" Ruthan bellowed, his gaze worried, but staying in control as he looked around.

The soldiers began retreating with relief on their faces, and Bran felt a pang of despair. Even if they could get out of the city, their chances of escape weren't good, and there was nothing he could do about it. He'd made the decision which had gotten them into this, and under the same circumstances, he'd have done it again, but that didn't make him any happier. He turned to fall back as well, sheathing his bloody sword as he did so. There was a wagon partly in his path, but he'd be able to use it as cover.

"Look out!" Ruthan's exclamation was loud, and almost panicked, but Bran didn't act fast enough, instead freezing for just an instant too long before pain exploded through his stomach.

Staggering, Bran looked down to see a bloody hole had been punched clean through his left side despite his plate armor, and a quivering steel arbalest bolt was sticking out of the wagon he'd been about to circle. He put a hand to the hole, his stomach lurching, then Bran fell to his knees. He would've fallen entirely, but then Ruthan was there, grabbing him.

"Sir! Just a minute, I'll get you patched up, and—" Ruthan began, but Bran shook his head, swallowing hard as he closed his eyes for a moment, then opened them.

"N-no. Get them out of here," he gasped, a hint of despair washing over him. "I got them into it. Get them out."

"But—" Ruthan began.

"GO!" Bran all but yelled with as much breath as he could muster.

Ruthan hesitated for just a moment, then bowed his head and nodded, murmuring, "Yes, sir. It's been an honor."

The man took a moment to lay Bran against the wagon, then stood, snapping out orders as he organized the retreat. For his part, Bran declined to watch, instead closing his eyes as his blood slowly poured out from between his fingers and back, his body steadily growing colder.

The sounds around him faded slowly, and for a little while he thought he was going to die like that. Then another voice spoke.

"Well, if it isn't Adjudicator Bran Darleth?" a woman's voice said, sounding idly curious, and he heard a soft chant, followed by a surge of warmth through his body, causing the flow of blood to slow. "I *did* think you looked familiar."

Bran opened his eyes to see Elissa of Silence looking down at him, a priestess of Medaea at her side, as well as a couple of golems. They all showed the signs of battle, but they also didn't look much the worse for wear, unlike Bran. He glanced down and noticed that while his injury hadn't been fully healed, it wasn't actively bleeding.

"I'm surprised you recognize me," Bran replied, looking up at her again, then sighed, wincing as he did so. "Why did you heal me? I *was* trying to kill you."

"Why? Because you likely have information we need, and besides, King Damrung would be most put out if he couldn't put you on trial," Elissa replied, grinning widely, and Bran couldn't help a sigh as he slumped back, defeated at last.

"At least I'll likely be fed properly until I'm executed," he muttered, resigned to his fate. Hopefully Ruthan would get the others out.

~

FAR AWAY FROM WESTGATE, Alexander tried to groan as he opened his eyes and immediately regretted it.

His thoughts were fuzzy, as they always were when one of his copies was slain. He'd likely remember most of what had happened after some time, but it was rarely pleasant, and a part of him wished that Mazina would let him die already.

That wasn't going to happen, though. The complex magical devices surrounded him in a tank formed of brass, one with a tiny crystal window in it, and across the room he could see another tank. That was where another copy of him would be made, then sent out into the world.

After a few moments of contemplation, Alexander simply closed his eyes again since he couldn't free himself from the bindings holding him in place anyway. Instead, he decided to rest and hope that maybe this time he'd figure out a way to break his original body out of the dungeon it was trapped in.

He also wondered why he could vaguely remember a bright purple halo, and why it was so fascinating.

TYRIA OPENED her eyes and let out a soft sigh of relief. Beatrice's prayers had turned to those of thanks, and the sense of danger from Westgate had come to an end at last, which relieved her. That didn't reduce the number of dead, sadly, but that was how life worked. Instead, she took the small victory as best she could and smiled, hope rising within her at last.

It was largely because of Sistina and the bravery of mortals that they'd survived, Tyria knew, though Zenith had also done everything the angel could, and Elissa and Nadis had contributed as well. She dared hope that their cooperation might help in the future.

And if the truth of Erethor and Eretha came out… perhaps that would help unite her faith. So Tyria smiled slightly, looking down as she murmured, "Thank you, Sistina."

Perhaps she imagined it, but it almost felt like the wind deliberately ruffled her hair in return.

CHAPTER 41

"This year has been *far* too eventful," Elissa murmured, and Nadis snorted.

"This year? Try the last two *decades*, thank you," the elf replied, her arms crossed. "You might only have had to deal with things for a year or so, but we've been dealing with Kelvanis for a long, long time."

"True," Elissa conceded, to Diamond's private relief.

It'd taken a couple of days for them to stabilize the situation in Westgate, as a large part of the market had been damaged or destroyed, and there had been more deaths than Diamond cared to think about. Still, most of the attackers hadn't been able to escape, and for once they'd actually captured some of the rebel leaders, as well as the head of Kelvanis's old assassin guild, so they'd been able to get information on what exactly had happened.

Now they were well on their way back to Beacon, which Diamond knew made all of the Jewels happier, as well as Nadis's guards. They'd been *very* unhappy to have their archpriestess run off without them, particularly when they'd heard what had happened in Westgate. As it was, Elissa had lost several of her guards permanently, and Westgate's prison was uncomfortably full, at least until they could extradite the prisoners that Kelvanis wanted to put on trial.

"To be fair, I'm not sure that you could put this all on Ulvian's plate," Diamond interjected, almost surprising herself, and the others looked at her, blinking as the carriage bounced along the road.

"Oh? Because of the cultists?" Nadis asked, looking at Diamond skeptically.

"That's right. What did you say about them, Ruby?" Diamond asked, looking at her wife curiously. "You spotted mention of their deities in the book about Medaea's old faith."

"Yes, I did. And it's just like you to foist this off on me," Ruby replied, a touch tartly, though her smile removed any sting from it. "According to the scriptures, Medaea's position in trying to get justice for the fallen led her to frequent clashes with Erethor and Eretha, making them something of archenemies."

"Ah, so you're saying that they were after us from the beginning, and just used the Adjudicator's desperation for their own ends," Elissa said, understanding dawning on her face. "That would make far more sense... and yes, it would mean that Ulvian isn't directly at fault for this."

"True, I suppose. Though the opportunity to deal with one of the last pockets of his regime *does* give me some pleasure," Nadis admitted, glancing out the window. "I just wish it hadn't cost so many people their lives."

"We did what we could," Diamond said, her mood dimming a little at the thought of the dead.

No one picked up the conversation after that, at least not immediately. When they did, fortunately it was to continue discussing the changes that Tyria was going to go through, and what effect it might have on their churches. Personally, Diamond was just happy the alterations had been delayed until after they returned to Beacon.

For that matter, she was also glad to have the company of the adventurers who'd killed one of the monstrous ruiners that'd attacked the city, as they would help if the cultists tried to attack again. Even if their leader, Adrian, had been asking a rather lot of questions about Zenith, to Diamond's amusement. He probably even thought he was being subtle.

On the other hand, she couldn't wait to get home to her own

bed, and to Phynis and Sistina. It stunned Diamond how much she missed them, even after only a few days apart.

~

"Oops," Wenris murmured, grinning broadly as she watched Lady Ryn Nocris screaming at her brother through the window, her tail lashing idly behind her.

Lord Allen Nocris hadn't been hard to seduce when she compared him to the majority of people Wenris had dealt with over the centuries. Indeed, his pride had made him even easier to flatter, and that had led him to bed with her.

From there it hadn't taken more than a few days to draw out many of his secrets, and Wenris had taken pleasure in spreading those secrets far and wide… and *exactly* in the right places to let his sister hear about them first.

Their plots to try and drive Phynis and the Jewels apart had *not* pleased the majority of the city, and they'd quite abruptly found themselves unwelcome, something that likely prompted the stunned look on the dark-haired human's face, and his sister looked *particularly* displeased as they packed their bags. Something about losing all her maids in a single night had upset the young woman, Wenris thought, and she was rather pleased with herself.

She *did* enjoy doing good work, in the end. And perhaps that would help her get approval from Phynis and Sistina to stay in the city longer. Anything that let her stay close to Diane made her happier, though she had to wonder why she enjoyed the elf's company so much.

"Because she's fun to corrupt, of course," Wenris told herself, looking away from the window at last. She stretched indolently, secure in the knowledge that she had all the time in the world to carry out her desires.

~

"How many days is it to Kelvanath?" Bane asked, adjusting his cap carefully.

"'bout three days, sir," the driver said, adjusting the contents of the trunk to fit Bane's bags. "Ya'd best be ready for lots of sleep in the coaches. We only stop long 'nuff to change the 'orses."

"Alright," Bane agreed, glancing back once, then stepped over to get into the stagecoach. It wasn't going to be the most comfortable trip, but he was looking forward to putting Westgate behind him.

Their plans had ended in a disaster, and a more ambitious man would likely have tried to finish the job, Bane knew. Umira was in prison, and as far as he could tell, Alexander and Erin were both dead, which only left him in the city. He could have tried to act himself, but despite that Bane had decided against it. He wasn't going to throw good money after bad, and the locals were on guard now. No, it was time for him to leave.

He *did* rather hope that Alexander had gotten out, though. He'd liked playing chess with the man.

CHAPTER 42

"Welcome back!" Phynis exclaimed, and Nadis's jaw almost dropped as the queen practically *threw* herself at Amethyst, who laughed, staggering as she caught the monarch.

Moments later Sapphire and Opal hugged the queen and their companion, and Nadis blinked, then looked toward the back of the room, where Sistina was standing, watching with a smile. Not that that lasted long, as Diamond approached and hugged the dryad, giving her a gentle kiss, which the dryad readily returned.

"Ah, Your Majesty, we *do* have company," Desa said, looking rather embarrassed, though she likely should have been after her greeting by Isana. It had been slightly more reserved than Phynis's welcome, but not by much.

Nadis had begun to wonder if there was something in the water in Beacon that caused women to form romantic relationships. Even if many of those who had were former victims of Kelvanis, and elves tended to be more open about such relationships, the sheer number of them struck her as odd.

"Oh, be quiet, Desa. I missed them, and I can ignore protocol if I want to. I *am* the queen, after all," Phynis replied, letting go of Amethyst and squirming out of the embrace to give Topaz a brief kiss. "Besides, we're going to go to perform the ritual in a bit. Oh! What did you think of the lift?"

Nadis winced at the memory, as the way the ground had lurched when the lift started moving hadn't exactly pleased her, but it was Elissa who spoke. "It was… loud and creaked a lot. On the other hand, I suspect it saved us about half an hour of climbing the city, if not more, so I shouldn't complain."

"*Always* complaints," Sistina said, looking upward and sighing. "Will fix. Have to decide how."

Nadis did smile at that since she was starting to get used to the dryad. However, she focused a little, frowning. "You mentioned the ritual… are you talking about Medaea?"

"That's right. I asked Albert to provide one of his recording devices, since I imagine you'll want to have that on hand, and he was rather grumpy about not being able to join us. Apparently, those adventurers who helped in Westgate are rather high-ranking, on the whole, and he had to be available to meet them," Phynis said, smiling as she added, "I've been busy coming up with rewards for them since they assisted so admirably. Tyria is waiting in Sistina's cavern, so we're going to have to go there if we're going to watch it."

"In her cavern?" Diamond asked, pulling her attention away from Ruby and Sistina, her eyes widening. "But… is there a lift for that, too?"

"I'm afraid not. Why?" Phynis asked, frowning.

"Well… I hate to say it, but I'm not sure that Elissa or Nadis are up to the hike," Diamond said, looking at Nadis as her cheeks flushed.

"Wait just a moment. Shouldn't we be the ones to decide that?" Elissa asked, frowning. "I'm a former adventurer."

Nadis added quickly, "Besides, how bad could it be, compared to climbing the mountain?"

THE BETTER PART of an hour later, Nadis regretted saying anything. Her legs were practically on fire, and they'd barely reached the bottom of the winding staircase. Worse, from the way Phynis and the Jewels were talking, there didn't used to be any alcoves to stop and rest along the way, which was a terrifying thought.

Elissa didn't look to be in much better shape, though her assistants were worse off than she was. The human wiped her forehead, then spoke softly. "Apparently I need to exercise more. Goddess, I thought I was in better shape than this!"

"It isn't *my* fault that you decided to slack off," Tyria said, smiling at them, her arms crossed in front of her as she appeared from nowhere. The goddess's voice was something of a surprise and caused Nadis to jerk upright.

"No, it isn't," Elissa agreed, looking up at Tyria with a smile, still leaning against the wall. "I just thought I'd been better than I obviously have. That is a *long* walk."

"True, it is. I'm fortunate that I don't need to take it, as with wings that would be decidedly uncomfortable," Tyria said, glancing at the shaft and pursing her lips. "On the other hand, I wouldn't expect Sistina to make it any easier in the future. Making it difficult to get here is a good way to keep herself safe. This *is* practically the heart of the dungeon, after all."

"Root might be a better term," Topaz said, looking depressingly energetic in Nadis's opinion. "She's a tree, after all."

"Heart, root. Both work," Sistina said, sniffing softly. "Is *mine*. I share it."

"For which I am very thankful," Phynis said, smiling at the dryad. "If you hadn't, I don't think Irethiel's plan would've failed."

The murmur of agreement that Nadis heard startled her, and she glanced over at Felicia, whose eyes were a bit wide. After a moment, Nadis spoke nervously. "If you don't mind me asking, why is that? Zarenya told me how Sistina destroyed Irethiel, in vague terms, but why do you think Sistina turned things around?"

Phynis looked at Sistina, pursing her lips as the queen thought. It was Diamond who looked most likely to answer, but in the end it wasn't.

"Without Sistina, I wouldn't have questioned my new path. I

would have fought Sifaren, and it would have fallen," Tyria said, her voice soft as she looked at Nadis, then at the Jewels. "Without her, the Jewels would have remained in the service of Kelvanis, and their power is immense. It was they who knew I'd been captured, and a great deal of information which proved crucial may never have fallen into the hands of Sifaren and Yisara. Furthermore, the assault which captured Jaine Yisara wouldn't have lost the majority of their reinforcements and might have been even more successful. Sistina's actions were like those of a pebble setting off a rockslide. One after another, they built on themselves into a torrent that ended with the destruction of Irethiel."

Nadis considered that, opening her mouth, then shut it again, a little stunned as she looked at Sistina. The dryad looked back at her, then sighed, murmuring, "Just made *sense*. Caught breath? Want this done."

Nadis thought for a moment, then bowed her head slightly, conceding the point as she murmured, "As you say."

The others led the way toward the end of the tunnel, which was blocked by a curtain of vines. Tyria simply vanished, stepping through the wall, something that disconcerted Nadis a little, but none of the others seemed to so much as bat an eyelash.

When she stepped into the cavern, Nadis stopped suddenly, her eyes opening wide as she took it in, her mouth opening, then just hanging there. Beside her, Elissa had also paused, looking around for a few moments before the human spoke, shock in her voice.

"I... did not expect this," Elissa said, looking around slowly. "No dungeon I've even been in has been this... this..."

"Beautiful?" Nadis suggested, her shock somewhat overcome by amusement at Elissa's reaction.

"Yes, that," Elissa agreed.

It was true, though. Nadis had seen exquisite gardens in Yisara's capital, particularly those maintained by some of the nobility who wished to flaunt their wealth, but none of them even slightly compared to what she saw before her.

The cavern was lit by a warm glow, almost like the sun itself, and Nadis could see that the source of the light were large orbs set into the ceiling, yet they were almost easy to overlook, when compared to the vegetation before her. Trees with vibrant purple blossoms the size of her hand lined a stone path, while glittering flowers of every color adorned bushes along the way. Many of the plants were common, but nearly half of them were magical in some way, and the way they were laid out looked carefully planned to Nadis.

Above all, though, was the tree. The white-barked tree stood nearly two hundred feet tall, its branches barely short of the ceiling itself, and fronds of green and gold swayed in a gentle wind around it, making it look like a weeping willow, at least after a fashion. If it weren't for the motes of golden light hanging in the air around it, in any case.

"We'll be heading to the pond," Phynis said, gesturing in the direction of the tree. "It's near her tree, at the base of a small hill, there."

"I see. So, you *lived* here?" Nadis asked, feeling a little incredulous at the thought, but she started forward as Sistina led the way along the path, and Tyria appeared, flying in the direction of the tree. "This is… is *incredible*!"

"Yes, I lived here, though I'm afraid it went through some, um, *renovations* after we left. And after Irethiel torched part of Sistina's gardens," Phynis said, glancing around and blushing a little as she hesitated, then added, "I think she got rid of the vegetables and other fields that Lily used to feed us, and not many of the plants used to be this magical. She's trying to revive some of the plants that were lost in the Godsrage, I think. Either way, all of the houses are gone, too."

"Aside from your private room, you mean," Diamond interjected, and the queen blushed brightly at that.

"Private room?" Elissa asked, raising her eyebrows. "Is it an actual room, or…?"

Phynis hesitated for a few seconds, then spoke, a hint of embarrassment in her voice. "Sistina… made a room for me, under a hill. It's just a bedroom with an attached bath, but I have the only key. It's nice, and one of the first gifts she gave me, after I gave up my claim to Sifaren's throne."

"Ah, I see," Elissa said, smiling gently as she glanced at Sistina, then murmured, "She really *does* love you, doesn't she?"

"Yes, she does. Even if she can be frustratingly closemouthed at times. We're *trying* to get her to talk more normally, but it's a struggle," Phynis said, and there was a snort from ahead of them.

"*You* try losing all sense of language and memories, then growing as a tree for several thousand years, and see how well you do at getting used to speech, hm?" Sistina retorted, the change to her speech startling after the short answers she'd given before. The dryad wasn't done, though. "I think I am doing *excellently* after just a few years, thank you."

"And... then she just says things like that," Ruby murmured, while the other Jewels giggled softly. "I don't think we'll ever understand her."

"If you say so," Nadis said, a smile creeping across her face as she took in the easy affection between them, Phynis, and Sistina. It was certainly odd, but she wasn't going to argue.

Soon enough they came into sight of the pond, and Nadis blinked at the sight of the gazebo on its edge, as she could see Tyria there, along with someone else she hadn't expected. Two someones, in fact.

"Is that Jaine and Lirisel?" Elissa asked, beating Nadis to the question.

"Yes, it is. Jaine really wanted to be here, and I thought Lirisel deserved it as well. They've been setting up the recorder and such," Phynis explained, nodding toward them and the goddess.

"And pilfering starfruit," Sistina added, letting out a somewhat wistful sigh.

Nadis laughed again, though she had to wonder what starfruit were, since she'd never encountered them before.

"Your Majesty, we're ready when you are!" Lirisel said, once they were close enough, and the priestess curtseyed deeply as she added, "Everything is prepared, save for Sistina's part."

"Not that there was much to prepare," Jaine added, a brilliant smile on her face as she looked at Elissa and Nadis, then mimicked Lirisel's curtsey as she added, "I'm glad to see the two of you safe!"

"The grace of the goddess protected us," Nadis said, though she blushed when Tyria glanced at her with an arched eyebrow.

Fortunately, Sistina distracted everyone when she ignored the byplay and walked over to the edge of the pond, bending down to touch the water. A shimmer of magic pulsed through the chamber, then the surface of the water simply… stilled. Another tap of her finger sent magic outward again, and Nadis watched as a circle of metal slowly drifted up out of the water, breaking the surface as it came to rest on top of the water, not a drop beading on top of the metal.

The circle itself was shocking, though, as it was made from adamantine, one of the strongest metals in the world, and it was a perfectly forged circle, yet still had thousands of tiny runes carved into the metal. Nadis recognized a few of the runes, but it was so far beyond her that she didn't know where to even begin to decipher what they were for.

"Sistina… I thought you said that changing Tyria back was *simple*," Topaz said, her tone dry. "That doesn't look simple to me."

"Want to make mistakes?" Sistina asked challengingly, looking at Topaz.

"No, of course not!" Topaz replied quickly.

"Then took precautions. Was given more time, did it right," Sistina replied, taking a step out onto the water, which held her like it was solid ground. "*Is* simple. Is still magic."

"What does that mean?" Nadis asked, unable to restrain her curiosity.

"It means that even simple things can go awry if you aren't careful," Tyria said, stepping out onto the water, testing it with one foot before nodding and approaching the circle slowly. "Transforming me might be simple. Getting the *exact* result I want… that is far more difficult. Like shaping clay into a bowl might be something any child can do, but only a master of the craft can make a masterpiece, except for the occasional lucky beginner."

"Yes," Sistina agreed, nodding and smiling as she pointed at the circle. "In the center. Will start ritual once you are."

"As you wish. I believe that's the cue to start recording,

Lirisel," Tyria said, and she stepped into the middle of the circle. The faint anxiety on her face startled Nadis, but she supposed even deities could be nervous.

Lirisel moved back to the gazebo, where a recording device had been set up, Nadis noticed. She also saw a large sack under the table, but she didn't dwell on it, instead turning back to watch Sistina and Tyria.

Tyria settled herself in the middle of the circle, taking a deep breath, then nodded, swallowing hard before she spoke softly. "I'm ready, Sistina."

"As you wish," Sistina replied, nodding gravely in return. Then the dryad leaned over to touch the circle… and she began singing.

"What?" Elissa murmured, looking almost taken aback as Sistina straightened, her voice rising in wordless song, and with each note the dryad sang, a different rune on the circle lit up. "What is she doing?"

"It's… something I've read about," Phynis said, her voice quiet as she watched the circle with an unwavering gaze. "Marin, Sistina's first life. She was the one who discovered that it wasn't the words that allowed someone to invoke magic, but specific tones. Words aren't required… and she studied music to learn the control needed to decipher what magic *truly* was, how it was put together."

Elissa inhaled sharply, but Nadis decided to ignore her, instead focusing on the scene before her eyes. The circle was lighting up faster and faster, and she could feel mana building in the air like a storm, enough to make Nadis shiver. Only now did she realize what it must have been like to be in the chamber when Irethiel died, and only now did she truly believe that Sistina might have been able to kill her. Knowing that she had wasn't enough, not even close to enough. *This,* though… it was power which Nadis had never felt from any mortal, not even the dragon that had tried to kill her a few days earlier.

Sistina's singing continued for a minute, then two, until at last Nadis saw only a few symbols were left, and she tensed, worry and anticipation twining in her stomach. A part of her had to wonder, would it really work? Then the last symbol lit, Sistina fell silent, and a column of light erupted upward from the circle.

The light should have blinded her, Nadis realized after a moment, yet it didn't. It was an incredible white that blazed brightly, enveloping Tyria entirely, and causing her clothing and hair to ripple upward as if in a high wind. Yet Tyria looked down… and smiled as the light seeped into her body, and she began to change.

First to change were her wings, which lost the faint purple hue that had imbued the feathers, changing into a glorious white almost as bright as the pillar. Then all the goddess's body seemed to change into light itself, something which Nadis couldn't quite describe, yet was glorious as well… and little by little, she came back into focus. First were her eyes, which glowed brilliant sapphire, like the deepest blue of the sky on those days when Nadis felt like she could fall upward and be swallowed by the sky. Then her hair returned to what Diamond had shown them, gold as spun sunlight, yet somehow even more vibrant than before.

As the goddess's body came into focus, though… not much had changed, yet at the same time everything about her had. Instead of the somewhat sharper edges of Tyria, she was softer, somehow more benevolent, and Nadis's breath caught at the sight of Medaea as the goddess's brilliant smile lit up the chamber, and her clothing began to settle once more. No longer did she bear the gemstones that had been forced on her by Kelvanis, and her clothing wasn't purple, but rather white accented by crimson and gold, and at last the pillar of light slowly faded to nothing.

"My goddess…" Nadis breathed, and slowly she fell to her knees, reverence rushing through her.

At the same time, a pulse of power rushed through the chamber, and Nadis saw Medaea blink, then look at Sistina, smiling wryly as she spoke, her voice almost even more radiant than before. "I supposed that's *one* way to generate a light node, Sistina. Thank you, for all of this."

"It was not intentional. A pleasant surprise, perhaps, but not intentional," Sistina replied, glancing down at the water, which

Nadis realized was now glowing itself. "And where there is light, there is also shadow. You are welcome, Medaea. Are you ready to break the bond between us?"

Medaea laughed with the sound of echoing bells, and belatedly Nadis realized that all the others save for Sistina were on their knees as well. The goddess glanced at them, amusement in her eyes as she murmured, "No, I don't think I am. I care for you a great deal, Sistina, and I'm not going to give that up yet. No, I think this is enough for now. I've changed a great deal from who I was… but I believe I've changed enough due to the whims of others."

"Lady Medaea?" Elissa asked, the name sounding a bit alien coming from her lips, but Nadis couldn't blame her.

"I'm saying that I'm going to make a few decisions for *myself*, Elissa," Tyria said, smiling back at her. "Now stand, all of you. Baldwin agreed to reforge my armor and sword into something more suited to me, and I think it's time to try it on. Who would like to help me with that?"

Nadis opened her mouth as she climbed to her feet, but it was Jaine who spoke first, her voice filled with eagerness. "Ooh, I would, please?"

The laughter that filled the room was infectious, and Nadis couldn't help joining it, as she felt contentment fill her at last.

EPILOGUE

"Goodbye, Urda," the Eternal Empress murmured, dropping the body of the man into the remains of the tree. His body fell toward the coals that burned within the tree, and she watched them go, then turned away. Urda was only one of thousands that she needed to lay to rest, so she wasn't about to stop now.

The ripple through the ley lines, though, *that* stopped her, and she smiled slightly as she looked up at the funnel surrounding the crater, at the winds which had been raging ceaselessly since the Godsrage. Before her eyes, the winds faltered, then began to die at long last.

Power rippled and surged beneath the Empress's feet, and she leaned down to touch the ground, closing her eyes as she reached out, drawing a breath ever so slowly as she tasted the power within the ley lines. It was a dangerous game, that much she knew, but the Empress had practice with it, and it wasn't as though the power would kill her. Maim her for a decade or so, perhaps, but not kill.

Through the ley lines, she was able to sense the sapling of the world tree, as well as the power it was pulsing with. The idea of it being *Marin's* soul within the tree amused the Empress to no end, considering how resistant the woman had been to becoming fey.

"'I don't want eternal life' indeed," the nymph said, laughing softly as she shook her head. "What twists and turns your life has taken, Marin. Still, I cannot say that I am displeased."

More importantly, from the power she sensed, Sistina had gained the power of all six nodes at last, and *that* made the Empress smile wider and stand once more.

Already the skies were beginning to clear, and the air was warming, to the fey's delight. She looked out across the frozen mountains, then laughed, her voice louder now. "The Eternal Wood isn't gone. It has merely been asleep, for generations on end. Now that ends. Now, my dear godlings… the hunt shall begin."

No one answered the Eternal Empress, of course. She hadn't expected them to, for the reawakening would take time, for those that had survived. On the other hand, she was patient, and could wait. After all, vengeance was a dish best served cold.

AUTHOR'S NOTE

Crisis of Faith was a hard book for me to write, for a variety of reasons. Some of you may have expected a fair amount of political infighting between the different aspects of Medaea and Tyria's churches, but I decided early on I didn't want to do that. Politics aren't my forte, I'm afraid, and it wasn't where I wanted to go with the story.

That said, the story was a long time in coming, and I evolved a great deal as an author since I wrote *Halls of Power*. There are definitely differences to the way I write a story now, but I enjoyed revisiting the main characters of *Ancient Dreams*, even if they weren't the focus of this story.

I deeply hope that those of you who enjoyed the original books enjoyed this one, and hope you enjoy many more of my books to come! For now, this closes another chapter of Sistina's story.

However, if Emonael has anything to say about it, that's only for now.

Made in the USA
Monee, IL
16 September 2021

78215299R00197